Ashton's mind stı event that could take pla.. ... ... days. is it about my birthday?" She shook her head. "What's so important about that? I turn eighteen."

His audible response was more than a growl, more than a groan. It was a guttural, painful bawl that forced her back a step. Mason leaned over, hands on his knees. Exasperation swarmed his body like an aura.

"Look at you." She gripped his shoulder. Angry or not, she loved him. "Whatever this is, it's hurting you. It's hurting us. Let me help you."

"You don't understand." He spoke through gritted teeth.

"Does it have to do with your dream-hunt in the woods? Those hawks crashing through my window?" Desperate, she touched his cheek, locked eyes. "Tell me what's happening. If not for you, for me. It's driving you crazy? Can you imagine how I feel not knowing anything?"

He pulled free, paced in circles, sand flying every direction.

"Mas, please." She stepped in his path, his gaze like burnt embers.

"It's big." His weight fell to her shoulder, and she cemented her feet in the sand to hold him upright. "It's bigger than the both of us."

She clung to him like a buoy in dangerous waters, unable to tell anymore who was saving whom.

Seam Keepers

by

Celaine Charles

Seam Keepers

Cover Art by *Kristian Norris*

The Wild Rose Press, Inc.
PO Box 708
Adams Basin, NY 14410-0708
Visit us at www.thewildrosepress.com

Publishing History
First Edition, 2021
Trade Paperback ISBN 978-1-5092-3544-5
Digital ISBN 978-1-5092-3545-2

Published in the United States of America

Dedication

To AH for challenging me to write this book.

To my family and friends for supporting my crazy whims.

To my outstanding beta readers for reading draft after rewritten draft.

To Christine Grabowski and Eilidh MacKenzie, editors extraordinaire.

To my PB-inspired critique group for always telling me the truth.

To SL, MS, AiH, SVS, MK, BV, AV, JW, and my TTT-Sunshine Committee (SL, ML, WS) for all your support.

And finally, a huge shout out to God for sending every hawk circling the sky above the evergreens—calling me, reminding me, nagging me to do the work.

Time to read, MW!

Chapter 1

Dream Driven

Ashton leaned back against the passenger seat, adjusted the journal on her lap, and began her four-thousand-seven-hundred-thirty-ninth sketch of an oak tree. The one she'd doodled every day since she was five. She knew it well, its knotted trunk billowing out as if eleven other trees had joined to make one. The oversized limbs, flailing in the illusion of air, always wrestled something invisible. Something she hadn't been able to put into words for the last thirteen years, yet still constantly drew.

Death could do that to a young mind, especially when it happened right next door.

Today, she imagined the leaves June green, but she never added color to her tree drawings, now distorted by the bumpy ride. She always worried color might reveal whatever secrets her oak held, and her little girl inside would never be ready for that.

"You're sure about the location?" She swung her feet onto the dashboard to steady the journal. As long as Mason drove straight, she could manage the familiar lines in her sketch.

He shifted the jeep into high gear. "Ninety percent."

Evergreens passed in a blur with the afternoon sun. He was in mission mode following some crazy list of instructions from his dream. Unable to argue the sanity behind it, she tagged along for moral support, as she always did. It had become her wordless best-friend mantra.

Hunched over, she gripped her pencil and continued shading deep layers of bark along the oak's trunk. Each stroke of graphite slipped with the vehicle's increasing speed. She made intentional short strokes against the white paper, shifting on her legs. But every line seemed to tick away the hours to graduation, the days until she and Mason would separate for college.

College. A momentous occasion, if only she could celebrate without everything changing. Too late.

Suddenly, the jeep lurched left into the oncoming lane, and she slammed sideways into the door. Everything flew from her lap. The engine groaned in acceleration, then lunged back onto the road, tossing her with a thud into Mason's shoulder. He flung an arm out to hold her back, as if the seatbelt wouldn't stand a chance against his almighty human-boy power. But her feet buckled from their perch on the dash, joining her sketchpad and pencil on the floorboard.

"What are you doing?" She glared, but he only squinted into the rearview mirror. When she looked back, there was a construction truck cruising along, probably at the fastest pace it could go. Not fast enough for Mason.

"Sorry." He shifted again, adjusting their speed to a less crazy version of him driving way too fast. "I need to find this place."

"You won't find anything if we crash." She didn't want to be a statistic. They were already wavering on the side of disaster, racing down an old road to find some clearing in the woods. She hated anything related to danger. Or adventure. Or outside. It all made her nervous, which was all the more reason to draw.

He grabbed her hand, gave it a squeeze.

His apologetic touch sent a little zing up her arm. But she pushed it back where it belonged. Friends for thirteen years, separate schools in two months; she had no right to change up her feelings. Besides, he was seeing Gianna now.

"Okay, I think it's up here." He slowed down, pulled off to the side. His thumbs drummed the steering wheel while his right eyebrow twitched in sync with the blinker. She was impressed he'd remembered to use it.

"Mas, are we really doing this? It's just a dream, and graduation's tomorrow." She laid a hand on his back, where muscles knotted in tiny mounds. Tension led the way instead of impulsivity. He wasn't himself, and she knew why. He hadn't slept in two weeks, his dream repeating night after night.

"I have to. It's the only way free of this nightmare. My life, my way." He pushed back long choppy curls, the ones he refused to cut because they annoyed his dad.

She chewed her lip for something to say, but nothing came. What could she say about following the instructions in a dream? It was crazy, just like his choice to move away without a plan, without a care for a future career path or claiming a major. He was leaving to escape the silent prison his dad had built in grief. And that meant he was leaving her. She wiped a tear.

He glanced sideways. "I'm sorry, I hate the idea of leaving you."

"Then stay here for school."

"I can't end up at the college where my dad

3

teaches." He frowned. "You'll be okay without me, maybe crack that shell of yours. Time for you to be the leader of your own life."

Lead her own life? Had he even led his? They'd done everything together since they were kids. She turned, hiding watery eyes.

"Whose floor will you bunk on when you feel lonely?" She regretted her words as soon as they spilled. It was a low blow. They never talked about his fear of being alone. Or why he camped on her floor so many nights since he was five. But she was desperate. They'd always been there for each other. "Why move so far from home? You don't even know your major."

"Not everyone has their art to hide behind." He pulled back onto the road. "I'll figure it out as I go. It doesn't matter as long as I can call my own shots. And I'll text you every night."

The spring colors outside blurred under the combination of tears and speed. She needed him as much as he needed her.

He shot her a knowing look but then turned his attention to the road.

"I missed it." He whipped a U-turn and drove slower than the truck he'd just passed.

The road was clear now. Moss-covered cedars lined the narrow shoulder. They passed an old farmhouse with a decrepit barn, leaning sideways but still standing. With faded green paint and broken windows, it seemed to say, "I remember a day…" Flashbacks of her childhood flared behind her eyes in muted hues. Six-year-old versions of the two of them digging for fossils in the dirt. Mason mocking her from the highest branch of a tree while she sat doodling at its base. On the way to school, they always walked cautiously along sidewalks for fear of stepping on cracks.

Every memory faded, as she thought of starting college life alone.

"I know it's near this green barn. I'm just not sure which side."

He was wound up tighter than she'd seen. Maybe it was the dream. Maybe it was the fact his dad was coming to graduation. Max Deed usually had classes to teach or was on a book tour during notable events— soccer games and karate belt ceremonies. He wrote a mystery series, taught at the University of Washington, and penned early civilization books. He was always busy, never home. And though Mason hated him for being gone, he secretly preferred it that way.

"Tell me the dream again." She blew out a breath.

He'd shared it a hundred times. Purple lights glimmering outside his window, each night shining farther and farther down the road from his house. Their hue beckoned him to follow, and in his dream, he did. He stepped out into the air from his windowsill and flew with wings to a forest clearing. Each night's dream he flew meant mornings of fatigue and agitation.

"Wait." He pulled off the road and set the emergency brake. "This is it."

Ashton stepped out onto the gravelly shoulder. She pulled off Mason's sweatshirt she'd borrowed, chilly from the jeep's AC, and took in a long breath of woodsy air. The weather had been warm for almost a week, Seattle's amends for eight months of rain, and she hoped it would last all summer. Tossing the sweatshirt into the back seat, she met Mason on the other side.

"You owe me two movie nights for this." She

peered into the woods. "This definitely counts as an adventure, and remember, you dragged me hiking last weekend."

"Ash." He looked serious. "You're not going."

"Of course I am."

He pushed more curls out of the way. "I have to do this alone."

What did he mean? They did everything together.

"I know, I know." He grabbed her shoulders, pulled her in for a hug. "This is insane. But this dream is killing me. I need to finish it. I'm not sure how I know, but I have to do this by myself. And you—" He leaned back to look at her. His amber eyes glinted with flecks of red, only visible when he was nervous.

"—are sworn to secrecy." She finished his sentence. "Fine. I'll wait here."

He tucked a piece of hair behind her ear. "You know I *always* love you." His familiar words eased the burn, as he peered past the tree line. If only he'd peered that carefully into his future choice of leaving home.

"Hey, who would I tell anyway?" She slumped against the driver's side thinking of her *long* list of friends: Mason, Mason's friends, her parents. Then she wondered about her parents. Were they still on the list? She'd always felt close to them. She shook off the thought. Of course, they were on the list. They'd made one mistake. A big one. White flashes of adoption papers splotched her memory like the cloud moving in to blotch the blue sky above. She had to believe her parents hid the truth because they loved her. Just…it still hurt.

Rustling and crackling branches faded, bringing her attention back to the tree line. Mason must have found his way in. She peered into the dense section of wet forest, thick with fallen logs, sagging cedars, and all kinds of rich moss. The sea of green felt almost symbolic of the space growing between them.

She plopped herself behind the steering wheel and slammed the door. Hopefully he'd figure things out so it could be her turn. That's how things worked in their lives. When one had a crisis, the other fixed it. So far, his childhood crises beat hers by a long shot. But she made up for it by being his everyone. His unconditional friend, a nurturing mother when needed, the sister he never had…

Ashton chewed her lip. No wonder he didn't have romantic feelings for her. When you're someone's everyone, you can't be their only.

Grabbing her sketchpad, she moved her pencil across the wriggled lines, skewed from the drive. "Stay focused," she said aloud. She wasn't anywhere close to convincing Mason to stay home for school, but he had agreed to help her figure out her past. Maybe finding her birth parents would help her find the strength to stand on her own. Even when she'd argued it was a *closed* adoption, he'd flashed his venturesome smile. "If it can be closed, it can be opened."

If only it were that simple. If only everything was.

****

Violet lights streaked from out of the forest like paint strokes. Ultramarine and alizarin crimson combined perfectly with the twilit sky, summoning Ashton from the jeep. She tossed her sketchpad and pencil onto the passenger seat and stepped onto the roadside, still barren. All the colors blended back to normal, but her shallow breathing painted a different picture.

What just happened?

"Mason?" she called at the forest's edge where she'd seen him disappear.

More lights flickered, shooting up from the trees just as he'd described in his dream. "Oh my God. It's real…his dream is real!

"Mas—" She ducked under the branches and into the woods. The air chilled as if she'd walked through a tunnel. She glanced back through overlapping boughs and could still see chrome on the black jeep. How far should she go? Gulping the uneasiness rising in her stomach, she pushed farther. What if something had happened? What if Mason was hurt?

The woods darkened with each step until she stopped to check her phone. Only one bar. Maybe she should call Mason. Or call home. Or 9-1-1? More lights! When she glanced up, there it was, as if the silhouetted cedars and firs were mere suggestions behind a lone oak. Her breath caught when the sky darkened, leaving this one tree illuminated. She would have recognized it anywhere. She had drawn it every day for the last thirteen years.

Colors swirled around the oak, forming visions before her eyes. She blinked. A hawk, perched on a low branch, stared at her. A man and woman stood on opposite sides of the tree. Ashton blinked again, and the woman turned, auburn locks flowing, placed both hands on the trunk, and pressed through the bark, disappearing. The dark-haired man peered at Ashton with empty eyes, holding no color at all. His glare forced her back until she caught her ankle between a valley of mountainous roots, falling into darkness, violet at the edges.

****

"Here." The inhaler forced into her mouth expelled

the needed dose of relief. Ashton held it in, allowing every last bit to fill her lungs. Opening her eyes, she found familiar brown ones staring down. Mason's hand gripped her shoulder. She could breathe.

"What happened?" Her voice cracked. Night air prickled goosebumps as she leaned against the seat. How much time had passed since they'd pulled alongside these woods in the daylight? "What time is it?"

"Late. You fell asleep." He adjusted her seat to its upright position, pulled his sweatshirt from the backseat, and tossed it on her lap. Jolting around to the driver's side, he revved the engine and pulled onto the deserted road. She stared at him, expecting more. He was the one who'd dragged them out to this spot in the woods. He was the one who'd gone mental about hacking his dream-encoded message.

Shaking from the blast of albuterol, she tried to piece together what had happened. The jitters from the medication danced in her chest, but thoughts about the last few hours felt as dark as the night outside. How did she get back to the jeep? Swallowing dry air, she reached for the water bottle in her bag. When had she fallen asleep? The last thing she remembered was streams of violet lights shooting above the trees and entering the woods to find Mason. And then...there was more. She knew there was more.

"Mas, tell me what happened in there?"

"Nothing," he snapped. Then he reached over, grabbed her hand. "Really, nothing."

A dusty sheen of filth coated his neck and face. Tracking down his dream was all he'd talked about for two weeks. Their graduation ceremony was in the morning. Now it was nothing?

"Something happened." His right eyebrow twitched, like it did when he was nervous. "You okay?"

"Yeah, I—" He stopped, leaned forward over the dash, peered up to the sky. Several clouds parted, exposing a hint of moonlight, eerily thickening the dark.

"Your dream? What'd you figure out?" She pressed her hands against her chest, took in steady breaths. She didn't want a second dose.

More silence, except for tires gripping asphalt. The droning engine filled the space with an unfamiliar awkwardness. Why was he acting so strange? "Mas?"

"Sorry, it was just a dream." He squeezed her hand again. "It was stupid coming out here." His breathless laugh sounded nothing like the Mason she knew. The Mason she knew, impulsive as he was, wouldn't frantically follow instructions from a dream. He was focused on one thing only: graduating and getting out of his dad's house.

"I saw the violet lights. It's all fuzzy, but I know I went in after you, and I—"

"What do you mean you went in? Into the woods?" He swerved along the road's shallow shoulder, jerked to a stop. "What did you see?"

Ashton grabbed at her seatbelt, tightening across her chest. "I didn't see anything. I mean, I don't know what I saw because I can't remember." She pushed on her temples, applying pressure to boost her memory.

Mason's glare burrowed into her. His usually tan skin turned pasty white, even in the darkness, as if it might be the end of him had she shared in anything he'd just experienced.

"Something happened to you."

"Nothing happened."

10

She glared back. Sweat pooled on his forehead. He was lying. He'd never lied to her.

"If nothing happened, why didn't you come back?"

He pulled the jeep onto the road as recklessly as he'd stopped. "I got lost."

"*You* got lost?" She gripped the sides of the seat, his speed increasing with each gear shift. How many summers of survival camp had he completed in his eighteen years? His dad always insisted there was yet one more survival skill to master, even if Max Deed never wanted to spend the time teaching it to his son himself.

Mason flinched. The vehicle veered slightly right as he regained control and glanced her direction. "Deer. Back there."

She hadn't seen a deer, but it was dark. "How did you get lost?"

He leaned forward over the steering wheel, peered up at the sky again. "Can we forget about this? I'm embarrassed enough."

Ashton rubbed circles into her temples, a headache building behind her eyes. She checked her cellphone. "Oh my God." Midnight.

"I know." He glanced over. "I texted your parents, told them we caught a movie."

"They were okay with that? Graduation's in the morning." She had promised her mom she'd set up for her family's celebration. A long list of to-do items flashed through her mind.

"Ash, it's okay. They won't say anything right now."

She stopped midthought, scowling at his nerve in bringing up the subject. Of course, they wouldn't question her. They'd been caught in a lie far too big to

11

apologize for. They'd tried. But their explanations never settled into the compartment of her brain where things were okay.

Compartments. Her mind worked like a file cabinet with rows and rows of files. There were illusions of files for every subject in school, long-term projects, and extra credit. They took up an entire drawer. Imaginary files for her artwork had another drawer. Each medium, each idea, each incomplete and completed endeavor, color-coded for easy retrieval. The drawer for her personal life was the smallest, with folders for only her parents and Mason. She had other friends, the kids she'd grown up with since kindergarten, but they all knew what she had always known: Mason was the only friend she needed. As an only child, her connection to her parents was unique. She was as close to them as Mason.

Until seven days ago when she'd discovered they weren't really her parents.

Mason caught himself, exhaling his mistake. "You know what I mean. They're giving you space. Let's just go home. It's been a long night."

"Maybe it's been long for you. I evidently just woke up." She knew she sounded snarky. Vibrations pounded against her chest, which could have been the albuterol, but more likely her nerves. As Mason shifted into high gear, the puttering construction truck from earlier flashed through her mind. That's the pace she needed. Slow and steady.

"You'll be fine in the morning. Gain a new perspective. Isn't that what your mom always says? And maybe—maybe I can finally sleep since I followed the dream through. To the end. It's done." He sucked in a shaky breath.

Ashton stared at her friend. His knuckles white as he gripped the wheel, jaw clenched sharp. His gaze scaled the skies above. He was anything but relaxed. And he was the one who'd always said she worried enough for the both of them. Maybe he was right. Mentally she labeled a new file in her mind, *Woods Experience*, placing it right behind *Adoption Lie*.

Ashton leaned against the seat and closed her eyes. If her heart beat any stronger, it would crack right through her chest.

Chapter 2

Shifted Reality

Mason dropped his clothes into a pile on his bathroom floor. Steam rose from the shower behind him, but the water would never reach a temperature hot enough to clean the horror. To scrub the blood off his back, or from the insides of his elbows, or behind his knees. He studied the drying bits of tarnished brown through the mirror, staring at the only evidence of the living hell he'd just experienced. And with graduation only hours away.

His freedom from home, now compromised. What had he been thinking?

Gripping the porcelain sink, the white of his knuckles flashed him back to the filtered glare of the moon. It had provided the only light in the darkened woods merely hours ago, until even that light faded to black. The thought almost broke through his throat, and he bent over the sink expecting to vomit. Again.

He jumped in the shower, letting the spray fall across his chest. Dipping his face in the force, he let his tears wash away, down the drain.

"Not Ashton—" He swore aloud, picturing the innocence in her blue eyes. He needed her to be okay when he left for college. But after tonight, would there even be college?

His dad was out of town until morning, always

important work to do. Max Deed never joked or laughed. Their relationship was more than estranged. His mom, dead thirteen years now. There was only Ashton, but *they* forbade him to tell her a thing.

Forbade in an unnatural way of spine-burning agony.

He ducked instinctively—the reminiscent sensation alive along the bones in his back. The same bones that had earlier curled atop themselves as he'd fallen to the forest floor. Coughing in the rising purple mist, he'd tried to take a breath, but it was no use. His body had folded over, his knees pushed into his chest, his shoulders turned awkwardly in on themselves, constricting.

His knees hit the shower floor, the smack against the tile only amplified the crunching of his bones from earlier in the night. Suddenly he was right back in the woods, recalling everything as if he was there.

The echo had filled his ears while his mouth pulsated in pain. His teeth, like knives, cut through his lips. He remembered screaming, but the sound was muffled by a thick layer of downy fluff. He was breathing tiny plumes of feathers, white and amber. Red blood ran over pink skin as his body ripped and tore until a final pulse of darkness swallowed him whole.

Once again, he was terrified, shaking against the wet tiles. The water pinged against his back, but he gripped the wet surface on all fours. "Stop!" He pleaded through the memories rolling over without mercy.

There he was again, in the thick of the forest. He blinked his eyes to better see, but they weren't his eyes. His head had pounded, rattling in a skull that wasn't his own.

When everything stopped, Mason became acutely

aware of his forest surroundings. Darkness hung, though the night was bright, as if each shade had its own hue separate from the others. He opened his mouth, but tiny hoarse shrieks were all that would come. His head jerked unnaturally to the side, then down to his feathered body.

"Oh God." The thought came to him as if he was still himself, though he was not. He was a bird, a hawk. Mason scanned the branches above. He tried standing on new legs, now tipped with awkward talons. Queasily, he opened his hooked beak, regurgitating whatever remained in his stomach from earlier in the day—when he was still human.

A chorus of hawk cries pierced his sense of hearing, demanding attention. The air swooshed about, almost knocking him down. The flock encircled him, a few yards out, as his vision extended farther than humanly possible.

Listen to us.

He tried answering with words he used to be able to speak, now suppressed with shrills and screeches.

Use your mind, Mason. The voices haunted.

What the— Furious, Mason forced his words in thought.

That's it. Use your mind to speak.

What's happening? Mason tried walking but stumbled on foreign limbs.

You were called through your dream.

He could tell which bird of prey was speaking. The voice was strong. Before him in rich brown and ivory flecked plumage, the dominant hawk stood a head taller than the rest.

Mason, still trying out new legs, staggered in a circle. *What do you want?* Speaking through his mind was easier than he'd expected and kept the eerie screeching to a minimum.

I am Gavan, Chief of Casts, here to guide you through this process. Are you ready for the information?

I think I have to be, since it's already freaking happening to me! He didn't mean to yell, if he was. It was hard to tell in his new form.

Suddenly, he thought of Ashton just outside the woods. No, by now she'd be looking for him, scared out of her mind. *Look, I need to get out of here. I left my friend back there.* But pointing in any direction was a lost cause. He didn't have a finger with which to point and found a wing full of sculpted feathers instead.

She is safe. Though you were told to come alone. The hawk took flight into the clearing Mason had entered as a human. The other birds of prey followed suit, perching in a barren tree across the field. Mason could see it as if it were right in front of him, though he knew the actual distance to be greater.

Keeeeee-arrr! Gavan sent an exclamation point to his orders.

After a few more curse words, Mason willed himself into the air, as if his body knew what to do in its feathered form. His wings spread clumsily but carried him across the clearing. The branch closest to where Gavan perched seemed left for him. Mason's talons attached themselves after the slightest of fumbles, and he waited for a message to penetrate his mind, with an uncertain trust he was now forced to rely on.

You are not human, Mason, but from the Spiritual Realm. You are a shifter, a seam keeper by birthright. We have come in hawk form to prove this point beyond

17

doubt. There is no time for denial or disbelief. You will be paired with Ashton once she turns eighteen in five days and joins you in age. As Gavan delivered this riddle of a fairytale, Mason impulsively argued with words that were of no use.

Bypassing the ridiculous reality of his current form, his mind lashed out. *How do you know about Ashton? She wasn't part of my dream.* Mason was already sick of being a bird and wanted his human legs back. His fists would be of use now.

She is the reason you are here. She knows nothing of this life, but once her birthday arrives, she will. Because of her appointed connection to the Human Realm, she is a crucial part of our world. Soon, you will both learn our ways in training.

For now, your duty is to keep her safe, unknowing of any outside Realms until she transitions. Only then will you both join us in the Spiritual Realm, you as a shifter and she as a warrior. Mason, we have called you to service early due to a danger that has arisen—

Danger? Mason's mind wrapped around the suggestion of Ashton as a warrior. She called him every time she saw a spider. *Is Ashton in trouble?*

She has been identified by a dark threat, a demon prince. For her connection to the Human Realm to be complete, you need to keep her fully human until she transitions.

Mason conversed through thoughts, with no pride in his ability mastering the skill. It already felt like second nature. He paid no attention to the other birds, his mind seeking only Gavan's jarring words.

Our cast will watch over her in hawk form, but you—you are linked to her, and the only one who can help us keep her safe.

18

Gavan's irritation was obvious as he slurred the word *you*. He seemed just as upset about the situation as Mason was. Mason's body rocked back and forth, his wingspan making him feel bigger. He couldn't take any more. *Demon? Linked? I don't understand. We start college in two months!*

Not anymore. Do not leave her side for the next five days. We will have hawks in play, but we don't want to scare her. Suddenly, purple lights flickered past the clearing, and the raptors took flight.

Wait! You've got the wrong people. I don't want any part of this. And I know Ashton won't either. She's terrified to leave home, let alone this Realm*! None of this makes sense—*

There won't be an Ashton if you don't help us.

What? How can I do anything in this form? The thought of a demon blew his mind. He lifted his wings to follow, but gravity had other plans. *Why am I a freaking bird?* His feathered body began twisting as Gavan's words warbled something about a destined pairing, the rise of demons at the borders of a Dream Realm, and angelic blessings.

No time to think. His body exploded in torment, disrupting any clarity Gavan may have tried to give. One second he grasped the branch of an old cedar, the next he thrashed on the ground listening to his flesh split and tear. His bones forced themselves back into their sockets. His arms and legs seared as they stretched into place. His heart thumped as his body hammered back together until he was human. Somehow uninjured and covered in the same jeans he'd pulled on that morning, he ran for the forest's edge.

Mason's head shot up, alone on the shower floor, the visions gone as the warmth on his back shifted to ice. He reached up and gripped the handle to stop the water. Pulling himself up, he stepped onto the bathmat. The mirror was covered in thick steam.

Five days.

It's all he could recite as he stood shivering in the cold.

Five days until Ashton's birthday. Five days to figure out what had just happened to his body. Five days to keep her safe from God knew what. He had five days to figure a way out of this hell…and then he'd get back to his own future plans. His own life, his way.

Five days.

Mason grabbed a towel when his dad's bookshelf came to mind. Only one thought: The demon stories his father secretly wrote must be true. The unpublished manuscripts, hidden behind his published series on ancient histories, were real.

He was never allowed in his dad's office, though that hadn't stopped him and Ashton when his dad was away. Years back, they'd rummaged through and found his manuscripts in a box on the top shelf. After their initial shock, they'd chalked it up to the fact he was a closet sci-fi, fantasy lover, that he secretly indulged in the fictional side of his typically expository personality. But his dad, a dedicated college professor and author, had never cared about fiction outside his mystery stories.

And now it made sense.

He thought about the silent prison his dad had built around their house. Always preparing him for everything, he took part in nothing. Mason had been forced to attend survival camps. He had a black belt in Shotokan karate. After-school sports were mandatory; free time was not in his dad's vocabulary.

Hiding grief behind his work was the Max Deed way. Any parental support was financial, not emotional. He'd made frozen dinners and canned soup for as long as Mason could remember. His dad had been the reheating expert until Mason was nine, old enough to manage on his own. After that, Max stoked the fridge with food—delivered weekly. Mason had a credit card for expenses. His jeep had been a gift on his sixteenth birthday. Every need met without face-to-face contact. And the older Mason grew, the deeper his anger rooted. He wanted to get as far away from his dad as humanly possible.

Now, after years of waiting to graduate, ready to leave his silent prison without a word to his dad, he needed to actually talk with him. He stared into the mirror. How might that conversation start? They barely mumbled salutations. But that was before the reality of monsters. Now he needed to know everything. Because somehow in his suburban neighborhood, in the twenty-first century, a demon sought his best friend.

The thought clenched his throat, and he threw himself over the sink.

Nothing.

Graduation had become his beacon to freedom, the fuel keeping him going when he felt shut out by his dad. Ashton shone in that beacon too, for different reasons. He turned on the faucet, splashed water on his face. He hadn't let himself think about what leaving her might mean. And now he couldn't. Morphing into a hawk had trumped his whole world.

He already knew he couldn't sleep, and he wanted to check on Ashton.

Not tonight.

She'd been so confused waking up in his jeep. He

could usually talk her down from her worry-craze. Not this time. She wasn't budging. How could she? He didn't understand it himself. And lying had never been a problem before, except...he'd never lied to her.

Hands trembling, he pulled on his T-shirt, then lifted his eyes to the mirror again. The steam had cleared enough to see dark moons form under his eyes.

He rubbed his face, a sense of doom beating with each heartbeat. He had to break into the home office and check out his dad's books before he got home. Though his dad had missed nearly every other important event in his life, he claimed he was coming to graduation. Just then, Gavan's voice triggered in the back of his mind.

Do not leave Ashton's side for the next five days.

Mason clutched the sink, afraid to move. Was Gavan in his head again? The bathroom sink dripped, bringing him back, and he pushed on the faucet. He swallowed a gulp of air, not unlike the wad of feathers he'd coughed out earlier in the night. He'd have to break up with Gianna. There was no way he could deal with all this and a girlfriend. It would have ended anyway, with school in the fall. He didn't want any hooks left to pull him back. Well, except Ashton.

She was the only family he needed.

His dad's books would have to wait. Pressure pounded against his temples, and he felt he would drop one way or another. Within minutes he was next door, turning the knob on Ashton's bedroom door, waiting their five-second rule before sneaking in. He quietly pulled his sleep mat out from under her bed. She squeaked something unintelligible and pushed over the extra blankets she kept at her feet.

Mason sucked in another dry breath, trying to

steady the pulsing in his chest. His gaze glued to the window, he prayed for fast sleep. Maybe he would awaken on graduation day, and all of the night's terrors would be part of the same dream haunting him for the last two weeks. Maybe it was safer there, in the back of his mind, just a nightmare.

Chapter 3

Highjacked Bliss

Graduating high school was supposed to be a celebration, not a sacrifice. With the recent news of her adoption and now the betrayal of her life-long friend…suddenly Ashton's senior year felt highjacked.

Relatively speaking.

Her parents and best friend stood alive and well in her backyard. Blue and white party balloons announced their presence to the onlooking sunset. Though she'd mostly forgiven her parents and could never stay mad at Mason, the girl inside felt no cheer in the moment, no joy in her accomplishment. There was no hope in her future, now lonelier than she'd imagined.

"*A new perspective…*" Mom's advice for every hardship whispered in the back of her mind. Mason had planted the idea, but from every angle, she was the one standing alone.

Her recent search for college-required vaccination records had proven more than her up-to-date inoculations. Her parents were not her parents. With no siblings to rant to, Mason was all she had. And he had been enough.

Until sixteen hours ago, when he'd lied to her for the first time. Who could she trust now? Who would understand her desire to know and not know about her past all at the same time?

Ashton leaned back against the lawn chair, her gaze falling across the now-emptied picnic tables. As an only child with no living grandparents, it had been a small gathering. Most of the guests consisted of her parents' work friends. The party, ending just moments before, left her in the only quiet of the day. Even that couldn't last when the subject of her newly agitated state slunk over with feigned puppy-dog eyes and a sentimental smirk.

"Your favorite." Mason pushed a plate of strawberry jam-filled cake across the table. Three layers of porous goodness, not unlike the childhood she thought she'd had, even layered with glossy red seeds of celebration.

"You're still mad."

It wasn't a question. He knew her more than she knew herself.

She forked the crumbling edges of soft dough, smushing the bits together. "Something happened to you last night." She could feel it in her bones. And more than that, she knew something had happened to *her*. Something strange and surreal. The sense of déjà vu from the woods had haunted her dreams until she awoke to foggy memories and a splitting headache.

Mason, who usually had something to say, wasn't spilling a word.

He had always been restless, impulsive. But delusional didn't fit the boy she knew. Even now, he had to be holding his breath to stay so silent, waiting for her to look at him.

"Come on, Ash." A small wrapped box flew her way, bounced off her lap, and clunked to the grassy yard. She glared his direction. Never would she have caught it, even if it wasn't a surprise. He was the

25

athlete.

"What's this?" She exhaled before stretching to reach it.

"Graduation gift." He shoved a forkful of chocolate cake into his mouth. His favorite.

"Are you trying to buy my silence?"

"Like I've had time to buy a gift since last night." His amber eyes flickered with that russet glimmer they got when he needed her. When he knew that she knew he couldn't say what he was really feeling yet. Though, he would when they were alone.

But they had been alone last night.

The silver wrapping paper reflected the day's fading light, even with its uneven folds. Clearly not gift-wrapped by a store clerk, unless the clerk was drunk or a toddler, but she was curious. He was a firm believer in gift cards. "They're straightforward and appreciated. No fluff required," he would recite to her objections in any gift-giving occasion.

He never bought her gifts. He was more of a "I'm taking you mountain climbing for your birthday" kind of guy. He always wanted to personalize experiences for her. She suspected it was to liven things up. It had to be rough when his best friend was a homebody and he couldn't wait to see the world. But he never left her behind. So she paid her dues in truly frightening escapades in exchange for casual movie nights at home. It was a balance, and surely a cause for some of her anxiety. She huffed at the ease he had in swaying her feelings. "I hate you right now."

"You know I *always* love you." He laughed and nudged his chin toward the package.

"You left me on the side of the road—for hours." Gift or no gift, that adventure crossed a line. A mentally disturbing line, and this time, she wasn't letting it go. Time would already tick away their last summer together. She needed him back to normal.

"You know I couldn't take you in there."

"It was a dream, Mas. They weren't real instructions. And I went in there anyway. I went in looking for you because—because—"

"Because you refuse to take your anxiety meds. That's why you can't let this go. Look, it was late, you fell asleep. You only dreamed you came in after me. Just like I—" He caught on his words. "—dreamed this whole stupid dream and thought it meant more than it did. But I get it, breaking curfew—"

"This isn't about curfew."

But he already knew that. It was his way of distracting her from the strangeness of the night before. She'd seen the violet lights flash the sky above the woods, the same woods he'd gone into alone. She remembered stepping into its denseness; the cool darkness enveloped her only a few steps inside. There were faces. She'd forgotten soon after her asthma attack, but the images resurfaced in her dreams. Vaguely in her mind's eye, a woman with hair the color of fall leaves pushed against an old tree. A man with dark hair stood staring, but she couldn't make out his eyes. If she had been afraid the night before, it hadn't registered in her weak memory. Now she was just curious.

"Open the box."

She stared at his deep-set eyes, pleading. His broad jawline clenched in hopes she would let it all go. It wasn't until the twitch started in his right brow that she decided to let him off the hook. For now.

Nestled in the box was a charm of an oak leaf.

Silver, delicate, and etched with life-like veins in its design. Its curly edges made it appear alive.

"It's beautiful."

He snatched it up, pulled at her wrist. Her charm bracelet fell free from under the cuff of his blue jacket, the one she'd stolen when the wind had kicked up. He attached the hook onto an empty ring and gave it a shake. It dangled between the sterling painter's palette charm from her mom, and the saxophone charm from her dad. All the charms glittered under the stream of twinkle lights draped crisscross under the patio eaves. The leaf's reflection outshone every other charm, almost unnaturally so.

Suddenly, the events from the last sixteen hours glared in her mind.

Her perfect family, imperfect.

And with graduation over, she had only one summer before heading to art school without Mason, far away at his university. Her heart slipped into that half-a-thump she often felt when she thought about him as more than a friend.

Her first tear hadn't dropped when Mason pulled her up.

"Stop it." He traced his thumbs along her cheeks. "No crying on graduation day." He held her. But even this close, she felt his head tilt back. He was looking to the sky, just as he'd done the night before.

"Ashton, what's wrong?" Mom approached, draping her arms around them both.

Mason didn't stumble in his response. "Hey, Mrs. Nichols. *Sappy* here just loves the new charm I got her."

"Let's see." Mom pulled at her wrist and goggled over the bracelet. Dad wasn't far behind.

"Well, it looks like you've done it again." Dad patted Mason's back.

"I pay attention sometimes." Mason winked at her.

Ashton stepped back. Dad and Mason exchanging trivial chit-chat, Mom complimenting his gift choice. Her head swooned in the illusion of how this very moment may have felt if only a few weeks earlier in time. When Maggie and Drew Nichols were her only parents. When Mason's dream hadn't sent him down a rabbit-hole. Perspiration collected on her forehead as the last seven days of her senior year fell like the final downy plumes of her youth, coming to rest forever on her bedroom floor.

Like a bird, she slipped out of her mom's grasp, fake smiling, before heading into the house and up to her room. Her mom called her name but wouldn't follow. Mason had been right. Her parents had been giving her space to heal.

Healing felt worse than any growing pains she could remember. She leaned against her windowsill, looking out into the neighborhood. Dusk covered the matching houses with a net of false security. She used to feel safe in her room, in the only home she'd ever known, next door to the only friend she'd ever wanted or needed or…desired. Now she felt like a wren forced out of the nest, looking back to wonder if there ever was a mama bird. Was this ever meant to be her home?

Drowning in self-inflicted pity, she jumped at the knock on the door.

Five seconds. She knew Mason was counting to ensure she was dressed. But all she could think now was five seconds to plan how she could force the truth out of him.

"Are you getting ready for Hicks's party?" He

leaned against the window, peering out at every angle.

"What are you looking for? You've been searching the sky since last night."

He looked into her eyes. "Maybe I'm searching for whatever you need to hear to *let it go.*"

Mason was much taller, but her gaze pierced to his level, catching his full attention. "Just tell me what happened. The purple light? The couple by the tree?"

"Ash, it was a dream. A stupid dream. You're worried about nothing." But he glanced out the window again. "Come on, we just graduated. Let's go celebrate. Anyway, I need BFF-help warding off Gianna."

"What? No."

"Hey, I need you. She's getting clingy, and I need my summer off before—before heading to school."

He was compelling as ever, but she'd caught his slip with words. He hadn't seemed irritated with his girlfriend a few days ago. The thought caused a twinge in her side. She should be happy he wanted to break up with Gianna. Even mad at him, she wanted more time together before leaving for college. But how could she let eight unexplained hours in a strange forest go? They would need to be alone for her to convince him to open up.

"It's been a long day, Mas. Let's just stay home."

"It's graduation night," he said after a long pause, then pulled her in, poking her sides.

"Stop," she huffed, but he didn't let up until she squirmed and laughed. He always had a way of fixing her moods. She wasn't going to let him do it this time, but there he was, painting a layer of light over the heavy dark pulling her into anxiety.

"All right, all right. I will go to Hicks's party with you, but on two conditions."

Mason had tickled her to her knees. "One, don't ditch you, because you're a gigantic scaredy-cat afraid to go anywhere social, and two—what could two be? There's only ever one."

"One, don't ditch me, period. I am not a scaredy-cat; I don't like crowds. Two, you're going to tell me exactly what happened last night."

Just like that, his mood changed.

"Nothing happened last night." But he looked outside again, like a new tic he couldn't control.

Ashton dropped her arms to catch herself as Mason moved closer to the window. She followed his gaze to a silhouette on a tree branch. Night had swallowed dusk, but with a gulp of the sun's lingering glow, the shadowy shape of a giant bird glared through the glass. It was thick storm glass, but this bird looked as if he might tap his hooked beak to the pane, and it would shatter in their laps.

"What kind of bird is that?"

Mason held statue still. "Hawk."

The glow from her bedroom light made it difficult to tell its exact coloring. She hadn't seen a large bird of prey perch outside her window before, only small wrens and robins. And she had lived there her whole life.

"I'll get my dad." She turned, but Mason swooped around to stop her.

"It's gone." His hand shook as he pulled her back.

She peered behind to see he was right. "That's so strange. There was a hawk in the woods last night. I mean, I think I saw one." Visions of a giant bird staring from a branch in the oak tree flooded her thoughts.

Mason froze. His glare pierced through the framed dark night as if he could burn a hole through the glass.

"Mas?"

He snapped his attention back. "It's graduation night; we're going out. I'll change and be back." Hiding his face, he pushed out the door, as fast as the hawk had vanished.

She slumped to her bed, wanting nothing more than to climb beneath the turquoise covers and hide under her ocean of safety. When her wrist tingled, she glanced at the bracelet. The oak leaf charm glowed for a moment, a luminescent tint of light. She gave it a shake in the ray of the desk lamp but couldn't find the right angle to make it shine again.

Ashton bit her lip, angry for assuming graduation would be blissful. Something to remember forever. Now, she only wanted to close her eyes, to transport back in time before Mason chased his dream into the woods. Before the day she found her adoption papers.

The memory, confronting her parents, still burned in her chest.

"Ashton, you've always been ours." Her dad had reasoned over her mom's sobs. "We'd planned to tell you, but then with every year that passed, it became more difficult. You were so happy. We all were. How could we burst that bubble?"

But the bubble had popped. It didn't matter that they loved her. They'd lied about who she was and claimed to know nothing about her past. The adoption, closed. Her birth parents wished to remain unknown.

How does that happen in today's world, where information is everywhere? And how did a seventeen-year-long family lie link with her best friend lying after thirteen years of friendship? All within days—even hours—of the graduation she was already freaking out about because everything was moving way too fast.

She pulled her bed quilt over her head. If time travel truly existed, she'd buy a first-class ticket.

Chapter 4

Conversations With The Moon

Ashton slammed the jeep door. She hated parties, dealing with obnoxious and contrived people, their sole purpose to hook up while under the influence of alcohol. She sucked in a breath to stay focused. Her sole purpose was to play the BFF card so Mason could ward off Gianna. That and celebrate their graduation. But celebrating was the furthest thing from her mind. She needed answers about what had happened in the woods. So, chin up, she walked into the craze of bodies alongside her much more confident friend.

"Deed!" Mason's head turned at each call.

The familiar banter shared by guy friends as greetings—last name calls, dude, and various curse words used as endearments filled the air. Hicks's father was a lawyer and his mother an admin bigwig at one of the hospitals. Their enormous house was filled with guests. Mason dragged her to Hicks's all the time, so she usually recognized most of the partiers. But his parents were throwing this one, so there were faces of all ages. Swags of blue and white crepe paper covered the walls. Bouquets of white roses filled the side tables while friends and family cheered, clinked glasses, and flashed pictures.

"Hey, Ash." She was an afterthought from every greeter, always in Mason's shadow. But it didn't matter. She was counting the hours before she'd have him alone.

Ashton's feet left the floor. Michael Hickson whirled her around in a hug, bringing her back to reality. He was Mason's oldest friend. "We made it!"

He smelled of celebration, but she hugged him back. He'd been her friend too.

"Yeah, yeah, on a mission." Mason high-fived Hicks and grabbed Ashton's hand. He pulled her along from one room to the next. Usually he chatted up everyone within earshot, but he seemed adamant on finding Gianna. Once they entered the kitchen, he came to an abrupt halt.

"Hey." Mason didn't drop her hand, which was odd.

Gianna lit up, beaming one of her perfect smiles, until she glanced at their linked fingers.

Mason and Ashton had grown up together, alongside most of their classmates. Everyone knew they were close friends. Some even wondered if they were more than friends at various stages in life, including Ashton. But never had they acted like a couple in public.

Ashton glanced his way, trying to get a read on another strange behavior. Since his dreams began two weeks ago, he hadn't been anything close to the boy she knew. Her stomach tightened more, and she shook her head to unclench her jaw.

"Happy Grad Day!" Gianna jumped into a hug with swift force, breaking through their clasped hands. Her posse all looked alike with dramatic eye makeup and flat-ironed hair, all wearing slinky dresses and ready-to-play attitudes.

Ashton stumbled back as Gianna's friends

swooped in to cut her off. Mason was caught in the attention, so she backed up against the kitchen sink.

"Ugh." She spun around, shirt soaked from the wet granite. She tried to catch Mason's attention, but he was laughing along with the gaggle of girls. Feeling conned into another party she didn't want to attend, she glanced around for a towel. Body after body streamed through the kitchen, so she pushed past them for the bathroom. A towel would be helpful to ring out her shirt, yet she also needed space.

Bolting into the hallway, she ran smack into someone entering the kitchen. "Umph!" Her hands flew up.

A tall guy grabbed her elbows to steady her. "Whoa, are you okay?"

She leaned back to gain distance and found blue eyes staring into hers. They were bluer than her own and contrasted with his short-cropped hair, black as night. The front of his hair, spiked up, exposed a broad forehead. When he smiled, the scruff along his chin caught her eye. Suddenly it dawned that she was staring, and she stepped out of his grasp.

"Yes, I'm—fine." She rubbed her arms where he'd caught her. They were buzzing, as if asleep. What was wrong with her?

He stood back to let her pass, extending his arm as if to say, *your turn*. She smiled her gratitude and slunk to the bathroom. Ignoring her soaked shirt, she peered into the mirror to find flushed cheeks. Was she blushing? She rolled her eyes and fingered her brown layers, fluffing the ends swirling at her shoulders. She hoped the knots in her chest untangled; she'd forgotten her meds again. It had been a warm day, but the sun had set. The cooler outside air was what she needed.

Pulling a towel from under the sink, she squeezed the water from her shirt. The back of her jeans was damp, but she didn't care. She was mad at Mason for dragging her there in the first place, angry she couldn't remember anything more about the night before. Now she was slamming into strangers and sweating off whatever remained of her makeup.

Her breath knocked inside her chest, as if it had nowhere to go.

Air. She needed air now.

Making her way to the front door seemed impossible with countless groups posing for pictures. She turned around, finding french doors opening into the backyard. Several people hung out under the decorative lights, so she headed to the other side of the lawn and found an empty sitting area. Crawling into an Adirondack chair, she decided to wait for Mason.

The moon was a full circle against the black sky. She inhaled a cool breath, letting it fill her lungs. Crowds made her nervous. Mason knew that but was obviously busy in his own realm of comfort. He hated being alone, so crowds were euphoria for him. She laughed aloud, wondering how they'd made it so long as best friends.

"I've often found the moon to be quite comical myself."

That voice.

She looked up to find the dark-haired guy from the hallway standing in the glow of patio lights.

"Ian." He pointed to himself before pulling up the other chair.

Ashton's heartbeat sped up. She'd never flirted, never dated. She never worried about other guys; she already had the only one she needed. Her relationship

37

with Mason wasn't romantic, but it was enough for her. She could focus on school and her art without distraction.

Though tonight she wished for her sketchbook, to draw this boy's face.

"And your name?"

"Oh, Ashton." Aside from bumping into him moments ago, she'd never seen him before. She felt flushed from their earlier encounter, chilled from the current cool air, and uncomfortable with his attention. "Are you friends with Michael's family?"

"You could say that." His smile revealed perfect teeth. "But you haven't shared your insight with the moon. Don't let me interrupt."

She knew he was joking but had no response to his playful tone.

"I'm just waiting for my friend." Part of her wanted him to go away so she could devise a plan to make Mason spill the truth. Yet another part of her hoped he'd meant to talk to her, that he wasn't mistaking her for someone else.

"Alone in the dark, with only the moon for conversation?"

"Well..." She suddenly felt desperate to sound clever. "I'm not alone now, am I?"

Oh my God—she sounded more needy than clever. She was not good at this.

"True." He laughed and sat back.

Ashton took it as a sign he was there because he wanted to be. Now if she could only figure out what to say. She hugged herself tighter to hide her shaking hands. Maybe she could salvage something from this depressing graduation night after all. And why shouldn't she? The last week of her final high school days had been a train wreck. Everything she'd believed in had crashed and burned in an instant. The file cabinets of order, tucked neatly in the back of her mind, were left with open drawers, files strewn on the floor.

"So where are you from?" She cleared her voice. More than scratchy, it was shaking. She was shaking. "I mean, I've never seen you around."

"I just moved here." He slipped off his hoodie and tossed it to her.

"Oh, thanks, but—I have a jacket in my friend's jeep." She started to hand it back.

"It's fine. It seems this friend of yours has left you cold and alone in the dark."

"He's dealing with something right now." She offered the sweatshirt again. But the strangest warmth from the cotton fibers encircled her wrist, traveled up her arm, and into her right shoulder. He made no attempt to take it, so she leaned back, unsure what to do.

She was no longer cold.

"Priorities are tricky things." He smirked.

She wanted to defend Mason. To correct Ian's assumption that she wasn't the most important thing in his world. Up until a day ago, she might not have argued with her own declaration. But somehow at that moment, she felt left out of everything having to do with her own life. She pulled Ian's hoodie over her head, the gray fibers soft and warm against her skin.

"So what brings you to Seattle?" Her voice was surprisingly steady.

"Art school."

"Seriously?"

"Is that strange?" The blue in his eyes deepened to midnight, and Ashton glanced up to see if the lighting had changed.

"No, it's just that I'm going to Cornish in the fall."

"We'll be classmates then." The blue in his eyes changed again, brightening another tinge, so blue she wondered what shades of paint she might mix to capture it on canvas. Azure? Ocean or royal? None of them would be right.

In any other encounter with an attractive boy who'd just announced he was attending her school, she would have lost her ability to speak. Her throat would have tightened, and she would have needed her inhaler to breathe.

In any other encounter? Her insides fluttered. There had never been any other encounter where she wasn't just a "Mason's friend-who-didn't-have-a-date" date to a school dance.

"What a coincidence." She tilted her chin, hoping to sound calm.

"If I had a drink, this is where I'd toast to my first Seattle friend." He stood up. "Shall I get us something?"

She didn't usually drink. She never talked to guys who weren't Mason's friends. But a tingle washed over her shoulders, spilling relaxation. She smiled up at him. "Sure."

When he disappeared into the house, she wiped away any mascara smudges that might have collected under her eyes. She fingered her shoulder-length hair, trying to adjust the layers, and surveyed the area for any type of surface reflection to see herself. When she glanced up, perched right above the garage eave was the shadow of a giant bird. At night? She squinted, bringing its shape into view. A hawk.

She jumped up and scuttled backward right into

another body.

"Hey, I returned as quickly as I could."

She turned, entangled with Ian for the second time in one night. His arms held up two plastic cups, empty now, since most of their contents had spilled over the both of them.

"I'm so sorry." She swiped at the beer covering her torso but glanced toward the hawk, now gone.

Ian stacked the two cups into one and tossed them into his chair. "It's okay. I'm sorry I spilled our celebration toast." He helped her pull off his sweatshirt, soaked.

"Sorry about your hoodie." A chill rushed up her spine, as she held it at arm's length. "I can wash it for you."

Ian's eyes grew darker as they stood in the yard, away from the outside lighting. "That's unnecessary, but then again..." His lips curved. "We'd have to meet up for you to return it."

Ashton's nerves flooded. "I guess so."

"Here." He handed over her phone. "I put my number in your contacts."

"When did you take my phone?" She closed her mouth, trying not to sound accusatory. Her other hand flew to her pocket. She hadn't felt a thing.

"Well, I didn't want it getting wet in our celebration spill. Preservation of future contact."

Her palms felt hot as she gripped the hoodie tighter. "I don't usually call guys I don't know." She was losing confidence fast. Where was Mason?

"A good rule to follow with strangers, but we're old friends now. We've embraced more than once, we're going to the same art school, and we even share clothes." His head tilted to the hoodie in her hands.

"Um…" Her stomach tensed, her chest tightened, but a strange warmth still pushed up her arms from her tingling fingers. "I—"

"There you are." Mason's voice swept over the uncomfortable moment. He dropped an arm over her shoulders. "Time to go."

She jumped, surprised for the third time that night. "Mason, this is Ian."

Ian held out his hand. "Nice meeting you."

Mason reluctantly shook it.

Ian's expression seemed to burn at Mason's touch, and even Mason pulled his hand back awkwardly.

"Same, but we have to go." Mason steered her toward the back gate.

"Bye," Ashton called before the side of Hicks's house blocked her view.

Mason led her to the front driveway. She should have protested. Was she even finished talking to Ian? But as she gripped the damp hoodie in Mason's mad dash to leave, her stomach lurched. She wasn't feeling well.

"What a minute." She stopped outside the passenger door. "I feel sick."

Mason sniffed the air in front of her. "Did you drink?"

"No." She took a deep breath to calm her sputtering stomach. "Beer spilled on me."

Mason glared back toward the house. "What a jerk."

"He's not." She pulled open the jeep door. "He was—nice." She couldn't help smiling.

Mason got in the driver's side and revved the engine. "Well, no thanks to you, I managed to break things off with Gianna."

"You're the one who group-hugged her and her friends."

"I didn't want to hurt her feelings." Mason scanned the sky through his windshield.

"Then why end it?" Her question was simple enough, but he froze as if he'd made a mistake. His mouth stuck in the formation of a word he'd planned to say, but somehow couldn't.

Ashton stared at him, waiting for an explanation. "Fess up."

"I just want to spend more time with you this summer." He looked over, softened his expression. "Is that so bad?"

Her heart thumped. She'd worked hard to bury romantic thoughts of him. Did he even mean it that way? She was usually better at reading him.

"Mas, you've been counting the days to graduation since freshman year. You can't wait to move away from home."

"Another reason I needed to break up with her."

They drove the rest of the way in silence. Mason pulled into his garage and turned off the engine. "Ash." He turned, pulling on her hand. "I do want out of here. But I'm still going to miss you."

"I'm going to miss you too. But if you want to make the most of our last summer together, why are you lying about the woods?"

"Stop it with the woods already."

"I saw faces in that oak tree. I can't place them, but I saw them. You must have seen them too." She gripped his hand. "I can help you, whatever it is. You can't say it was nothing when you keep acting so strangely."

"I'm not acting strange." He pulled his hand back, gripped the steering wheel. "Did it ever occur to you I might be a little messed up graduating without my mom?"

He threw it out there like he'd meant to hurt her.

"What?"

"It would have been nice to have her in the audience, like your parents." His voice, barely audible.

"You mean my parents who lied about being my parents until a week ago? Those parents?" Shame leaked as the words slipped out. She knew it wasn't the same for him. She hadn't known her birth parents existed until a week ago. How could she miss them? But part of her did. She'd been wondering who they were with every passing day. Why had they given her away? Then she writhed in guilt because she loved the parents who raised her...the same ones who had lied. She needed more answers than a closed adoption file could give. And she would find them. But she couldn't do it without Mason.

And now, as emotional as he seemed, was he lying again? She couldn't tell anymore.

She knew he missed his mom; he carried her in his pocket everywhere he went. Literally. Mia Deed had been a geologist, collecting rocks and minerals. He carried one of her favorites every day, a small dime-sized sphere of nuummite. It was black with streaks of gold, still beautiful even though he fiddled with it daily and left it clunking against loose change. He hadn't talked about his mom at any other significant date...becoming a teenager, turning sixteen, getting his driver's license. But then, maybe graduating was different.

"Mason—I'm sorry."

He ran his fingers through his hair. "Let's get some sleep. Summer vacation is official tomorrow." He didn't even pretend to sound excited, another telltale he wasn't himself.

The awkwardness in the jeep expanded as they climbed out into the garage. Mason stalled for a minute before hugging her goodnight.

"Do you want me to come over? My dad's home, but he won't notice."

"He will notice, so no." She pushed him back, but playfully, trying her best to lighten the mood. She headed next door to her house. "See you tomorrow."

He seemed uneasy. But she'd had enough strangeness for the night. And a certain energy stirred up her wrists as she held the damp gray hoodie in her arms. A nice reminder that in the midst of a depressing graduation day and worrisome week, something unexpected had her smiling.

Chapter 5

Awake

A familiar blaring tone ripped Mason from sleep. He squeezed his phone to shut off the alarm. Six in the morning. He rolled over to fall back asleep, when thoughts from the day before spilled over his semi-conscious state.

He sat up, rubbed his eyes. Sleep would not be in his near future. Too many thoughts raced through his mind, and the sun was barely up. Was this what Ashton felt like every day?

Careful not to wake his dad, he crept down the stairs. He threw a pod of dark roast into the coffee maker and glared at it to brew faster than the machine was capable. By the time he swallowed his first drink, he was already twisting on a bar stool in the kitchen, contemplating a break-in to his dad's office.

There was no way of knowing when his dad would wake up. He was unpredictable. Even though his college classes had ended, he may or may not need to go into work.

Mason sipped his coffee, wondering about his dad's hidden books on demons. Now that he was some kind of creature himself...He gulped another drink. The thought of his teeth slicing through his lips, unsettling.

Nope. He pushed the thought to the back of his mind. His own issues had to wait. Right now, he needed to learn what type of monster was after his best friend. Or whatever Gavan had said she was to him. Mate?

"Oh, God." The reality of his thoughts hit him, and he squeezed his eyes shut. What kind of nightmare had he stirred up tromping into those woods? Why hadn't he just taken melatonin? And Ashton. She'd been his rock since his mom died, since his dad had fallen into a thirteen-year-long bout with grief. But what about his grief? What about him? He was losing control again. Graduating was supposed to buy him freedom from this big, lonely house, not imprisonment to a cast of otherworldly raptors. He rubbed his head with a free hand, groaning, regretful for even thinking about his dream.

"I will get Ashton through this, but then it's back to the original plan." He spoke to the quiet kitchen. "I'm outta here—"

"You're up?"

Mason's dad stepped into the kitchen and tossed his own coffee pod into the machine.

Startled, Mason sat up straighter, set his mug down, and hid his shaking hands in his lap. "Forgot to turn off my alarm." Had his dad heard him?

"I have to run into work."

He popped the lid on a to-go mug and headed for the garage. The door fell shut with a loud bang. Seconds later, the familiar click of the car door closed. After that, the churning of the garage door opening and shutting played its tune until the house was still and far too quiet for Mason's nerves.

"I had a great time at my grad party, Dad. Thanks for asking." He snorted to the empty room.

Shaking off sarcasm, he jumped to his feet. His dad could be gone for a few hours or an entire day. It was too early for Ashton to be up. She had surely remembered to turn off her school alarm. She thought about things like that in advance, and in advance of advance. He slugged another gulp of coffee and slipped into the room he was never invited to visit.

Mason pulled the manuscript box from the top shelf. His dad kept a tidy office, so there was nothing in his way as he piled the books onto the desk. He thumbed through the titles: *Demons, Shadow Demons, Dream Demons*, and two untitled journals.

He opened *Dream Demons*, figuring he might as well start where it all began, with a dream. Settling into his dad's leather chair, he immersed himself into the world he'd mocked as a child. A sci-fi realm was somehow trying to claim him and Ashton?

Not if he could help it.

After several hours, Mason set the manuscript down and stood to stretch. Confusion rested heavy on his back. Nothing he'd read clicked with what Gavan had shared. Seam keeper warriors or shifters weren't mentioned, unless it was the shifting of monstrous forms from shadows or dream demons that summoned their victims through nightmares. His dad only spoke of Heaven and Hell, fallen angel stuff, and various debunked claims about possession.

Gavan had spoken about a Spiritual Realm, while his dad had written clinically about demons lingering on Earth, appearing as unidentifiable creatures. Somehow humans gave them power through an unknown magnetic source. Constant in their torments, they would hound a person to the point of death. His dad had speculated it as sport to the Underworld. There was no mention of demon princes or hawks or other realms. Nothing.

With Gavan's condensed version, and his dad's sketchy, imaginative one, Mason didn't feel any closer to the truth. How could he bring the topic up with his dad? Did it even matter?

He grabbed one of the journals and opened it to the middle.

The Colorless are demons who link to one particular person, connecting to them (for life?). Can they look human? Fades materialize in and out, smaller, not as connected. Do they work for the Colorless, or are they more like animals? Fades feed on human fear. The Colorless are attracted to that fear (is there a hierarchy?).

Fades? Colorless? Mason flinched as the words filled the quiet space, then glanced around as if caught in the act. His shoulders hunched over, relieved and embarrassed at the same time. It was after ten. He wanted to text Ashton to see if she was awake but dreaded the confrontation he knew would greet him. She would be more than anxious about the wall between them.

All he could do was add more bricks.

****

Ashton awoke to chirping birdsong, welcoming her first real day of summer. What an enchanting way to wake. But when she rolled over, reality struck. Memories of the night before flooded just as her phone buzzed a text notification.

—I'm an early riser, text when you wake up.—

Ian. She leaped out of bed, then placed the phone on her nightstand. She couldn't text him. Well, not at six in the morning.

Instead she grabbed a pair of yoga pants and one of Mason's old sweatshirts and sequestered her phone in her bedroom. With tea in hand, she found her mom painting in their studio. Classical music played from the speakers in the ceiling. Mom, engrossed in her work, hadn't heard her sneak in. Art always eased her thoughts. Or at least that's what her mom always said. Would she still have been an artist if she hadn't been adopted. Was it even her destiny?

Ashton's mom stroked big brushfuls of blue across a canvas. They hadn't worked together in over a week. Ashton blamed it on the busyness of graduation. But really it was the adoption lie hovering between them. And guilt. Guilt for wondering about this other family she belonged to, somewhere out there in the world.

Mom crinkled her nose, then dipped her brush to tint the hue. Ashton's heart jolted. Everything about her mom was her. They were the same. Or so she had always thought. Of course, Mom wasn't anxious about anything. She enjoyed being outside and playing golf with Dad. And she had never once mentioned being afraid to leave home. Maybe they were more different than she'd realized. The tingles in Ashton's chest bloomed.

"Good morning." Mom's cheerful greeting pulled her from her thoughts.

"Morning." She sat at her worktable, trying to shake off the stress. She needed to draw. Picking up a piece of charcoal, she began sketching, setting her mind to work. She needed the calming effects of her art and let her hand dance across the page. But it wasn't long before distraction clouded her mind in the shape of her oak.

Her fingers knew this design by heart, so her mind wandered to the night in the woods. How did that woman disappear into the bark? Who was the man with the eerie eyes? What did it all mean? And the hawk! She'd seen one in her vision, one outside her bedroom window, and another at Hicks's party. All these thoughts wrenched in her stomach, so she stopped and grabbed her cup.

Jasmine tea coated her growing worries. The forest. Knots over Mason's secrecy. Nervousness about calling a boy who wasn't Mason. And the deeper ones brewing about art school far away from her best friend and across town from her parents—

"Wow. I've never seen you add color to your tree before."

Startled, she looked down at her paper. Then jumping up, she almost spilled her tea. The oak was the same design she'd always drawn, but this one...rich with color. She'd added violet lights in the background. The start of sap-green leaves and raw umber branches came to life in a corner of the page.

"Oooh, tell me about the eyes." Mom's voice took on a spooky tone. Ashton looked again, just making out a set of eyes hiding in the branches, this part not yet colored. The ominous black and white of them forced her to take a step back.

"Are you okay?"

"Yeah." Ashton scooped up her pencils, dropped them into the mug. "I think I'm just hungry." She eyed her drawing again. Color? She never added color. Her tree was always just a doodle. An exercise to warm up before a surge of inspiration. But she couldn't look away. The hue glared in its contrast, like the bright red of her vaccination file, tucked behind the one labeled Adoption Lie. She blinked as her mind traveled back to the day she and Mason discovered the truth.

Ashton Magnolia Nichols. Her name, scribed in old

blocky typeset, had looked foreign, like it belonged to someone else.

"Who's adopted?" Mason's voice flashed in her memory. The world had stopped for a full minute. Maybe more. She remembered her voice catching as she read the legal jargon across the ivory sheets.

"I am."

How was she adopted? She was an artist like Mom. Quirky like Dad. She shared in her mom's brunette hair and her dad's bright blue eyes, his off-beat sense of humor. There was no way these two people weren't her parents.

The paperwork had a date, July 1. Her birthday was June 15. That seemed unusually close. Her mom was her friend. But friends don't lie. For seventeen years and eleven months.

They don't lie.

"I made muffins." Mom's voice pulled her back to reality, down the hall, and to the kitchen. The muffins were already on a tray, but she'd heated more water for tea.

Ashton shook off the memory and closed her mind to the strange color she'd added to her drawing. "I don't know why I got up so early." She tore the paper cup from the bottom of a blueberry muffin, hoping to rip up her ill feelings toward the adoption. She didn't want to be mad at her mom anymore. She had enough on her mind.

"I'm sure you're just coming down from all the graduation hullabaloo."

She studied her mom's face. She still looked young, even in her early fifties. Her carefree attitude probably kept her youthful. No matter what, she could always count on positive thinking and encouragement from her, even when she didn't want it. Dad was more left-brain. He was a surgeon, a straightforward, reserved, but with-a-secret-love-of-jazz kind of dad. Her parents were the most opposites-attract couple she knew. They'd been married thirty years. It must have been his musical talent that first wooed Mom. When she thought about it, she could always hear Dad playing his saxophone from the back of her mind.

"Don't you think?" Mom poured in a splash of hot water to warm her cooling tea.

"Probably." What was the matter with her? Did she need to pinch herself? "I guess. I'm just distracted today." Oops, why had she said that?

"It's the first day of summer." Mom laughed. "Or is that what you're worried about?"

She *was* worried about that. She'd worried about it since Mason announced his decision to move out of state. Since they'd planned to possibly open her birth records. Summers always passed in a blink. Everything was happening too fast.

"I can't talk about it right now."

"Remember, art school doesn't start for weeks. And we have our trip to New York in July." She raised an eyebrow, blue paint staining her temple. "That's something to look forward to."

Ashton reached out to accept her mom's olive branch, to let her magic touch work, as it often did. She missed sharing herself with her mom, and she needed to put those strange eyes she'd drawn behind iron doors.

"I met someone." She blurted the first thing she could think to say.

"What?" Mom plopped the teapot down and grabbed her hand. Her eyes wide. "From Michael's party? I want details."

Ashton couldn't help but laugh. What a relief to think about something new and hopeful. Something lighter than family lies, best friend strangeness, and now scary eyes perched in her oak. She pulled her fingers through her hair, fluffing up the slept-on layers, and told her mom all about bumping into Ian. "And he wants me to text him. I think he wants to get together."

"What's this I hear? A boy wants to date my daughter?" Dad waltzed in and kissed the top of Mom's head, winking at Ashton.

"Dad, it's not like that. He's new to the area, and we're going to the same art school in the fall. I'm just his first friend in town."

"Where's he from?"

"I'm not sure." She sipped her tea to think. She remembered asking but couldn't recall his answer.

"When are you going to see him?" Mom cooed.

Dad cleared his throat. "I'm not sure she should be seeing some boy she just met, especially when we don't know where he's from." He fiddled with the coffeemaker.

"If anything, we'd just meet at CC's Café." She reasoned, "I mean, if I even meet up with him. He loaned me his hoodie, so he might just need it back."

That was it. Her stomach flip-flopped. Of course, he wanted his hoodie back.

She sprang up. "That reminds me. I need to wash it." Up the stairs she ran, two at a time to her room. As she lifted it from the back of her desk chair, her fingers sizzled with static electricity. "Ouch—" She dropped the hoodie but snatched it up again, along with her laundry basket.

She turned the dial on the washer, then slowly walked to her bedroom, even slower to the nightstand.

Stretching her neck to see the screen, as if something terrible might happen if she got too close, her heart leaped to her chest. Six new notifications from Ian.

The first one. —*Are you up?*—

Butterflies took flight in her stomach.

The second. *—Craving coffee.*—

The third. *—Isn't Seattle famous for that?*—

She was smiling now.

But her mouth dropped open at the fourth message. —*Wouldn't a caramel latte taste perfect right now?*—

Caramel lattes were her favorite coffee drink. It was jasmine tea everywhere else but always caramel lattes from a coffee shop. A warm tingle ran up her spine.

Her heart pattered at the fifth text. *—Painting now.*— She liked that he was an artist too.

His final text had her giggling at his playful tone. —*Don't mind being interrupted.*—

Ashton had never dated but still knew texting seven times in one morning was pretty needy. Yet the smile crossing her face relayed a different message entirely. She liked him. What could be the harm in meeting him for coffee?

Her hands shook as she typed her response.

—*CC's Café by Mountain High, 9:30?*—

Excitement flowed from her toes to the top of her head. Maybe she could recover something good out of her graduation after all. She jumped in the shower. The warm spray and lavender scent of shampoo awakened her more, as she started thinking. Her whole world would open wide once fall term began. With her school only thirty minutes away, she could come home at any sign of homesickness. A safety net. Maybe meeting Ian was a sign of times to come. Maybe Mason was right when he said it was time for her to be the leader of her own life. If only she knew who she really was, she might recognize the person Mason was trying to make her see.

Mason!

How long had she gone without thinking about him? He was usually her first thought of the day. It didn't matter that he'd broken up with Gianna; he was leaving. It was all he'd talked about for four years of high school. Graduate. Get out of Seattle. Away from his dad.

His friendship was everything, but she'd never be anything more than that. She shook her wet hair. It was still only ten after eight, the morning after graduation. Mason would tease her if he knew she was awake this early. Besides, he'd been weird about Ian anyway.

She swallowed a tiny morsel of regret and pushed him out of her mind. If he could have secrets, maybe she could too. Maybe this new Ashton didn't tell Mason everything.

Chapter 6

Coffee Date

Ashton walked into CC's Café at nine thirty-five, on purpose. She didn't want to seem desperate but was also a stickler for promptness. Ian was already there holding two to-go cups. She liked him more already. Every table was full, so he stood by the counter with the same grin he'd worn at Hicks's party.

Unsure of what to say, she smiled as she approached.

"Hello." He offered her a cup, motioning to the filled space. "It's packed."

"I see that." She wondered now if this was a sign it had been a mistake to come.

"We could check outside?"

But when she turned to the covered patio tables, they were also taken. She had never seen the place so crowded.

"We could sit in my car?" he offered, his blue eyes looking surprisingly green in the overcast daylight.

Ashton could see her dad frowning at that. "Let's sit in my car, if that's okay." She tried smoothing her voice to stop the nervous shaking. It only made her enunciate strangely. "I have your hoodie. I washed it but forgot it in the back seat."

His smile settled her nerves a bit, and she led the way to her mom's old hatchback. It had been handed down to her on her sixteenth birthday, old but still chugging along.

Ian didn't seem to be alarmed by Old Blue, as her parents called it. He hopped in and adjusted the seat back even farther, although he wasn't any taller than Mason, who was the only passenger who ever sat in that spot. Then he turned, angling his body toward hers. "Tell me about yourself."

She laughed. "I don't think so. You go first." She took a careful sip of her latte, still steaming hot. Sweet caramel. Delicious. She smiled again.

"What's to tell? I moved from the east coast to study art. Not something my father is proud about. If I like it here, I plan on staying. Creating a home of my own."

"Wow, you have things planned out."

"Why not? Seize the day, right?"

Ashton nodded. A few drops of rain hit the windshield, creating tiny splashes. "So your father doesn't support your art?"

He laughed gruffly. "My father doesn't support any of his children's interests. He's more of a lone rider, you could say."

"I'm sorry." All she could think of was Mason's dad. But it wasn't that Max was a lone rider. He'd just never stopped mourning the loss of his wife and buried himself in work. He was always too busy to notice Mason. She wondered what the story was with Ian's father.

"It's okay. My art takes the place of any paternal inadequacies I felt as a child."

Ashton didn't know what to say. Her dad was the kindest man on Earth. Maybe she should go a different direction. "You have siblings?"

"Brothers." He snorted with as much endearment as he had mentioning his father. "Another reason I'm building a new life for myself, away from all of them." Then he stared out the window. The rain was picking up.

She gathered his family wasn't close. The sudden lull in conversation bubbled in her chest, and she placed her latte in the cup holder. He did the same.

"I'm looking forward to Cornish. How about you?" His tone, now upbeat, lightened the mood.

She was happy about the change of subject but not thrilled the topic was onto her. "I guess so." Unlike him, or even Mason, she didn't like the idea of moving away from home. Mason had encouraged her to give it a try her first year. But she had already seen herself moving home at winter break. Of course, now…

He lifted an eyebrow. And once again, she wished for her sketch book. With his perfectly shaped face, she could already see where she'd shade the bone structure along his jawline.

She caught herself staring. "I'm the opposite of you. Even though our school's only a short drive away, I'm still nervous about leaving home. I've never lived anywhere else."

"That's okay. When the right move comes along, you'll know you should take it." He leaned in a little closer. "Tell me about your art."

She smiled. She could talk about art without thinking. "Well, pen and ink is my medium of choice, though I also love sketching in charcoals. I paint too, watercolors mostly. How about you?"

His eyes sparked hazel green. She wasn't sure how she'd missed it the night before. It must have been too dark.

"My art..." He leaned his head back, his left hand brushing her fingers as she gripped the edge of her seat.

Butterflies swarmed behind her ribcage at the warm rush. She didn't move an inch.

Thunder boomed outside the car, and she flinched. He took her hand and gave it a squeeze. "Just a little thunder."

Should she let go of his hand? It felt warm. She swallowed her obvious insecurities. High school as Mason's sidekick had not prepared her for any of this.

"Your art?" she reminded him.

At the mere mention of the word, flashes of canvas rushed her thoughts, splashed with unending green and gold paint. The air thickened while separate pieces of canvas melded together to form the parts of one grand picture. Was she dreaming? She squeezed her eyelids, but the visions continued, vivid and colorful. Inviting.

Magically, she found herself in the painted vision before her. She could see herself in the setting. A forest. She must have gasped, because she could hear her breathless shock carry in the wind. A beautiful golden dress draped along her shape. There was no rain here, instead the sun's glow rose in the background, breaking through the surrounding evergreens. Her hair was longer, laced with strands of gold, and it danced around her waist in elegant waves.

The image kept shifting, like layers of the same picture overlapping with the original. Then from the far corner, she glimpsed a mist forming its own design: Ian. His eyes, more blue than green now, sparkled like those of her own, and he swooped in closer and closer until his hands opened before her. She, the Ashton in the vision, smiled at his embrace, and he looked at her longingly before engulfing her in a kiss.

A kiss so rich she tasted it on her tongue and felt it in her toes. Her tiny feet stood between two larger ones standing atop the cool padded leaves, his hands secure around her waist.

Ashton shivered as the visions transformed into reality and she found herself in Ian's arms, somehow comfortably over the center console of the car. He was kissing her. Surprisingly, she was kissing him back, although she wasn't sure how the vision had materialized into truth.

He pulled back, smiled down at her. His eyebrows lifted in question, as if asking to continue. The color in his eyes looked as green as the forest she felt they'd just walked through, and she wanted to return. Her wrist tingled against his back, and she shook her bracelet, her oak leaf charm snagging on his sweater.

All concentration blurred when he leaned to kiss her once more.

She could almost feel the forest surroundings until the kiss ended abruptly, and she awakened fully to the flapping of wings and screeching outside the car. She couldn't see through the rain-covered window, but the blurry forms of raptors screeched chaotically, matching her screams. Several of them swooped down over the front windshield. Talons aimed straight through the glass. She covered her face as the windshield shattered in an explosion of frenzy.

****

Ashton's safety compromised. Head outside at once!

So many thoughts flew through Mason's head, it took a minute to make sense of the new voice barking orders. It came to him the same eerie way Gavan's hawk voice had breached his senses the night before graduation. He jumped out of his dad's office chair anticipating the pain of crushing bones.

"Who are you?" He spun around the room, looking for anyone. The noise in his head boomed with a sense of urgency.

Shunnar, second-in-command of the Northwest Casts. No time to explain. Out back now.

Mason gripped the hair on his head. Fear engulfed him, like it had the day his dad told him his mom was gone. For the first time in all his years of preparation, he couldn't think of one tip from survival camp that could help him now.

Move!

At least his years of athletic training paid off, because without understanding why or how, his legs picked up his feet, and together carried him through the house and out the back door. Rain poured from gray skies. Squinting, he tried to keep the weather from his eyes when he noticed several hawks lining the fence.

There was no time to react. His knees buckled, and his body dropped to the wet grass. Elbows stretched out, forcing his shoulders from their sockets. His chin tucked into his chest while teeth tore through his lips to form the hooked beak of a hawk. Bones snapped, and feathers somehow choked down the bile rising from inside. His eyesight shifted into something more powerful.

His new body knew what to do, even if his inner heart writhed. He fell in behind the other birds of prey taking flight with ease. Shunnar's message loud and clear in his mind: *Save Ashton from evil.* He didn't understand how, but the pure will emitting from under his rustled plumage executed the cast's plan without need for explanation. He'd never flown so high so fast, and then, in an instant, dive-bombed straight down to Earth again.

They were above the parking lot of a strip mall when he saw his mark.

Why were they crashing through the window of Old Blue? Was she in the car? Mason's human concern seeped through his hawk's potent focus, but whatever animal instinct pumped through his veins screeched in battle cry, *kiiiiiii-arrr!*

Shunnar, in the lead, pulled up at the last second and used his long talons to pierce the glass, which crumbled the windshield like an ice sculpture crashing on a tile floor. The two larger birds behind Shunnar flew into the car. Without knowing what to expect, he intuitively knew his target.

Demon.

People in the surrounding area rushed the scene. Screams sounded from every direction. Rain continued its downpour, unconcerned with the confusion it added. Suddenly black smoke oozed from the car and choked out the commotion. Or was it smoke? The familiar scent filled the air, like a match striking, or sulfur. Mason could hear nothing but Ashton's scream coming from the driver's seat. On the left, sat the guy Ashton had been talking to in Hicks's backyard.

Not guy. Demon.

His hands were raised, not batting at the birds aiming for his head, but directing a liquid light. The white glow of it spread over him and Ashton, turning green and then brown and then black. The heat singed the air around the car, creating a buffer to keep the fighting raptors back.

The hawks didn't stop. One after the other, they dive-bombed the forcefield. Mason's rage bubbled in the heat. If the hawks were still in pursuit, it meant this guy's defenses could be broken. This…*demon*…could be destroyed.

And it was with Ashton.

He smacked the glowing wall of black light.

****

The birds' loud cries pierced Ashton's ears as the windshield crumbled into tiny glass cubes in her lap. Ian threw himself over her body, crushing her, but she knew it was for protection.

She'd called out, but the car filled with smoke, or something else. The pungent smell forced her mouth closed. Heat filled the space as dizziness filled her head.

Ian climbed over the passenger seat. Then he pulled her to the back seat, her back scraping on the console.

"Ashton, I'm sorry for this. You weren't meant to see it yet. They will lie to you. But I will always tell you the truth about who you are." He kissed her forehead. "My One Hundred."

"What are you talking about?" She tried sitting up, but his hands pushed her gently back, soaking her to the bone with warmth from where his fingers gripped. Like sinking into a hot bath, her eyes closed, and the upheaval surrounding the car faded away.

Chapter 7

Hidden Truths

"She's waking up."

Ashton's mom's voice broke through the strange heaviness keeping her eyes closed. Her toes tingled as she forced her legs to move.

"Hey, sweetie." Dad's voice.

"Ash." Mason.

Was her whole family there?

Her eyes fluttered open, and she was greeted by a room full of faces: Mom, Dad, Mason, and even Mr. Deed stood in the square, sterile space. She was in a hospital bed.

"What's going on?" She lifted her head but lay back when the spinning began.

"Not so fast." Mom leaned over her. "The nurse gave you something for the nausea. It knocked you out."

"Do you remember the car accident?" Dad asked gently.

"Um—I remember the birds breaking the car window."

"Birds?" Mom questioned. "It was a thunderstorm. The pitch of the crack shattered the windshield."

No. She thought back to the incident. Hawks broke the car window, and Ian...Ian!

"Is Ian okay?" She rolled to her side, slower this

time, pushed herself up.

Mason propped her pillows. Dad fiddled with the bed, adjusting the back to rise.

"Ian wasn't there," Mason said flatly.

Dad added, "Because of your anxiety, Dr. Will thinks you may have fainted from the shock. But there are only a few scratches and some nausea. How do you feel?"

"Okay, I think." Her brain stretched to fill the empty spaces from her memory. Where had Ian gone? What about the angry birds? "There were hawks. They broke through the window. Ian and I were both in the car because CC's was full."

"Sweetie, the café called 9-1-1, and they rushed you to the emergency room because you were unconscious. Ian wasn't with you. Maybe he'd already left before it happened." Dad rubbed her foot through the blankets and then headed for the door. "I'm going to let the nurses know you're awake."

"Hey, Ashton." Mr. Deed peeked his head around Mason. "I'm glad you're okay. You had us a little worried." His smile looked foreign.

"A lot worried." Mason chimed in, plopping next to her in bed. "All I could think of was the time you fell out of that tree." He snagged her hand, holding it with both of his.

He must have really been worried. He hadn't mentioned the tree incident in years. It had happened when she was seven, playing with Mason in the greenbelt behind their houses. He'd tried teaching her how to climb trees like a ninja. She hesitated, falling six feet into a blackberry bush. Scraped up and embarrassed, she'd only suffered a sprained ankle and one lasting scar under her right eye. It had healed well and faded over the years to a faint white line she covered with concealer. Mason had doted on her for the rest of the summer. It was also the first time he'd told her he *always* loved her.

"I'm sorry I worried you." She squeezed his hand. But inside, the familiar twists of anxiety tightened in her chest.

He tucked a strand of hair behind her ear. "I'm just glad you're okay."

A booming voice broke through the door. "I'll be the judge of that." It was Dad's friend, Dr. Will, smiling behind his round glasses and white mustache. He'd been at their house for barbecues and Christmas parties over the years.

"Hi, Dr. Will." She smiled as he washed his hands in the sink.

Mason slipped off the bed so Dr. Will could check her over. He listened to her heart and shone his minilight in her eyes, then patted her on the leg.

"Good as new." He smiled up at Dad. "All tests are clear. I think the fright of it all caused her unconsciousness. She's okay to go home."

"Thanks, Tim. I appreciate it."

Dr. Will slapped her dad on the back. "Of course. Now you have no excuse to get out of the golf tournament tomorrow. You too, Maggie. We're playing for charity."

"I know, I know," Mom sang.

Dr. Will winked at Ashton again before leaving the room.

"Honey, I don't know. One of us should stay home with Ashton." The wrinkle between her eyes deepened with worry.

"He said she's good as new." Dad squeezed her

shoulder. "It's too late to pull out now."

"I'll stay with her." Mason sat back down on the bed.

"I have a better idea." Mr. Deed stepped up, resting his hand on Mason's shoulder. Mason swallowed a visible lump in his throat. "Mason and I planned on heading to our beach house in Lincoln City tomorrow night. A little graduation celebration. It might be a good place for Ashton to recover. The weather should be warming up by the end of the week, so the kids could rest and play some board games. The ocean air will be good for her."

Ashton was speechless. She looked to Mason, but his expression was unreadable. He would never have agreed to go anywhere on vacation with his dad. When she glanced at her mom, she only looked to her dad, who looked to Ashton.

He nodded. "What do you think? You love the beach. I know we'd miss your birthday, but we can celebrate on our New York trip in July. I think you should go."

Mason chimed in. "It'll be fun. Come." He smiled strangely. His amber eyes gleamed with tiny ruby streaks. There was more he wasn't saying.

Mom kissed her cheek, then started collecting her things. A nurse came in to help them with paperwork. Mason pulled on her hand. "Come on. Let's get out of town and hang out at the beach."

Ashton exhaled. Maybe time away was exactly what she needed. If she knew Max Deed, he'd be working remotely most of the time. She'd have Mason all to herself...to finally pry out the truth. And this time, she wasn't taking no for an answer.

****

The drive to the Oregon coast was long. Even traveling later in the day out of Seattle, they hit traffic heading through Portland. The rain didn't help, slowing all travelers well under the speed limit.

Ashton dozed on and off in the back seat, Mason next to her. Max Deed drove in silence as she'd expected. He never wasted words, even for family, which she assumed he considered her by now. His speech in the hospital room the day before was lengthy.

And Mason. She glanced at him sitting next to her. No earbuds clung to his ears. The radio wasn't even on. He just stared out the window, gaze up to the sky. The inside of the car was uncomfortably quiet; the only melody was the soft hum of the engine. The tempo changed only when Max took an exit off the freeway.

Ashton swallowed a drink from her water bottle and pulled out her phone. She hadn't responded to Ian's latest text.

—*Our coffee date was nice. I hope I can see you again before school starts.*—

It didn't make sense. Didn't he remember the hawks crashing through the window? Or the kiss? Or the way he'd whispered, "I will always tell you the truth about who you are." It hadn't been long after her release from the hospital before she'd remembered the whole event. When she did, she questioned her own mental state.

Could her family be right? Was it the thunder cracking that shattered her car window? Had her anxiety caused her to pass out and mix everything up? Or had she dreamed it all, like Mason's strange dream two weeks before graduation? She needed to talk to him alone. If her parents found out about any of these possibilities, the crazy birds or insane dreams, they'd put her in therapy. Her dad was too left-brained to wait it out, even if her mom could somehow support the strangeness.

She tossed her phone into her bag. What could she say to him? *Do you remember hawks crashing through the windshield? Did we really kiss in the illusion of a painting?* He'd think she was crazy. And she liked him, or at least thought she could. They'd be going to the same school in the fall. Maybe once they arrived at the beach, she could figure out what to text back. For now, she was on her own.

Which reminded her, depressingly, she was on her own in more ways than one. Pulling her phone back out, she typed into the search engine *opening closed adoption files*. She had planned to wait for Mason to help her. But he was too busy in his own head, now buddy-buddy with the dad he'd hated for years. She wasn't sure she wanted to open her birth records, but taking charge of this part of her life seemed to give her a needed lift. If she did find her birth parents, it wouldn't change how she felt about her own mom and dad. Would it?

No. She turned her phone over in her lap. She couldn't face this yet. Stress was ruling her life at the moment. And since she might be losing her mind—literally—she wasn't sure about opening that door. She exhaled as she made a mental note to contact the county clerk and fill out a petition form. She would handle it when she got home. Alone. Suddenly, her bed with her ocean-blue covers tugged at her soul.

****

Finally, Max pulled onto an old gravel road, winding through dark silhouettes of low pines and green brush. The surrounding trees were much sparser than the dense forests back home. When they pulled into the driveway, the ocean wasn't visible. She vaguely remembered it being a short walk to the beach.

The little shack-like beach house wasn't exactly run down. No one had been there in so long, it just needed some tender loving care. Once inside, Ashton was pleasantly surprised to find Max already starting a fire in the fireplace. It might be June, but on the Pacific Northwest Coast, with the forecast of rain on the horizon, she was freezing.

Mason plowed through the door carrying both their bags in one arm, tossing her his sweatshirt with the other. Then he motioned for her to follow him down the hall. She traipsed behind taking in the sea-color decor, walls washed in coral and sky-blue hues. It felt like forever since she'd been there. Maybe once or twice in the last thirteen years. It had always reminded Mason of his mom, then he'd feel sad. His dad was always sad back then. Ashton couldn't figure out why they were even there.

Max's bedroom and their room, conveniently called the "bunk room," were the only two bedrooms in the house. Theirs had two sets of bunkbeds, one on each wall. A blue-painted shelving unit sat against the back wall, complete with boxes of board games. She couldn't imagine playing games with her mind so full. And she couldn't hold in her thoughts any longer.

"So what's the story?" She pulled the door shut, dropped his sweatshirt on the bed. "Why are we here?"

Mason tossed their bags on top of a dresser. "What do you mean?"

"I mean, why are you suddenly agreeing to go on a vacation with your dad? You guys don't do vacations."

He paused before responding. He'd been doing that

71

since the woods experience, and it was driving her crazy. That and staring up at the sky.

"He wanted time with me at the coast before I leave for school."

Ashton clamped her fists until she felt her nails pierce her palms. Nothing in his response felt like the Mason she knew. "I'm caught in *The Twilight Zone*."

"You're probably tired after all the grad stuff. We're at the beach. Relax. Find your Zen." He faked a smile.

She stared open-mouthed. Was he serious? She'd thought if she got him alone at the beach, he might open up. But his story was the same.

"I need some air." She left the room and walked past Max to the back door. Once outside, she found the dark overgrown path leading to the water. The mounds of sand slowed her march, but the sound of ocean waves told her she was headed in the right direction. When the narrow path opened onto the horizon of ocean, she halted. Its welcome roared even if she couldn't see it well in the dark. Bonfires flickered up and down the shoreline casting light. Waves crashed against the sand. The leaf charm on her bracelet seemed to hum at her wrist until she gave it a shake. It was comforting in a way, or at least distracting. It was exactly what she needed to step out of her life. For a moment.

She wasn't sure how much time had passed. It didn't seem to matter with everything out of control. She sat down and kicked off her shoes, toes curled around thick clumps of sand. Each grain, coarse against the soft pads of her feet, reminded her she still felt something. The cold coastal wind whipped up her back like a slap across the face.

She wanted to go home. But where was that...really? She had a mom and dad out there somewhere in the world she never knew. Did she look like them more than she thought she looked like Drew and Maggie Nichols? Did it matter when she loved them as if they were the same parents she knew them to be two weeks ago? Two years ago. Twelve years ago.

"Hey." Mason's voice rolled over the ocean waves, pulled her thoughts back to shore. "My dad started a fire. Come inside." He didn't sit down.

She let out a long breath...one, two, three, four. Counting her fears away. "So this means you're going to tell me what's going on?" She didn't stand up.

His pause surged with the crash of waves, and she felt almost hopeful in the friend she thought she knew.

His sweatshirt dropped across her shoulders. "Ash, there's nothing to tell."

"You mean there's nothing you're willing to tell." She pulled on the sweatshirt.

He shoved his hands in his pockets, gaze still on the dark horizon.

"I'll stay here."

"It's freezing. Come inside."

If he raised his voice, she couldn't tell. The wind swallowed his tone.

Anger rumbled through her chest, which could have been the windchill, but there was no stopping her now. How could he lie to her? After thirteen years of friendship. She stood up before she could back down and pushed him. He stumbled, pulling his hands from his pockets to catch his balance. He wasn't shocked. They'd jokingly roughhoused enough times. It was the look of defeat she didn't recognize in his eyes.

"Tell me what's going on!"

"I can't say anything. Give me two days, and I'll tell you everything." He drew both hands through his hair. "Please."

"What happens in two days?"

"Can't you just trust me?"

"Trust you!"

"Two days."

Ashton's mind stretched around every possible event that could take place in two days. "Is it about my birthday?" She shook her head. "What's so important about that? I turn eighteen."

His audible response was more than a growl, more than a groan. It was a guttural, painful bawl that forced her back a step. Mason leaned over, hands on his knees. Exasperation swarmed his body like an aura.

"Look at you." She gripped his shoulder. Angry or not, she loved him. "Whatever this is, it's hurting you. It's hurting us. Let me help you."

"You don't understand." He spoke through gritted teeth.

"Does it have to do with your dream-hunt in the woods? Those hawks crashing through my window?" Desperate, she touched his cheek, locked eyes. "Tell me what's happening. If not for you, for me. It's driving you crazy. Can you imagine how I feel not knowing anything?"

He pulled free, paced in circles, sand flying every direction.

"Mas, please." She stepped in his path, his gaze like burnt embers.

"It's big." His weight fell to her shoulder, and she cemented her feet in the sand to hold him upright. "It's bigger than the both of us."

She clung to him like a buoy in dangerous waters,

74

unable to tell anymore who was saving whom.

"On your birthday, you—we—we're going to change. We aren't from—"

Mason stopped short, pulling them both down to wet sand. His back arched, face contorted in pain, shoulders constricted against some invisible striking force.

"Mason!" she screamed into the wind, picking up even more. "Max!" she called up to the beach house, well aware they were too far for his dad to hear.

She rummaged through pockets to find her cell phone. One bar. Hopefully enough to connect 9-1-1.

"No." He knocked the phone from her hands, slumped over, coughing as if he was the one with asthma.

"Mas, are you okay?"

"Yep." His breaths were shallow now. "Muscle spasm."

"Muscle spasm?" She pushed on his shoulder as leverage to stand up. "You're kidding me, right?"

"Two more days, Ash." He rolled onto his back, amber eyes pleading. "Please?"

She stormed away, suddenly stopping short at the path back to the house. The shadow of a hawk perched in the branch of a low pine ahead. Its eyes glinted in the night.

Chapter 8

Distractions

Mason waited for his dad to call it a night, a full hour after Ashton. He'd caught her knowing glance when she announced she was going to bed. She wanted him to follow her so they could continue talking. But there was no way he'd be trapped in a room with her rantings. Once she clung to something she never let go. If anyone could get her to try, it was him. But even he knew his limits.

Another ten minutes crawled by. No movement in the bedrooms. Even the crackle of soot-fallen logs in the fireplace stopped hissing. The faraway hush of crashing waves against a black night shore was the only sound seeping through the walls of the beach house.

It was time.

He slipped out the back door into the salty air, knowing better than to speak out loud.

Gavan. Shunnar. Somebody, he thought into the night, unsure how it worked. The hawks had always made initial contact, but he was done with their random invasions into his mind. Ashton's anti-anxiety meds were looking more enticing with each passing day. He walked in circles to the back yard, knees bent, hands up to block, as if something might dive at him. None of his black belt skills could save him from the supernatural, could they?

Lack of confidence tasted foul on his tongue.

Where are you? He gripped the back of a rusty lawn chair until his knuckles glowed white in the dim porch light.

No response.

He pitched the chair across the lawn, breaking the silence. There was hardly enough room to pace in the small fenced yard. He pinched his right brow to stop the twitching and tried again. *Gavan! Shunnar!*

You need to calm down. It was Shunnar.

What the hell did you do to me? That wasn't anything like the crap you pulled with my dad.

Shunnar drew out his exhale. *Your dad still believes in his demon monsters of fiction. I'm not concerned with him, although leaving his books out on his desk was careless.*

You called me to shift. I can't control this—this thing happening to me.

Running into his dad after witnessing Ashton's accident had been the most difficult thing he'd faced. He had tried to be quiet about another realm controlling his every move, but his dad was a poker player. A good one. He wasn't budging until Mason fessed up.

The whole event replayed in his mind. "Dad, I can't do this right now. Ashton's hurt. I have to get to the hospital."

"What do you mean?" His dad grabbed his keys.

Mason couldn't believe his bad luck. His dad was hardly ever home.

Suddenly Mason's shaky legs buckled. He fell against the kitchen island. He didn't know if it was the adrenaline pumping from shifting, the shock in seeing Ashton hurt, or the fact he couldn't seem to control his environment anymore.

"Dad, I have to go."

"What happened?" He shouldered Mason's weight, heading out the garage door. "Did you get into an accident? Why didn't the ambulance take you?"

"No. I wasn't in the car."

Max pulled out of the driveway and sped down the street. His voice typically steady. "I need the full story. They'll ask questions at the hospital."

His dad's sedan took the corners with ease. Mason's heart pounded. He imagined Ashton forever messed up by what she'd seen, about whatever that creature had done to her, about this barbaric future some shifting hawk told him they were part of.

His head spun faster than a carnival ride. Shunnar's voice rang through, but he couldn't make out the words.

"There's a demon after Ash. I—"

Spasm. His already trembling body tightened into one giant spasm, then jackknifed over the seatbelt.

"Dad—"

His dad pulled over and jumped from the car. He ripped open the passenger door and pulled out Mason's legs. This gave him more room to breathe. But why did he stop? What if he really needed a doctor?

"I know what this is. I saw it happen to your mother." He forced Mason's stiffened chin up to face him. "I'm not letting you go. Do you hear me? You stay with me!"

An imaginary vise gripped Mason's body. Every nerve, muscle, bone morphed into one solid lump. It wasn't pain so much as full constriction. He was immobilized.

His dad rambled on about his mother running from demons. His words wrapped around Mason's head like cartoon birds, flying circles after an animated knockout.

Responses wouldn't come, but it didn't seem to faze his dad, who kept chattering away.

Finally his rantings faded until he spoke to himself in a whisper. Mason's torso buzzed, as did his fingers and toes. His dad leaned against the car, his face in his hands. Mason had never seen him look so defeated.

His expression faded in the night's chill, bringing Mason back to the beach house.

You were told to keep Ashton human until her birthday. You were warned. Shunnar's voice, sharp in his mind, brought back the pain in his spine. The dark backyard, not nearly black enough to hide his anger.

She's going crazy. I can't go two more days like this.

You must. Distract her—

Distraction? That's your advice? She's not a little kid. The muscles in his back tightened, and his stomach knotted. There was no way Ashton could handle any of this. A mountain hike or scary movie, he could sway her into experiencing. But this?

You'll need to give her something else to think about. Take the next step in your relationship. You'll be paired soon anyway.

What does that mean? I suddenly have no choice in my own future? Heat rushed under his skin, pushing his thoughts through to Shunnar with intensity. Graduation had been his ticket to freedom, his way out. Now this impossible nightmare—he didn't want any of it.

You are destined for greater things. Grow up, Mason. You're not a child in our world either.

What do you mean our *world? A world where I painfully morph into a freaking hawk? Where demons are real, and choices don't matter? What kind of world is that?* He felt himself losing steam. Exhaustion pulsed under his skin. His heart skipped beats. Or was it—

"No!" He fell forward onto his knees, body contorting at unnatural angles. "Make it stop." He coughed, teeth piercing through his top lip, blood spilling onto his hands, no longer gripping the grass in his tiny back yard. Talons twisted into place, wings forced their way through the back of his arms, snaking down to what used to be fingers. His neck sliced the air, back and forth, until the violet shade of hawk vision clicked into place.

The pain you've experienced tonight ought to be enough deterrent not to blindly disobey orders again. Shunnar's voice, curt. *Change back.*

I can't do it on demand. I don't even know how it happens.

Although we can see well at night, hawks from the Human Realm cannot. You can't be caught flying here by some naturalist. It will draw unwanted attention. We were patient as you ransacked your father's office for his fairy tales on demons. We even supported your decision to bring Ashton here, away from home. It may buy time from the Dark Realm. But this little tantrum is over. Go to bed.

There was no way he was going through all that pain to change back. A part of him, somewhere deep and unknown, wanted to fly. He needed to feel his wings stretch above the wind. But no sooner had his body ascended, than it crumpled back to the ground.

Shrieks escaped his beak, the sound haunting as human bones began the crunching journey back into their sockets. His neck coiled into place, as feathery plumes forced their way down his throat. Gagging, he coughed up blood, finding his own human hands and knees, carrying his full human weight.

Distract Ashton for two more days. We'll keep watch. Shunnar's voice held an edge of finality.

Mason rolled onto his back as the rain started, each drop an icy reminder his life was not his own. For now. He would follow orders long enough to keep Ashton safe. Then he'd find a way out. He wasn't going to be a pawn in somebody else's game, especially when the game was haunted with demons and morphing hawks.

****

Ashton woke to breakfast smells. Eggs and bacon, and hopefully toast with jam. Mason was sacked out in the bottom bunk across the small room. He didn't look peaceful, even in sleep. How far could she push him today?

The pain that had floored him the night before was far too real. And she'd been through many a muscle spasm with him in the past. Everything in her life was a mess. Should she call home? Mom would consult Dad, and Dad would think something more serious had happened to her in the car accident. If you could even call it an accident. Her shoulders shuddered at the memory of those talons breaking through the windshield.

Far. Too. Real.

No, she couldn't call her parents. Not yet. How bad could another day be?

Ashton's stomach growled. She couldn't think of anything else until she had some proper caffeine. Crawling out of bed, she pulled on leggings and one of Mason's sweatshirts. Then she tiptoed down the hall to the kitchen.

"Well, good morning." Max greeted her with more vivacity than she'd ever witnessed. "Just a minute here."

He turned around, lifted a bright yellow teapot off the stove, and poured steaming water into a mug. "Do you want tea or hot chocolate? Mason mentioned you don't drink coffee unless it's a latte."

"Um, tea would be good." She scooted onto a bar stool facing a dining area with a big picture window on the opposite side. She couldn't see the ocean from her spot—the beach was farther down a winding path—but she could hear its soft roar. Outside was gray and breezy. The possibility of rain teased her hope the clouds would burn off. She could use some sunshine.

Max set a mug on the counter in front of her, followed by a box of jasmine green tea bags. She smiled, knowing Mason had to have mentioned it earlier.

"Thank you." She set a teabag steeping while fixing her gaze out the window. The cloudy morning matched her heavy heart. Her mind rattled with questions. Perhaps sunshine wouldn't matter either way.

How had Mason put it? Something big was happening to the both of them. What big thing? And how could it hurt Mason without being present? Her mind started thinking of spy movies or sci-fi technology…or magic. All of it fiction. All of it impossible.

"Would you like some eggs and bacon?" Max fiddled with the stove and pulled a sheet pan of bacon from the oven.

"I don't think I've ever seen you this cheery before," Ashton chanced, smiling coyly so he wouldn't be offended. He wasn't the joking kind of man.

"That's because he's never been this cheery before." Mason's sleep-filled voice rang as he slid onto the bar stool next to her. "What's up with you, Dad?"

Ashton couldn't help smiling at Mason's messy hair, shagging every which way. He really was comfortable around her, right down to his baby blue boxers and wrinkled T-shirt. "I see you dressed for breakfast."

Mason pretended to karate-chop her, faking left and going right for a teabag himself. For a minute, it felt like old times. Then she remembered the wall he'd built between them.

"For your information, I have plenty to be happy about this morning." Max smiled, as Ashton and Mason exchanged confused glances.

"Do tell." Mason hopped off the stool to fetch water for his tea. He never cared where he got his caffeine: tea, coffee, Red Bull.

"Well, for starters, I don't feel crazy anymore. I can finally breathe in this world full of secrets. Secrets that were slowly making my life hell," he said, flipping eggs without a spatula.

Mason shifted uncomfortably. "Dad, watch it. I can't talk about anything."

"Excuse me?" Ashton inserted.

At the same time, Max carried on. "I've known about this possibility for the last eighteen years, and I'm not hiding it anymore." He set a platter filled with eggs and bacon on the counter, followed up with plates and forks.

"Dad, I've explained explicitly how I'm the one who gets burned, pretty much literally, when you talk about things you shouldn't."

"Don't worry, Mason. I am only talking about the things I've figured out on my own. I'm referring to my own validation."

"Validation about what? You don't know anything." Mason scooped eggs onto his plate, then stopped mid-spoonful, offering the platter to Ashton.

"Validation of something I believed to be true but was too afraid to admit. It just hasn't come up since your mother's—" His voice broke. "Death."

"Really, Dad? You're going there with this?"

He spun around. "*There* is the only place I know. The day Hell took my wife? Then yes, I'm going *there*. I'm staying *there*. I will learn all I can until I find some kind of peace *there* so your mother didn't die in vain."

Mason stood up. "You can't do this right now."

"Mason," Ashton chastised. She didn't know what they were talking about, but it was getting out of hand, fast. They never spoke about his mom's death.

Mason sat down, stabbed his eggs. "I can't talk about this. You both know that."

Ashton caught his collective "*you both* know that."

"I didn't talk about it for eighteen years. Look where that got me." Max opened his mouth to say more, but instead, left the room.

"Mason, talk to me." She nudged his shoulder. "I know this has to do with what happened to you last night."

"I can't talk about it!" He jumped off the stool, dumped his dishes in the sink.

"Wait a minute. I'm on your side. I'm always on your side, we're a team."

He froze, before slowly turning to face her. His gaze met hers, more than tired. Deeper than longing. Saturated hues she didn't recognize. What paint colors would she combine to match them? There wasn't enough Kelly green or wisteria to blend with clay brown. Never could she mix the chroma behind his expression.

He shook his head and walked out of the room.

She would give him one more day.

Chapter 9

Tap Tap Tap

The tap on the bedroom window was so soft it was almost undetectable, absorbing into Ashton's already bizarre dream. She had been walking on the beach, hawks building in numbers along the scattered fallen logs. They seemed to be trying to tell her something, eyeing her, nodding their heads, hopping from log to log. With bare feet buried in the sand, she stared at them. Two, then four, then swarms of them. Danger pricked her skin, but she couldn't move.

Then came the tapping. It was quiet at first until the sound of tiny pings against glass pulled her attention from the birds. She twisted her body to peer behind, where a shadowy shape loomed on the path back to the beach house.

Ashton squinted through the gray, overcast day. It was the only way she could think to bring the hidden object into form. Recognizing the disturbance, her jaw dropped.

Then she awoke with a start.

Ashton lurched to a sitting position in her bed before her brain fully caught up. She held her head to settle the dizziness, until—

Tap, tap, tap.

She heard it before her eyes found the source. Glancing over at Mason, she pointed, giving her visitor in the window a heads-up that he was sleeping. Why? She didn't have an answer for that. But when the one who kisses you until your insides melt and protects you from attacking birds stands at your window bearing two latte cups, you alert them to possible detection.

Ian winked, motioning to meet him outside. She nodded, then crawled out of bed before she could change her mind, remembering to be quiet as an afterthought. A quick glance at Mason confirmed he was still asleep, and she tiptoed to her suitcase, grabbing clothes. Once she was safely down the hall and into the bathroom, she allowed herself to breathe.

After dressing in yoga pants and a sweatshirt, she shoved her bare feet into flip-flops. She brushed her teeth and swooped her hair into a ponytail. It would have to do. Gulping courage, and a little foreboding guilt, she slipped out the door, heading straight for the shore. The sunrise from behind the beach house burned bright, even veiled by the marine layer of cloud cover.

Then she saw him.

"Caramel latte?" Ian met her on the path. Her favorite coffee drink again? It was better than birthday cake.

She wasn't sure how to respond, worried what Mason would think. Worried if what she thought she experienced on their coffee date really happened, and even more worried he didn't seem to remember it in his texts. But it was her birthday. And his arm felt warm on her back.

"Thank you."

"You didn't respond to my texts," he said playfully. "I thought maybe your friend was taking up too much of your time."

"It was a last-minute decision to come. How did

you find me?" She sipped her latte, ignoring his comment about Mason. It was still hot, warming her insides from the chilly morning. A coffee shop must be close by.

"Let's just say a little bird told me." He smiled up at a hawk perched in a pine. She followed his gaze to the next tree limb, where a small cluster of them sat ready to strike. She stepped back toward the beach house, anxious about another attack.

Just then, a brisk breeze blew up the wide arms of her sweatshirt, like a sign. Even far enough from the shore, she felt the dampness like a wake-up call. Questions rattled behind her eyes. What was it with these hawks? What was Ian doing here? Had he followed them?

"A little birthday vacation?" He took her hand, pulling her attention from the birds of prey, away from her thoughts, his eyes pleading to walk farther down the beach. Her heartbeat sped up in her chest. She wanted to see him, though unsure how far she should venture from the house. Goosebumps rose on the backs of her arms. But Ian didn't seem worried, and his grip felt warmly secure.

"How did you know it was my birthday?" Her feet didn't follow as he started toward the beach, her hand dropping away from his. She stood, reluctant, and took in the sight of him. His short black hair looked freshly cut. He was tall, and although his body hid under a black sweater and cargo pants, he radiated an essence of fitness.

He turned, bringing that intensity of his eyes. They were brown today. She had only seen him twice before but couldn't remember them being brown. Or could she?

His eyebrows arched, and he tilted his head toward the beach.

"I…" She shifted her weight from foot to foot. "I think I should stay close to the house."

"Mason's asleep." He smirked.

Ian touched the side of her arm and infused her with that strange rush of warmth she'd felt in his touch before. Standing for another moment, woozy from the relaxed feeling surging through, she shook her head and walked with him down the path.

Suddenly her ears filled with a radio-blaring call of a hawk. Her earlier dream of giant birds trying to tell her something registered in bursts. Ian increased their pace to the shore. But when another shriek filled the air, Ashton ducked low and looked to Ian.

With his eyes on the hawk, he pulled her up. "Must be a storm brewing. The fire pit's right there, not too far." He pointed to the circle of rocks, closer to the water. His hand on her shoulder felt as warm as her latte, and for no reason at all, she followed him.

They sat side by side on a fallen log, and a fire somehow sparked to life. Staring at the flames, Ashton wondered when Ian had lit it, but let her gaze drift over to the crashing waves, rougher than the night before. The hawks cried again, and she jumped up, breaking contact with Ian. A rush of frigid air wafted over her, like awakening from a dream. Something was wrong…something like the hawk attack through her windshield.

"I think I made a mistake." Tingles in her chest started their fear-dance. But Ian reached out, squeezed her shoulder. The warmth from his touch warred with an internal flutter trailing up her stomach, icy and sharp. She let him pull her down to sit. His touch warm.

89

His face charming. His eyes blue…weren't they just brown, like chocolate?

"How can a coffee date be a mistake?"

She slowed her breathing, to get ahold of herself. "Coffee date?"

"Well, you didn't expect a toe-curling kiss in a coffee shop parking lot, only seconds before escaping angry deranged birds, to be our first date, now did you?"

Her mouth fell open. He did remember the hawks.

Traveling up her back, his hands smoothed away every concern she started to form. All she could think about was his kiss. That kiss emerging from the vision of his artwork. The beautiful forest in greens and golds. She sucked in the ocean air; high school was clearly no training for this.

"Toe-curling?"

He smiled, presumably unmoved by the gathering hawks. "Well, it was for me. Forgive me for assuming you enjoyed it, too."

"I-I did." She was in trouble now, unable to think clearly. But more than that, something kept zinging her back to reality, like the continuous tapping sound waking her from her dream. She looked at her wrist, the source of irritation, and her oak charm gleamed like the sun. Feeling stronger, she stood and stepped away from his touch.

"What is it?" He rose and reached out to steady her, though she didn't need it this time.

She took another step back. "How did you know where to find me? We didn't tell anyone." Her brain kick-started into motion, but not quick enough, sputtering before she could finish a thought.

He was smoothing her shoulders again. "Are you

sure you didn't mention it?"

Not only was she unsure, she couldn't remember what he thought she'd mentioned. Keeping her from further thoughts was the green of his eyes, reminding her of the foliage outside her studio window back home. Green like the crispest apple on a fall day. Green like the Emerald City in *The Wizard of Oz*. Perhaps he was a wizard himself, because she knew his eyes hadn't been green a few moments ago.

"Your eyes." She slapped a hand over her mouth. "I mean, what color are they? Do they change in the light?"

He paused. "They do." Then he pulled her in close. The heat from his arms drowning out her inner voice, the one whispering alarm.

"I think I can trust you, Ashton."

What was he talking about...*him* trusting her?

"I'm sure you've figured out there is something bigger happening." He waited a moment, perhaps allowing her thoughts time to register. "Something involving you."

"I-I know something's happening today, on my birthday, but I don't know what." Nervous red flags planted deep in her chest; this topic had been off-limits with Mason.

"You are important, Ashton Nichols. The One Hundred, and I want to tell you what that means." The breeze picked up, and his fingers brushed strands of hair from her face, very Mason-like.

"The One Hundred?" She longed to know how she fit into everything, and Ian seemed more than willing to share, very un-Mason-like.

"Ashton, you are bound for greatness, and together we can do marvelous things. I can tell you everything if you come with me now. Just *say* you want to be with me."

Parts of her wanted to agree. His warmth mesmerizing, the truth inviting.

"Ashton, you are extraordinary, and you deserve to know all you are capable of—"

Before he could finish, a flash of movement rushed between them in a peppering of amber and white. Horrific screeching filled the air. Ashton fell back onto the sand, pushed by the force of displaced air. Ian dropped to his knees, protecting his body from the pounding of hawks.

He closed his eyes and raised his hands, palms faced out, recited words from under his breath. Black flames jetted from his fingertips, searing feathers on each hawk circling down in rotation. Extending his arms, he pushed the flames farther out, forcing the raptors back.

Chaos bled. Birds hovered. Plumes fell. And shrieks carried in wait for the smoke to clear.

Ashton backed away from the bizarre scene. Hair on her arms prickled in fright. Pushing through the strange compulsion to stay with Ian, she raced toward the beach house. The farther she ran, the more her head cleared. The closer she got to the house, the more she realized what a horrible mistake she'd made.

****

Waking to the call of danger thrust Mason from bed. His bones snapped with a crash to the floor, while screeches flooded his mind in a cacophony of orders. His hawk eyesight deepened like a zoom lens; blood pumped at hyper-speed. As his body contorted, his brain translated Shunnar's message of Ashton in trouble. He tucked his head, protected by fear and drive alone, and broke through the bedroom window.

Raptors swarmed the beach, free of onlookers due to the early hour. The sea raged violently, as if long clawed tendrils shot out from under the dark swirling masses. Each progression of waves striped the beach closer and closer to where Ian held Ashton in his arms. Mason's vision bled green. What was she doing? Just as in CC's parking lot, fragmented pictures played in his mind, and he knew his role.

Repeatedly he dove his body into his enemy, willing him to fall. Then he dropped in line with his cast, swooping up and around, repeating the motion. The mission: attack continuously, hard and fast, giving Ian no time for retaliation. His feathers cemented to his body, like armor at his speed. He didn't tire, he didn't falter from the pattern. He hurled himself at the target, regrouping midair before dive-bombing again.

By the third round, Ian stood with new confidence, chanting words Mason couldn't understand. Jet-black flames exploded from his fingertips. Mason's feathers smoked, clouding his vision, pinching his air flow. But he pushed through, realizing the flames snuffed as he lunged back into the air at high speed. He fought through another round when groggily he lost hold on the lift of the wind, collapsing on the beach below.

****

Mason woke in human form on the sand, sore and surrounded by brethren. The man in charge had to be Shunnar. He stood solemn in black camo gear, with cropped brown hair and a stern expression. In a flash, his hazel-green eyes reminded Mason of a beach glass charm Ashton once linked to her bracelet, though now they glared at him. It was exactly what Mason needed to snap out of his daze.

Shunnar closed his eyes, chanting something about the "glory of good." A golden light rushed over them, and when Mason looked down, his damaged body healed. The experience left him gasping. But Shunnar didn't seem in the mood to explain, whipping into command mode.

"Damian, report to the Seam. Des, you're on watch at the house. Connor, take the remaining cast and fall in behind Ian. I'll get coordinates from our Healer, Bethesda. Mason, you're on clean-up."

Clean-up? Going after Ian was all he could think of. What was Shunnar asking?

"Fix this with Ashton."

"It's her birthday, we're done."

Shunnar crossed his arms. As pain pricked the top of Mason's spine, the others scattered to follow orders.

"All right!" Mason fell to a knee, too drained to fight back. "Tell me what to say. She's too smart to believe she didn't see fire come out of that monster's hands, or a swarm of birds go Hitchcock crazy."

"You're right. She is smart, and somehow she still wants to trust you. Her transition begins at the human hour she was born, 11:50 p.m. We wait until then. For now, you can tell her about Ian. She will have to accept there is evil in the world. As for the hawks, she is only aware of us as raptors. Keep it that way."

"She's going to wonder how I'm involved, especially when you keep shocking me."

"Earned consequences," he snapped. "Her human mind can't handle the absurdity of you shifting. We need her humanity as intact as possible. It's our only way to stay connected to a world that's advancing at accelerated rates. Her transition may already be compromised."

Mason pushed himself to stand, head shaking, eyebrow twitching. The sense of adventure he swore by weeks ago felt decades away. Ashton would be confused. What little he knew already stabbed at his insides. He struggled to accept a few hours of humanity as critical in what seemed like a magical world, but what did he know? Regret. That stupid recurring dream he'd followed into the woods was now a nightmare in reality. He had to finish it. For Ashton. "What do I do?"

Shunnar turned toward the settling waves. "We only need a few more hours. She will know everything after tonight, and Ian will have missed his opportunity. You see, as much as Ashton's human experiences will help the Spiritual Realm protect the Dream Realm, she could unintentionally assist the Dark Realm in their ploys to spread evil."

"Then why wait around like sitting ducks?" Mason approached him at the water's edge, though he kept his distance. The sun pushed through cloud cover, preparing for the first sunny day since they'd arrived. What a setting for Ashton's birthday, now spoiled by real evil.

Shunnar broke his gaze from the vista. "We've never had a demon aware of our Centennial before transition. Ian knows the importance of her humanity. That's why he's fighting for her free will. He's unlike the lesser demons you and Ashton will fight at the Seam. We aren't sitting ducks, Mason. We're his constant reminder of our stand."

"Free will? Centennial? The Seam?" Shunnar and Gavan kept bringing up concepts he couldn't follow. "I don't understand."

"We're all gifted free will. It's a powerful armor if used correctly. Ashton is our Centennial, an infant sent to the Human Realm every one hundred years to grow up linked to human minds. What humans conjure up without care becomes reality in the Realms. Together you and Ashton will work to protect the Dream Realm borders. It is the place human souls travel when they sleep—and where demons slip in, gaining fuel for power from negative human emotions. An ongoing battle longer than you can imagine. You will learn of this in your training."

Shunnar's answer only created more questions, but one stood out as Mason rubbed his right brow to stop the twitching. "If she's the Centennial, then who am I?"

"We're all wondering the same thing. Now go. Keep Ashton human for the rest of the day."

Mason expected any other answer than the one given. Shunnar transformed effortlessly into his hawk form, something else Mason intended to ask about soon.

Shunnar's winged silhouette circled above, and he shrieked his final message before disappearing over the horizon.

Mason took in a salty breath to clear his head. He had to let his unanswered questions go. For now. He ran up the path toward the beach house. Once he got Ashton to her birthday hour, he could figure out how to get out of this mess. He approached the bathroom window, hoping to slip inside unnoticed. When he pushed at the glass frame, he wasn't surprised to find it locked. He and his dad had set up their surroundings like Fort Knox, not that the supernatural needed locks to keep them at bay.

A hawk on a tree branch behind him, Desmond he thought, cried out and soared to Mason's shoulder. He was surprised he wasn't more freaked out. Des tousled his wings, tapping the glass with his beak. One crack. A crack growing in design until it encircled the lock, tipping out just over the latch, allowing Mason to get his hand in free.

Mason slid open the lock and pushed up the window. Des flew off as Mason hooked his arms onto the ledge. Using upper-body strength, which seemed enhanced since learning of his new shifter abilities, he hurled himself through the open window. His thud to the floor made him freeze, worried he'd been heard. When footsteps rushed down the hall, he jumped to his feet and flushed the toilet. Then he messed his hair, opened the bathroom door, and faked a yawn.

When Ashton ran smack into him, he pretended to be shocked and backed up in mock morning crankiness. "What the—"

"Mason." She jumped into his arms, voice cracking. He hadn't expected this. "Where were you? I'm freaking out!" She was whisper-screaming, so maybe his dad was still asleep.

"What's wrong?"

She pulled him into their bedroom and shut the door. "Look!" She pointed to the broken window. "I came back to the house after another hawk attack, and you're gone, the window's broken—"

Mason sank to his bunk. He didn't know how to explain the window in the bathroom, let alone this one. He fingered through his messy clumps of hair, relieved she was safe, but angry she'd left with Ian.

"You know what happened, don't you?"

"I just came from the bathroom, Ash." He thought he'd at least try to lie.

"What happened to the window?" She looked pale as a ghost, the tiny scar below her eye aglow.

"I woke up when it broke. I think a branch fell from that old pine out there. I wanted to try and board it up before my dad woke up." His lying words felt like his body had back at the beach.

"Why couldn't I find you when I came back?"

He needed to buy time. "Well, where did you go?"

"I, um, I went outside to get some air and…" When she started tearing up, he knew he had to save her.

"So you left with Ian?" He pulled her to sit.

"You knew. And you were going to let me lie?"

He rolled his eyes. "You don't know how to lie."

"I can if I need to." She shook her head. "Just tell me what's going on. It's my birthday. I waited like you asked. Now fess up."

He leaned over, moaned into his pillow, "I can't yet."

"What do you mean? I gave you the time you asked for."

"It has to be your birthday hour. 11:50 tonight." His body tensed, waiting for the freak-out. When it didn't come, he peered up from his pillow. She'd moved to her suitcase, shoveling clothes in without a word.

"You can't leave. Wait until tonight. If nothing happens, I'll take us both home." He leaped from the bed, pulled her from the suitcase.

She was crying.

He had to turn things around. Fast. "Can you tell me what happened outside?"

She froze, defeat shadowing her face. Then she pushed him away, staring out the broken window. It was quiet for too long, when she spoke without looking back. "I had a strange dream and woke to a tapping sound on the window. It was Ian holding up lattes. It felt innocent enough." She turned to face him.

"Why wouldn't you tell me about him?"

"You go out with girls all the time. We're both used to that. It's just never happened for me before." She wiped away tears.

What could he say? She was right. He stifled the part that made him furious under his ribs. Packed it in tight. He had no reason she shouldn't see other guys...or maybe he had every reason. But it didn't matter. It couldn't be Ian.

She walked closer to the window, stepping over glass and undoubtedly eyeing the hawks outside. "You realize this all makes us sound crazy. Like mentally crazy."

"Ash—"

"No. You're acting strange. Your dad isn't himself. I don't really know Ian, but odd things happen around him with hawks on steroids."

"You can't trust Ian." He tried to slip that in, though she was teetering on overload.

"You don't get to decide that, do you? I want to call my parents, but Dad would have me admitted. After what happened to your back last night, I'm wondering if we need to call a doctor...or the police. I just want to go home."

Mason put his arms around her middle, rested his head on her shoulder. If he hadn't felt his own bones crush under the weight of a shifting hawk, he'd have been right where she was. As much as he saved her from all the typical evils that used to fill their world—social anxiety, exam jitters, the occasional spider-kill—he knew he would always need her more. What could he say to earn her trust for a few more hours?

"The hawks." Her voice broke the silence.

"They're the same ones that attacked my car, aren't they? They're watching us."

He wanted to whirl her away, jump in the car, and head home. He wanted to snuggle under her ocean of blankets and watch movies and eat sour candy until their tongues hurt. But how could he when spiritual hawks spoke through his mind. When a demon was the new bogeyman…living under her bed.

"They are."

She didn't seem surprised, staring out at them. The sun began brightening up the outside world, but if he couldn't get her to her birthday hour, no amount of light would matter. And according to Shunnar, she could land herself in a far more serious mess than the dark. He had to stay strong. Get her to her birthday hour, then get their lives back on track.

"Mason," she asked without turning around. "What does the *One Hundred* mean?"

Chapter 10

The One Hundred

Ashton couldn't look at Mason when she asked about the One Hundred. She already expected the long pause standing between them. Next would come the lie. And now the excuse to wait until her official birthday hour.

"I don't know what you're talking about? One hundred what?"

"Ian referred to me as the One Hundred."

"Ian doesn't know anything about this. And you need to leave it that way."

"Excuse me?"

Mason grabbed her hands. "I didn't mean it like that." He tilted his head in that way when he's trying to look past the anger fuming inside. "We're going through something huge, and he's in the way. How did he find us here?"

"I don't know. I don't even know how I feel about him. I know I like being with him. Then those hawks show up, which is frightening. But no matter what's happening with him, you don't get to tell me who I can or can't see. You're acting—"

"What? I'm acting what?"

"Jealous." She pulled her hands away, plopped onto her bunk.

He sat down on his bed, worry scratching his brow.

"I don't want you to get hurt. Can't you stay away from him until we get through this?"

"Then what? You've been lying to me since you went into those woods. What do you expect me to do?"

"Well, I sure as hell don't expect you to run out to meet up with the devil himself."

"What? He's *is* part of this, isn't he? He has to be. That's why he started telling me things. Twice. They didn't make sense at the time. But that's it, isn't it?" She dropped her head in her hands. "I don't even know who to trust anymore."

"You're supposed to trust me." Mason swept past her, pulling the door closed. The click echoed in the morning silence, clanging in her ears.

"Mas!" She punched her pillow, the act itself shocking her into reality, whatever reality was left. It wasn't long before guilt pressed. Why had she gone outside to begin with? What was it about Ian causing her to go against her typical norms? The ones that told her to ignore drama and focus on school. She could never imagine her life away from Mason. Then again, why didn't she feel the way she *thought* she felt about Ian with Mason? Or did she? Clearly a playing field she avoided at all costs, because going there would mess up what they had. And messing up things with Mason wasn't an option. Ever.

She wiped away an escaped tear and grabbed a clean change of clothes. Max and Mason's voices carried from the kitchen, but she shut herself into the bathroom. It was time to go home. All she needed now was a shower.

And an Uber to a bus station.

****

Mason left the bedroom, his heart dragging like

dead weight. He hadn't wanted his feelings for Ashton to change, but they were doing just that. Changing, turning a new path, and crushing the only comfort he'd felt with her. Was it because he wanted to feel more for her? Or because he was supposed to?

Seeing her with Ian struck a nerve.

Shunnar had said she was his destined partner. Being paired with Ashton wasn't the problem; he'd loved her his whole life. It was just a different kind of love, one he'd grown up with. One he didn't mess with.

He knocked his head against the wall. A week ago, he was deciding which major would keep him busiest the longest. He didn't care what future career he chose, as long as it took him far away from home. Now his dad rattled on about demons killing his mom. His own body shifted into a supernatural creature, soon to be living in a completely different Realm. He banged his head again, feeling none of the pain.

Shunnar knew why Ashton was in this Realm. It was planned from the time she was an infant. So if they only sent one seam keeper every century, why was he there?

Shunnar, come in. Mason leaned against the hallway wall. He knew he had to talk to his dad, update him on the latest events, but he needed to hear from Shunnar first. If the hawks made them leave the beach house, he would need to find a way to convince his dad.

Our connection isn't like using a walkie-talkie, Mason. Just focus on me when you call my name, and I will know to respond. We give you privacy until we hear our name...or a topic of interest, which does tend to be more your style.

Mason cut to the chase. *I don't know how much my dad knows. I won't be able to stop him if he decides to flee the beach house.*

Gavan's word is to wait. We've only hours to go, and knowing where the enemy will strike is the edge we want. We can defend.

Mason's head dropped to his chest. Dealing with Ashton was all encompassing. Just the thought of keeping these life-changing events a secret from her was impossible, and now his dad, the man he hadn't exchanged real words with in ages. At least nothing past homework and college admission deadlines. *What if my dad wants to leave?*

We won't let that happen. Gavan's contacted the Blessing Council.

Blessing Council?

Better observed than explained. Although security has been increased, keep your eyes on Ashton. I will contact you soon with details. For now, don't leave the house.

Mason felt the connection sever. It wasn't a dial tone, just a feeling. One to mix in with the exhaustion and frustration he was already feeling. He rounded the corner to find his dad in the kitchen. "Good morning?"

His dad cocked an eyebrow. "Is that what you're calling it?" He continued packing up their groceries.

Mason couldn't figure out if his dad knew something had happened, or he was just being his typical awkward self.

"I heard the window break, saw the hawks gather, and found the two of you missing."

Mason's head shot up, meeting his dad's icy glare.

"Do you want to put the pieces together for me?"

Mason sighed. "You know something big is happening. I only know bits and pieces. I can't even share what little I do know until later tonight. It has to be the exact time Ashton was born—11:50 p.m." He waited, bracing himself for the pain to run down his spine.

"You know what? I accepted that dark shadow over my life when your mother was alive. I accepted it from her because she begged me to, without even uttering a word. She wore her fear on her face. I didn't realize the consequences of what she knew. But now, all these years later…" His voice quieted to a whisper, as if he was remembering something private from his past. "When I found your room empty and the window broken, all I could think about was the night she died. She was running from them. She led them away from us, and I knew not to follow. I stayed back to protect you."

"Dad, I'm okay." Mason forced himself not to bring up his mom. He still didn't know how she fit in with everything happening but knew inquiring would get him zapped.

"The world we know, Mason, it isn't real. It isn't anything we thought it was." His dad stared at the counter as if the moment had been on hold, waiting for an opportunity to erupt. "I'll repeat what I said in the car the other day. There are demons and angels out there, other realities. I don't know how it all works, but your mother was from that world. She must have been…" He looked directly into Mason's eyes, his own like a dark cave. "I don't think she was completely human, and so maybe, neither are you."

"Dad, I know about who I am. I—"

"No, Mason." He looked to physically swallow the shock of hearing Mason's confirming words. "Your mother never wanted to be a part of that world. It must be why she left it. I-I've been stunned by this new

105

chapter in our lives, but I'm pulling it together now. I failed before, but I'm going to honor what she would have wanted. I need to get you out of here."

"No. We can't hide." He spoke over his dad suddenly taking interest in his life.

"I'm not losing you too, Mason!" His voice rose, and Mason flinched. He didn't want Ashton to hear. They both glared in statue form until his dad gripped the edge of the counter with both hands. "Pack your things. We're leaving."

"Think about what you're saying. You know the danger that's out there. My connections have told me to stay here. They've upped security. They know who we're dealing with. We must get to Ash's birthday hour, then I can tell you everything. I can understand the truth of it myself. I can even try and find out what happened to Mom."

"They, they, they—" His dad shook his head.

He didn't want to hear anything Mason was saying, but Mason had to make him listen. He knew Shunnar would be chiming in soon. How did things turn upside down? There was nothing special about him, and as much as he adored Ashton, she was typical too. How did some Spiritual Realm even exist, and why would they ever have interest in the two of them? Maybe it did have something to do with his mom. He would ask about that soon. But right now with some sort of Blessing Council forming, Ashton freaking out, and Shunnar barking orders, he needed to calm his dad.

"Listen, I know you miss Mom. I know you're frustrated with being kept in the dark. I can't figure out why this is happening to us, but it is. And we're not running. It didn't work when Mom tried. I've been chosen for this, and I'm strong enough to do it." The words flew like a blow to his jaw. As if he almost believed them himself. And compelled to end with a definitive thought, he added, "I need you to believe in me."

Max's gaze dropped before slowly lifting to meet Mason's. Silence vibrated like a ticking time bomb. "That's exactly what your mother said to me before she died."

Chapter 11

Tea Time

Steam filled the tiny bathroom, coating every surface with a foggy glow. Ashton had stayed in the shower until ice crystals replaced any temporary comforts of heat. Now wrapped in a towel, she swept a free corner across the film-coated mirror. Dripping hair clumped at her shoulders, each drop signified an impossible obstacle. She smirked at her watery reflection. What obstacles had she ever had to fight?

In her eighteen years of life, she'd lived a boring suburban existence. She had both her parents and attended a good school. She may not have been athlete of the year, or on the popular side socially, but she could paint. She knew loyalty in friendship. Until two weeks ago, her biggest burden was separating from Mason for college. Now a life-long lie about her adoption hovered. And this. This unbelievable nightmare of Mason's somehow coming to life. Was she just going to leave him?

Her gutsy will had washed down the drain. She'd promised to give him time. He, and whoever else, might creepily be waiting for her birthday hour. But she had a voice. Even if she didn't know what she wanted to say. And tomorrow, when the world continued to spin, she would find her way home.

Sniffing back tears, she rubbed her eyes to focus on

the reflection staring back. Instead of finding her own face, foreign eyes hung behind an anomalous space inside the mirror. A nameless face coming back to her from a dream...no, the vision in the woods.

The woman's skin, honey-gold, was a canvas for her blue eyes. Chestnut locks, longer than Ashton's, rolled off her shoulders like the waves outside the beach house. Ashton's mind churned, flashing back to the vision where this woman pushed her hands into the giant oak.

"My Ashton." Her voiced chimed like a songbird.

Ashton's heart thumped to the bottom of her stomach. Her feet, cement blocks. She screamed when the woman reached a hand through the mirror and clasped her shoulder. But any sounds muffled beneath the whirring ceiling fan. She screamed again, louder, but it was the kind made in dreams, open-mouthed while no sound escapes.

Violet lights seeped from the mirror, flooding the bathroom in a distraction of color. It danced through the steamy air and clung to her body. She dropped her towel, swatting at the sticky light, but the colorful magic transformed her skin and bones into a fluid-like substance. In horror, she watched her skin melt away. There was no pain, only a warm tingling sensation. She tried to call for Mason, but her lips disintegrated into her chin, into her neck. Like a dream she disappeared in a flurry of purple radiance.

Barely a minute passed before her body rematerialized through the mirror. When the spinning stopped, she was naked on a wooden floor, nowhere near the Oregon beach house. That, she knew right away.

This new space was small and grand at the same

time. Closed-in circular walls, but with a high ceiling. She couldn't see the top. The purple lights had vanished, giving way to a natural white glow that seemed to fall from the space above. Where was she?

She bumped into a bed to her left and snatched up the blanket. A wooden wardrobe stood to her right. There were no windows. When she looked back at the bed, shades of lavender doused pillows glistened in the natural light from above. She peered again to find the source when a knock on the door triggered her third heart attack of the day. She froze, but the door opened anyway. It was the woman from the bathroom mirror, the same one from the woods. Ashton stepped back, not that it mattered in the small space.

The woman stopped in the doorway. "I mean you no harm." She stood slightly taller than Ashton, a gentle smile on her face. "My name is Althaia. I know this must be confusing for you. I promise it will all make sense soon. For now, you are safe." The woman's voice felt reassuring, but why should it? Hadn't she just traveled through a mirror? Was she dreaming?

"Why don't you get dressed?" The woman, Althaia, pointed to the wardrobe behind her. "Then join me for a cup of tea." She backed through the door. "I'll be right out here."

Ashton stared as the door clicked shut. Then she searched the room again, but found no windows, no other doors. How would she get out of here? Where was *here*?

Althaia's face replayed in her mind. Ashton knew her, but how? Hearing the clink of dishes outside the door, she reluctantly turned and opened the wardrobe. Escaping would be easier in clothing.

Her fingertips grazed the denim jeans and yoga

pants folded neatly on shelves, colorful T-shirts and sweatshirts hung on a rod. Clothing someone her age would wear. She rushed to dress, pulling on a pair of jeans and blue T-shirt. After finding running shoes, she wondered if she could get back a different way than she'd come. Taking a deep breath to calm the pattering of her heart, she twisted open the bedroom door.

There was only one way to find out.

"You look lovely." She jumped at Althaia's voice. The woman motioned her to a large wooden table in the center of the room.

Ashton glanced back to see three doors side by side. There was no hallway; they all opened to this one larger space, round like the bedroom. How could the doors stand so close to each other? Her mind began working the way it did when she was stuck on a math problem. The solution was near, she just needed time to work on it. Time she didn't have.

"Tea is ready."

Althaia set the table with two decorative teacups. A floral aroma swirled above a pot on the stove. A small kitchenette sat off to the left. It was all very simple, old-fashioned even. Ashton scanned the larger space for a way out. There were no windows in this room either. No doors except the three side by side behind her. Just as in the bedroom, the same natural light poured through a ceiling she couldn't make out.

"Have a seat. I will explain everything." Althaia placed a hand across her heart. "Well, almost."

Ashton didn't move. What would Mason do in a situation like this? What had he taught her from his survival camps? From karate and self-defense? Step one, she remembered, remain calm. It was every step after that hidden in the shadows of her mind.

"Thanks for the clothes."

The face from her vision smiled sweetly. "Please have something to drink. It's my own blend of jasmine tea. Your favorite, correct?"

"How would you know that?"

"There is much that I know, and you will learn all you need in due time."

Ashton studied her face, all the while the vision from the woods replaying in the back of her mind. Althaia's blue eyes, her long auburn hair. Her hands pressing through the bark of the tree. As she looked around, her mind almost clicked, like a piece of a puzzle snapping into place, and she knew at once where she was.

"We're inside the oak!" She spun around, noticing the tiny fossil-like lines trailing down the walls like lace-patterned wallpaper, but it wasn't wallpaper. It was the soft underside of bark. The round room towered above, with no end in sight. The realization knocked, and she grabbed the back of a chair to help settle the dizziness.

"I know this is difficult for you to comprehend. Trust that it will all make sense by morning." She motioned again for her to sit down. Then she took the pot off the stove, filling the two cups with sweet-smelling tea.

Ashton's heart filled with sprigs of nervous energy, telltale signs to grab her anxiety pills. She hated taking them and worked hard not to, but her insides were trembling.

"I don't understand what's happening." Any ability to remain calm vanquished. What would Mason do next? Run? Escape? Something more than standing like a statue. Tears welled in the corners of her eyes.

"Don't be afraid. You are a part of something remarkable." Althaia sat down, nodding at the empty chair. Her smile filled the room with a fresh breath of air. A warm waft touched at the back of Ashton's arms. If this woman was dangerous, she couldn't figure out how. She was dressed beautifully in a green silken wrap. Pleated layers of fabric flowed toward her brown belt, then blossomed underneath. The hem draped long over dark tapered pants, tucked inside calf-length suede boots. She looked like a maiden warrior from a fairytale.

Ashton pinched herself to wake up.

When nothing changed, she darted. It was impulsive, channeling Mason after all, but she made it to the middle door, throwing it open. Blinding white light, as if alive, wailed. Each electromagnetic wave somehow fought the other in a battle to shine the brightest. Ashton slammed the door, glancing back.

Althaia hadn't moved. She only looked patient, sad.

Ashton opened the third door to find another bedroom. It was slightly bigger than the first, making space for a large standing mirror. But where the other room carried hues of lavender, this one was spruced in greens. It was lovely, bringing more tears to Ashton's eyes. Her mom always spoke of mixing greens, the right shades from a paint tube were impossible. Maybe because they were all here in this room.

Ashton closed the door. She sat down at the table. "Let me guess. I'm part of something big you can't tell me about."

Althaia let a sigh escape. "I will tell you enough to tide you over. It is the best I can do, as I assume you've been told the importance of preserving your human

113

experience."

"Human experience?" She blurted the words before thinking. Had she pretended to know anything about her *human experience,* maybe she could have found out more. Maybe it had to do with her parents. "I mean, yes. Mason—my friend—he said I needed to wait until my birthday."

Althaia nodded at the cup of steaming tea before her. Ashton couldn't place the scent, sweeter than jasmine, but it reminded her of her childhood, or at least she thought it did. She wrapped her fingers around the cup, letting the warmth rush in. Feeling a little like Alice in Wonderland, she took a sip. It tasted like walking through a garden growing more than jasmine. Sweetened with more than any local organic honey her mom had served. She took another sip. Unnamable goodness.

Okay, she thought. *Time to figure things out.* "Exactly, why am I here?"

"For your protection. This tree is the northwest portal between the Human and Spiritual Realms. Guarding it has been my role since you were bor—" She choked, eyes glossing.

"Since I was…born? Were you going to say born?" The words came out as she pushed away from the table. Memories of adoption documents found in her mom's file cabinet flashed behind her eyes.

She needed her inhaler.

"Ashton." Althaia stood, reached out a hand.

"I need a minute." She leaned over, breathing in slow, shallow breaths.

Althaia's blue eyes never left Ashton's.

Ashton's balance wobbled as she wrapped her arms around her middle. Her stomach lurched and swayed.

She looked at the woman who had pulled her through a bathroom mirror.

"Ashton, it's the tea. It's turning the key on your memories. Just a touch before your transition tonight."

"You poisoned me?" She turned, tapping along the circular walls to find an outside door. There had to be a way out.

"I'm helping you. I hate seeing you suffer. You're my—I mean, you're important to our world, and you were supposed to remain human until tonight. Somehow everything's been compromised." She sat down at the table, rambling, unconcerned with Ashton's search for a way out. "I don't know how evil found you. But I'm not losing you in the last days of your Centennial duties."

Ashton stopped at the word Centennial. Her memory flashed again, only this time to the backseat of her car, windshield shattered, Ian whispering to her about being his One Hundred. Could it be the same thing? The same *big* thing Mason alluded to at the beach house? "What are you talking about?"

Althaia bit her lip, a tiny wrinkle appeared across her otherwise smooth forehead. "I can't tell you—"

"Then what was the tea for?" Ashton startled at the volume in her own voice. She never yelled. At anyone. Even frustrated with Mason, the silent treatment was her strongest vice.

"The tea was to loosen the lock on your memories." Althaia stood, found her composure, smoothing her silken robes. "I am aware you need to transition home as fully human as possible. I'm going against protocol. But I was worried for your safety."

Ashton placed both hands on the table, allowing it to support her weight. Something to ground her in place. "I already have a home. I have a future. I'm going to art school."

"Look at me." Althaia stepped closer.

Ashton peered into the woman's eyes, as blue as her own. Her long brown hair had the same natural waves Ashton battled since she was a little girl. She'd chosen to lop hers off in a mess of long layers to camouflage the craze. But it was the same.

"*This* is your home."

Adoption papers, the bathroom mirror, purple lights…Ashton's knees weakened. Althaia caught her weight, hooking her ankle around the leg of a chair, and sat her down. "Allow your memories."

The scent in the room ignited once more. The tea, making its way through her veins, sent tingles down each limb. "You're—you're her. You're my birth mother." It wasn't a question.

Althaia nodded.

Ashton started to cry. She was at her limit, the one Mason typically sensed before she did. If he were here, he would have sat her down before this point, held her until everything disappeared. He'd wipe away any escaped tears and make her laugh.

She craved his obnoxious way of fixing things. Now, more than ever.

Althaia didn't comfort her, and for this she was relieved. She cried until she wasn't sure how much time had passed. Light still brightened the room, but it felt as if she'd been gone from the beach house a long time. She wiped her face with the neck of her shirt and looked up. Althaia was waiting patiently at the table.

"What happens next?"

Althaia frowned. Ashton wondered if it was due to her response. But she didn't know how she felt about this woman being her birth mother. She'd only learned a week ago she was adopted. Finding her birth parents had been part of her summer plan. But right now?

It would all have to wait.

Althaia broke the silence. "This was supposed to be a time of celebration. But the Dark side discovered you. They have never known about our Centennials before." She looked away, as if pondering the idea, but shook it off, returned her focus. "We are elementals from the Spiritual Realm."

Ashton's heart dropped to her stomach. Again.

"You were chosen to live in the human world, as human, until your eighteenth birthday."

Ashton's breath pushed, short and quick.

"It happens every hundred years, though it's never an exact date, to keep the Centennial hidden. But somehow…" She walked to the stove, stirring the contents in the pot. "Somehow, a demon prince found you. I understand why Gavan sent the hawks in early."

This snapped Ashton from panic. "The hawks are attacking *me*."

"Not attacking. Protecting."

Ashton's mind almost clicked aloud, turning and twisting the overload of information. "From—"

"A demon very interested in your Centennial gifts."

"But I don't have any gifts."

"Not yet. When you were chosen, it was promised you would receive blessed gifts upon your return. The Realms have anticipated your homecoming for eighteen years. Now you can become the seam keeper you're meant to be."

Her mouth dropped open. She wanted to speak, to argue in the absurdity of her words, but nothing would come.

"Keepers protect sleeping human souls, all of which you will soon learn about. But your Centennial gifts will be special, qualities a typical keeper doesn't hold."

Ashton shook her head, but Althaia continued.

"You see, as you've lived in the Human Realm, you've absorbed their lifestyles, their troubles, their fears. This knowledge is transferred to the Spiritual Realm upon transition and helps us to better protect the Dream Realm."

"Okay, stop." Ashton stood up. "This is too much. You said I'm from the Spiritual Realm, and now there's a Dream Realm? And a Dark side? And demons?" She held her head, trying to stop the spinning. "I can't be a *seam keeper*. I can't do any of this. It's a mistake."

"This is why the Centennial stays human until her eighteenth birthday hour. It's too much for you to process otherwise." She laid a hand on Ashton's shoulder.

Ashton didn't shrug it away, as she thought she might. The contact felt needed. She only wished it was Mason, or her own mom from home. She slumped back down into the chair.

"I will answer to the Blessing Council for pulling you out early. But don't worry, I will send you back before your transition. I simply don't trust Cillian." Her eyes fluttered to the floor. "Ian, to you."

"Ian? What does he have to do with this? And what Blessing Council?"

"Oh, my sweet, you will learn everything you need in training. It's what comes after transition. I must believe all will be well with you in the process. But please know, Ian is not who you think he is."

"He protected me from the attacking hawks you say were helping."

"Ashton, the Ian you know is Cillian, demon prince, Lucifer's son."

Ashton stood again, stepping back into the wall. "That can't be." She wiped her forehead, perspiration collecting on her brow. "He's my age. He's going to my art school in the fall. I don't understand."

"He is whatever age he needs to be to accomplish his goal. I don't know for sure why he has his eyes on you, but I assume it's your Centennial gifts. He needs your free will. But you are safe now. He can't find you here. The Dark Side has never crossed the portal boundaries."

Ashton's jaw dropped. She liked Ian. Liked it when he kissed her. Knots tangled in her stomach, buzzed up her chest. She started walking the small perimeter of the room. Then she walked around again. Mason was the pacer. But she didn't know what else to do with all the energy, desperately needing to wake up from this nightmare.

"Things work differently here. The Blessing Council oversees all the Realms. They consist of five elders from the Spiritual Realm, three from the Dream Realm, and one from the Heavenly Realm."

Ashton paced faster, nausea rising.

"Since they manage all elemental business, it won't escape them I've interceded. I didn't ask for permission. But you are my daughter." Althaia approached her in a lap around the room, smoothed the hair drying around her face. "I will do anything to protect you."

Ashton pulled her face away but didn't move back. "I'm not ready for this."

"I understand."

"I don't think you do. I'm just a girl who likes to draw. I'm nothing special." She thought of Mason forcing her out of the house on weekends. The only extracurricular she took part in was watching him play sports. He was the one with the recurring dream. He was the adventure guy. There must be a mistake. She felt it in her bones.

"You were chosen."

"What if I don't want it?"

"There are many Realms in the Universe. Ours is the Spiritual Realm, and it is an honor to serve in this way. But the Centennial is a warrior who has sacrificed her childhood for the good of the cause. Her knowledge fortifies the Dream Realm with a blanket of energy. Ashton Nichols, that honor goes to you."

"No, I don't want it." She pulled free from Althaia's arms.

"If you refuse…if you deny your gifts, they are lost for another hundred years. The Dark Realm continues to multiply, and the Dream Realm weakens."

She slowed, enunciating every word. "If that happens, every fear from the Human Realm will grow, saturating the Dream Realm and filling the Dark with more power than ever before. What kind of world would you go back to?"

Ashton had no response.

Althaia pushed the teacup toward her. "I promise this will ease your confusion. It isn't strong enough for your full memories to flow, but trust in the process. When you realize who you are, you will proudly accept this honor."

Ashton still couldn't move. Her racing heart skipped beats to the fantasy Althaia described.

"Okay. I will tell you more." She took a deep breath. "Our work with the Dream Realm, the place where human souls travel as they sleep, is crucial to keeping balance in the Human Realm."

Maybe it was desperation, maybe the overload of information, maybe she really was dreaming and couldn't wake up. But with no doors leading out, she channeled Alice again and drank the tea. If she'd started something that would ease any amount of confusion, she needed to finish it.

Althaia looked relieved. "Demons are from hell, sent from Lucifer himself. They cannot be killed, only driven away. They are as powerful as humans allow them to be."

"Humans allow demons power?"

"Stress carries a powerful charge. In the world today, people worry and fret to great degrees about their lives. Anxiety and fear equate to potential demonic power." She tilted her head. "While humans sleep, they work out their emotions through dreams. Demons feed on the negative energy emitted in the process."

"So people create demons through bad dreams?"

"People don't create demons; they provide higher demons power and strength to create evil, while lower demons do their bidding. But if we allow them more power, who knows what they could do in *any* Realm."

Ashton thought about her own life. She worried every day while she was awake. She had a prescription for it. How much negative energy had she emitted each night without even thinking? And she had far less to worry about than others in the world.

"Mason won't tell me how he's involved."

"You and Mason are bound in destiny, but only he can divulge that truth."

"So that's it, I'm left in the dark. Can I even trust you?" Without understanding why, she felt confident this woman was, in fact, her birth mother. But what if Althaia was just like Ian? What if the hawks were? Ashton was beginning to feel like a pawn in a game.

Just then, her bracelet caught on the hem of her T-shirt. She brushed it with her other hand, feeling a light tingle. A splash of light caught her eye before it was gone, reminding her she could trust herself.

Althaia smiled and touched her hand to a brooch in the folds of her silken wrap. It was an oak leaf, identical to Ashton's.

"This charm is from you?"

"Mason doesn't know. I had it delivered with instructions to gift it to you. As you know, he hasn't been in a position to refuse orders. I'm sure he feels terrible hiding the truth. It will all be in the open soon."

She knew Mason had been lying. She also knew he was being hurt. None of this sounded as if it were for good purposes.

"I am risking much for you. Our Realm believes it is imperative for the Centennial to transition fully human, without any knowledge of other worlds. I believe you are strong and will transfer effortlessly to the Spiritual Realm, but you must choose to trust now."

Ashton thought about the risks people were taking for her. Max had broken a long-time silence with his son to hide them. Mason suffered some kind of corporal punishment for revealing too much. Now there was a Blessing Council involved. What could that mean? Maybe Althaia couldn't reveal the whole truth because she would endure some awful consequence.

"It will all be clear on your birthday hour. Your earthly time will be done, your spirit will remember everything, and we will have a lifetime together. I promise you. Just tr—"

"*Trust.*" Ashton finished the word. The same word Mason had resorted to lately. But what if she didn't want a lifetime in another Realm? What if strangely, she wanted to go back to that little girl clinging to the only family she thought was hers, especially after Mason's mom died. What if she took her anxiety medicine every day so she'd never feel stress again?

Could she go home then? Make more of a difference? Take yoga and spread the word about positive thinking?

Chapter 12

Trusting The Light

Mason leaned back against the chair adjacent to the short sofa his dad now slept on. He hadn't accepted the news that they needed to stay put. Instead he tossed the groceries and his clothes into bags, bellowing orders for Mason to grab his and Ashton's things while she was still in the shower. The whole event was like a get-away scene in an action movie.

Mason smashed his fist against the arm of the chair. Why had he said those final words? "Dad, staying might be the right move here. Mom ran. Look what happened to her."

Only seconds after, Max Deed had passed out over the side of the sofa.

We don't have time for this. Shunnar's voice boomed in his head. *Our healer has stepped in. Your father will awaken in twelve to fourteen hours.*

But Mason had caught the look on his face. He'd twisted the knife in his dad's thirteen-year-old wound.

Mason swung his dad's legs around the best he could on the tiny cushions. He looked like a sleeping giant. But at least now he could check on Ashton.

The morning was in full bloom outside the windows when Mason realized he couldn't hear the water running in the shower anymore. How long had he argued with his dad? How long had he sat waiting? Too

124

long. It had to have been almost an hour. Was she going to hide out in there all day?

Mason held his ear against the bathroom door. "Ash?"

Nothing.

"Ash, I'm sorry." His forehead rested against the wood. Her silent treatment was underway, the only play she had left.

"I know I haven't been honest. But you're not the only one going through this. There's even more to *us* than I've been told. I don't know what it entails—and I *hate* it!" He clenched his fists, forcing down the heat rising inside. Angry emotion wouldn't lure her to open the door.

"Do you see how messed up this is? I hate that we're both being forced into it. I don't understand it myself, and it's not like I'm allowed to ask questions. But if there's one thing, Ash, at least we're together. You know I always love you. Can't you see that? You've got to cut me some slack. Please, Ash. Open the door."

It was quiet with only faint sounds of snoring coming from the living room. But behind the bathroom door, nothing. Was she so angry she wouldn't hear him out? She'd always shown compassion when he shared his thoughts. She'd never left him with raw feelings this long before.

Never. And then he knew.

BAM! The thrust of the door busting open was more dramatic than needed. The house was old. Mason wasn't surprised to find the bathroom empty. He was only furious it took him so long to figure it out. Folded clothes sat untouched on the ledge by the window, worn clothes on the floor. Ashton's eerie absence felt like the morning he'd learned his mother was dead.

Shunnar! Mason bellowed in thought, barely able to contain himself.

Shunnar's human form appeared from down the hall, looking as unruffled as he had on the shore. Expression serious.

"She was taking a shower. Now she's gone!" Mason paced the hallway outside the bathroom.

Shunnar was joined by two other shifters, also in human form. One was Desmond, broad with long black dreads and piercing dark eyes. Somehow, he knew him from his hawk form, the one who'd helped him with the bathroom window. The other had red buzzed hair and freckles. He was stocky, while Des was leaner, both carved with muscles Mason could only dream of having one day.

"This is Des. Connor." Shunnar thumbed to each of them.

Mason raised his chin in welcome, then peered at Shunnar. "What are we doing about this? I thought you had security in place?"

"Security *is* in place." Shunnar eyed him, and Mason knew he'd crossed a line. He stepped back to allow Connor into the bathroom.

"It had to be internal." Des spoke to Connor. "I've been on post all morning." Two more shifters arrived, their bulky size crowding the small space.

Shunnar and Connor spoke privately before Shunnar addressed them all. "Ashton was pulled through the elements. The residue left behind is Light, so we know she is safe. Orders are to resume with the illusion she is still in the beach house. Everyone to post."

Harmonious responses of agreement filled the

house, and the men scuttled out the door. Mason felt out of the loop. When would the make-up class be? He was tired of feeling one step behind. "What does that mean?"

Shunnar and Mason stood alone in the quiet, Shunnar nodding as if he understood. "The residue in the bathroom is of the Light, the side of good, so Ashton was pulled through to the Spiritual Realm by another elemental. It must have been someone powerful, although we are unsure of the origin at this time. The point is, she is safe. If evil had taken her, the residue would have been Dark. It is crucial Ian believes she is still here, so all guard posts will keep the façade. Since your father is out of commission, shift and train with Connor. The Blessing Council meets in a few hours."

Mason's fists clenched and unclenched. "I need to know if Ashton's okay right now."

"She was taken by Light, evidence of our Realm. Have faith and trust she is well." Shunnar's hazel eyes gleamed in the already bright room. The sun was up, filling the space around them, and though a change in weather was exactly what Mason had wished for, he couldn't help feeling encased by darkness.

"Our Realm? I don't even know where that is. I can't protect her if I don't know where she is." His voice small, defeated. Any recognizable sense of himself diminished.

"The Spiritual Realm is your new home. Trust the process. Now shift. Connor's waiting outside."

Mason checked on his dad one last time. Asleep, Max looked younger, his hair still neatly in place even after his earlier tirade. His father always looked pulled together in any situation. To his neighbors, he was the perfect doting dad. At the university, he was the distinguished professor. At his wife's funeral, he was the humble and quiet widower, appreciative of all condolences. He was everything expected on the outside, yet nobody Mason could relate to on the inside. The man before him was as much a stranger now as he'd ever been. And who was he...ranting about demons?

Mason found Connor waiting outside. Glaring sunrays broke through the overcast sky in giant blue patches. The brightness distracted him from the analysis of his dad. Stressing was a job better left for Ashton.

Connor stood in the yard with three other men, but they dropped and shifted as he approached. Mason, dreading the feeling of broken bones, stopped when Connor ushered him back into the house.

"Shunnar said to shift and train."

"I want to test something first." Connor pointed toward the bathroom.

"Did you need to go?" he asked uncomfortably, not sure where this was leading.

"Your shifter senses have jumpstarted." His voice low and rough, but without agitation. Mason assumed it was his normal tone. "Most of your strengths won't enhance until your mate comes of age. It's a package deal for most seam keepers. But let's see."

"Okay." Mason shook off the sting of certain trigger words, like mate, strengths, and seam keepers. Though putting off the bone-crushing shifting experience to learn a little more about the perks sounded like a good idea.

"All right, let's test it out." Connor pushed open the bathroom door and stepped aside. "What do you see?"

Mason laughed, the nervous feeling like a lump in his throat. Connor didn't budge, so he entered the bathroom and looked around. The tub still dripped from Ashton's shower. Her clothes sat abandoned on the window's ledge. Smoothing his fingers across the folded blue T-shirt, he smirked a half smile. She always preferred his shirts to her own. He rubbed the soft cotton, as if it might deliver a message to her whereabouts. When it didn't, he pushed the shirt away and looked back to Connor. Connor only nodded, as if he was onto something.

Mason rolled his eyes and continued surveying the room. He saw typical bathroom items, all of them disturbing reminders of his helpless state. What was he supposed to see? He studied the coral-colored towels, remembering Ashton's frown when he had mistakenly called them orange. She'd corrected him. *Coral is a softer, warmer hue than orange.*

He found her travel bag holding miniature-sized tubes and jars of who knows what; since Ashton hardly wore makeup, he couldn't guess what they were. Her toothbrush was still wet, next to the tube of toothpaste, neatly rolled from the bottom. The clothes he'd seen her in that morning lay crumpled on the floor. He bent to touch them, hoping they still held some of her warmth, but his heart slipped when the coldness mocked such a naïve thought.

"I don't know what I'm supposed to see." He tossed her clothes aside.

"Don't look with human eyes. Use your hawk vision," Connor stated matter-of-factly, as if Mason knew how to do that.

"You want me to shift?"

"No. Use your hawk vision in your human form."

129

He said it like he shared a secret.

When he didn't move, Connor added, "Concentrate on your inner hawk."

"We can do that?" Mason had referred to himself as part of the collective group. He didn't know why but sputtered to correct what felt like a slip. "I mean, I can do that? How?"

"Focus on your hawk inside. He's always there. Push energy to your vision, holding the shift back. You'll feel it when it's right."

Mason squinted at the sink, fixing his eyes on the red stripe of the toothpaste tube. He tried looking deeper, beyond the striking color to see something smaller, more detailed, maybe a fingerprint. His insides stirred as a tingling sensation drew up along his spine, curving around the back of his head, resting warmly behind his eyes. Then, his vision altered. Details of texture became ultra-clear, growing larger in scale for a few seconds before his body painfully contorted on the ground.

Bones snapped, muscles constricted…

"No!" Connor's hands were on his back pushing him down hard. "Don't shift!"

The force of Connor's touch felt like a blow to his gut, and he resurfaced human, coughing as if the wind knocked out of him. "Whoa." He leaned back on his knees gasping for breath.

"You started to see, didn't you? Before shifting?" Connor looked pleased.

Mason pulled himself to stand. "I guess so. It didn't last long enough. I couldn't stop the change." He ran his fingers through messily clumped curls.

"Try it again." Connor didn't miss a beat.

Mason rolled his eyes. It didn't feel good to shift in

130

the first place and starting and stopping midshift felt dangerously close to death. But this was for Ashton. He had to try. Closing his eyes again, he sought the tingling sensation from the back of his mind. There it was. That spot behind his eyes.

This time when the warm feeling swooshed up from his center, he held it down, like holding a stick shift steady on a hill without the brakes, that balance of pressure between accelerator and clutch. He swallowed the pain while sweat dripped down both temples. Connor's voice ranted something about pushing down and forcing through. He switched to autopilot, as he had done a thousand times in soccer games or during sparring matches in karate. His competitive nature took over, allowing him to multitask and think strategically. The warm knot forced its way up his middle, and he willed it down with refreshed power. This allowed the tingle behind his eyes to push out, and when he opened them, he was gripping the sides of the sink.

His human brain flinched as the sharpness of detail assaulted his senses. The dirtiness of the bathroom was striking. Bacteria and grime were visible in jumbo size, but more alarming was a purple glow radiating from the mirror itself. It shone brightly in the center, softening around the rectangular edges. "I see purple. Is that the light you're talking about?"

"That's it." He seemed content with Mason's achievement and patted him on the back so roughly it knocked his inner hawk-sight out like a flashlight. Everything went black, leaving the pulse of a headache in its place.

"So does this mean I have some of the powers I'm supposed to get?" Mason asked, rubbing his head.

"Powers?" Connor looked at him dumbfounded.

"We're not superheroes."

"Whatever." He opened the mirror to find a variety of medicine bottles, sunscreen, and lotions. He pulled out a bottle of pain medicine and threw two back, swallowing them with a gulp from the facet. "The purple stuff. Tell me about it."

"The *purple stuff,* as you call it, is the residue of Light or…goodness from God. If it was dark or gray, it would be of the Dark Realm. Demonic."

"God?" Mason swallowed a gulp of air.

"Of course. Who do you think we work for?" He shook his head.

Mason blew out a breath. This was obviously bigger than he'd imagined. "So how did the *good* light take Ashton through a mirror? Did she travel at warp speed or something?" Mason closed the mirror trying to see the purple light again but settled on trusting it was still there.

"When spiritual elementals enter the Human Realm, or travel from realm to realm, they leave particles of light behind. All *good* light comes from above; it's angelic. It leaves a purple residue. Demonic light is dark, ashy-gray." He led them to the front door.

"So because there's purple residue, we know Ashton's safe? How can you be sure?"

Connor turned to face Mason. "We don't have to understand it to believe it. We have faith in what is good, and we keep fighting the fight. We strive through danger believing that good will always prevail. If humans fought *that* fight, maybe they would be lifted by inner encouragement, instead of doubt and fear."

"Then why fight at all?"

Connor shook his head, shoving Mason in the shoulder on his way out the door. "Dude, it's *because* we believe in the prevalence of good that we keep the upper hand in battle. Life is balance, and death is part of that. Just suffice it to know Ashton is somewhere good, and in the meantime, there is still a demon to hunt. Ride on that confidence and let's go."

****

Ashton finished her tea, curious about the ease it was supposed to bring. But she only felt more exasperated as Althaia insisted on the secrecy of the Realms. She warned humans couldn't handle knowing demons existed. For all Ashton knew, she was telling her more of the truth than Mason or Ian had ever tried.

For this reason, she listened.

"If humans knew about the power they leaked to demons, and how powerless they are to stop it, it would cause worldwide panic. Misery loves company, and humans are far too full of sorrow. It could empower the Dark Side completely, offsetting the balance."

Ashton leaned back in the wooden chair. "I don't understand. If people knew their pain fed demon powers, then wouldn't that be inspiration to stop? To be happy?"

"Would it?" Althaia challenged. "Could the human race simply put aside their jealous emotions and doubts? Could they stop worrying about finding better jobs, or fretting about where money was coming from to pay bills? Could the young across the lands relent in trivial concerns, like passing school finals?" She lifted an eyebrow, striking a nerve in Ashton.

She wasn't ready for this woman to presume she knew her that well. She refused to feel guilty for striving to do her best in school. Her sense of pride pricked, stretching to protect her mom and dad's honor, their expectations for her to succeed in life. The pause was slight, but she was sure Althaia caught it. Maybe finding her birth mother was more of a complication. Maybe she didn't want to know who she really was after all.

"And if they stop in their competitive nature, would they continue in a forward motion at all? Or would they simply worry about the realism of it, thus providing strength to evil regardless of their understanding?"

Ashton didn't have a response. She couldn't imagine a world without stress, but she couldn't imagine one with the knowledge of demons either. Instead, she looked around to find the source of light coming from no visible windows. Though a natural sense of radiance filled the room, it had dimmed. She knew her world would be changing by midnight. The anticipation of her official birthday hour fell on her like a shadow of gloom, and she knew no way of escaping worry about that.

With time ticking away, more questions grew in her chest, like twisting vines searching for sunlight. She sparked a second wind, or maybe it was the tea. Bluntly, she faced Althaia. "If you are my birth mother, who's my birth father?"

Althaia blinked. "Your father lives in our Realm. He leads the—I've said too much already. You will meet him soon. He was unhappy the council chose you as Centennial. Many things happened at that time. Much loss." Her eyes fell mournfully. "It was too much for him to bear. He thrust himself into his work, which took its toll on our relationship. We may be spiritual elementals, Ashton, but we are not perfect."

"I'm sorry." It was clear she'd trespassed on painful memories. As much as she wanted to ask more about this man who was a leader in the Spiritual Realm and her birth father, she changed the subject. Mason would have pushed on. She longed for even an ounce of his endurance. "When do I go back?"

Althaia slipped from her chair and knelt in front of Ashton. Her blue eyes glistened, as she stroked her palms down Ashton's face, softly brushing her eyes to close. Ashton's instinct was to resist, but she was weary from the overload of information, especially without Mason's support. The warmth from Althaia's hands flushed her cheeks. Violet lights sparked behind her eyelids, growing brighter before finally blinking softly to black.

Chapter 13

Blessing Council

In hawk form, Mason's body squeezed through a maze of tree branches, following Connor up and around and through small spaces at shocking speeds. He didn't know their location, but the terrain had switched from the sporadic pines by the shoreline to a thicker forest.

His vision was freakishly precise, but when Connor flew into a tiny dark cave set into a mountainside, Mason's hawk-body gulped.

Nature's obstacle course, Connor sent from inside the cave.

Mason pushed back the vision of his own feathers and blood slapped against the mountainside and followed. Buzzing through the hollowed-out cave passages, the skittering of rodents scattered, the coolness tingled, then the stale air pushed him out another opening just as fast. Connor appeared after Mason, his laughter echoing through Mason's mind.

Flight training lasted hours. It was the longest he'd stayed in hawk form, and his arms jittered, his legs wobbled. But part of him couldn't wait to do it again. As he was about to drop, Connor informed him they'd also train in human form.

What? More?

Just outside the caves, Connor set up targets on several tall tree trunks. Mason thought they might be

Douglas firs, but he wasn't sure. With Ashton gone, he'd begun looking at colors and nature as she might. Everything was muse for her art. He shook the thoughts from his head and pushed sweat-drenched hair from his eyes. He needed to focus.

"So I thought we'd warm up with some basic hand-to-hand combat." Connor stepped back, bending his knees into a fighting stance.

Mason put both hands up in surrender, not even blinking at how fast he'd conceded defeat. "I'm a human black belt, dude. But I'm pretty sure that's nothing compared to someone who fights demons."

Connor cracked his neck and smiled. "We'll see."

Mason stumbled over weighty feet in the dance Connor engaged. Stalking around in circles, he tried reading Connor's first move. But Mason's human vision was as heavy as his feet. "How are you not wiped out from the flying and that bone-breaking shift?"

Connor grinned wider. "Practice."

Before Mason could respond, Connor's right leg flew up and smacked his left shoulder, spinning him round before a crack to the back of the head. Mason dropped to the ground, his head in his lap. He thought of his dojo back home, his sensei pushing him all those years...for what? With his insides still rattling, he turned around to gawk at Connor. How long would it take for him to become that good?

Then it hit.

He wasn't only Mason from the Human Realm. Somewhere in his unknown bloodline, he was more. He smiled until his cheeks hurt.

"Have you gone mad?" Connor laughed, his red hair like a flag in a bullfight.

Mason stood up. Something in his bones snapped, not shifting but settling into place. He wasn't in the dojo anymore. He wasn't human to begin with. Relying on human karate skills wouldn't work in this realm. And somewhere buried deep, his seam keeper inside knew this.

Mason was ready to learn. "Show me."

Connor grinned, satisfied with Mason's readiness, and lunged into a fighting stance. Mason pushed his hair up again, inhaled a new breath, and reached farther into his lungs.

"Let your body remember who you are." Connor threw a punch.

Mason, a quick learner, punched back. They continued this way, Mason mirroring Connor's every move, throwing punches, kicks, and blocking them upon return. His karate skills had supplied a foundation for stamina, but just as in flying, his seam keeper side took over. He felt the residual jitters from his earlier shift smooth over each muscle in his arms, his legs, his chest, and his back. It felt as if an invisible layer of armor attached itself to his body.

And it was *his* final roundhouse, sweep, and blow to the side of Connor's ribs that brought his trainer to the ground.

Now Mason was the one smirking, Connor on his back in the dirt.

After their warm-up, as Connor called it, they focused on the shifter weapon of choice, small weightless throwing knives. With little introduction, Mason handled them like an extension of his arm. Tiny silver bursts of light cut through the air in flashes with each toss. His accuracy, spot-on from the first throw, boosted some of his confidence lost at the start of sparring.

Connor explained again that it was his true nature resurfacing, after living in the Human Realm for so long. He also said Mason's precision would increase once his mate turned eighteen.

There was that term again, mate. It nudged at Mason, like an opponent strategically brushing past him on the field. It didn't matter that it was with Ashton. It was others telling him what to do with his personal life. He'd had enough of that. Plus, he'd never thought of Ashton that way. Or if he had, one lazy summer night watching movies on her bed, two years ago, he'd stuffed those feelings away.

She was his lifeline.

Finally, Connor announced the end of their training. They shifted, a longer process for Mason, and lifted into the air. Mason searched for landmarks to map his way, but somehow the unfamiliar forest terrain skipped to the familiar Pacific coastline in a blink.

Conveniently, the beach house was secluded from the main road and nosy neighbors. As they landed in the backyard, all appeared quiet. Mason assumed his dad still slept and was relieved. Every obstacle weighed on him, adding to his physical and mental exhaustion.

"Let's fuel up. Things will start hopping after sundown." Connor nodded toward the door.

Mason shook off the pain from shifting and followed Connor into the house. His dad snored from the front room as they walked straight to the kitchen. Mason threw together some sandwiches, and they both devoured the meal without a word. He'd been hungry after soccer games, but this was something else. His whole body tingled and buzzed. "I feel like I'm vibrating."

Connor snorted, practically inhaling his last bite. "It's adrenaline. Shifting does that, especially if you've been training or fighting." He downed a glass of water. "It'll fade."

Mason had barely swallowed his last bite when Shunnar popped his head in the kitchen, informing them it was time for the Blessing Council.

"What exactly *is* the Blessing Council?" Mason chugged his water.

Connor grinned, his response to everything.

Mason followed him outside, into the tiny yard. Several lawn chairs were pulled into a circle. Hawks lined every free edge of fence. He couldn't help wondering what kind of show he would witness with a group of rusty, un-matching lawn chairs on a forgotten, dried-up lawn. The sun had set, dropping a blood-red curtain on the horizon behind.

"Better to witness it," Connor finally replied.

They both stood behind the empty chairs. No one spoke. Mason wondered why he wasn't in hawk form while so many others were. He stood silently with Connor, Des, Shunnar, and a new face he'd never met, or had he?

This questionable man stood across from the group, dressed in the shifter uniform Mason was beginning to recognize. He wore dark camouflage pants, a black T-shirt and vest, surely concealing an assortment of throwing knives. He was tall and muscular with short dark hair, but it was his frost-blue eyes that haunted in his glare. As he stood, his broad jaw clenched and unclenched. Mason thought he wouldn't want to cross him unexpectedly. At the same time, he looked familiar.

The man peered at Mason, his icy scowl hurling

disgust. It knocked Mason in the chest, and he looked away, swallowing down scratchy lumps of awkwardness.

Coming to his rescue, bright lights flared around them, pulling his attention from the mystery man. Energy filled the air, like an electrical storm on a scorching summer night. Every time his eyes adjusted, a new body mysteriously appeared into an empty lawn chair. He didn't know where they'd come from, but they couldn't be human, even with nothing inhuman standing out about their features. Soon, the eight chairs filled leaving only one vacant.

Everyone stood silent before the obvious aura of royalty. There were five individuals wearing neutral colors of white, off-white, and beige. Ashton might better have described their hues with a hundred other names for the color white. Another group of three wore velvety garments of purple. *Indigo*, he smiled to himself.

Curiosity about his backyard guests pricked, and his impulsive side swelled like a balloon. Connor knocked him with his shoulder, and he fell into a new stance, trying for shifter-focus, a first for him.

All was quiet. The birds must have nested early, the bats not yet awake. Waves from the ocean somehow muted for *this* meeting. Then, nothing.

What was everyone waiting for?

Are we doing this telepathically? Mason thought he was missing the meeting.

Connor nudged him again.

Finally, soft music trailed on the winds, growing louder until a flash came down from the sky. When he looked up, an impressive glow hovered above the last empty chair. It was so bright he squinted his eyes at the light. Whoever it was shone so radiantly he appeared the brightest of blues, like tropical seas. The Pacific Ocean, just yards from where they all stood, paled in comparison.

Everyone in the small yard tipped their heads and closed their eyes, including the hawks lining the fence. Mason's eyes, reduced to slits, watched. He wasn't about to miss a thing.

The melody from above grew stronger, when it began to seep warmly into his mind, like millions of microscopic organisms slipping in through every exposed pore. Notes from unknown instruments entered his body and rushed through his bloodstream, sharp and stinging.

In a panic, he scanned the group, but everyone else wore peaceful, smooth expressions. So he inhaled a breath and let it out slowly, relaxing into the music. It was…beautiful. He wanted to watch the being covered in blue light, but it was blinding. And the weight of the music, unreal. The melody somehow forced his eyes shut just as the song infiltrated his mind.

It was a message.

The wordless rhythm swirled into code, and Mason deciphered it with ease. He laughed aloud, awed by both the bizarre delivery and the fact he could understand it. His eyes flew open to notice a blur of turquoise light shooting up from the yard. Was it visible by other humans on the beach?

Their small assembly bowed their heads as if in prayer while more lyrics of a language felt, not spoken, coursed through his veins. The force pushed his chin into his chest, and his eyes squeezed tight once more. Blood pumped through his motionless limbs until finally, his body released from the hold of the presence above. The beautiful song, filling the ugly backyard, dissipated. When Mason opened his eyes, the turquoise light, and the being behind it, was gone. The individuals in ivory and indigo took their seats.

Mason looked around. Everyone was focused on one of the five dressed in white. His long white-blond hair fell to his waist, yet even with the amount of respect everyone paid him, he was simply dressed. All of their clothing appeared casual. The females wore loose dresses reminding him of a grandma's nightgown, minus the flannel roses. They flowed long, emitting an inner light through the seams. The males wore loose tunics over what looked like looser pajama bottoms, but far from sloppy.

The male in white lifted his hands in greeting, with his palms up and arms spread wide. Before he spoke, he looked upon each guest sitting in a rusted lawn chair, then nodded to every hawk standing in human form. He turned to acknowledge the hawks in bird form lining the fence and surrounding tree branches. His golden eyes seemed warm and inviting when his gaze fell on Mason. He didn't show recognition but didn't show suspicion either. The setting felt wildly out of place, but Mason knew he would probably hold this kind of power anywhere.

"We have been blessed and meet now in highest expectation of greatness to come. Our Centennial elemental is safe, though not as expected. We have failed to keep Ashton's human-linked mind inside the Human Realm for the entirety of her eighteen years. Yet not all is lost. She is of the first century of the third millennium, as the Human Realm measures. She is strong, and goodness prevails as always, though not without creative measures. We thank you, Clan of

Northwest Hawks, who fight collectively for our cause. As primary advisor for the Spiritual Realm, I come to you, devoted members of our Blessing Council, to gain perspective in this heightened quandary. We have faith that Ashton is safe, so at this time our focus is Cillian and his measures to intervene in the promotion of our Centennial for his own dark gain." He turned toward one of the females wearing violet.

She was exquisite with black tresses swaying in sync with the folds of her gown. Her eyes slanted slightly, the color, darkened honey with glints of red. They were so mysterious, Ashton might have described their luster as scarlet or ruby. The woman looked as if she were made of glass, like a delicate statue.

Memories of Ashton flashed behind his eyes, his best friend, the girl he'd grown up with next door. The one he could talk to with food falling out of his mouth. The one he rolled on to force out the secret whereabouts of her hidden sour candy. The way the Blessing Council spoke of her now was honorable, important. Who was she going to be?

Connor elbowed him in the side. He was distracted. Maybe his shifter mind wasn't as locked down as he thought.

The female in purple spoke in an airy voice. "The Dream Realm is in support of the Spiritual Realm's declaration and feels at ease in the safe return of our Centennial. We have faith in the outcome. Therefore, we agree in uniting our focus solely on Cillian. Lucifer's prince has ventured closer than his typical confrontation. Let this be settled."

The man in white, who had spoken before, responded. "The angel Sandalphon has blessed our cause. We will attack at nightfall. Ashton's captor, although not revealed by the angel, knows of the necessity of her transformation *inside* the Human Realm. While she will return in time, we must not allow Cillian a foothold. Gavan, are your warriors equipped?"

The mystery man Mason had wondered about acknowledged the Council. Gavan, the first voice Mason had heard in his mind as a hawk, stepped forward and bowed his head to the man in white. "Aye, my liege, we are. Several casts will depart at once. As you are aware, Ashton's safety is my—our—primary focus." His gaze snapped to Mason.

Mason blinked. The fury in Gavan's eyes was bone-chilling. He couldn't tell if Gavan was angry at Ian or at him for failing to protect Ashton. The more Gavan stared, the more it enraged Mason, and the heat of his hawk inside itched to get out. To fight.

Connor's shoulder barely touched Mason's, grounding him, and he blinked away.

The formality of the meeting broke as quickly as it began. Final words of blessing barely soothed Mason's muscles, now twitching from Gavan's expression. The council members stood, with small groups forming around them. Private discussions here and there, none of which Mason could hear. Connor hadn't budged, and so Mason stood ready next to him. When he looked around for Gavan, he was gone.

Connor's voice trickled through his mind. *It won't be long now.*

They'd used their voices all day, except in hawk form. How strange to speak to Connor in his mind while he stood right next to him in the yard.

Are we going after Ian? Mason's heart thumped in his chest, wondering what an offensive attack might feel like. He'd only ever fought in two defensive

145

strikes. Now, after training all day and jabbed by Gavan's strange eye-contact, his adrenaline stirred.

We, yes. You, no. Connor elbowed him.

What? Why not?

Enough! Shunnar's voice rang sternly in Mason's mind.

It must have been a dual message because Connor straightened beside him. Suddenly the calm of the meeting erupted in flickers of light. All the beings clad in whites and purples blew out like birthday candles. Hawks took flight. Men shifted.

Connor broke his stance and leaned over in a rush. "I have to shift. Sorry you aren't in on this one, but demons never die, so there'll be other opportunities." He laughed as he dropped to the ground, easily shifting, and lifted into the orange and pink sunset sky.

Mason rolled his eyes, then scanned the yard for Shunnar. The once-orchestrated event unraveled in chaos like a battlefield. He backed up, leaned against the door of the beach house until Shunnar found him there.

"I need you to stay here tonight. Your father will wake soon. Wherever Ashton is, she will return in time. Once she reaches her birthday hour, you will transition to the Spiritual Realm together."

"So I will see her again?"

"Of course. You *are* hers. It may not sound bold to your human side, but in our Realm, it's very honorable." He set his hand on Mason's shoulder.

"I still don't get that part. I know we're some kind of team, but how are we supposed to work together if I'm *serving* her?" He rolled his eyes again, though that even felt a strain after the weight of the day.

"You will provide her safe passage as *together* you

fight off evil. How much more *team* do you need?"

"Passage?" Mason's eyebrows rose.

"Get some sleep, Mason. Your entire world changes tomorrow." He patted him on the back before heading to the beach. "One more thing." He spoke without turning around.

"Yeah?"

"Shower first. You stink."

This time, Mason was too tired to roll his eyes or respond at all. He clicked the door shut to face the dark quiet on his own.

His dad had slept through the entire day of fiction. Ashton was *God knows where* with everyone else fully confident in her unknown safety. There was an army of raptors outside his door, where spiritual beings had appeared and disappeared on his lawn. And an angel had appeared!

This new world felt like a page from one of his dad's demon books.

He did need a shower, but he also needed sleep. There was no way that would happen, especially without Ashton, or stressing out about transforming into another Realm.

Shunnar's final words replayed in Mason's mind...*Your entire world changes tomorrow.*

Hadn't it already changed enough?

Chapter 14

Heart To Heart

Mason dropped into the chair across from his sleeping dad. Every muscle in his body felt like bricks, as if standing up would take more than he could give. Shunnar had said his dad should be waking about now. What would happen after that? How would his dad react tomorrow finding him gone…thirteen years after his wife died?

He leaned his head back against the cushion and wiped the stress from his forehead. Somehow, he had to say goodbye. This hadn't been the plan before his dream turned everything upside down. In August he would have moved away for school, and his dad wouldn't have even noticed. But now…

Suddenly, Max stirred in his sleep, almost rolling off the sofa. Mason swooped down to break his fall when his dad's eyes flew open.

"It's okay. You fell asleep." Mason pushed against him, supporting his weight until he sat up on his own.

"What time is it?" He rubbed his shoulder.

It had to have been uncomfortable sleeping fourteen hours on a half-sized sofa. Mason waited for him to settle, then moved to the chair by the empty fireplace. The room felt wintery, opposite the warmth from earlier in the day. Without Ashton there for advice, he took a more impulsive approach.

"Ashton's birthday hour is tonight, just before midnight. We'll be gone for a while." There, he'd said it. He closed his mouth and looked for an expression of understanding on his dad's face, hoping for a typical Max Deed response of a few words.

His dad's lips thinned into a straight line. Then like a match striking, he straightened his back and stood, towering above Mason.

Mason pushed to stand, matching his height but feeling smaller than he should have.

"Mason Gabriel Deed, if you think I'm staying behind while you disappear from my life, you're out of your mind."

"Do you think I have a choice?"

"You have a choice in telling me exactly what's going on."

He had him there. Mason's gut wrestled with the idea of being honest.

I know this is difficult, but he needs to let go. Shunnar's voice sounded more lax than his usual curtness. *Our Healer will tint his dreams to allow for understanding. Your family and friends...they won't ask about you.*

Ever? Like we're forgotten?

You and Ashton will always be remembered in the Human Realm, but in all minds associated with you both, it will be as if you're off traveling. It is for the best.

Mason was getting what he always wanted, finally gaining freedom from a man who never found time for him. Why was he worried now about his dad's loneliness? He was ready to leave home and lead his own life. It just wasn't supposed to be *this* way.

What did it matter? He had to do whatever it took

to get Ashton back. He was too close.

"Dad, listen to me. I don't have a choice. I have to get some sleep. I'm going to take a shower and go to bed. If I'm gone in the morning, know that I'm okay. I'll be fine—and—I'll be back." Though he didn't know if that was true. "If people ask, say that Ashton and I went on a summer road trip."

"No!" His dad's voice rose. "This is crazy."

"Please, do this for me. If not for me, for Mom. It's her world that's calling. I can't tell you about it, just like she couldn't. You honored her wishes then; please honor mine now." His eyes burrowed into his dad's. He needed this. And he didn't care anymore about the spine-burning consequences that might follow.

His dad dropped his gaze and turned, walking from the room at a defeated pace. Before he was gone, he called over his shoulder. "Mason."

"Yeah?"

"I will honor what you need right now, but I want answers once this *big event* is over. I let your mother go, afraid to talk to her about it. Afraid I was the crazy one. I failed to protect her, but I still need to know the truth. I deserve that." Then he turned around, locked eyes with him. Waited.

"Fine, yes. I will tell you everything I can after things settle down. None of this is your fault. Mom wouldn't blame you. And, Dad, don't go seeking me out. Just go back to normal as best you can and cover for us until I contact you. Okay?"

Mason moved to stand in front of his dad, feeling more level with him now.

But his dad shook his head, showing more emotion than Mason had ever seen. "I know I haven't been there for you."

"It's okay. Really." Any other time Mason would have appreciated his words. A breakthrough to a long overdue conversation. But tonight? He couldn't begin to heal those wounds and instead started down the hallway toward the bathroom.

His dad reached out, grabbed his elbow. "I want you to know it's been difficult. I'm sorry I was distant for so long. Being with you these past couple days has been…nice." He sucked in a breath. "You remind me so much of your mom. Unfortunately, it was to the point I couldn't look at you. Your face was a daily reminder she was gone. I thought I could protect you from that world. I tried. I thought if you were busy with sports and school, you wouldn't have time to notice anything darker. I didn't know what you were up against, but I needed you to be safe while I escaped my own pain. I guess I pawned you off."

The break in his confession was the loudest silence Mason had heard. There wasn't a creak in the floor, no faint sounds of ocean waves in the far-off distance.

He ran a hand through his hair and kept going. "The Nicholses were happy to step in, and I let them. But it haunts me, Mason. For years, it's haunted me. That's why I started writing about it. The more I wrote, the more I could bury myself and forget. I don't know what's happening. I guess I'm still mourning the family I never got to have. I'm going to miss you."

Mason had never had an honest, heart-to-heart conversation with his dad before. Speechless, he stared into his eyes, a darker version of his own, holding them quietly. Somehow his gratitude must have penetrated his dad's thoughts because they both gave each other half a smile.

His dad hugged him, long and awkward,

whispering that he loved him, and then closed himself into his bedroom. Mason stood in the hall for another full minute, still processing his dad's long, belated words he hadn't realized he so desperately needed to hear.

Slowly, he walked to the shower.

Later, lying in bed, every bone and muscle heavy on his sheets, he prayed for sleep. But with new emotions pounding through his veins, it was just another choice he wasn't allowed make.

****

The clock ticked 11:37 p.m. when the purple glow eased into the space around Mason's bunk. It wafted from a picture frame on the dresser, an old snapshot of the shoreline outside the beach house. He bolted upright, afraid at first, as the glass in the frame warped and distorted the photo. As more violet hues reflected from the frame, Mason remembered what he'd learned from Connor; purple light was good.

In a blink, Ashton sat in a heap on the floor.

"Ash." He pulled her up, hugging her to the point of crushing. "Oh my God. I didn't know when I would see you again. I was going crazy. Where did you go?"

"I'm sorry, Mas. I know you were worried. I wasn't with Ian, though." She gripped his shoulders, something she did to ground him when he was upset. But he was only relieved to have her back.

"It's okay." He didn't want her feeling guilty.

She hesitated, so he pulled back, nodded for her to go on.

"I was in the Spiritual Realm."

"You know?" His eyes grew two sizes. "How much do you know?"

"Not enough. But I know about the Realms. And

demons. And I met my—birth mother." She collapsed onto Mason's bunk bed.

He slumped down next to her. "Wait. What do you mean?" The secrecy from the past week had been paralyzing. He'd been waiting for Ashton to know the truth. Only now, so close to the hour, he hadn't expected it.

"It was my birth mother who took me. To protect me. All I know is that I'm not from the human world, as crazy as that sounds."

Mason's head spun. He looked at the clock. 11:45. His insides were a million pixels of white blobs at the thought of transitioning into a Spiritual Realm.

Before he could put together any words of wisdom for Ashton, she reached for him to hold her, something she did when she was scared. He wrapped his arms around her and pulled her close. "I had no idea, Ash. Are you okay?"

"I don't know. I feel like it must be true because of all the madness that's happened." Her voice wavered. "I wanted to know who my birth parents were. I guess I'm getting that now. But I'm done with trusting the process, Mas. It's our lives being messed with."

"Listen, I don't know what's going to happen in a few minutes, or hours, or however long it takes for this transition. I only know that if we must go through it, then I'm happy it's with you. And don't ever leave me again like that!" He tightened his grip around her middle. He felt stronger after training, but would his newfound strength ever be enough?

Her head, nestled against his chest, reassured him. He wasn't sure what would happen after midnight, and so he pulled her closer. All the lies he was forced to tell had to have been worth something. He buried his face into her hair feeling relieved the most important person in his life was back, safe in his arms.

For now.

****

Mason howled.

Blood rushed to his head, heavy with sleep and confusion. He wanted to push away whatever force held him down. But his struggle only activated the strange pressure more. When he opened his eyes, he was on the ground, branches and dried needles scattering from the disturbance, and Ashton, unconscious, clutched to his chest. Unsure of his location, he made out blurry clusters of tall trees, the scent of evergreen swirling the scuffle.

"You're transitioning." Connor's voice seeped through the mayhem. "Relax."

Connor's mouth moved, but his words echoed like loud clanging. Trying to hold onto a motionless Ashton was a burden, but he refused to let go, forced himself to stand.

"Release her." Shunnar's deep voice broke through. Pressure pounded against Mason's spine, as gravity forced his body back down to the ground.

A woman strutted into view with an air of authority. She wore brown leather boots and cargo pants, a stocked utility belt displaying various weapons. Her long unruly curls, red as fire, demanded their own direction of cascade. Her gray eyes, set sternly in sharp bone structure, stared at Mason. She was small in stature, yet her rugged attitude radiated from every porcelain pore.

"Although she is your bond, Mason Deed, she is now my duty. Step down." Her voice rang like a dinner bell, loud and commanding. The sun hung overhead, teasing Mason's sense of direction and time. The skyline looked nothing like Seattle, or the Oregon coast, and though he had no idea how long he'd been asleep or where he was, it felt far from home.

Mason directed his question to Shunnar, unsure if or how he should address this fiery new character. "Bond? And what does she mean, step down?"

"This is my mate, Rory. She's in charge of training new warriors. You belong to Ashton, but not the way you're thinking. For now, you need to let her transition. Centennials do that without us. Come with me." Shunnar nodded, and two unknown shifters bent down to lift Ashton away.

Mason tightened his grip, hopeful he wasn't leaving bruises.

The two shifters looked at Shunnar.

"I'm staying with—" Another nod from Shunnar, and Mason's words cut off. The two shifters forced his arms open, while a third appeared, lifting Ashton away. Mason cursed and fought against their iron grip but only managed to twist himself further. He was tired, weak. He'd only worried about Ashton transitioning, not the effects on himself.

Rory blared over the ruckus. "All right, keepers, when Ashton awakes, she will know everything, yet nothing at all. It will take time for her human and seam keeper memories to bind. I will work with her exclusively. Hawks report to Shunnar; riders stand by. Move out."

Before anyone disagreed with this little spitfire's demands, the men behind Shunnar dropped to the ground, morphed into their hawk forms. Mason didn't want to shift, but his bird of prey inside had a different idea. His body tucked and molded clumsily before talons appeared where his feet once were. Screeching filled his throat where a demand to wait once was. He called out, Ashton's name at the edge of his mind, but apologies were lost, his body taken over by the hawk.

Twisting back, his last glance fell on Rory. She was kneeling next to Ashton, rubbing a bouquet of green leaves across her cheek.

Fall in! Shunnar belted orders. *I want you in the front line.*

Mason inched away, not about to blindly follow orders anymore. He had done what they'd demanded before Ashton's change, for her safety. *I promised her we'd be together when she woke.* He held back the colorful words he would have rather spewed, as a familiar heat crawled up his spine.

And you will. Your job right now is to fall in line, soldier.

I didn't sign up for this! Mason spat back, his hollow bones constricting.

Destiny did it for you. Let the Centennial transition on her own. It is our way. The words stung, but the burn under his feathered skin subsided. *Don't defy a direct order again. We're in the Spiritual Realm now.*

Mason moved to where he was directed. It was hard to break the rules when he didn't know them, but as soon as he did, he would break every last one to get back on track with his own plan. He stretched to see Ashton, hoping she was okay, hoping she understood he'd tried to stay. He followed as the cast lifted in flight, but his mind settled on one thought. When he did see Ashton again, she would surely make him pay for not being there…Another broken promise.

Chapter 15

Transformation

Ashton dreamed of her backyard garden. The fragrant bushes and plants in every shade of green. Hues her mom relished mixing, like a scientist, using brushes and trays instead of beakers and microscopes. Green umber and viridian were never true, but she beamed at the right amount of phthalo blue and hansa yellow.

Somewhere between dreaming and consciousness, her mom's smile faded and the colors called, *time to wake up.* As if on cue, a soft breeze pulled her awareness from her dream.

She opened her eyes to the outside. *Outside?*

In one swift motion, she sprang to her knees, greeting an unknown face, crowned with a long red mane. Weaving back and forth, she placed both hands on the ground for balance. Steadying her body was easier than her heart, pounding against her ribs. The scent of evergreens pulled her attention to the circle of trees enveloping the area behind the red-haired woman. She wore a military-style uniform and held a bouquet of green herbs.

"Welcome home, Ashton. My name is Rory, and I will be your trainer. Can you stand?" The redhead spoke kindly, though with a certain edge of authority.

Ashton looked past Rory to the crowd collecting.

They were all women, about her age, dressed in Rory's same uniform, light camouflage cargo pants and white T-shirts. Looking down, she wore the same, complete with brown leather combat boots. As she stood up, a thick belt pulled at her hips, the pockets filled with gem-stoned gadgets. She pulled out a jade-handled dagger. The short blade, almost triangular, blazed with luminescent green light. Her mouth dropped open, but before she uttered a word, Rory's hand slipped over, swiped the knife, and sheathed it.

"Weapons training comes soon enough."

"Weapons?" Ashton swayed again, then took a wider stance.

"Yes, first we must restore your seam keeper memories, then you will feel like yourself again and we can get to—"

"I already feel like myself." She grabbed at her chest. "Where's Mason?"

"He's training. You need to drink this tea, nourish yourself with a blessing, and presto, you'll be ready. It takes time adjusting back to our realm. After all—" She chuckled. "—you've been human for eighteen years."

With the wave of her hand, another woman appeared carrying a tray. She offered Ashton a small cup of steaming pink liquid and chunk of bread.

Ashton glanced at the platter. "Ready for what?"

"Ready to remember. Your memories have already been unlocked, due to a slight deviation from the plan." Her giggle flitted around the space at a high pitch. "But rest assured, all is well. Since your birthday hour has struck, your body just needs to give your memories the go-ahead. So go ahead." She beamed expectantly. "Bon appétit."

"I don't think so." She backed into two women

behind her. "Sorry." She changed direction. "Mason?"

Rory approached her one small step at a time. "The sooner you drink, the sooner your memories will settle, and everything will make sense."

Just as Rory's voice cut through her indecision, a memory of drinking another strange tea tugged inside, from her birth mother...Althaia. Didn't she say it would help? Ashton already knew she was a seam keeper, but was that from Althaia telling her or from the tea?

For a split second, her mom, Maggie, flashed through her mind, pouring tea and serving muffins the morning after graduation. It had only been a week, yet already seemed far away. Ashton looked at the circle of uniforms growing around their group, and her mom's image melted away. When she blinked, Althaia stood before her, glorious in her green silk wrap and leather boots.

"My darling Ashton, this will answer all your questions. This is the reason I accepted the loss of your childhood. It's the hope I've held onto, that your sacrifice will bond our elemental duty at the seam." Althaia's eyes glistened. "Please drink. Eat."

This is what Ashton had wanted, wasn't it? The drawers of her imaginary file cabinet cracked open in her mind. Hadn't she wanted to fill the file labeled *Adoption Lie* with truths about her birth family? Didn't she want to know who she was supposed to be?

Rory cleared her throat and nodded at the tray, the sound snapping Ashton from her thoughts.

Althaia smiled, and Ashton picked up the teacup, sipped the syrupy pink drink. A warm rush sizzled down her throat, causing her eyes to water. It was much spicier than Althaia's concoction. After a quick breath, she picked up the bread. It was bigger than a bite, but smaller than a biscuit. Should she bite into it or plop the whole thing into her mouth? Before her spectators' piercing stares, she tossed it back and gulped the last of the tea to help it down.

"Now what?" Ashton set the cup on the tray, breathing out the fiery flavor spreading through her insides.

Althaia's expression held concern, while Rory covered a laugh.

"Now, we wait."

Rory's response unraveled Ashton. Maybe it was the tea, because the heated sensation traveled down each of her limbs. But did this woman just ask her to *wait*?

"Oh, no." Ashton backed up, careful to look behind her this time. "I'm not waiting any longer to find out what's going on with my own life. Where's Mason?" Every direction she walked, more women gathered wearing the same clothes she wore, the same belts of jeweled weapons suspended from their hips. They all stepped back as she approached but didn't leave an opening for her to see past.

"Mason!" she called into the air.

Just then, it hit.

Vertigo seized without warning, without building in intensity. Ashton doubled over. Her head pounded through the visions flooding her memories. Visions in various stages of her life, but *not* her life, played like a movie in her mind. Althaia was there, but then it was Mom and Dad, Maggie and Drew, from her home in Seattle. Their house, next door to Mason's, with their garden in the backyard. Mason was there, climbing trees as a young boy, opening her sticky locker in middle school. She knew these visions to be true. But he was also there fighting monsters from her nightmares, in battles she'd never seen before.

How could this be?

Pictures, factual and fiction, flashed at rapid speeds. Images from her past blew through a storm of new memories, familiar and unfamiliar, forcing their way in. Through it all Mason stayed the only distinguishable constant until finally, with a jolt, her mind stopped spinning, and the visions slowed.

Ashton fell, gripping the earth again for support. She was grateful for the hand on her back and didn't care if it was Rory's or Althaia's. She didn't want to be alone. Even with a newfound strength brewing inside her chest, she didn't think she could stand.

Rory called out and more hands helped to lift her up. Ashton's brain was mush. She wanted to speak but couldn't form the words. Rory watched her intently. Althaia's lips were a thin line. Silently, the large group behind them waited. What were they waiting for?

In a blink, she knew.

She was a seam keeper. The title floated at the surface of her mind, but what did it mean? She protected humans...from evil. From demons.

From Ian.

Her brain produced information like an old-school computer printer, zigzagging back and forth, without waiting for her to catch up. She was a warrior.

A warrior?

She had to tell Mason. Where was he? Her insides burned with the realization of her new self. But her old self was also there. All of it made her dizzy.

"Mason," she called louder, straining to see over the surrounding heads. "Where is he?" She focused on Althaia, realizing no one else would answer. "Please help me find him?"

Althaia scrunched her nose, glanced at Rory, who set a hand on Ashton's shoulder.

"He will join us soon. First, you need to find your memories."

"I need to see Mason first." Surprised by her own sharp tone, she planted her feet in the dirt for balance.

Rory's hand dropped. "The connection between rider and hawk is strong, I understand. We've never had the Centennial's mate live in the Human Realm before. There is no protocol for it. But you need space for your memories to merge, without distraction. The process takes time. So let's get you settled into training camp."

What did she mean? Mate? Protocol? Merging memories? Ashton couldn't keep up.

Before she could question, Rory pointed out various women around her. Names flew in one ear and out the other, yet with each introduction the matching faces seemed familiar. Rory pulled her farther down a dirt path to the opening of an elaborate canvas tent. Althaia followed.

Ashton glanced around at a camp site on steroids. Enormous flares of colors popped between wide pines and old cedars, so tall she couldn't see the tops. These castle-like tents appeared in all directions, like enormous bright-hued mushrooms. Mushrooms that reminded her of fairytales.

There she was, being pulled down a rabbit hole, masked as a bright blue tent. The same blue in Althaia's eyes, matching the color of her own. Maybe the truth of her past could be revealed in a blink of the tent flap and she could wake up back home, safe and sound in Seattle.

****

Mason closed his eyes and leaned on an old cedar in the clearing. His body pulsed from training. Yet the bumpy bark against his spine was nothing compared to the bruises from shifting. Shunnar claimed the marks would be gone before he hit the shower, but with the ache reaching deep into his lungs, it couldn't be true.

Shunnar had been called away, giving Mason the only time he'd had alone since he and Ashton transitioned. Everyone had been waiting for their Centennial to arrive, but he was some kind of *plus one*, and from what he picked up around the whispers and stares, nobody knew what to do with him.

"Nap time?"

Des's voice brought Mason to his feet at once, looking up to the much taller seam keeper. How did he get so close without a sound?

"Whoa, sorry." He grabbed his lower back, his surprise jump to attention, jarring.

Des's long dreads shook when he laughed. "Shunnar had an emergency, so you're done for the day. I'll show you where you're bunking, and then the showers." He covered his nose. "Or maybe the showers first?"

Mason was too tired to laugh but tossed his chin up in response.

When they walked out of the clearing, long rows of colorful tents sprouted up from between the tallest trees Mason had ever seen. Was Ashton in one of them? He hoped her training wasn't anything like his. He couldn't imagine her enduring that kind of exertion. She'd complained on every hike he'd ever dragged her on.

"This must be strange compared to the Human Realm." Des walked at a relaxed pace, and Mason was relieved. Shunnar had one speed: expeditious.

"I guess so. I mean, I haven't done anything except break my bones to fly, then break more bones to spar."

Des laughed again, as if Mason was joking.

"I still don't quite get why I'm here."

Des stopped walking, turned to face him. "I don't know how you ended up in the Human Realm, but somehow you're a shifter. You do belong here. We just don't have a proper plan."

"Then why can't I train with Ashton?"

"The Centennial needs time for her memories to return. It's tricky at first because she never actually lived them, but she would have. So we train while we wait."

"And my memories?"

He shrugged as if it sufficed in all the information Mason needed.

"Okay, I get it, I'm a surprise. Can't I just opt out?" Even though a part of him revved at the thought of flying, following orders wasn't in his future plans. He'd only gone this far to keep Ashton safe. As soon as he could see her, say a proper goodbye—the thought stuck in his throat—he wanted his own life back.

Didn't he?

"No." Des didn't blink. "It doesn't work like that. It doesn't matter *how* you're a shifter; you are one. Your life's been chosen for you already." He started down the path.

"By whom?"

But Des just shook his head and kept walking.

Mason lagged behind, scanned the surrounding trees for any other option to get out of there, then reluctantly followed Des. For now. His shoulders slumped, and he pushed away the idea it was in defeat. None of this felt right. None of it made sense.

Or did it?

Transitioning *had* changed him. He felt stronger and faster, and aside from the physical pain of morphing into a hawk, flying was in his bones. But if this was some kind of destiny, why all the secrecy? Why was he a surprise?

Mason picked up his pace. "So if I am destined to be here, what do we actually do each day?"

Des turned down another path, past a small group of tents. Mason took in his surroundings, trying to mark where he was, something he'd learned to do in every survival camp his dad had sent him to, but he couldn't keep track in this new place. He looked at the sun setting in the distance. The sky looked like one of Ashton's mom's paintings, the silhouetted tree shadows like Ashton's pen and ink drawings.

Des glanced at Mason. "Humans are a fretful lot, always falling asleep with stirring thoughts."

Mason thought of when his mom had died. He couldn't close his eyes and be alone at the same time. That was when he'd started spending nights with Ashton. Heading solo off to college had been his plan for conquering that pain once and for all. His mom was dead. It was time to get over it.

Des went on, his soft voice a contrast to his great size. "Positive thoughts emit a feather-light energy…excitement, anticipation, happiness. These all cushion the Dream Realm, ensuring the safekeeping of human souls as they sleep."

"Like a force field?" Mason tried to help.

Des lifted an eyebrow. "Well, it's more like a current. Like waves in an ocean, lulling souls safely along."

All he could picture were sleeping bodies floating

in the sea. His image didn't look very peaceful, more freakishly eerie instead.

"But worry, fear, envy, hate…" Des's jaw tightened. "The energy emitted from negative emotions is heavy. They collect on the bottom of the Realm like muck, pulling souls down. Lesser demons are sent in to feed on their energy, returning to their higher demons to be siphoned." He crinkled his nose. "It's disgusting. The monsters return again and again, happily engorging themselves for their masters to milk. What's worse?" He stopped and peered over with dark eyes. "The more negative energy extracted, the more humans exist in their waking sorrow. Souls can't rest. Misery begets misery, Hell's assurance of continued power."

"So humans stay angry and hateful the more they go to bed angry and hateful?"

Gravely, he nodded. "Humans fight monsters for their thoughts every night, they just don't know it because it happens in another realm. It's no wonder children are afraid of the dark…" His declaration stained his face. "They should be."

Mason shuddered, though a spark of pride struck in his chest…to be a part of something so crucial. But when he pictured the whole scene more realistically, he was even more confused. "So seam keepers clean up the mess?"

"We can't mend humankind; damaged souls are damaged. Their healing isn't up to us. But we can guard the realm to keep the demons out. Seam keepers work in casts, six pairs of riders and hawks, trained and blessed to protect the borders. Different teams work at varied locations, and together we stop the lesser demons from entering."

"What about the muck pooling at the bottom of the

Dream Realm—or the ones that get in?"

"Internal keepers manage that. If we do our job at the seam, they have an easier go of it."

Mason opened his mouth to say more, when a group of keepers ran down the path ahead of them. Des turned, as if listening to a private conversation in his head. The mental telepathy thing was strange. Mason was still trying to figure it out.

"Showers, the white tent ahead." He patted Mason on the back. "I've got to run. Demon activity at the portal."

"What? Here?" Only hours ago, in training, Shunnar had claimed that demons never crossed Spiritual borders, and keepers never passed into the Dark Realm. It was only the in between they had to worry about. "Can they get through?"

Des called over his shoulder, "Of course not."

Chapter 16

First Flight

Ashton clung to the back of a hawk, her fingers
clenching thick downy feathers, her legs gripping its
hollow-boned body. The wind roared past her ears,
mixing with her own heartbeats, and melded into one
continuous buzz. As she pressed her face behind its
neck, her stomach fluttered out of tune with the strum
of broad wing strokes, somehow carrying her weight
through the air.

How was this possible? Did she shrink? Did the
hawk grow?

A little of both. A familiar voice rose on the wind.

Ashton opened her eyes, still hunched low over the
hawk. She glanced to the right to see Rory on a hawk
just ahead, her fiery red hair flailing through the air.
She was too far away for her voice to carry. To the left,
there was only space and sky.

Ashton.

She looked around again, still clinging to the bird's
back she was riding. Rory had said this was a practice
flight, to adjust before flying with her team...*cast*, her
seam keeper side corrected, always a step behind. They
had passed a cast of six hawks and riders earlier in the
day. The flying cluster looked like a formation of geese.
Maybe another cast was coming up from behind. She
wrenched her neck to see.

Ash, it's me.

"Mason?" Nausea rose in her throat. This couldn't be happening. Then, just as she settled on disbelief, a deeper part of her understood. In seconds, her seam keeper side relayed the reality that the hawk she clung to was Mason. Yet somehow, he was still himself.

Shifter. His voice filled in the term her memory worked to name.

"How?" she cried. Her tears chilled her face.

But she already knew the answer. She had stood right there in the flight arena with Rory when the hawks had flown in. They grew larger on approach, while she grew dizzier. When it happened, her equilibrium pulled from every side. Her seam keeper thoughts were confident she could mount, while crushing the poor bird only confused her human mind.

"Mason?"

Yeah, it's me, kiiiiiiiiiiii-arrr!

The hawk—Mason—ruffled his feathers. He rocked her slightly, sending a clear message to hold on. If her knuckles had been glove-free, they would have been ghost-white, she clenched so tightly. Suddenly, he pulled up, soaring into the cerulean sky and wafting atop an air current. Then he whirled twice before falling into place behind Rory. The change in elevation caused the wind song against Ashton's ears to change tempo. And her stomach…

You won't be sick. You just need to remember your body is made to fly.

A part of her knew he was right, but the part that didn't wanted a barf bag.

Stop thinking about it.

"How are you talking to me?" she called into his neck, still not ready to sit up like Rory.

I'm kind of in your head. It's a mental thing.

"You can hear my thoughts." A reprimand, not a question.

If it's any consolation, I can only hear your thoughts in hawk form. It's for our safety on the job.

"I don't like this one bit." Worry bubbled with the nausea.

Try it, Ash. Think something to me.

Of course, make it a game. He was trying to distract attention away from his ability to invade on her thoughts, even if it was only in hawk form. Just then Mason swooshed them over a low cliff. She gripped his thick plumes, the color of milk and cinnamon. As brave as her seam keeper side seemed to be, her human side didn't want to fall off on her first day.

You're not going to fall off.

"You could have inferred that one. Why can't I hear all your thoughts?"

It's mostly white noise, until we direct a message toward each other, or seek it. I'm trying to communicate with you, so the flow is open, narrowly. I'm still learning how to do it myself, but I can't read your every thought.

Ashton focused on Mason, the human boy she'd grown up with. The one who owed her movie nights with sour candy after every scary adventure. This had to count for a year's worth!

It doesn't count if I didn't choose it.

"Stop reading my thoughts." Though he was right. Neither one of them had chosen an otherworldly life. Her seam keeper side was ready to learn…ready to remember who she was supposed to be. That side of her wanted to talk more with Althaia and to meet her birth father. Maybe her human side wanted that too, but her memories only trickled now, like a slow drip from a broken faucet.

Stop using your voice. Think something to me.

Still clutching his neck, she leaned over to brave a glance below. *Where are we?*

Mason tipped them slightly, circling wide in the open air. Below them was a forest's edge. Evergreens and deciduous trees lined one side, creating a natural border between the forest and a rushing river. Even more stunning was the afternoon glow coming from the other side of the water. Colorful spray leaped from splashing ripples in a rainbow of bright light. Each watery bead seemed to explode in the breeze, camouflaging the shore on the other side.

Ashton tried looking above the luminescent spray, to make out the terrain on the far bank. All she could see was mist, sparkling with hues of bursting pigment. It reminded her of a waterfall painting her mom had recently done.

Her mom.

Ashton blew out a breath. Maybe the hidden shore was like her old life. She knew it was there, she just couldn't see it clearly.

It's the seam. The border between the Human and Dream Realms.

Mason's soothing voice pulled her from gloom. She didn't have to guess which side was the Dream Realm. The kaleidoscopic water sprays, blurring the land behind, was telltale.

Suddenly Rory changed course. Mason fell in line behind her without a hitch.

Sorry, orders from Shunnar.

"Shunnar?" Ashton coughed, spitting out a fluffy bit of down.

Think it, Ash.

Who is Shunnar? She closed her mouth against any more feathered fluff.

Rory's hawk, my boss.

Boss?

Trainer, boss…he's evidently my new handler. I guess graduation didn't really mean freedom.

What could she say? He was right. And she was just as confused.

Hold on.

He lifted his wings, and they dropped in elevation, slow and steady. When Rory and Shunnar dipped lower toward the forest side, he followed. With each dip, her belly flip-flopped and her eyes glazed over, but soon they were low enough she could have reached out a hand to touch the treetops.

Landing on the human side seemed impossible; even her keeper side knew they were larger than standard hawks. But it didn't stop them from descending onto the highest of tree branches, fitting effortlessly. Was the blur between Realms making everything possible?

I think so. This is my first time too, with a rider, I mean.

Ashton sat straight up when her stomach lurched again, but still she gripped her fingers around Mason's plumes. The temperature felt warmer this close to the human side. Sunshine warmed her back as Mason's talons gripped and regripped a branch she thought couldn't hold their weight.

Rory's voice carried from the branch next to theirs. "When you are with your cast, you will scan the area below. Notice every color. Every texture. Examine the prickles of dark soil begging for light. Look for the

172

deep pores of bark creating valleys and canyons for the tiniest creatures. See through the eternity of greens lost in the quilt of leaves and needles below, all similar, yet unique. Know them. Recognize them. Observe every detail. It is the only way to identify lurking demons. They become the land around them, colorless, until you decipher a shimmer in their slightest movements."

It seemed impossible, especially while flying. Before she could ask, Shunnar lifted into the air. Mason was right behind him, the jolt forcing Ashton to tighten her grip. The trees grew smaller as the blue sky opened wide. Cool air rushed past her ears.

Again, dizziness waved through her insides but settled faster this time. Her heartbeats steadied, as her keeper memories began filling in some of the unknowns. Her body was changing size as needed. She would be able to detect prowling demons. She would be ready to kill—*No!*

Mas, I don't think I can actually kill anything. It was safer to think the message because putting it into words painted a completely different picture in her mind. One that made it far too real.

I know, it's weird. Just demons though.

She thought of Ian. He didn't look anything like a demon. If that was what she had to kill, then they had the wrong girl.

Mason was quiet.

But that nagging keeper inside wouldn't shut up. She stuck out her figurative chin, proud to guard the borders of the Dream Realm. Her memories glowed with honor and courage. Ashton just wanted to cry. Maybe she already was. It was hard to tell with her face smothered in brown and ivory feathers.

After a while, she opened her eyes, her head still

resting on Mason's neck. She looked down along the side of his body, catching the late day's light glinting on one of her weapons.

Carefully, she loosened a hand from Mason's neck and poked at the strange instruments tucked in her belt. There was the jade-handled double-sided dagger she had unsheathed earlier. She sat up an inch more to check out the one next to it, an amethyst-handled knife. It was long and slender, with a slight curve tipping the blade.

Mason soared steadily, so she sat up a little more, one hand still hooked to his neck.

There was a sapphire dagger, carved with intricately pierced cutouts. It looked more like a piece of art. But her seam keeper side knew the edges were essential in tearing through demon tissue.

Whoa! She swallowed wind-filled breaths to calm her nerves.

You already know how to use them. You just need to remember and practice. Mason's voice seeped through, encouraging her as he always had.

I don't know about that.

She switched sides, looping her left hand around Mason, still gripping her legs around his middle, and leaned up on her other side. There she pulled out the largest weapon on her belt, an amber-handled half-sword, thick with a serrated edge. She gulped as she slid it back into its sheath.

What are these? She cupped a leather pouch.

I think they're tiny explosives. Mason responded through her thoughts. *I can't remember what Shunnar said about them.*

But her keeper side knew he was right. She pictured three rose-colored glass spheres in her mind,

174

without even opening the pouch. They were like giant marbles, but not as effective at the seam as her sharper options.

Ashton shook her head, leaned back into Mason's neck.

It's scary that I recognize these weapons. Even more, that I know what to do with them. But using them?

We'll find a way to figure this out, Ash. Maybe we won't have to.

Did they have a choice? Ashton's head spilled with memories and emotions. Hadn't she tried to tell Rory and Althaia that she might not be interested? They wouldn't hear of it.

They said once my memories are complete, I'll only want to be a seam keeper.

Mason flapped his wings, increasing the speed and whipping the wind more through her hair. She snuggled in deeper.

I wouldn't know. You're the only one with returning memories, Ash.

****

Ashton held her breath until Mason turned the corner on the path from the flight arena. "Mas." She jumped into his arms, happy to see him in human form. It was the first time since their transformation into the Spiritual Realm.

"Hey." Mason exhaled into her shoulder.

"This all feels like storybook fiction." Her arms buzzed at their reunion, but she let go and stepped back so they could walk together. Trees like skyscrapers surrounded the path, creating a protective barrier for the training camp. The sun had dropped curtains of gold behind the tree line and cast shadows, dark as night, in splotches across the forest floor. They had flown the whole afternoon, and dusk was settling in.

"I can't believe you finally know." He ran a hand through showered-wet hair. "I didn't know how much longer I could keep it from you."

"About that..." She fake-slugged him in the gut, and he feigned slumping over, kicking up dirt from the path. They both laughed, and for a minute it felt like she was back home.

"Sorry, what could I do? I was being electrocuted every time I slipped up."

Ashton stopped in front of him, creased her brow. "You did good. I'm proud of you, Mas. I couldn't have done it myself."

"You can do anything."

She stared back. What had changed in his features? He looked taller, more defined, when he was already fit before. His skin was tanner, and the amber in his eyes had flecks of deep garnet. "You look the same, but different." She touched his cheek, expecting softness, but jumped back at the zap.

"What's wrong?"

"Your skin." She touched his face again. "Can't you feel it tingling?" She thought it was her own body shaking from emotion when she'd hugged him earlier.

He pulled away. "It's adrenaline from shifting."

Ashton shook her head. "I can't believe you turn into a hawk."

He exhaled a deep breath, then dragged her off the trail to a grassy spot under an old cedar. He slumped down to a bulging root, patting the spot next to him. She sat down crisscross.

"What's it like shapeshifting?" The word felt foreign on her tongue.

"Painful." He laughed, but there was no joy.

Ashton looked up at the lanterns hanging along the trees. They lit up the darker parts of the path. "What's happening to us?"

"What have your memories told you?"

"It's all a mix. One memory from my childhood pops up next to a new memory I've never seen before, but they're both me. One side of me is confused, the other side understands. At first, they all poured in at once, pushing my old memories to the background. Then everything shuffled. Now I can still see myself at school or at home in my room, but it's like those things happened a long time ago."

"Is there anything about me in them?

"Yes." She pushed her hair back, took a breath. "You're all over in them, old and new. It's not like I've lived two lives, but more, pieces of this other person are waking up inside. It's strange realizing I'm both— elemental and still me. I don't know how it feels for you, but aside from a few killer headaches, I feel stronger. I just don't understand how. And seriously, Mas, these weapons!" She whipped out the topaz-topped dagger, flipping it around with ease.

Mason didn't flinch.

"You didn't even blink. I'm swinging a dangerous weapon in your face."

His voice was low, serious. "Because when I transformed, it was *for* you. I have to be able to read you, so our thoughts can be joined in battle." He pulled up fistfuls of grass, lining the mounds atop his legs, avoiding eye contact.

"What's wrong?"

"Nothing. Tell me more about your new memories." He looked eager, but there was a storminess behind it.

"What's up?" She took his hand, ignoring the vibrations pelting through his palm. She knew a million things that could be upsetting to him right now, but where to start? He had never been so quiet. The Mason from home leaped off park benches, twirled her in the air, hyper with energy after a big event. Her seam keeper side knew their first flight together had to feel bigger than winning a soccer tournament. But her human side knew closed-up Mason meant he was hurt or scared.

"It's a lot to take in. I don't have memories pouring into me. Nobody knows why I was in the human world to begin with. It's never happened before. I don't get where I fit."

She squeezed his hand. "Your dad knew about demons. He thinks your mom was involved with them, right? So your mom must have been from this world. Maybe that's how you have shifter blood." Ashton's mind stretched to find answers.

"I guess. That's what Shunnar says." Mason stood up, brushed the grass off his pants. "Come on. I've got to get some sleep."

Ashton's mind ticked away with sleep being the last thing she could think of. But she let him pull her to her feet. Songs of crickets and tree frogs chorused in the background as they walked. Were they the same night noises from home? Could Mom and Dad be listening to them now?

Where was she in relation to them?

Her memories jarred again, with one part of her relieved to be back at the seam, eager to reunite with her birth family. The other side, a much larger part, longed for her uneventful life back home, with the parents she'd grown up with, and the secret of her adoption buried deep.

Chapter 17

Holding On

Ashton waited for Rory at the wooden table in the blue office tent. Her entire body was numb after hours of sparring with her team. They had all grown up together long before she transitioned into their world, and already, they were becoming kind and patient friends. But they didn't go easy on her. Every block, kick, or punch she threw was a surprise to her human side. With every blow she received, she got back up. She thought about all her disappointed PE teachers from high school. What might they think of her now?

Rory told her it would be this way; she was the destined Centennial seam keeper. She was a strong warrior chosen to protect the borders of the Dream Realm...or she would be if she remembered and believed. But there was a problem with Rory's expectations.

Her memories weren't resolving, resulting in a persistent headache instead.

"I apologize for my tardiness." Rory's red hair spilled through the tent flap. "Frankly, with all the increased demonic activity at the seam, it's a good thing training ends tomorrow. We need you."

Ashton's stomach dropped at the news, yet at the same time, her hands fisted in anticipation. "That's the problem. My keeper memories are at a constant battle with my regular memories…I mean, my human ones."

"Are you still getting headaches?"

Ashton nodded.

"I thought they would be gone by now, that your memories would settle. But every Centennial is different. Have any of your gifts emerged?"

She bit her lip, afraid to answer. She hadn't felt anything that might be considered a gift. Past Centennials had developed effortless strength, levitation, even the ability to see through walls. Ashton had dual personalities and a constant headache.

"Maybe I'm not the right girl." Her voice shook.

Rory tilted her pointed chin. "That's impossible. There are no mistakes in the Spiritual Realm."

"Then what about Mason? He was a surprise."

"Good can come from bad."

"Mason's not bad." Ashton's tone sharpened.

"Of course not. I only mean, *good* always prevails. It's just the battle between the good and the bad we need to worry about." She pulled Ashton to stand before she could say another word, then closed her eyes. A pink glow radiated off Rory's shoulders.

Ashton took a big step back.

Rory opened her eyes, closed the distance between them, and laid a hand on Ashton's arm. The rosy glow pulsated around the two of them, appearing lavender at the edges of the blue tent, then snuffed out as if it were never there.

"What was that?"

"A little something I've earned in rank. Your memories are a bit snagged. I thought it might help."

She waited for Rory to explain, but she only stood quiet, as if deep in thought.

"Well?"

"You're holding on to something."

Ashton slumped down to the long table. Of course, she held on to something. She held onto everything…her parents, Mason, her old life, this new one. When did she *not* hold every part of herself behind neat folders and bury them deep inside her mind's file cabinet? But thinking of her imaginary color-coded files only reminded her of her art studio back home, the color a comfort in who she was.

"Maybe if I could see my parents again."

Rory moved to the desk, returning with a large bundle of paper. She unfolded it atop the table, smoothing out the worn creases. It was a map.

"Seattle is there." She pointed to the northwestern part of North America. "We are here." Her finger traveled farther northwest, past the borders of everything familiar.

Ashton recognized the continents and oceans she'd learned in school. But beyond that were three more spheres, thinly drawn outside the universe, like rings from a pebble tossed in a pond.

Their names were labeled in script. The Dream Realm was the closest sphere to the locations Ashton recognized. The Spiritual Realm was the ring after that. The Heavenly Realm was the farthest away. Across the center continents were the words *Human Realm*.

Ashton touched a finger to Seattle, then to a small dark circle floating ominously in the center of the Atlantic Ocean. It was about the size of Washington State, and darkened in the center of the page. Her mom might name the paint color *Mars black*, mixed with added metallic to catch the light. It appeared to roll like thunderclouds through its center.

"That's the Dark Realm," Rory said.

Ashton half expected the blackness to bleed through to the backside of the map.

"You will see your human parents again, if that is your wish."

Ashton's head snapped in her direction.

"They remember you, though they aren't burdened with thoughts of you. It's something our healers do to manage the Centennial's family, to help in transition."

"What do you mean, not burdened?"

"They know you and love you, but they also believe you are away, safe and sound. It's for their own benefit."

Tears collected in the corners of her eyes. Of course, she wouldn't want her parents to worry. Worrying was her own self-appointed job. But now there were new memories mixing in with the old ones, all filled with new things to worry about. The nagging ache in her head altered into a full thumping. She pressed her palms against her temples.

"Maybe if these memories could stop for a while. I could rest. I feel—I feel like I'm losing myself."

Rory reached a finger, dried a tear on Ashton's cheek. "Your human side will never be taken from you. But there is also a destined warrior deep in your soul. She is every part of you and more. She is the Centennial. And we need her."

Ashton thought about the past days of training. All the workouts she'd hated as a human, she excelled in as a seam keeper. And Mason had been right about remembering her weapons. She knew how to use every one of her four blades and exactly which one to access against each distinct type of demon.

She'd learned how to use the soul-spherules, those little rosy explosives in her leather pouch, though they required an emotional link. And when it came to killing the lowly demons at the borders of the Dream Realm, her cast had told her not to worry. Seam keeper emotions shut down in battle. But did that only mean she'd remember and feel guilty later?

No, they were demons, like Mason had said. Why couldn't she keep things straight? "It's a lot of pressure." Her human side pushed back.

Rory tilted her head to catch Ashton's gaze. "Remember, you were chosen. Let your memories flow. I believe if you do, your human side will be quite impressed. Have faith. This is your destined honor."

Rory's gray eyes brightened, looking hopeful the weight she'd placed on Ashton's shoulders wasn't too heavy. Somewhere deep, her seam keeper side was eager. Tingles ran up and down her arms like the zings of adrenaline she'd felt after sparring or using her weapons against a haystack. Always that scary ruthlessness took over her other emotions when she practiced killing something.

Killing...there it was again.

Ashton's human side still shook.

Chapter 18

Discoveries

Mason walked back to his tent after his third day of training. He'd split ways with Ashton only moments before, ready for bed, and unapologetic for his new desire to sleep over going out. How quickly times had changed.

He focused on each footfall heading toward his tent, the night chill soothing against his sore body. It was a good sore. He could fight. He could fly. He threw knives as if he'd grown up with them. So how was it he ended up teamed with the Centennial and the entire Realm had no idea about it?

He was just as stuck here as he was growing up in Seattle. His dad, silent about his mom's past, had shut himself away for the last thirteen years, leaving Mason in the dark. Now, back in the world he was supposed to be from, he was still trapped in the dark.

He stopped walking, lifted his chin into the night air, and sucked in a large breath. It was Ashton's trick to calm down. Deep breaths.

Tomorrow they would find out their official post. Surely a destination far from Seattle or any kind of human future. He ran a hand through his hair. Wasn't that what he had always wanted? To get as far from his dad as possible. He rolled his eyes. Maybe this was a little too far.

Just then, quiet murmurs drifted through the moon-tipped branches, the name Mia Deed ringing through his ears, his mom's name. He bent around an old fir to listen. Two voices seeped from behind a cluster of brush.

"It belongs to Mia, all right."

He knew that voice well. Shunnar.

"Did you read the whole thing?" Rory?

"Yes. I can't believe Mason's mother is alive." Shunnar whispered more, but Mason's heart pounded loud against his chest. He held his breath and strained to hear.

"Just as we suspected. Do you think Max has seen this?"

What were they looking at? With the dark knitting blackness between tree branches and shadows, he couldn't see a thing.

Shunnar went on. "She hid it from him well."

"Let me guess." Rory gasped. "She has a secret lair?"

"Safety deposit box. She—" Shunnar paused.

Mason wasn't sure if he detected his presence, or not. He was still putting together the mental telepathy part of being a shifter. His thoughts were only open if another shifter focused on them. He'd been caught so many times in the beginning because he was being watched twenty-four seven. But now, if it worked as Mason understood it, Shunnar shouldn't be able to hear his thoughts unless he was specifically trying to. That is, if Mason was doing it right.

"How often does she go? Won't she know the journal's missing?" Rory asked.

"According to the records, she checked in every month for the last thirteen years, and then suddenly, stopped. I believe the timing coordinates with Ian's detection of Ashton. Hawk coverage increased. It must have scared her off."

Shunnar lowered his voice, so Mason leaned in more. "I can't imagine she'd leave her son to that beast, but with the hawks' protection…maybe? And if she did trust the hawks, then does she still hold faith?"

"She's been gone a long time."

"Ian can't possibly know the truth. If he did, he would have intervened sooner."

Rory's voice scaled up a notch. "Or maybe he does know. Maybe he *wants* Mason planted in our realm? Perhaps it provides his way in. I don't know how Mia has hidden herself all this time, but shouldn't we take it to the Blessing Council?" Her question fell into the night.

Shunnar's response was slow to come. "I know we *should*. What would happen to *him* though?"

Him, who? Mason wondered. Him, his dad, unprotected back home, or him, himself?

"Poor guy." Rory's whisper cut through the night to where Mason stood, hunched at an uncomfortable angle.

"Mason has no idea," Shunnar added. "He shifts without fail and fought against Ian in two attacks. His intentions are for good."

"Let's investigate more ourselves, and then, of course take it to the council." Rory's voice quivered nervously, a quality he hadn't sensed in her before. "For now, let's keep our eyes on Mason."

"Agreed. In the meantime, see if you can track Mia. She'll be safer on our side than theirs."

Suddenly, keeper voices carried from down the path, scaring Shunnar and Rory away. Mason, just as startled, lost his footing and fell over a root.

What had he just heard? His mom was still alive? Questions swam through his mind, along with all his dad's misconceptions. Everything he'd written in his books were false, yet he still knew demons existed. He blamed them for his wife's death, for causing her car accident. But there was no way he could have known about the other realms, about the hawks protecting them, or the possibility Mia could still be alive. Max had shut himself away in his office, in his grief, because he had only ever wanted to protect her. Something he could never have done. Not against something like this.

Mason couldn't breathe. He pulled himself up to all fours, digging his fingers into the dirt. Breathe. Breathe. Breathe.

As the other voices grew closer, he forced himself to stand and changed direction. Exhaustion would have to wait. He needed Ashton.

****

Three days had passed since Ashton's eighteenth birthday, and she hadn't even celebrated. The realm hadn't celebrated her being the Centennial either, but maybe it wasn't their custom.

Had she missed every rite of passage into adulthood?

With each step toward her tent, the path grew darker. It was just as well, the dark outside matched her gloomy mood. Talking to Rory hadn't made her feel any better about being the Centennial. It only dredged up more guilt about what she was hanging onto.

What was blocking her memories from finishing whatever it was they needed to finish?

Her parents? Her home? Her art?

Mason?

Maybe she wanted all those parts of herself back and was mad for not fighting more for them when she could have. She should have forgiven her parents sooner over the adoption lie. And she never even considered other art schools outside of Seattle. Why would she hide away her talents? And Mason! She should have told him how she felt about him long ago. He never cared what school he went to, as long as it was away from his dad. Maybe they could have found a compromise and gone somewhere closer. Together.

She stopped on the path, chin dropping to her chest. She should have been more honest with herself.

Moonlight gleaming through the treetops caught her eye, urging her to keep walking. But with each step, like always, she wondered if it was the same moon spilling through her kitchen skylight in Seattle. Now that Rory had shown her the map, she felt even farther away.

Arriving at her tent, she pushed open the giant swooshes of yellow fabric on her makeshift home. *Home*, never the right word in this realm. But it would do for tonight because there was a big comfy bed, and even her gloom felt tired.

She struck a match to light the candle in her lantern. Then she plopped onto the bed, brushing out her hair, mangled from training. It was already longer now, strangely growing several inches in only days. Her keeper side felt comfortable. But a little human voice in the back of her mind called, "Don't forget me." It reminded her of the green barn she'd passed with Mason that day he'd chased his crazy dream.

She, too, was still standing somewhere in her own body.

Maybe, like the barn, she just needed a little paint

and some new windows. And a new structural beam so she didn't collapse. She laughed as she slipped out of her boots and onto her bed. She was done thinking, ready for sleeping.

"Hey." Mason's voice.

He let himself in five seconds later, just as he would back home.

She jumped up eager to see him without the audience of Rory and Shunnar or the rest of the trainees. For the last two nights, they'd worked well into the evenings, hardly seeing each other before bed.

"Can we talk?" His tone, serious.

"Come here." She pulled him in for a hug. "It's good to see you. Alone."

"I've missed you," he whispered.

She gripped him closer, happy to feel something like her old self, if only for a minute.

They sat down on the bed, and he leaned back against the satin-covered headboard. The shiny fabrics in apricot and gold were contradictorily cheery against his dark mood.

She waited as he pulled off his boots and adjusted himself, quiet. Deep in thought. Not the Mason she knew. Maybe they were already too far from home.

"I've been thinking about my dad and what little information he knew about all this." He threw both arms in the air as if to include their new surroundings and life changes together.

Ashton sat up straighter, against her aching body's objections. "I don't think he knows anything about this." Neither of them had seen Max since they'd transitioned into the Spiritual Realm.

"That's just it. Everything he told me, all those books he wrote thinking he knew what was going on—

he didn't know anything." He yanked on the tassels of a decorative pillow.

What was he getting at? Was it the fact his dad wrote nonfiction books about demons? Or because Max Deed, after ignoring Mason for most of his life, had suddenly taken an interest in him and helped them hide?

She reached for his hand. "What exactly are you worried about?"

The look in his amber eyes sent a chill sizzling down her already aching spine. He enunciated each word. "I think my mom might still be alive."

"What?" Ashton's voice rang out before she could catch it in her palm. "Why would you think that? Your mom died in a car accident."

"I don't think she died." He leapt off the bed, pacing back and forth around the tiny space. Draping fabrics rustled under his quick movements. "I overheard Shunnar and Rory use my mom's name. They had her journal from a safe deposit box, somewhere she *recently* visited."

Dark memories of Mia's funeral filled Ashton's head. Then, just as her leaf charm on her bracelet zapped her wrist, her mind clicked. The sensation was like a key turning a bolt lock. Her seam keeper side recognized the tether holding back her human side, an image of a little boy losing his mom. That was when she first latched on to Mason and never let go.

"She's somehow hiding from both sides, Light and Dark. And Ash?"

"Yeah?" She shook off the chaos in her own head.

"They were worried about *me*. They're keeping their eyes on *me*! Shunnar defended me, at least, and they agreed to keep things quiet from the council. For now."

"What are they worried you'll do?" Her mind jumbled, making room for another problem to solve, another file to open. Why Mason? Hadn't he followed all the realm's instructions, even before she transitioned? Hadn't he endured their recurring dream and the lies he'd been forced to tell? What could they possibly be worried about?

"I don't know. It's freaking me out." He ran shaky fingers through tangled hair, still wet from the shower. Suddenly he froze, head tilted, eyes slanted down.

He was waiting for someone to discover his thoughts. There were no secrets in the shifter world when your mind was an open book. When he began to move again, she stood, intervening with his insane pacing. He needed her right now. It didn't matter if her seam keeper self wasn't sure how to help, her human self knew how to start. Pulling him down to the edge of the bed, she crawled up behind him, smoothing warm hands across the tense muscles flaring in his back.

"How could my mom be alive? She died, Ash. I saw the car. I went to the funeral."

"Ask Shunnar about it? You said he defended you."

"No." He flinched as she worked out the deep knots wreaking havoc. Training had been tough on them both. Mason could handle the physical; it was the mental strain he struggled with.

"She's your mom. You deserve to understand your shifter history."

"I don't know." His head fell forward as she moved her fingers up to his neck.

"Well, what has Shunnar told you so far about your shifter blood?"

"He said I must carry a gene for it but didn't go into my history. There hasn't been a lot of time for questions with Ian on the hunt for you. And when I do ask, nobody seems to know."

Guilt swept across her chest, but she forced her hands to keep moving. She was the reason he couldn't really pursue his past. He'd been too busy protecting her, getting her to this place with her free will intact.

Well, they had arrived! And she was safe now. Even though her insides were a muddled mess, she could still help Mason figure out his mom. She knew *that* Ashton. She'd done it before, all those years ago, after Mia's death. She would do it again.

"I guess we can rule out the gene coming from your dad, right?" She let her fingertips wriggle up under his shirt, working the muscles along his spine.

"Already have, but how did I end up a shifter who grew up in the human world? Shunnar said it's never happened before. Always a Centennial rider, never a hawk. But now they're telling me I've always *belonged* to you, my destined path. And if that's right, why is my mom still hiding?"

"Rory said that pairs are officially destined by their tenth year. They train together until they're eighteen. But the Centennial's *mate*—" She stopped short, the word sticky on her tongue, her hands unmoving against his skin.

Mason turned around, took both her hands in his. "Go on. What did she say?"

"She said he trains alone. When they finally meet, everything falls into place. Their memories entwine, and they know how to work together. To work with their cast. To be one." Her gaze dropped to her hands. His thumbs swirled tiny circles on her skin.

"It's weird, isn't it?"

"What do you mean?" she asked.

"Thinking about us as more than friends."

He'd said it. His impulsivity sparing them both from the awkwardness of their unspoken reality, the one everyone else seemed to already know. Ashton leaned over, burying her face in the bed cover. Mason pulled her back up as if her newly gained muscles were nothing.

"How do you feel about that?" he asked.

How did she feel? She'd felt more for him before any of this otherworldly chaos began. When he'd started dating Gianna, the color green took on a new hue in a dark part of her mind. She'd thought it was anxiety about separating for college, but maybe it was deeper than that. Maybe it was because they *were* destined.

"How do *you* feel?" She turned the question back on him. The sound of her heartbeat clanged in her ears, like the ocean crashing outside the beach house from a world too far away. She was no good at this. She loved Mason but had accepted he was always and only her friend. She'd never had the guts to take it further.

And hadn't she felt something for Ian, at least when she believed him to be an actual person? His name stabbed in her chest like a sparring blow.

Mason looked directly at her. "I always love you, Ash. This destiny thing, whatever it is, has put a huge dent in our future plans. But at least we have each other. And I think it's okay for us to define ourselves our own way."

"What do you mean?"

"I mean, maybe we don't let them decide every part of our lives. Maybe we can control our own

194

feelings without their tampering."

Her stomach tightened as she held back a gasp. He didn't want to be more than friends. And how could she be upset by that? Their friendship was the foundation of her core. Thirteen years of genuine love and companionship was a reality she could hold onto in the midst of this fairytale craziness.

And she would.

"Agreed." She shook off her hesitation to say more, pushed away her feelings just as she always did back home, and forced a smile.

He leaned back against the headboard, still squeezing her hand. "Let's figure this world out, and maybe we can figure our way back home."

"I miss home too, Mas, but Rory showed me a map. We're pretty far north."

"Well, my mom did it."

Chapter 19

Celebrations

Ashton walked along the path toward the assembly area, where she would soon attend the Culminating Ceremonies. She wasn't in a hurry. It was the first morning without Rory running her like a work horse. And she had a lot on her mind after Mason spilled the news about his mom and about maybe going home. But when her human side wondered how possible that might be, her keeper side clenched her fists. Her nerves rattled on a whole new level.

Instead she exhaled a deep breath and marveled at her surroundings. She had no idea where seam keepers stayed after training, but the forest draped around their camp with colorful tents like flowers in a giant's garden. She longed to sketch them and knew her mom would have been over the moon to paint them. It had been so long since they'd worked together on a piece.

Her mom.

She'd never missed her so much. And now…could Mia Deed really be alive?

With her hair tucked in a ponytail, the camp's constant breeze felt cool against her neck. It had offered relief during training. So far, the Spiritual Realm felt like a make-believe forest from a fairytale, always set with mild, comfortable weather. But there was something about that constant comfort tipping her anxiety. Everything felt too perfect.

"Where are my gifts?" she whispered to the wind, impatient. Rory had said they would develop in their own time. Could they break through her human hang-ups? "And if they don't..." She tilted her face to the morning sun. "Can I just go home?"

"Who are you talking to?" Mason popped up behind her, scattering her thoughts.

Ashton jumped into a fighting stance, her hand on her belt. "Oh my God!"

"Jumpy much?" he teased. He wore the shifter uniform of dark charcoal camouflage and a black T-shirt. Ashton wore the same, only khaki and white. His dark blond curls were more golden in the sun, practically touching his shoulders now.

She glared in response but continued down the path, not wanting to admit she was talking to herself. And she didn't want to share her fears. Mason had enough to worry about.

He fell in stride next to her. "Sorry. I'm on stress-overload."

Of course, this whole thing with his mom had him strained. She stopped, pulled him in for a hug. "Your heart's beating like a drum."

"I'll be okay, always am. Let's just get through this ceremony. Then—" Mason scanned their surroundings.

"Then what?"

He tucked a strand of hair behind her ear. "Then we figure out what *we* want." He put a finger up to his lips as if the forest listened.

What was he up to?

But she nodded, and they walked in silence for a while. She didn't know how to solve either one of their problems, and without her anxiety medicine, she focused on the trees as they made their way along the path. She let the colors and textures of the forest calm her nerves the way working in her art studio used to help.

"Shhh—" She stopped, a finger to her lips, the other pointing to the rustling in a tree. She held her breath when two brown wrens hopped out on a branch.

She glanced at Mason, but he was smiling at her.

"Do you think they're the same birds from home, flying between realms?"

He laughed, scaring them away, and pulled her along. "I don't know."

Ashton sighed, turning her thoughts to the day ahead. Maybe quiet mornings to think weren't in her seam keeper future. "Do you have any idea what to expect at the ceremony?"

He kicked a stone off the path. "Shunnar tells me nothing."

Of course he was grumpy. He'd accepted his mom's death years ago, but not without compromise. His fear of being alone had been an unspoken hitch in his healing. It was another reason she didn't understand his need to go away for college.

"Are you going to talk to Shunnar about your mom?"

"I have to make sure I can trust him." He looked over with a familiar smirk. "I'd like to see that journal first."

Ashton stopped dead in her tracks. She knew that look. "You're not thinking of—"

"Shhh, Ash. Seriously." He leaned in close. "Of course I am."

"Are you crazy? We can't sneak around stealing journals after training to be fighters for the good. How would that look?" But she knew him too well.

Mason rested his hands on her shoulders and shined his all-knowing smile. "We?"

"Well, I can't let you ruin everything on your own." She shook her head. He was racking up movie night points, if that was ever possible again. Plus, she owed him for all he'd done to keep her safe before they transitioned.

"Good, we agree to look for the journal then." He started down the path, and after an exasperated breath, Ashton followed.

Rounding an oversized pine, they came upon the assembly area. It was like a giant fire pit with concrete seats built in, three rows deep in a big semicircle, but with a central podium instead of a fire. Teams were arriving, sitting in their assigned pairs.

Nigel and Bronwyn would be part of their cast. Nigel had jet black hair with dark skin and eyes to match. He was taller than Mason, around six foot five. Bronwyn, his physical opposite, with crystal white hair and light blue eyes, stood maybe five foot one. They were an interesting duo because tiny Bronwyn did all the talking, while giant Nigel responded in as few words as needed but always with a kind smile.

Then there were Adam and Hannah. They were the same height and looked exactly alike. They both had brown eyes that seemed to be hiding secrets of some kind. Their skin was milky white with the lightest of freckles in all the right places. Adam had short brown hair with coppery highlights. Hannah's was the same, just longer, curling at her shoulders. They were both pretty quiet, always leaving Ashton wondering what they were collectively thinking.

"It's starting." Mason pulled her attention to the

front podium where Rory and Shunnar stood.

Before they addressed the audience, sparks of light flickered as a new group appeared and descended into the pit. They looked almost luminescent until they were solid. Five beings clad in billowing ivory frocks, three males and two females. Next to them, a smaller group dressed in violet, one male and two females. The hum of voices dispersed around them as the ceremony began.

Rory spoke first, introducing the new visitors as representatives from the Spiritual and Dream Realms. Before Ashton could question, her keeper memories stretched over her human ones, settling her wonder for the moment.

"We are thrilled to have new casts of seam keepers protecting the Dream Realm. Our hearts are full for our destined pairs who will fight for God's free will. As you know, we do our part to bind the walls of the Dream Realm, to keep out evil wills bartering for the souls of humankind. Humans are unaware of the importance they hold in this process. Nor do they understand the immeasurable *power* gifted to their souls. It is our responsibility to bind the seam, easing the demand pressing from inside. Our internal keepers have reported an increased outpouring of demonic energy. This may be how Cillian was able to identify our Centennial. Honoring our duty at the seam amplifies the efficiency of our internal keepers. This is your calling. Your destiny. Your duty."

Applause soared, and Ashton's pride swelled. Maybe this *was* her destiny, except for that sting of human doubt jabbing her ribs again. Why couldn't she keep her feelings in check?

She peeked around at the other keepers. Their

gazes were glued to the podium, while proud smiles plastered their faces. They had all been born here knowing who they were meant to be. They all had courage.

Would she ever feel that kind of confidence?

She squirmed on the bench, her head starting to ache. Her seam keeper beamed with assurance, but her human side was on a roll. After only three days of training, her new physical strength was impressive, but was it enough for her and Mason to be leaders?

They were both emotional messes! How could they be heroes?

She shifted on the bench again, her insides starting another dance of doubt. Like a skip on a music track, she played all her worries on repeat. How could she be this important? How did they think they could count on her? Maybe her gifts weren't coming. Didn't Althaia say her birth father had left her after Ashton was chosen as Centennial? He must have known from the very beginning it was wrong.

Rory had said there were never mistakes in the Spiritual Realm, but with Mason being a surprise and her memories stuck, it was all sounding like a big blunder.

Mason glanced over with raised brows, eyes wide.

She snapped out of her anxiety-ridden craze. He needed her. So she slid her hand with the charm bracelet into his.

"Thanks," he whispered, thumbing the charms. "I keep thinking about last night."

She leaned into him, knowing they couldn't talk yet. The ceremony continued.

Shunnar spoke next, introducing the shifter Mason had spoken about earlier, Gavan. He was the overseer of all casts. Ashton had never met him before, but his pale skin and familiar face intrigued her. His dark blue eyes were serious, almost frightening. His face reminded her of someone, but she couldn't place who. He had short hair, dark as coal. Wearing shifter gear and a stern expression, his presence demanded attention, something everyone gave, including Ashton.

"As you are aware, this is the year of our Centennial." Gavan's eyes found Ashton's, and she flinched. There was a brief pause before he withdrew his gaze. "It hasn't come soon enough. The humans of today are far more discouraged in their lives than their ancestors were. In previous centuries, we learned to protect each generation as it battled the time's lurking evils: survival of the elements, survival of expansion, survival of industry. Today's humans, consumed with information, have somehow erupted into the survival of themselves. We now protect this race from their own minds.

"That, my keepers, has created an entirely new level of power for demons, changing the game. The evil side is hungry, and lesser demons hunting for fuel are multiplying in vast numbers. The insight and gifts of our new Centennial, Ashton, have strengthened our ability to protect the realm more efficiently.

"We've assigned your casts, and tomorrow you will begin your work at the seam. Ashton..." His eyes looked almost sorrowful. "...and Mason will thrive in Toria, bordering the northwest, but the *sacrifice* of the Centennial links to us all. Welcome to your new posts, my warriors. Enjoy the celebrations of today, for tomorrow we embark on new journeys."

Ashton caught Gavan's break between her name and Mason's, and his strange emphasis on the word *sacrifice*.

Rory returned with a few words of inspiration, announcing them all officially as seam keepers. She elaborated that it didn't matter if two of their cast weren't raised in the Spiritual Realm. Ashton and Mason had regained their elemental selves and completed training onto level ground with their peers. "Faithful blessings be upon you all."

As if on cue, an orchestra of notes filled the air, pulling all gazes to the sky above. Brilliant lights flickered down, and Ashton blinked. She glanced at Mason, expecting his shock at this new energy filling the space, yet he was calm.

Holding her breath, she squinted her eyes and peered back to the scene above. A towering form glowed in blue, like turquoise tropical waters. Words to properly describe the sight were lost, until her new memories erupted at last, recognizing the angel Sandalphon.

Just then, she felt it. The hum of music inside her chest formed into something coherent in her mind. The rush threw her off balance, and she almost tumbled off the bench. But Mason's arm slipped in around, holding her steady. Leaning into him, she let the message wash over her mind. Eyes closed, she nodded in comprehension, physically and mentally extracting understanding from the beautiful notes pulsing through her veins.

How had she come to this place? Not two weeks ago, she'd stood on the edge of those woods outside Seattle, quietly wondering if Mason had lost his mind. Now, here she was with an entire realm believing in her destiny to protect sleeping human souls.

Her seam keeper inside cheered so proudly she

smiled.

If only her human side could stop lagging, unsure of her ability to be as important as the angel had just blessed her to be.

Chapter 20

Snooping

Guilt raced through Ashton's veins. It had only been an hour since the ceremony concluded. The angel Sandalphon had just blessed their new cast, and here she was traipsing behind Mason on his insistent journal-seeking mission. She could only imagine what the consequences might be if caught.

Mason wanted to start in Shunnar's tent, then move to Rory's if unsuccessful. There wasn't a step after that, because his stubbornness couldn't see past *not* finding it in one of those two places. Ashton glanced back at the joyful noises emanating from the center of camp, music and voices bubbling through the branches of cedars and firs. They had gone to the celebration, making sure to be visible. But when small groups broke out picnicking or playing games, Mason pulled her away feigning an innocent stroll.

In no time, they were down the path that veered off toward the trainers' camp area. Mason yanked her into a gray tent with elaborate fabrics splashed in blues and charcoals. The colors crisscrossed down, forming an entry into the living space. The darker colors mixed with shade trees from outside and created an ambiance both mysterious and private.

"You take that side, and I'll take this one." He pointed for her to go right. He didn't wait for a response, and she knew why. This was about his mom.

She set to work, wanting to find the journal and get back to the celebration before discovery. Shunnar had a small armoire on Mason's side, and a tiny three-drawered nightstand on hers. Bracing herself for snooping, she started with the top drawer, finding nothing but a couple of old books with worn titles. When she opened them, what looked like game plays filled the pages. They must be plans or drills for missions and hawk flights. The contents of the next drawer caught her eye, a woman's nightgown folded up next to other lacy items.

"A-hem!" She cleared her throat to get Mason's attention. Holding up the goods, she smiled. He chuckled back, showing her more women's clothing from the armoire he was searching.

"They're mated. I don't know why they bother with separate tents. I wonder if it's a training thing." He continued searching.

Ashton replaced the nightgown and opened the third drawer. She bit her lip, eyeing the most interesting object of all. It was a locked metal box, about the size of her English composition notebook and perfect for a small journal to fit inside. She motioned to Mason. He was over the bed in seconds pulling at the lock.

It wouldn't budge.

Mason pried it with a pen from the nightstand. Frustration flew from his lips in colorful four-letter words when she felt it. A warm tingle, permeating from the back of her head, spread until she felt her cheeks flush. Without realizing why, she shoved in next to him, covering his hands with her own. She took deep breaths to steady the beating in her chest.

"What's wrong?" His expression twisted.

"I don't know." She forced the box to the bed, pushing his hands away. "But I think I know what to do. I can feel it."

He stood back.

Ashton traced her fingers along the heavy padlock. The heat from her head flowed down her arms, traveling to the tips of her fingers. Visions of vines growing intricately around each other unraveled in her mind. She realized with every heartbeat the vines untwisted further, so she set her mind on the rhythm inside. Before long, the lock snapped open.

Mason's eyes were bug-huge, and he nodded approval before returning attention to the box. Instead of the journal, they found a wallet, cell phone, and ring of keys. She hadn't seen a cell phone since transitioning. Even with its dead battery, it seemed remarkably out of place in their current surroundings.

"Why would a shifter from the Spiritual Realm need a cell phone?" She wiped her forehead as her body's temperature returned to normal.

"He wouldn't." Mason snatched up the wallet to find ID and American cash inside. "Shaun Wright?" Mason showed her the Washington driver's license. It was Shunnar's face in the picture.

Mason's eyes darted from side to side. "How often does he go to the Human Realm?"

He rummaged through the rest of the wallet, then fixated on something from between the folds. Ashton gasped as she peeked over his shoulder. It was a photograph of his mom. Mia was standing on the far side of a green turf, behind a statue. But it wasn't just any statue, it was the bronze mustang from the courtyard outside their high school.

"That—that's our school, Mas." The statue had

been erected their first year of high school, *four* years ago. "This is how he found your mom."

Mason stood silent, a sign Ashton never liked.

"Mas, this is good news." She switched gears, tried to reason with him. She couldn't deny her fear of being caught snooping; they needed to get out of there. But the picture had him spooked. "It means she really could still be alive."

"If she's really alive, then where's she been for the last thirteen years?" His eyes glossed over.

Ashton slipped the picture back into the wallet, fumbling to put everything in the box. She clicked the lock and replaced the box in the bottom drawer. With a new sense of leadership, something she usually left for Mason, she pulled him to the tent entrance. Somewhere in those moments, Mason's competitive side took over and he snapped into gear, guiding their strategic exit.

Standing on the path outside, nerves tingling under her skin, a new sense of accomplishment rushed to her cheeks. It wasn't the time to bring it up, but she was sure she'd discovered one of her gifts. Smiling, she looked to Mason for direction. This was his mission, and he seemed in control again. Were they returning to the party, or tempting fate further and heading to Rory's tent?

Before choosing either direction, Mason suddenly lunged, pushing her back against a tree. His breath heavy in her ear, his heart pounded against her chest. His weight slid against her, and even though they were always close to each other, this new proximity sparked butterflies in her stomach.

"Don't move," he whispered urgently. Both hands gripped her waist.

Ashton's heartbeat leaped to her throat. Moving

was the least of her concerns. *Had he changed his mind after their talk last night?*

"Hey, guys." A voice rose behind them. "The festivities are at the assembly. Can you take it on down the road?" It was one of the weapon trainers, Liam.

"Oh, hey. Sorry." Mason released his grip and pulled Ashton onto the path. "We were just...taking a walk."

"I can *see*." He snickered as if in on some private joke with Mason. As an afterthought, he looked over to Ashton. "Everything okay?"

Mason squeezed her hand.

"Oh, yeah. We love this place, and we'd never been this far down the path."

"I understand, but you really aren't supposed to be here. There's better food than the grub at training, and some new games beginning. You should head back." He was grinning, and suddenly Ashton's cheeks were warming. What did Liam think he interrupted?

"No problem. Thanks, dude." The guys shook hands while Ashton's cheeks burned even hotter.

Once they were far enough away from Liam, Mason let go of her hand. "We have to get into Rory's tent." But then he stopped short, turned to her. "Hey, I'm sorry I shoved you. Are you okay?"

"Yeah, don't worry." She straightened her shirt. "But what must Liam think?"

He snorted. "What do you mean? Like we need permission to be a couple?"

Was Mason calling them a couple?

"Well, I mean...we're supposed to be these...I don't know, leaders of the cast, right?" Why was she feeling anxious? "Doesn't it look bad if we're off *alone*, doing...um, I don't know..."

Mason chuckled.

She peered under defensive brows. "What?"

"Ash, I thought you said Rory told you about the teams?"

"She did. But I thought you said you didn't want any part of being told how to feel."

His head tilted as he exhaled a breathy half laugh. "Ash, I'm just using it to our advantage. You heard what Liam said; we're not supposed to be here."

She straightened her back, reality cutting against her spine. "So you want them to see us together now, thinking we're something we're not, and then dump me later when we're back with the cast. Do you realize how that makes me look?"

"What are you talking about?"

"It's just…" She held back tears. What *was* she talking about? Why did it matter if they faked making out? Who cared what the trainers thought when they already believed the two of them would be a couple? But the more she thought about it, the more *she* cared. "I don't want to look cheap, Mas. I'm the Centennial. I'm not going to fake a relationship you don't want. We could have just said we were taking a walk." She started down the path back toward the ceremony.

"Whoa, slow down." He grabbed her elbow. "We're breaking into tents right now. I had to think fast. I'm nervous too." He looked at her with those amber eyes of his. "I'm sorry."

She held his gaze, silently erasing the feelings his feigned interlude had drawn. For that split moment, she'd thought maybe…

"Listen, we've got the whole day. Let's grab some food, and we'll try again this afternoon."

Reluctance swarmed, but she let him pull her down

the path. He'd done it again. Always deciding what she needed to do. Just like he decided the outcome of their relationship. Who cared how she might feel?

She stopped walking and pushed her hair back. Feelings darted through her torso without rhythm. If she were back home, she'd grab her anxiety pills.

"Mas." She wanted to be honest, if only she knew how she really felt. With new memories weaving under old ones, she wasn't sure anymore. If Mason wasn't feeling more for her, that was fine. But she wouldn't have a false relationship. His friendship meant more than that, and it was enough for her human side, even if it confused the seam keeper inside. Rory had never described the Centennial pair as *just friends*.

Another reason she couldn't be the Centennial Seam Keeper. She must be a fraud.

Mason took her hands. "I always love you, Ash. I didn't mean to hurt you." He pulled her into a hug. Frustration tensed each muscle, but with his chin tucked into her neck, his hands clinging fistfuls of her shirt, she melted into the comfortable curve of his arms. The same arms that had held her during Seattle thunderstorms and scary haunted houses. The arms that told her he'd always be there for her. And for the moment, she let everything pressing fall away.

While they were still embraced, a murmur of voices came toward them. They turned to find Shunnar and Rory. Quickly, Ashton and Mason straightened and started walking toward the assembly. Mason grabbed her hand again.

"You two are pretty far off from the celebrations." Rory laughed.

"We were just taking a walk. How's the party?" Ashton was now relieved by Liam's earlier interruption.

Surely, they'd have been caught in the act had they gone on to search Rory's tent.

Ashton looked at Mason as he and Shunnar locked eyes. Mason didn't flinch, but neither did Shunnar. There was a long silence.

"Enough mind-chat." Rory pulled at Shunnar, causing a break in their concentration.

"Well, we're hungry and looking to grab some food." Mason put an arm around Ashton.

"Enjoy yourselves. It will be your last day off for a while," Rory goaded over her shoulder. She and Shunnar continued toward the training tents, where not too long-ago Ashton and Mason had broken and entered.

The walk back to the arena was quiet. Too much had happened in a short amount of time. Ashton wasn't mad at Mason, just bewildered. She shoved it down because she knew Mason was frustrated too, and it wasn't only about their little spat. Finding Mia's picture had shaken him, supplying the real possibility his mom was alive. And they still hadn't found her journal.

Even more, Ashton was confident she'd discovered her first gift, if she could call unlocking a padlock with a feeling a gift. She'd been excited to share it with Mason, but that was before he used her emotions for his own gain.

Chapter 21

Summoning

The fanciest of hors d'oeuvres awaited them at the buffet table. Tiny wedges of cheese, dolloped with fruit and colorful jams, bite-size toasts and crackers, swirls of meat rolled into interesting designs, and glass goblets of steaming soup sat ready to be devoured by new friends and teammates.

Mason had to admit he was hungry, and since Ashton was barely speaking to him, he dove into his plate. The smells were intoxicating and each interesting bite delicious, until thoughts of his mom popped every food bubble. She was alive.

Why had she left him alone all these years?

"Massy, did you try this delicious soup?" Ashton's words came out slurred, her body falling sloppily against his shoulder.

Massy? He eyed her closer. "You okay?"

She looked up after slurping down the last drop. Her eyes were only hints of glossy blue, blotted by dilated pupils. With flushed cheeks, she looked almost…high.

He slid her chair back. "Let's get you out of here."

She was dead weight, giggling. "Wait, I want more soup. Did you try the soup?"

"Okay, let's go." He glanced around for help, but the trainers had cleared out. Other keepers were middrink or halfway through a game, looking more relaxed than he'd felt in a long time. He didn't want to raise any more suspicion, already caught out of bounds twice on the same day. So he heaved her up like a scarecrow. If things downshifted too quickly, he would call for help.

It took all his strength to walk Ashton out of there unnoticed. As she leaned and swayed, drunk-like, he pretended alongside her, laughing until they were out of sight. Then he beelined straight to her tent. Once there, he sat her down on the bed and glanced around for water.

"I want to go back to the party." She rubbed her hair out of her face. In the struggle getting her there, it had fallen out of her ponytail in wispy clumps.

"Did something happen?" Her forehead felt warm, but not burning up. The pink from her cheeks had spread to the backs of her hands, enhanced from the yellow tint of her tent.

"Why such a *party-pooper*? I thought you knew how to have fun." She poked him in the chest.

"I think you're sick." He thought back to the food she'd eaten. It was everything he had, save for the soup. If she stayed put, he could go back and talk with the chef, but she wasn't cooperating.

"Mas, I—I need to get out of here!" She crawled across the bed to get up. Mason grabbed her leg as gently as he could when she peered back, pleading. "I need air. Help me."

Panic swept across his chest. There's no way she had an inhaler here. He locked his gaze on hers, letting her know he was going with her. "Okay, let's take a walk, maybe check in with sickbay."

She stared in response, head cocked to the side,

unnaturally. Something was wrong. As soon as he led her outside the tent, she bent over, hands on her knees, inhaling deeply.

"Ash, can you walk with me?" He pulled her close, taking on her weight.

"Okay." Her giddiness was gone, her voice frail and breathless. She leaned on Mason for support as he walked her down the dirt path to sickbay. The tent was to the left of the training arena and closer to the party. He peered around for someone to help. He couldn't lose her…not now.

"Connor!" Mason yelled.

Connor was carrying a box from the office tent. He glanced up, then parked his box on a rock, and ran to them. "What happened?" He lifted Ashton's other side, continuing in the direction of sickbay.

"I'm fine. I mean, I do feel a little dizzy…" She passed out cold.

"What happened?" Connor's expression flashed concern, which translated to Mason that something like this was uncommon, and maybe worse than he thought.

"Food poisoning? It happened after she ate the soup. She was acting strange, and I took her back to rest, but then she couldn't breathe."

"Sickbay it is." Connor picked up his speed, and they arrived within seconds, greeted by a healer, Leeza. She'd iced Mason's shoulder on the second day of combat drills.

"I thought training concluded yesterday?" Her eyebrows rose in question, but her arms motioned them over to a ready cot.

"She was fine until she ate the soup, then she started acting strange."

"Strange how?" Leeza checked her pulse.

Mason glanced at Connor, then back to the healer. "Well, drunk. Slurring and behaving silly."

Leeza looked directly to Connor. "Send me Jasper. He was in charge of food today." Connor nodded and flew from the tent. Mason moved to the side of the cot, taking Ashton's hand. He didn't interrupt anything Leeza was doing as she ran her tests, and she didn't ask more questions. She continued working with a purpose, and to Mason that meant she must be working her magic.

Connor returned with Jasper, the camp chef. Shunnar and Rory filed in behind.

Shunnar pulled Mason outside to review what had happened. He didn't want to leave, but Shunnar wasn't asking. Rory and Jasper huddled around Ashton, while Connor stood at the door.

Mason listed the events from the time they had seen him and Rory on the path. Shunnar was deep in thought as Mason spoke, unrolling a finger for each next part. When Mason finished, Shunnar backed into the tent without a word. Mason followed, but Connor blocked his way.

"Let's go for a walk." Connor grabbed his shoulder.

"No." He pulled back. "I need to know she's okay."

"Shunnar wants us out. Sorry. Orders." He pulled him away with more momentum.

Mason looked back, his muscles tightening, hands fisted. Panic spun like a web across his chest, something Ashton always described with her anxiety. He needed back in there. But when the blistering jabs of pain threatened his spine, he knew he had to obey Shunnar's orders. For now. Reluctantly his body moved with Connor, but his mind raced to Ashton.

What had he done? Their last conversation was arguing over defining their future relationship. Gripping handfuls of his hair, he realized she'd never really answered his question about being paired together. He kicked at the ground, with lack of anything else to hit.

"You need to calm down." Connor slowed his pace, turning to face him. "This won't help her."

"I need her to be okay." The last time he'd seen her passed out was with Ian, in the back of her car. The only time before that was when she'd fallen from a tree he was teaching her to climb. They had only been kids, but when he saw her on the ground…his seven-year-old heart sank. When she was finally okay, he was forever in love with his best friend. He hardly left her side. Now he thought of their new future *together* and knew wholeheartedly he needed her in it. Of course, he wanted to be paired with her.

Why couldn't she understand that wasn't the point?

****

Ashton gazed dreamily down at her own sleeping body, her features blanketed by the healer's gray hair. The woman fussed over her while Mason held her hand.

Was she dead?

She touched her hands together. Warm skin told her she was still solid, just lighter, and floating farther away from her body.

Without warning, she maneuvered through the top of the tent, every cell separating and streaming through the fibrous holes without friction. She was flying through cobwebbed skies, her tummy unusually calm, until the familiar doorway of the beach house stood clearly in view.

In a flash, she was back on the Oregon coast. She

wiggled her toes, lifted her foot, opened her hands. She was real, though her thoughts were as muddled as the overcast day.

When she took a step from the front door of the beach house, a dim light bounced from beyond the fence. It flickered in front of her feet, jumping toward the path, to the shore and back again. She started to call for Mason and Max, then closed her mouth. Innately she knew she was alone. In the quietude of the gray day, she followed the soft glow.

The bouncing light traveled in rhythm with the tide the closer she got to shore, growing in brightness and size until it burst before her. Ian. He stood on the beach as real as she almost felt she was. His face readable, his smile aimed right at her heart.

"Ashton Nichols."

"Ian." Did he have a last name? At once goosebumps pricked her internal alarm. She knew who she was now—a seam keeper, strong and powerful. And she knew exactly who he was.

She marched toward him, unafraid, confidence in every step through mounds of sand, until she lost her balance. It was slight, and she caught herself, but Ian was there instantly, reaching out to steady her. His touch tingled in her shoulders. The warm sensation macerated her insides, and suddenly, she forgot what she was going to say.

"Ian?"

"I've missed you." He pulled her to their spot on the logs. A fire roared up in the pit.

"I, um…" Fog. All she could see was the blue gray of fog. It swirled inside her mind just as it hovered atop the shore. Hadn't she felt a heightened sense of danger? She shook her head to remember, but his face brightened as if he'd been waiting for this very moment.

He smiled, teeth gleaming like the ocean spray behind. Though something was different. She leaned toward his face, his blue eyes holding her in place. Blue. Had they always been blue? Suddenly, it didn't matter as long as he was smiling at her.

He leaned in to kiss her. Their lips almost touched when he paused, his nearness stirring. "May I kiss you?"

"Yes," she said, ignoring the twinge in her heart. A fleeting thought of Mason flashed through her mind, but Ian's eyes were longing. She wanted him to kiss her. And he did. Softly at first, barely making contact until he pulled her closer, his warmth smoothed away any hints of danger he may have initially sparked.

Ian's hands brushed slowly up her back to her shoulders. In turn, she slid her arms around his middle, gripping tightly, kissing him back. Everything felt...

"Wait a minute." She pulled away when he tucked a piece of her hair behind her ear...the way Mason always did. A twinge poked at her side. Something was wrong. But when Ian looked into her eyes again, her uncertainty vanished into the foggy mist outside. His lips were tempting. His fingers trailed over her arms, up to her shoulders. Then, tenderly he held her face in his hands.

"Come with me," he whispered. "Together we can create masterpieces."

Behind her eyelids, art appeared, as if she stood in a gallery. She recognized Ian's green and gold painting, the one where he'd first kissed her. When she looked further, her own pieces from home drifted into view. Her pen and ink drawings of feathers falling from a setting sun, a fawn sipping water from the eye of an earthly being, waves crashing in wheat fields...but then a watercolor of peonies grew larger than the rest. She'd sketched it as a gift for her mom to paint. Mason had helped them hang it in their kitchen nook.

Ashton blinked. She could see Mason's face in her mind. What was he saying? Oh yes, he was explaining they had no choice, that they needed to define themselves their own way. She didn't want to be his consolation prize. Maybe she *could* make a choice in the matter. What about these hands holding her now?

Ian leaned in to kiss her again.

Mason didn't want her. How could they be destined together when he had never made a single move? Ever. She kissed Ian back, fueled with anger and frustration. It was about time she made her own decisions. Wasn't that what Mason had said in the jeep, that day they followed his dream? *Time for you to be the leader of your own life.*

Ian's kisses trailed along her jawline as her heart swooned. She wasn't worried. She wasn't afraid. It was passion. She couldn't remember feeling anything close to this emotion before. And then...

There was Mason's face again, pulling her thoughts away, nagging for friend-interference to ward off the girls he didn't want. That's what he needed her for? How were they supposed to be a lifelong team, paired forever, when he had never once kissed her?

Ian planted soft kisses down her neck, her stomach flip-flopping in sync with every touch. Mason had never made her feel this way. But then, she'd only recently thought about him romantically. Their friendship had always been...comfortable, reliable. He'd never awakened feelings like this.

Or had he?

"Ashton." Ian pulled back. "I will tell you the truth of your potential. You are bound for bigger things, and you deserve all of it." His fingers brushed her hair behind her shoulders. He looked so desperate. "I will *always* adore you. Come with me, choose me."

Always? Something snapped. A flush of cool running water filled her veins. The icy chill traveled from her right wrist, up to her shoulders, and down her left arm. She glanced to her bracelet, the leaf charm glowing in the marine-layered light. When the coolness reached the bottom of her feet, she stepped away.

Her mind flashed to Mason again.

Five years ago, he stood in her room wearing his karate *gi*, his face beaming; he had just earned his black belt. He could have gone out with the guys to celebrate, but he had burst into her room, throwing her onto her bed in one of his prized flips. He'd tickled the joy right out of her, and she'd laughed and laughed. His hands felt right on her body, as he gazed down with amber eyes. He glowed with pride and just a hint of regret. Sorrow his mom would never know the gains he'd made. Anger his dad would never ask about it. *Love* that he had her to share it with. He planted a fat, juicy kiss on her cheek before lifting her up with both hands and smiling enough for the both of them. Her heart pulled toward Mason as the vision faded, and she found her hands against Ian's chest, holding him back.

She needed to think. She needed to breathe.

"Ask me to take you away and I will. I will make your destiny perfect. I love you."

He loved her? Did he even know her? His words felt foreign until she translated them to a native truth; Mason *always* loved her. He showed her every day.

221

Moments flashed behind her eyes.

The day Mason had leaned over her injured face after falling from the too-tall tree he'd begged her to climb. "I always love you, Ashy. Please be okay."

The day he picked up her up off the floor because she'd discovered her parents weren't her biological parents. "*I* will always love you, Ash."

Just a week ago, at this very beach house, he suffered internal shocks of pain *for* her. He'd done everything *because* he loved her. She'd felt it her whole life.

Just like that, she remembered who Ian was. The son of Hell. What was she doing?

"No!" She pulled away from Ian's grasp, and in slow motion, his face turned from desire to confusion to anger. He shook his head, wanting to communicate something, but his blue eyes burned black to the very back of her mind.

She faded away like a memory…until her body drifted somewhere white and overcast, high above the shoreline. Flames from the fire pit crawled up, misty and gray, suspending around her. She squeezed her eyes shut against the smoke, coldly aware of the distance away from Ian's warm touch. She didn't want it anymore. Her body shivered, ready to go home. She pursed her lips and blew the swirls of gray away, like dancing snowflakes under the moon.

"Mason?" she called into the dimming light.

"I think she's coming around."

Rory's voice echoed as Ashton's soul settled into her body, still resting on the cot at training camp. Her tethered spirit latched on and anchored back where it belonged.

"Get Mason," Rory commanded.

Movement scuffled around her bed. She tried opening her eyes, but the pull was hard, as if her body might lift into the clouds, back to the beach house, back to Ian. Her body tingled under the weight of resting hands gripping her arms and legs, grounding her from flight.

There was a struggle of pressure holding her body in place, and then a familiar voice breathed softly in her ear. Mason. His scent familiar, his words pleading for her to come back to him. She opened her eyes.

"Mason." His cinnamon gaze sprinkled comfort. "You did it."

"*I* did it?" He raised a brow, then smiled with relief. "How are you?"

"I'm cold." Her teeth chattered. Her gaze spilled around the room finding Rory, Connor, Shunnar, one of the healers, and even a chef staring back at her.

The healer tucked a blanket under her chin. "Ashton, you were poisoned. I've given you fluids to flush the toxins, and a remedy to wake you. How do you feel?"

"I thought I was dreaming."

"It was the soup. You passed out. Do you remember?" Mason pressed.

Ashton thought back. She remembered soaring above herself in the pale thin air, everything peaceful. She remembered the beach house and Ian waiting, arms open for her on the shore. He had kissed her, and she'd kissed him back…until Mason tugged in her heart. The flashbacks of him brought her back. Reminders of who he was, and who they were together.

She exhaled a breath, clarification that it didn't matter whether Mason loved her romantically. The Spiritual Realm and their ways had complicated things.

He loved her, completely, in every other way. This was the truth flooding her memories now.

And it was all she needed.

"What is it?" Mason's face was serious, distant from the adventurous tree-climbing boy she knew him to be.

Rory whispered, a hand on her shoulder, "You can tell us."

The whole group seemed to close in, as if she might reveal a secret. Ashton's cheeks warmed, shame filling her veins. It wasn't a secret; it was a seducing.

"It was Ian. He lured me away through my dream. At least, I think it was a dream."

"What do you mean? You dreamed about Ian?" Mason's tone short.

Silence filled the already tight space. Rory and Shunnar whispered something to each other before Rory addressed her. "Ashton, Ian is a high demon prince, masterful at his game. There is no shame in his trickery. What matters? You are here with us now. You won the battle."

Ashton looked into her pale eyes. She had been weak with Ian, like a schoolgirl with a crush. But Rory praised her bravery? She didn't understand.

Rory glanced at Shunnar. "I told you she was a powerful one."

"Wait, what happened?" Mason demanded.

Rory gave another knowing look to Ashton before explaining to the group. "Ashton wasn't poisoned; she was summoned by Ian. The soup was a coincidence, his enchantment needing warmth to trigger. Then, he slipped in through her open heart." Her eyes fell to Ashton. "He can be very charming, and he'd appealed to you as an interested suitor in the Human Realm, am I right?"

Ashton only nodded, afraid to look at Mason.

Rory continued, "His behavior confirms our assumptions as to the magnitude of Ashton's gifts. He wants her, even after her transformation."

"But I don't have any gifts." She forced back tears. Opening locks wasn't anything amazing.

Rory touched her forehead. "He doesn't know that." Then she glanced at Shunnar. "How did he get this close to our realm?"

"Ian is Cillian, the lowest of high demon royalty, compared to his father and brothers, as you know. Our sources show he's gained quite the small army of lesser demons here in the Northwest. But it's all under the radar of his siblings, from what we can tell. He must be doing his own bidding. I will put more shifters on it." Shunnar turned to Connor, and after a silent exchange, Connor flew from the room.

The healer added, "It would be best to handle this situation discreetly, one demon prince at a time."

Ashton got the impression the healer spoke from experience. They would need to handle Ian without bringing attention to Hell.

The room was quiet until Mason pressed on. "Ashton, how did you get away?"

She wasn't sure how to explain.

"When you first woke up, you said *I* did it. What did you mean?" His right eyebrow twitched.

Rory stepped in again. "Although he never fights fairly, Ian can only take those who choose him with free will. You are strong, Ashton. You must have refused him, breaking the enchantment. Do you remember the memories that pulled you back?"

Ashton stood on the confidence Rory had begun

building. "Well, it was the charm on my bracelet at first. It blasted a cool rush through my body, helped me focus." She blinked at Mason. "Then it was you. I remembered times in our lives when you cared for me or showed me love." She must have spoken the words he needed to hear, because finally she felt him relax.

"You see, Ash? I will *always* love you." He leaned his head against hers.

Ashton's tears breached. How close had she come to losing him? To losing everything. She had all she needed in Mason, and it didn't matter anymore how it was defined. Their relationship was their own.

"You're safe now." Rory smiled.

But was she?

If Ian was crossing impossible borders to get to her, even after her transition into the Spiritual Realm...how safe was she? How safe were the people around her? Or the sleeping human souls lost and unknowing in the Human Realm? She gripped the edges of the cot with both hands, her legs heavy now, like wet cement.

Would she have the strength to fight him off again? Especially without her seam keeper gifts?

Chapter 22

First Kill

Ashton's hands trembled as she sailed through the air on the back of her hawk. Seam keeper memories told her she was a confident warrior, yet her human side still wanted to hide under a wing.

Your shaking is throwing me off. Mason's voice seeped through her cloud of dread. It wasn't the fear of flying, it was the purpose of the flight.

We probably won't see any action. It's our first day.

"All the more reason we will see action," she said. "Sneak past the newbies." They'd only just arrived at their official post, and already they were on guard duty for the Dream Realm.

Mentally, please. We don't need to announce our presence.

Ashton closed her eyes. Pressure from her new memories had slowed to a constant trickle, a thin waterfall, barely there, yet running endlessly along a ravine. Her head ached less, though the residual pain was still there. Rory explained it was because her seam keeper memories would have been hers had she grown up in the Spiritual Realm. The more her human side understood her destiny, the more comfortable she would feel all over. Right now, though, on their first official mission, she wasn't so sure.

I'm scared Ian will try something again.

His feathers fluttered around her. *Shunnar says it's impossible. He can't physically cross the borders. And you're wide awake in the action, so no chance of another summoning.*

Hadn't she been awake the last time, too? She sank into the warm down beneath his contour quills, and a shiver ran up his spine. Was he scared too? She shook her head. He wouldn't admit to a lack of confidence.

You're right, we can do this, she sent, hoping he hadn't picked up on her reluctance. She didn't want to pile on the pressure. He didn't have memories telling him he belonged.

What kind of destiny was that? Why would only half of their anticipated pairing be known? With their whole world expanding overnight, shouldn't clarity now trump all reservations? She closed her eyes as the answers became clear. It didn't matter what realm they were in. The problems from their human lives had followed them. He was still stuck. She was still worried.

Ash, not now. After we figure out my mom, we can plan out the rest of our lives. But first, we are seriously demon hunting here.

Ashton's seam keeper side agreed; it was time to focus. She closed her human mouth.

The next hour along the seam was uneventful. The river splashed below with magnificent colors. Mason's body relaxed, his wings barely stroking the wind. They soared back and forth along the river, drifting to the Dream Realm side of glimmering lights, hiding any surface in which to land, then glided back to the tree line, thick with velvety foliage. She wondered about the Dream Realm, longed to see what it looked like on the ground, if there were such a thing. But there had to be somewhere. She'd met three of its representatives on the Blessing Council.

Focus.

Such a strange word to hear from Mason. Typically, she was the one slipping her wrist into his hands, so he could fidget with her bracelet. Or she'd run her fingers along the muscles in his neck. He was the one with the attention deficit.

She sat up straighter, trying to sense their environment the way Rory had taught. Looking. Listening. Lowly demons could be invisible until they were not.

Mason flew toward the forest side. The river rushed wildly below, crashing along. When they flew low enough, the melodies from the trees created a constant beat. Insects hummed, scavenging for food. Chipmunks chittered, preparing nests, she imagined, for their young. Sometimes the sounds would pause, as if a universal signal of danger. Then a chorus of smaller birds chirped an "all safe" response, and the melody would pick up again.

Ashton lifted her head, allowed the breeze to fall through her hair, to whip against her cheeks. Her shoulders arched with a new sixth sense. A sense Ashton had never felt before. It pushed to the surface, wanting release. And like the warrior her new memories told her she was, she soared with newfound confidence.

Time passed, though she never lost her level of alertness again. Just at the end of their run, the rolling waves of branches crested, and she glimpsed it. She wasn't sure what *it* was, but her head snapped to attention.

Mason must've seen it too, because his wings quivered.

Get ready! She scanned the land below. He circled back around, and their cast spread into a new formation. *There!* She saw it again, like a blurry spot on a photograph, or a glitch in a computer game. Raking her vision across the tree line, she caught sight of its form move only a few yards from the edge of the seam.

Got it! Mason spun faster than a carnival ride, ducking them back, around, and down. Straight down!

Ashton gripped her legs tighter than could feel good to Mason, but she was in fight mode. Her hands twitched to grasp a weapon as her mind assessed the situation, calculating the exact formula needed to succeed.

Mason's mind joined with hers, their thoughts becoming one. *Execution time.*

She wasn't surprised when he dipped even lower, maneuvering around bristly branches, down to the foliage-littered ground. He wasn't landing, rather shadowing the strange movement on its course. The creature had no form. It was like chasing something invisible, when suddenly Ashton could see it again.

A colorless blur one moment formed into a slithery, snake-like eel the next. Gliding low across the ground, it looked about a yard long, and fast. If it had any color at all, it would be the lightest of gray, like fog rolling in. Its dull wrinkled skin reeked of sulfur.

A cerulean hue shone in Ashton's mind, and without looking down to her belt, she snatched at the sapphire-handled dagger. Its engraved designs glowed with the same power piercing from behind her eyes. She felt its song in her mind, blessing her abilities. A tear fell from her cheek, and she wiped it with the back of her daggered hand. It wasn't a tear of sorrow but of gratitude for her training. Her keeper memories filled in what her human mind couldn't imagine. Her emotions shut down, leaving behind only the cognizance of the outcome.

The other warriors in their army of six had prevented the demon's choice of escape. It was surrounded. Ashton thrust her arm away from her body, palm down, dagger out, and swung at the demon as if she'd slain dragons her whole life. It snarled an outrageous clang of racket.

Like an alarm sounding, four other eel-looking monsters appeared from behind. They joined in the first demon's cry. The cacophony of noise sliced like a knife, thwarting Ashton's follow-through. Wincing, she kicked her heels into Mason's side. She'd only nicked it.

The teams split up synchronously, though Mason stayed the course.

The noise. It threw me. Go again! A side of herself, one she never knew existed, craved its blood. Mason veered onward, clawing its slimy tail.

Ugh! Suddenly, the world grew black as night. Ashton squinted to see through a strange inky mist the monster had strewn from its tail. And the smell…rotting garbage! Mason slowed. The vapor was hot, clinging to them, weighing them down. He dipped lower to the ground as her boots kicked up leaves and dirt from below. Was the substance forcing them down?

No, Mason had lowered them *under* the haze. She ducked her head, gazing up at the black gas floating away. New ink spots dotted the sky as their teammates battled the other demons.

Mason picked up his speed, flying up and over the

231

scene, but Bronwyn and Nigel were already closing in behind the creature. Just then, an agonizing sound exploded in Ashton's ears. Bronwyn had wounded the demon further. Ashton's dagger grew warm in her palm, and she kicked her heels into Mason's sides, willing him into action. It was unneeded; he was already descending.

She had never been this excited. Never had she come close to a feeling so riveting it threatened to be the death of her. And she wanted more.

The demon had slowed, compromised by its wounds, but let out more of its inky black haze. Mason stayed with it, soaring just outside the gas, then approached on the opposite side. The demon turned its head toward them…with no visible eyes. Ashton shuddered.

Just then, Mason screamed his battle-hawk cry, syncing his plan into focus. She injected her blade without a blink. Her hand sank deep into its flesh. The cold slippery texture, a shock upon contact, but not enough to slow her down. Her glove, saturated through to the skin, boiled so cold it burned, yet her sixth sense refused to give into the pain. When she plucked her arm back in a twist, the demon exploded in a gas of black fumes.

Success.

The thing was dead—or at least gone for a hundred years. Her heart pounded in the aftermath. Black oozing liquid dripped from her dagger. But the sapphire glow from her weapon forced through the ichor and wound up her arm, leaving a cooling effect in its wake.

Mason cried out in triumph, and their cast responded in cheers. They too had banished the other creatures.

Ashton's body tingled, elated with pride, and finally, she accepted a small part of her destiny in play. The others may have grown up aware of their callings, but she would never forget this feeling. She didn't believe any of them would. It proved their cast had what it would take to fight together.

As the sun melted into the horizon behind them, Ashton held her head high, soaring home on a new wind of hope.

****

Ashton bounced from heel to heel, waiting for Mason to shift back. Their first mission was a success and she wanted to celebrate, uncaring how much Mason might tease her for all the times she had complained about going out. All those parties he'd dragged her to in high school...but who knew her prerequisite for fun was demon hunting?

What was taking him so long? If she glared at the arena gates any more her eyes would dry up. Instead, she turned toward their new town, Toria, sitting over the hillside. They'd just moved in, and already her seam keeper side felt at home. Her human side, shadowed since the hunt, tried to imagine her parents happy and not missing her, as Rory had promised. But she liked Toria too.

The town looked more like it belonged in Munchkin Land. She especially loved the charm of colorful hut-like cottages. Only in the Spiritual Realm would buildings the colors of peacock blue or tangerine look natural in their wooded setting. With matching roofs of moss and tree bark, they sat perfectly, dotting cobblestone streets.

The shops on Main Street looked more touristy, reminding her of Leavenworth. They sold everything from herbs to arrow heads. All seam keepers' needs could be found at one of the venders. Currency was the trickiest thing to wrap her mind around. It was unneeded. All wares were a gift in exchange for their service at the seam.

"Are you joining us at the café?" Hannah's voice drifted through her thoughts. Ashton flung herself around, realizing her energy level was still racing, and bumped into Adam. Of course, they were side by side. They were always together. Always quiet. And so far, always kind.

"I'm so sorry—" Ashton stepped back.

Adam smiled. "It's okay. It's been quite a day."

"It has. And yes, I'm waiting for Mason." She looked back to the arena gates, waiting for him to burst through.

"We'll save you both seats." Hannah linked an arm around her shoulder in a half hug. Ashton's heart burst even more. It hadn't even been a week, and Hannah hugged her as if they'd known each other longer. Making friends was new for her, but she liked it.

"Thank you," Ashton said, as they disappeared down the hill, into town. Shadows began their twilight blend into each other, stitching the dark around the stores below.

She'd already learned the layout of the town, with quaint cafés offering baskets of unnamed pastries, alongside the most delicious concoction of coffee and tea. She had no other description for it. Rich espresso steamed like a latte but always leaving an herbal flavor on her tongue like lavender or basil. Keepers called it café-awake, served hot or cold, but either way, divine.

Along the hill beyond Main Street, lined in neat rows, were the buildings that housed active keepers.

Riders roomed with riders and shifters roomed with shifters in what looked like boardinghouses, called flats. Paired couples lived in separate houses more like townhomes. There was a bonding ceremony where mates pledged eternity to each other, like marriage. Until they mated officially, they lived apart. But everything in Toria was close by.

Ashton roomed with Bronwyn and Hannah, while Mason shared his flat with Nigel and Adam. The rest of their cast lived down the hall. It was all very much like a dorm might be, not that Ashton knew. College felt more than a lifetime away. And at the moment, after slaying a demon, she didn't mind.

"Hey, there."

Ashton blinked as Bronwyn made her way over. Her moonlit hair picked up the last slivers of light from the day.

"Waiting for Mason?"

"Yeah, he doesn't like shifting in front of me—oh! Please don't tell him I told you that."

"I get it. He didn't grow up shifting. It'll be easy for him soon enough. But cross my heart, I won't tell." She smiled, exuding the positive attitude Ashton was already beginning to expect from her.

"Thanks. Where's Nigel?"

"I'm meeting him at the café. I was helping Rory in the armory." Her smile, intoxicating. Ashton wondered if she ever had a bad day.

"Of course. I'll see you there soon." Ashton hugged her good-bye, comforted by her touch. Her list of friends was growing.

The sun set low, painting the sky with a final streak of apricot, making Ashton hungry. She closed her eyes, fighting the urge to go back to the arena and drag

Mason out. But when she opened her eyes, he was only a few steps away, wearing his familiar cocky smile. He had a bounce in his step, likely hyped up with the energy of their first kill. Maybe this distraction wiped away some of the stress about his mom or the fact he was still being watched. Either way, they were celebrating!

"Hey, partner." She greeted him, and he kissed her with a smack on the cheek.

"Time to celebrate," he sang, and threw an arm around her shoulders, steering her in the direction of Main Street.

He wouldn't have to drag her anywhere tonight.

"Did we really kill a demon today?" They hadn't really killed it. She'd learned they could only send them away for about a hundred years. But that was enough for her.

"Yeah." He ripped up his shirt revealing a bruised stomach, blossoming in hues of indigo and violet. "You sure know how to grip."

She reached out to gently touch him. "I'm so sorry."

But he dropped his shirt as if it wasn't anything big and moved down the path. "Seriously it's fine. My body will heal by tonight. Anyway, that beast will be dead for our lifetime." He laughed.

Ashton beamed, happy about their successful battle. But more, it felt good to see Mason laugh again, the crinkle gone from his forehead. There was an energy surging under his skin she hadn't seen in him since…since home.

A whisper from inside reminded her she *was* home. But even feeling elated after their first demon kill, she hadn't fully decided yet where home was. She imagined a tumbleweed rolling in the wind. The freedom might feel good, but sometimes choice in destination matters more.

They arrived at the café in no time. Toria was small, no need for cars. Since it hardly rained, traveling anywhere by foot was the easiest mode of transportation. When they turned the corner to the café, their full cast stood waiting.

Shouts of "Dude!" and high fives exchanged from one shifter to the next, while the riders hugged their hellos. Even Hannah and Adam were smiling, their typically serious faces rosy.

"Nice kill." Clara, keeper from the third line, put her fist out to Ashton, and she bumped it, feeling giddy again. This was a first demon slaying for the whole cast. Everyone was smiling. Clara's pixie cut flickered gold in the glow of street lanterns, matching her brown sun-kissed skin. Ashton had toughened up in a short time, but she hoped sculpted muscles like Clara's might define her own arms one day.

"Thanks, it feels good. Surprisingly." Ashton shook her head, her human side still trailing just behind.

Clara leaned into her mate, Ren, who grabbed her around the waist. They were always joking around, and if one of them wasn't laughing, something was probably wrong. Ren was built even sturdier than Clara and wore his long black hair pulled back. They fit together like the perfect puzzle, and in a battle, she wanted them at her back.

"Let's eat." Ren spun Clara in release, clasped her hand, and started toward the buffet.

Ashton followed, filling her plate with bite-sized meats, veggies, and fruits topped with unusual, flavorful sauces. Everything was served tapas style.

With so many scrumptious choices, she could see why.

Soon the whole gang sat around a long wooden table. Mason and Ashton on one end, side by side, and Bronwyn and Nigel across. Hannah and Adam sat next to them, always connected at the hip, and the other pairs sat down the rest of the table length, Lily and Seth across from Helen and Abram. Clara and Ren at the opposite end. There was a hum of voices carrying across the large space, with other casts enjoying their meals, while craft elementals (or craft els, as Ashton had learned) bustled around delivering trays of delicacies.

Ashton had asked about the workers behind the scenes, the ones who prepared the food and ran the shops. Bronwyn explained they were artists of their crafts, just as seam keepers were warriors of their trade. Chefs prepared foods with unusual flavors and sculpted them into beautiful plates of art. Shopkeepers took pride in their hardware, displaying their works and designs as if in a gallery. Every elemental's position was honorable in the Spiritual Realm.

Near the end of the meal, a craft el flowed from table to table serving wine for dessert. He looked older than anyone she'd seen in Toria, but his eyes danced with youthfulness as he gleefully filled glass after glass. It was a vibrant mulberry color and tasted velvety on Ashton's tongue. The warm liquid offered a sweet closure to their savory meal. She was tired now, the adrenaline from the mission settling, and she leaned over onto Mason's shoulder. He was talking to Nigel, in a voice softer than usual.

"So how often do keepers go into the Human Realm?" Mason asked nonchalantly, but Ashton knew he was seeking information about his past. She was hoping he might have enjoyed the whole night before stressing about his mom again.

"They don't," Nigel said.

"What about Shunnar and his hawks?"

"Not that I know of, I mean, not until the Centennial." He smiled at Ashton and then back to Mason. "Not until going in to train you."

Mason shook his head, contemplating. Ashton knew he was wondering about Shunnar's wallet with fake ID, car keys, and the cell phone they'd found in his tent.

"Yeah, the realm was all abuzz with the discovery of a hawk in the Human Realm." Bronwyn chimed into the conversation, still smiling.

"Why do you think that is?" Ashton tried to sound as nonchalant as Mason.

Hannah leaned in, tucking a coppery wave behind her ear. "It's never happened before."

"Word is Gavan found out and took personal interest in you. He sent Shunnar in early. We don't know why." Adam swirled the wine in the bottom of his glass.

"I thought it was because Ian discovered me before my birthday," Ashton said.

"That's the part that doesn't make sense." Adam narrowed his eyes. "Ian found you, but he shouldn't have. The Centennials are heavily protected, even from themselves. And the assigned hawks allowed entrance to the Human Realm can do their job of protecting. The whole bit about you hiding out in the beach house—it would have been unneeded had Gavan not intervened." He swallowed his last sip of wine, not realizing the weight of what he'd said.

Ashton thought about the recurring dream Mason

had endured for two weeks before he was drawn into the woods. He'd told her it was because Ian had detected her early, and her human side needed protecting. So they trained him ahead of schedule. But she hadn't met Ian until the day after they visited the woods. A chill ran up her spine. Had Ian been creepily watching her before they officially met?

Mason let out a breathy half laugh and downed the rest of his wine. "Whatever. I'm beat." He pushed back from the table and stood.

"Yeah, me too." Ashton joined him. "Good night, guys. See you two back at the flat." She eyed her roommates.

"Same." Mason lifted a chin to Nigel and Adam. "Night, guys. Nice work today," he called to the rest of the cast.

Mason clutched Ashton's hand as they left the café and set out on the path toward the flats. She wanted to ask him what he was thinking about, but she already knew.

"So it was about me. They went in early to check *me* out." Mason thought aloud.

"Maybe it's like Hannah said. It had never happened before, and they wanted to see if you were really a shifter."

"But it exposed you!" His stride increased.

She pulled him to slow down. "I'm okay."

"Thankfully," he whispered but his eyes still shifted back and forth, his brow twitching. "Were they searching for my mom and found me instead? Maybe that's when they followed her to find the journal. Or maybe they found me first and used me to find her."

She could feel him adding more bricks to the invisible wall he kept up between the other hawks. His unknown past separated him from any true comfort.

"I still need to find that journal. If any of this is true, how did my mom get there? How did she meet my dad if keepers don't go to the Human Realm?"

"Why does it matter? We're here now. Part of me feels like it's where we're supposed to be. Like it *could* be home for us." Her words of comfort surprised even herself. This time, he pulled her to stop before they headed into their flats.

"And the other part of you?" He tucked her hair behind her ears.

Ashton looked down. Her human side continued to betray the new warrior inside. She hadn't wanted to burden Mason with it. He wouldn't know how to help her. He didn't know his own story, let alone why she was chosen as Centennial, or where her precious gifts were. So far, she'd discovered she could open locks. So what? How would that help in patrolling the seam for demons? And even if it could, it wouldn't unlock any bolted truths for either herself or Mason.

Chapter 23

Claim Who You Are

It was a friendly competition, a training game before their first planned night mission. Mason's heart pulsed in the tips of his fingers as he pressed his blade snugly against Adam's throat. Des called match point to Mason, but Mason's blood boiled so loud in his ears, he couldn't pull back. Drowning out Des's warning, "Dude, we're done," hissing sounds slithered up his spine.

You know who you are. I know who you are. Claim who you are.

Mason froze, his hand shaking as he listened between heartbeats. Then suddenly, he flew across the room, landing flat on his back, his head snapping the ground with a thud. "Ah, what the—" He propped up, his hand moving to the wetness behind his head.

"What's your problem?" Adam leaped across the floor until held back by Des and Connor. The group circled around them like a schoolyard fight.

"Yeah, what's up? I'm kind of bleeding here?" Mason snarled back just as angry as Adam. The group was silent around them, and Mason wasn't sure the cause for such an audience. He struggled standing up, as Adam broke free and shoved him down again.

"You want to bleed? I can help with that."

Des pulled the back of Adam's shirt, pushing him

into Connor.

"Take him out of here," Des directed at Connor, then addressed the group. "Showers, now!" He waited until everyone had cleared out, including an angry Adam wrestling against Connor's strength.

Des glared down at him, and Mason wished he was the one with dreads to hide behind. "What the hell is wrong with you?" He walked to a shelving unit and grabbed a silver metal box. After rummaging through, he returned with first aid supplies.

"Adam attacked *me*." Mason continued applying pressure until Des pushed his hand away and not too gently dabbed the blood up from the back of his head. Mason sat like a child on the floor with his head pushed between his legs. "And who threw me across the room?"

"How hard did you hit your head?" Des was dumping something cold and wet over the wound. "Don't move. Head injuries take longer to heal."

Mason froze, quietly swearing Des held his head down harder than needed. After a few minutes, Des let up and stood. When Mason looked up, he was thankful for quick reflexes. Des returned his knife, dropping it without warning.

"Shunnar will want to see you."

"Wait a minute." Mason tried standing too quickly and slumped back down to his knees, the blood whooshing in his head. "Aren't you going to tell me what happened? Why did Adam attack me?" He found his way to his feet.

Des ignored him, putting away the first aid supplies before stalking over. "You attacked Adam. You drew first blood. *I* pulled you off."

Mason felt like he'd been struck. "I don't

remember that. I-I heard you call my point, and then I don't know. I only remember being thrown back." He rubbed at the back of his head. It was buzzing now, half from the pain and half from his body healing itself.

"Wait until Adam calms down, then *you* need to clear this up. He's rightfully angry."

"Of course, I'm sorry."

Des tossed him a sorrowful look and left without another word.

Mason stormed out. He didn't want to run into anyone and headed the opposite direction of Shunnar's office and the showers. He didn't even wait for Ashton. He knew if he hurried home, he could clean up before Nigel and Adam arrived.

Almost there, he noticed a familiar silhouette standing at the entrance.

Shunnar.

"I heard about the incident." He held the door open for Mason. "Let's talk inside."

Mason shut the door to his flat and turned to face him. "Look, I don't know what happened. I thought Adam attacked me, but Des said I initiated. I don't remember any of it."

Shunnar didn't speak, just stared.

"Did you hear me? I don't know how it happened."

"Tell me what you do remember."

Mason recapped the match, Des calling game point, someone throwing him across the room, Adam freaking out.

Shunnar remained silent again, and Mason wondered if he was having a mental conversation in his head. Maybe to Gavan?

"Mason, you're different from the other shifters because of your time in the Human Realm. We understand how the Centennial transitions, that it takes time for her memories to weave together, time for her gifts to emerge. You are a unique case. Come to me if you remember anything, and we'll keep an eye on things in the meantime." He turned to leave.

"You mean *continue* keeping an eye on *me*," Mason said smugly. He almost blurted the part about his mom being alive but left it wedged in his throat.

Shunnar turned around. "Of course. We keep an eye on all our cast. It's part of the job." And, as if that was enough, he turned to leave.

The door clicked shut, ringing loudly in Mason's ears. *What just happened?*

****

Mason stood as the shower sprayed over his flesh. He was sticky from training, the back of his head still coated in dried blood. His wounds were healing, but the residual pain pulsed under his skin. Suddenly, flashes of the incident resurfaced. His match with Adam flickered vividly in his mind, Adam's throat as Mason put pressure on the blade. It was still a fair fight in the rules of the game. Then he remembered a rush of adrenaline shutting like a makeshift curtain, separating him from the outside. He had stopped hearing or even seeing the others around him. It was just his blade on Adam's throat.

Blood pounded in his head again, just like it had with Adam. The clang of noise clattered in his mind, alone in the shower. Everything fogged over. What was it? Why couldn't he see through it?

Claim who you are.

Mason jumped back, shutting off the water. He stilled himself to hear more clearly. But the voices weren't coming from inside or outside the bathroom.

The raspy whisper came from behind his eyes, from *inside* his mind.

"Stop it!"

Silence slapped him out of his craze, and he clambered out of the shower. He checked around the small bathroom as if someone might be hiding. After finding the space empty, he dried off. Was he going crazy? Maybe his human side couldn't handle the Spiritual Realm? Maybe Shunnar *should* be watching him.

He listened from behind the bathroom door before slowly turning the knob, hoping Adam had stayed clear a while longer. He couldn't sense Adam or Nigel nearby, though something felt off. He shook his head. His rage must be messing up his signals. But when he stepped around the corner, a body stood silhouetted against the window. Without thinking he was across the room, his body on top of the assailant in record time.

Mason's hand pressed against the second neck of the day, but this time, instead of being thrown off, he felt heavy on top of something entirely too small to be an attacker. Her breathless squeals of alarm penetrated his sense of danger. Blinking, he cleared his blurry vision bringing Ashton's face into perfect view.

"It's me—it's me! Mas, stop!"

"Ash? I could have killed you!"

"What were you thinking?" She pushed him off.

He stood up, adjusted his towel, breathing through the adrenaline blazing through his veins. "How did you get in here? I locked the—" He rolled his eyes, remembering her gift.

Her eyes grew with guilt. "I needed to tell you something."

"Did it ever occur to you that I might need some

space?"

"Since when do you need space?" Ashton threw back. "I am your space."

"You're right. I'm sorry." But he turned and scooped up the clothes he'd dropped on the way to the shower. After a minute, he walked back out wearing clean sweats and pulling a black T-shirt over his head. "What did you want to tell me?"

She waited for him to settle on the gray sectional before sitting down. She was keeping her distance.

"Ash, I'm sorry." He took her hand.

"What happened? I couldn't find you after training, then I saw Shunnar leave the flat."

He stared at her wondering if he should tell her now or stretch it out until he caved. Keeping secrets from Ashton was difficult, as it proved to be before her birthday, although this one might be necessary. Defeated, he searched for the scar under her right eye, reaching his hand up to trace the faint line. "It's practically gone."

"You're stalling. Tell me what's going on."

"Tell me what you wanted to tell me first."

She glared at him, and he glared back, his lips curving at their familiar banter. He was breathing comfortably again, calm in her presence. This was something he could do. He could be himself around Ash. He could be honest. But just as fast, his mind flashed to his mistaken attack on her, his strange attack on Adam. He threw his head back onto the sofa cushion, breaking the staring contest.

"Something *is* wrong," Ashton said. "You never give up that easy. What happened?"

"Okay. I'll tell you, but please don't overreact."

She nodded, but when he shook his head to chicken

out, she grabbed his face with both hands. "I promise. No overreacting. Just tell me."

He gently wrapped his fingers around her wrists, pulling her closer. "Something weird happened at training today. Something bad." He looked away from the swirling currents of her expression. "I attacked Adam. By accident."

Ashton leaned back. "Like you just attacked me?"

He shook his head, too exhausted to get excited anymore. "*You* surprised me in my *locked* apartment. Adam and I were in a sparring match, and I sort of blacked out at the end. The next thing I knew, I was flying across the room and Adam's freaking out. Des said I wouldn't back down after the match point, and—I guess I drew blood." He was desperate for her to understand. "Ash, I don't remember seeing his blood. I don't remember hurting him. But later—" He leaned closer. "In the shower, I remembered what happened, and I heard it again."

"Heard what?" Ashton reached out, rubbing circles on his back, like she always did when he was tense. He closed his eyes into the reassurance of it.

He peeked over at her, head still hanging in response to the comfort of her hands. "I heard this whispery voice in my head. It told me to claim who I am." Startled by the click of the door opening, he jumped up. Adam and Nigel walked in.

"Adam." Mason shifted from foot to foot. Nigel put himself in between the two of them. Ashton stood next to Mason for support but stayed quiet. "I'm really sorry. I messed up."

Adam's tight face said nothing, though his freckles were bright, distinct like animal spots. He was still upset. Nigel nodded to Mason as if to be patient.

Finally, Adam shook his head, meeting Mason's eyes. "It not okay, but—okay, I guess."

"It won't happen again. I'm really sorry." He'd already apologized. Now he was coming across as weak. And how could he promise not to hurt him again when he didn't know how it had happened in the first place? Doubt chipped at his confidence.

"Yeah, it won't." Adam smirked. "Because if it does, I'll end it." Adam's shoulders relaxed and he nodded, maybe trying to save face.

Although they had only known each other a couple of weeks, a sense of trust had grown over the last few patrols. He didn't want that trust compromised for their first night mission scheduled in a few hours.

Mason half smiled, tilting his chin up before sitting next to Ashton. When he glanced her way, she winked. As if nothing had happened, she rattled on about her day, covering the awkward tension in the room.

"So as I was saying, I think I figured out another one of my gifts."

"Better than breaking into locked apartments?" Mason egged her on as he watched Nigel and Adam retreat to their rooms.

"Actually, yes." She smiled proudly.

"Seriously?" Mason laughed, bringing his attention back to her. He was curious about her gifts, of course, but he also needed stress interference.

She eyed him funny, he knew because he wasn't going back to the big topic he'd spilled before Adam and Nigel arrived. Thankfully, she understood and continued talking. "Rory put me through some scenario testing this morning. I passed everything with perfect scores. She said she'd never had a keeper score so high."

"Ash, you're a perfectionist, and you actually care. It's why you always wanted to study on Saturday nights," he said. "Of course you aced them."

Mason felt more relaxed after getting initial contact with Adam out of the way. As for the haunting voice in his head, he would ignore that a little longer. Glad for Ashton's news, he listened without engaging in the conversation. He mumbled appropriate responses as she described Rory's tests.

She said something about her ability to unlock working in the abstract. She said it had to do with how she analyzed everything and jabbed him because he always teased her for overthinking things. Her voice was soothing, replacing the darker one attacking him earlier. She looked beautiful today. She was pretty before, but since transitioning and seeing her fight, it was a definite turn-on.

Whoa! Where did that come from?

Ashton missed his return to reality, continuing with the descriptions of Rory's tests as if he hadn't just checked her out. He tried not to, but all he could think of was her hair. It had grown so long, so soft. He reached out to feel the silkiness of it, letting it fall through his hands.

She went on with her story without notice. "Rory put me through all kinds of scenarios and recorded my responsive instincts. As the scenes changed around me, I had to respond in different ways. Sometimes I had to use physical strength, other times I had to think things through, like I did when I was summoned to the beach."

She paused, bringing his full attention back. The beach summoning still scared her. He gave her a squeeze until she went on about her work with Rory. Maybe she could figure out the haunting voice from his head. He couldn't ask her with Adam and Nigel in the next room. He'd have to wait.

"So that's one of your gifts then?" He fingered another handful of her hair, and she turned around, resting her head on his lap, her feet over the arm of the sofa. This gave Mason's hands full rein over her long, bronzed waves. Idly, he drew them out into patterns across his legs.

"Rory doesn't know what to call it, but she thinks it might be due to the influence of the computer age. It's not something specific like manipulating water or creating smoke. It's not a spell or power I can wield when I want. It's just something my mind clicks to when I need it, I guess. It actually feels like little clicks in my head. But I can't really control it yet." She twisted, trying to look up at him.

"Don't move," he murmured. "I have hair art happening here. It's a masterpiece."

She laughed sweetly, a familiar sound reminding him they would be okay. They were always okay when they were together.

Ashton was quiet. She shut her eyes as he traced designs into her hair. He almost thought she'd fallen asleep when her whisper broke the silence. "Tell me about the voice."

He looked down at her closed eyes. She was as tired as he was. They had both worked hard figuring out their new destiny. More than physically draining, it was mentally pressing. Ashton missed her parents, and surprisingly, he wondered about his dad. Now he was hearing voices in his head and attacking his friends. He had to figure things out.

Not wanting Nigel and Adam to hear, he leaned closer. She smelled like lavender and honey. It must be the new shampoo in the realm. She had always smelled nice before, but this was different. She was different. Her eyelids fluttered, so he refocused, speaking in the smallest voice he could. "It was a quiet whisper inside my head. It said it knew me and to *claim* myself."

Ashton opened her eyes. She didn't say anything at first, though she looked like she wanted to. How could she respond? How could anyone? It was weird, even in the Spiritual Realm. Then abruptly, she swooped up to face him, the warmth from her hair suddenly removed. "Wait a minute. Maybe I could treat this like one of the tests I went through with Rory?"

"Actually, I was thinking the same thing." He nodded his head toward Nigel and Adam's rooms.

She dropped her voice at his cue. "I can try." Then she hopped up onto her knees, placed her hands on his head, and closed her eyes.

Nothing happened at first until her fingers started massaging his temples, which felt incredibly good. He tried not to groan because it might distract her, so he worked at keeping it inside. Like a sneeze, though, his guttural noise of relaxation escaped.

"Mason, stop," she reprimanded, still focused on her task.

"Sorry, it feels good."

"Shhhhhhh." She kept her eyes closed and continued pressing on his head.

He tried to relax and let his mind wander, but no matter what, his thoughts came back to his mom. Everything wrong in his life right now led back to her. It was why Shunnar and Rory were watching him to begin with. Or maybe they were the ones behind this? No, he was obsessing. He focused his thoughts to his new position as shifter, protector, demon hunter. He felt lighter as she rubbed away the pressures from his day. But then the words that had haunted his mind at training and in the shower replayed, only this time as an echo. *You know who you are. I know who you are. Claim who you are.*

Afraid to disrupt Ashton's focus, he held back the strange sensation inside. The words were there, but not as strong as they had been. A warm rush filled his head, until suddenly the place her fingers touched burned hot. His eyes flew open to Ashton's, though hers were sealed tight. She was deep in *whatever* she was doing, so he tried leaning away to get her attention. It was impossible. Her fingers glued to his skull.

She was in a trance when he reached up to grab her wrists. He pulled, but she was strong and held on. It felt like his brain was swelling, and he couldn't take it anymore.

"Ash, stop!" He tried ripping her hands away again, but she climbed onto the sofa cushion, stood over him, pressing harder, her eyes open now like wild blue flames burning down at him.

"Hold on! Hold on!" she screamed.

Nigel and Adam raced from their rooms.

Abruptly, Ashton released him and jumped from the sofa, stumbling back.

"What happened? Did you figure it out?" He didn't quite know how to name what it was she was trying to do. He glanced at Nigel and Adam, watching from the sidelines, then stepped closer to her. "Are you okay?"

"I heard the voice in your head."

Adam stepped up, his voice gentle. "Ashton, you heard someone else's voice…through Mason?"

She nodded, her hands squeezing her arms, like she was cold. But she wasn't cold. It was fear.

"I don't mean to pry." Adam stepped closer. "But I believe you experienced a thought transference of some kind. I've heard of this happening, but it's rare."

"I don't know what I experienced." Her gaze fell to the floor.

Mason looked to Adam, silently urging him to go on.

"Well, I don't know what you were hoping to find in *his* head, but seeing you two connected like you were, I don't know what else it could be. We've all been waiting to see what your gifts are. Maybe this is one of them."

Mason decided to fill in the blanks, hopeful that trusting his roommates was at least one safe bet. He knew he couldn't go to Shunnar. "She was helping me figure out..." He paused, unsure of how to say it, and looked to Ashton.

She nodded. "He heard a voice in his mind, delivering a strange message. It's what happened at training when he accidently attacked you." Mason's eyes widened, not angry at how she'd said it, but more how it sounded when she did.

"I'm not crazy." Mason turned toward Adam, who put his hand up to stop him.

"Dude, it's okay, I don't *think* you're crazy." He half laughed. "At least I hope not. But, Ashton, can you tell us what you saw in maybe-crazy's head here?"

Ashton glanced at Mason again, and he shrugged his consent. "I heard Ian's voice from inside Mason's mind. Ian told him he knew who Mason was and that he should claim himself. But I don't know what it means."

Mason could tell Ian's voice scared her, and he reached out to take her hand. Ian was now using him to get to her.

"We should take this to Shunnar," Nigel said.

"No," Mason blurted. "I mean, not yet."

"Mason, we're treading in dangerous waters."

Adam nodded. "Ian's contacting you through thought, that's big. He's not some minor demon."

"I get that, but I think this has to do with my mom. My *dead* mom, who just might not be—" He sucked in a breath. "Dead."

"Then the rumors are correct." Nigel shook his head. "They've said demon activity is higher than usual. Ian is planning something, and he's working solo. Demons don't cross our borders. This is huge."

The room was silent for too long when Adam spoke up. "All right, let's sit down. Can we all agree to keep this between us for now, at least until we put more pieces together?"

"Won't everyone know soon enough? The shifter-mental thing?" Ashton asked.

"No," Nigel said, joining them on the sectional. "Mason just needs to learn how to better lock down his thoughts." He turned to Mason. "I can show you."

They all nodded in agreement.

Mason shared his experience with the voice in his head, his attack on Adam, and then told them about the night he overheard Shunnar and Rory talking about his mom, her journal, all of it. In the end, he felt a wave of relief. At least Nigel and Adam knew this world. He could use some inside help.

They agreed to think on things and separate for now. The hour before their first night mission was closing in. They would regroup in the morning. Mason was relieved to have their support, feeling a little stronger against Ian's ploy to get to Ashton. He would need the help if protecting her from Ian now involved protecting her from himself.

Chapter 24

Night Mission

Shunnar and Rory briefed the group as several evening casts trickled into the flight center. The flow was seamless, teams overlapping fluidly like a well-oiled machine. Groups were separated into different shifts: morning, afternoon, evening, and night missions. They rotated every few days.

Ashton felt guilty not sharing her thought transference with Rory. There hadn't been time between the experience and the night mission to understand it herself, so maybe she hadn't really deceived her...yet.

The guys went out to shift as the riders double-checked their weapon belts. It still blew Ashton's mind how everything worked. But her seam keeper side clarified any confusion as soon as the questions formed in her mind.

When she walked from the armory out to the terminal, her senses heightened. The smell of soil underfoot permeated the air. The sound of the breeze against her leather jacket filled the arena like an anthem. And there was a tingling under her skin itching for action. She teetered between fear and anticipation as she waited.

There were six separate platforms, each about the size of a small stage. Riders climbed their own set of stairs attached to each platform to mount their hawks. With every step, her perspective blurred. The waiting hawks doubled in size as the riders' bodies adjusted to fit. Her body shuddered as a burst of energy flew up from her feet, causing her insides to flex, forcing her new size. In the end, she felt the size of a fourth-grade schoolchild. The dizzy spell lasted only minutes, gone before she could really complain. When she'd asked Mason if it was similar to how he felt shifting, he'd grunted and told her to think more bone crushing.

The Dream Realm border was both strange and beautiful in the daytime, and she couldn't deny her curiosity to see it at night. For the moment, all her problems paused: her freakish detour in life, missing her parents, wondering if the clicking gift Rory identified was anything at all. She pushed out Ian's haunting voice from her best friend's head. And Mason. Mason and his troubles were joined at the hip.

But she wasn't thinking about any of that now. Instead, her warrior inside mounted Mason's hawk form as if she'd done it a thousand times.

Once free of the terminal lights, Ashton squinted to see through her night-vision goggles. It wasn't long before her eyes adjusted, and they flew through the air portal, a cloudy substance hanging over a grove of trees, to the Dream Realm. The wispy whiteness of the portal thinned to the deep blue of night, and Ashton's seam keeper confidence expanded in her chest.

Excited a little?

Mason's voice filled her mind, and she smiled in the chilly air. *I can't help it!* Physical adrenaline was not a sensation she'd grown up with. The only adrenaline she'd ever felt regularly was the stressful kind, like awaiting exam results.

Their cast flowed behind them in a V formation, Bronwyn and Nigel to the left in the second line, as Hannah and Adam flanked right. Clara and Ren were center third line, with Lily and Seth to their right and Helen and Abram to the left. She knew Mason, and maybe Nigel and Adam, might be thinking about Ian speaking telepathically. They might even be suspicious of her mind-transfer ability. But out here at the seam, she could let it all go. Her human side stayed hidden in the background while her keeper side led onward, at peace with her destiny, innately breathing through the duty of it without a worry about the two uniting.

Ashton peered through her night goggles into the forest's edge, the soft violet glow causing the treetops to float disjointedly from their trunks. A mist covered the ground, steeping the forest floor like tea. Fresh scents of pine and evergreen, Christmas to her overstimulated senses, rose in the vapor. The river below lay nestled between the Human and Dream Realm, lapping at the edges with long tendrils. The dark sky reflected indigo in the goggle-tinted moonlight. And the moon! It was a lantern in the sky. Could it really be the same moon she'd seen night after night from home?

Stay focused, Mason delivered, and she didn't take offense. She beamed at his authority. His confidence and composure had renewed after his floundering earlier in the day. She shook off her wonder for the mission at hand and scanned the terrain below. It was difficult with the lack of light, the unfamiliar goggles, and the mist, but she concentrated on her surroundings.

Unexpectedly, they altered direction. She glanced over her shoulder. At the edge of the northwestern borderline, another formation of six paired seam keepers materialized into view through the mist. The riders raised their hands in greeting and turned in retreat, their duty at the border completed for the day.

How do we see through the fog down there? she sent to Mason.

We look for anything that stands out, same as we do in the light.

The formation broke with hawks dividing out on their own. It wasn't abnormal—they'd done it during daytime outings—but typically they stayed together, unless...Ashton surveyed through her artificially enhanced vision, stretching to see what might be there.

We're spreading out. No signs yet. It's easier to cover the grounds this way at night. Mason flew down to the rim of the forest's edge.

The water's dampness kissed Ashton's cheeks. Even with the filtered colors coming through her goggles, the landscape glowed in the moonlight.

They dove into a thicker part of the forest, winding in and out of tree trunks, and under low canopies. Did the lantern-moon just blow out in the wind? How quickly their surroundings shaded, until just as fast they returned. She searched for any strange motions or goggle-tinged colors not belonging. But even this deep in the forest, the darkness appeared mockingly darker than it should.

There it was again. Only this time, the black nothing became something before splitting apart.

Hold on! Mason sent.

He cut north, whirling straight up, reentering the open night. The moon, bright again, stood high and clear, a beacon in the violet sky. Crossing through its light path, a cluster of shadowy monsters shot through the air.

There they were.

Ashton couldn't tell how many demons were flying, maybe ten or so, but Hannah and Adam were closing in above them. Mason hooked underneath, closing off their escape below. The rest of their cast framed in from opposite sides.

Ashton's heart raced in her chest, but rhythmically and controlled. Only her human mind was worried about the outcome. The warrior inside pushed out, replacing panic for strategy.

Mason, in full throttle, barely communicated. They didn't need words right now. Together they needed only instinct and courage. Action.

Bronwyn and Nigel plowed up through the center, and they all scattered. Bronwyn's white hair glinted lavender between the moonlight and Ashton's goggles like a banner at a finish line. Ashton's thumping heart steadied into something less fluttery, more tribal.

Hannah and Adam dropped down over the pack, taking on one of the demons escaping. Ashton could see the emerald strikes flying from Hannah's dagger as it lashed out at the pterodactyl-like creature. Ear-piercing shrieks smothered the sound of the wind against her ears. The monster pulled up from its own formation, bringing the pair to a halt. Its giant legs, reared up, striking viciously. The rest of them blew past, leaving Hanna and Adam behind.

They're okay. Lily and Seth have their backs.

Ashton's hand hovered over her weapons belt. She didn't have to look to feel the glow of amber in her mind. She unsheathed the blade as its blessing crawled up her arm and into her chest, the rush flooding down to the tips of her boot-covered toes.

On point. One by one, pick 'em off.

Mason's instructions painted a picture in her mind and her keeper-side knew what to do.

Go!

Mason rose underneath one of the prehistoric-looking creatures. Ashton's arm strummed out into the underbelly of the dark, scaly membrane. It had been about to attack Clara and Ren from above, surprised by Mason's ascent from below. Ashton stabbed her half-sword directly into the heart. The beast shrieked until it exploded into a flurry of foul-smelling smoke, and she held her breath as Mason flew them through the deathly fog.

She glanced back to her team, all of them in the throes of battle, fighting on night's edge. Mason slowed and dipped under another demon. Its two dangling claws ripped back, attacking in retort. This time Ashton sliced her sword into the creature's middle, trying again for a strike through the heart.

She missed.

Wounded, the demon dipped in its course and veered away from its pack.

Mason redirected, dropped down atop the next beast. Ashton's sword slid seamlessly into its beak-like head. But, squawking in pain, the demon reared up, butting the bottom of Ashton's boot with its leathery wing just as Mason pulled away. Such a small movement, yet enough to throw her balance. She grasped for Mason's neck, but her fingers only filled with feathers as she toppled into the night.

Ash! Mason's call like a siren.

Ashton's body tumbled aimlessly. Flailing through the dark, her human side feared the cold rush of the river below. Innately her seam keeper side knew Mason would swoop down to rescue her. When she opened her eyes to look toward the rumble above, all she could see were the purple-tinted collisions of battle, demons clawing, keeper weapons glowing, wailing snarls from the dying beasts, and Mason's hawk cry from somewhere behind it all.

I—wait—Nigel, help... Mason's voice broke through, saturated in panic.

She was going to get wet.

Preparing for impact, she pressed her arms to her sides, trying to crash at an intentional angle—feet pointed, knees slightly bent. But before the expected splash, something caught her body in freefall, tearing her away to the left. Her head snapped right, ripping along her neck muscles; the moonlit night faded quickly to black.

****

Ashton opened her eyes only to squeeze them shut. The pain in her neck pulsed to its own raucous beat. Her waist, swollen after jack-knifing mid-air, throbbed to its own tune. But even with the distraction of injuries, she knew she wasn't in the Dream Realm. Air lined her throat like a blanket with each breath, heavier somehow, and it hurt to swallow.

She opened her eyes, slower this time, and searched her surroundings.

As her vision adjusted, a new panic bled through. She wasn't in the comfortable setting of the clinic at the seam. Instead, like a prison, concrete walls enclosed her on all four sides. Held on a cot in the center of the room, each wrist and both ankles were attached to medieval-like chains, fixing her in place. How long had she been out?

There were no windows in the tiny room and only one door. The giant bolts clamped tight; she was trapped. *Mason!* She stretched her mind, pleading for him to respond.

Nothing.

The empty quiet cut into her already wounded body, and she tilted her chin down to inspect herself. The movement seared her spine, but her gear was intact, save for her weapons belt, which was missing. The room held only the cot in the center. She stretched a shackled hand up to feel her neck but couldn't reach with the short chain. She guessed her stomach was bruised, not that she could lift her shirt to check. A flickering chandelier hung from a fifth chain above her, an odd choice in the dungeon-like setting. The ceiling was so tall, Ashton couldn't see it through the shadows.

Mason! her human side thought desperately.

After no response, her keeper side remembered she could save herself.

It was difficult to concentrate through the pain, but finally the clasped shackles fell open. Maybe her gift was sluggish due to her injuries. The chains had pressed her skin raw, but she would recover. Although moving off the cot proved to be more difficult.

Images of broken ribs crossed her mind, and she cursed her other unknown gifts. Why hadn't they surfaced yet? What were they waiting for? Lying there in the dark, trapped and all alone, her question of late reemerged: How was she supposed to be the Centennial?

****

"What the—" Mason slammed his fist against the door, splintering the wood. "Tell me what we're doing to get her back. I'm tired of speculating!" The pain in his fist only pulsed in comparison to the anger roaring through his body.

The meeting room was filled with keepers, alongside Mason and his angry ego, the same one he used to challenge his dad with when he was younger. Along in the gathering were his cast, Shunnar, Rory, and Gavan, with Isleen, a representative from the Dream Realm, and Nurzhen, representative from the Spiritual Realm. There hadn't been time to assemble the full council.

They had discussed the situation for longer than Mason could stand. He was dirty and worn out from fighting the monstrous bird-shaped demons. It had taken their entire cast's focus to put a dozen down. Two of the demons had escaped, one carrying Ashton's body away through the dark forest. They lost them in the rising mist, and Nigel forcibly turned Mason back to the seam, their team depleted.

"This isn't helping, Mason. We can't search for her without a plan," Shunnar countered. Mason leaned over the table where Gavan sat at the head. Isleen and Nurzhen sat stoically across from him. Everyone else littered the perimeter of the room.

Connor and Des entered through the door that had just taken Mason's abuse. "The blessings are complete. Bethesda has done the readings," Des reported.

Mason had met Bethesda once before. She was a healer, but also a spiritual navigator, locating demonic and elemental energies.

"She gave us Ashton's location. It's one of Ian's outer structures, in the Human Realm," Connor said.

Mason interrupted. "Why the Human Realm?"

Gavan responded to the group. "It makes sense he would take her there. Now that she's transitioned, her abilities are lessened in the Human Realm. He isn't sure how powerful she is and probably doesn't want to take any chances."

"Are you saying she has no strength there?" Mason couldn't handle the idea of Ashton out there to begin with. Now she was helpless.

So far, they were aware of Ashton's fighting strength and her ability to manage situations, including opening locks. Mason knew she could perform a thought transfer, or whatever Adam had called it, but aside from him, Adam, and Nigel, no one else knew. He didn't want to share it yet. If he did, he'd have to admit Ian was working through him. Shunnar would surely lock him up, and he wouldn't be able to join the search team. He could feel Adam and Nigel's glare but ignored them, hoping they got the hint. None of them dared speak mentally with Gavan in the room. He locked his thoughts down, as Nigel had taught him.

"She has all her strengths and gifts, only dulled. A restriction put in place for all elementals to assure the safety of humans," Gavan explained, then turned to Shunnar and Rory. "Ian isn't fully aware of her potential. Bethesda found her *because* of her gifts."

"Will he hurt her?" Mason's fists clamped and unclamped.

"No." The room echoed in chorus.

Rory stepped around the desk to face Mason. She put her hands on his shoulders, a tether to calm him, just like Ashton would. "He wants her alive, Mason, and the rules are the same as before. No one's spirit can be taken without their will. He will only try and wear her down, but he won't hurt her, exactly."

"Exactly?" Mason's eyebrows rose.

The room fell quiet. Nobody wanted to respond.

"Exactly what?"

Rory looked at Gavan for a silent sign before

answering. "Ian has his own abilities, minimized in the Human Realm or not. He will use trickery to confuse her, to entice her to his side. Her human link in elemental form is too much for him to walk away. If he can sway her, he increases his power tenfold. We've discovered an increase in his army of lower demons. He's been slowly building his numbers and keeping to himself, even away from the Dark Realm."

Mason glanced at Nigel and Adam. They had just spoken about rumors like this.

"Ashton's gifts are enough to push his reign above our control. All the knowledge Ashton has miraculously shared with us could be swept away to Ian. He would have more power than his brothers or any other higher demon, short of his father." Rory's tone was serious. "We need to get to her quickly. Mason, do you think you can do this? We can use you. Once we're close enough, in hawk form, you can speak to her, help her prepare from the inside. But if it's too much for you—"

"I'm fine. Let's go."

Gavan gave his final words. Isleen and Nurzhen blessed their mission, the power in the room thick, though for Mason, his insides shredded with angst. The *fix-it* inside him, as Ashton called it, desperately needed to do its job. He had to find her.

Within the hour, Mason stood in fresh gear, accompanied by Shunnar, Rory, Connor, and Des. A small group because they were entering the Human Realm. The rules were different, and they had to conceal their energies from Ian. Mason had wanted Nigel and Adam to go but discovered Nigel was right when he said seam keepers never went to the Human Realm, and there was no time to argue. Shunnar's team was some rank above, so the rule didn't apply.

Connor approached Mason, offering an open hand. A smooth green stone sat nestled in his freckled palm. Mason lifted an eyebrow, questioning the strange gift.

Connor laughed. "Blessed malachite. It helps cloak your energy in the Human Realm."

Mason continued staring at him.

"Just put it in your pocket, dude. I'm not proposing." He dumped the stone into Mason's hand and walked away, smirking.

Mason rubbed the stone between his thumb and forefinger. It was about the size of a dime, rippled with streaks of deeper green like pools of algae-covered waters. It reminded him of the stones scattered around his house when he was younger. His mom kept all kinds and colors in every room.

His mom.

Shaking his head of the memory, he closed his hand and pocketed the malachite, following Connor out of the armory.

The five of them walked across the arena to the main gates and exited into the surrounding woods. They headed over a small hill into a clearing to the west. Mason stopped dead in his tracks. The simplicity in Des and Shunnar's next actions blew his mind. The two merely walked into a grove at the clearing's edge and disappeared. No smoke, no lights, no fuss. Just gone.

Connor grabbed Mason's jacket and pulled him into the center of the grove. There was an ancient oak tree, which reminded Mason of the hundreds of oaks Ashton had doodled over the years. But his memories were cut short when Connor pulled him through the trunk of the tree, his body smooshing through bark. Then they traveled through another door from the center of the tree, flooded with blinding white light. He blinked through the spots forming in his vision before walking into what appeared to be a warehouse. Wherever he was, it was far away from the seam. The air was dense and filled with the foul stench of rotten eggs and garbage. Mason felt like something had ripped off his skin and then stretched it back on again.

Once all five were through the portal, Mason shook off his discomfort, following them out of the dark building, into the glaring sunlight. After the shock of transporting through realms, he could only laugh at the view in the distance. Greeting him like a welcome home sign stood the Space Needle.

They moved quickly, walking along the streets of Seattle. He had just been there last December, shopping with Ashton. Well, she had done the shopping. Mason was a firm believer in gift cards. But Ashton dragged him to see Santa Claus every year, justifying the visit by saying his inner child needed it, even when they'd grown too old. It was tradition. At the end of the day, they shared salted caramel chocolates…

He shut his eyes to close the memory; keeping up with the group's pace was priority.

"Let's go." Shunnar pulled keys out of his pocket, motioned toward a white van parked in a lot across the street. They jumped in. Shunnar started the engine and merged into traffic. They drove about thirty minutes along the water to another vacant warehouse. It was the simplest of plans, walk into a warehouse, battle Ian, and save Ashton. No problem. At this point, Mason didn't care what the plan was, he just needed her back.

They parked a block away from a huge gated lot. It held three oversized buildings surrounded by tall cyclone fencing. The sun burned down, melting the pavement beneath their feet. Mason wondered if his boots were leaving imprints in the cement. When he had last been home, the city had only begun warming up from its rainy chill.

"Des, Connor, take the east side. Mason, Rory, and I will take the west." Shunnar adjusted a backpack he had slung over his shoulder. "Go!" he ordered.

Mason looked up at the sun, like a foreign object in Seattle's skyline, already starting its decline. Based on the ease of getting there, how smoothly might things go? Would they be back home before sundown? He followed Rory, who followed Shunnar around to the north side of the first building. There was no sign of activity.

Shunnar whipped out wire cutters from his backpack, slicing through the metal gate. From every spy movie Mason had ever seen, nothing was this straightforward. Though he'd never seen a spy movie with seam keepers and demons before. The group crawled through the makeshift door and split up, Mason following Shunnar and Rory to the west, keeping flat along the edge of the building.

Smelly black soot marked the ground. What were the buildings used for? Aside from the KEEP OUT postings everywhere, there was no signage showing the name of a business. He covered his nose and mouth with one hand, avoiding the odors of burnt sulfur. His other hand drew a blade from his vest.

Rory had daggers glowing in each hand, one yellow, one blue. Shunnar motioned for them to stop, then peered around a corner. Loud thumping noises followed by short eerie screams chilled Mason to the bone. He held his breath as their small trio inched around the corner, finally joining Des and Connor, and three new spots on the ground holding the remnants of what Mason deduced were demon remains. They stepped over the vaporizing mounds to a side door in the next building.

Once inside the second building, Mason inhaled the dusty air, relieved to rid his senses of demon death, or at least demon removal. The shaded dark was welcoming after the blinding sunlight, and as his pupils adjusted, the vast empty space took shape.

A jet aircraft could have fit in the massive warehouse. Above them was a makeshift loft, with a spiraling staircase. Hanging chandeliers dangled from long chains, an odd lighting choice. The only natural light came from clerestory windows on the north and south sides. But in such a large building, this place had to be grimly dark at night.

The group halted. Shunnar and Rory whispered something privately between the two of them. Connor leaned into Des. Did they have paired mates somewhere? But before he could question further, Rory turned a circle in the center of the room. Both of her hands were open, eyes closed, until she approached and laid one hand on Mason's shoulder.

A soft pinkish light radiated off her body. With her coppery-red hair, she projected the lightest of sunset auras. He didn't mean to stare, but she glowed beautifully, his own shifter senses picking up the power behind it. He had believed only the Centennial had gifts. There was still so much he didn't understand.

Rory dropped her hands and opened her eyes, the pink residue fading. "She's in the third building, west side, back right."

"You got all that by touching my shoulder and spewing pink light?" Mason asked.

Shunnar turned to Mason. "Go back outside." He

pointed away from where Mason knew Ashton to be. "Get about a block away from the building before you shift. Stay in hawk form for only a minute or two. Do you understand? Your spirit is traceable, and Ian's surely monitoring. Warn Ashton we are coming and to be ready."

"Then what? Do I come back here?" Mason was heading to the door already, eager to connect with Ashton.

"Meet us at the van. You'll drive."

"I'm the getaway driver?" Irritation bled from Mason's tone.

"You are where you need to be. We work as a team. Now go!" Shunnar's authority delivered with a sharp twinge of pain down Mason's spine.

Mason breathed out some choice words but followed orders. He didn't want to waste any more time. He slid himself into the shadows alongside the first building. Retracing his steps, he made his way to the van, luckily without demon interference. A block farther, he found a deserted gas station and crept along the crumbling brick to the back alley. He made a mental note of where he was, in case he needed to return with Nigel and Adam. He knew Ashton wouldn't have any peace until Ian was gone.

None of them would.

Mason dropped to the ground to shift, his heart pounding, not from adrenaline, not from the pain he was about to endure in the change, but from hopeful anticipation of finding Ashton.

And killing a demon prince.

Chapter 25

Knight in Shining Armor

The door jostled before the weight from the other side broke through. Ashton prepared for someone entering, but the face busting into her confinement startled her more.

"Ashton, are you okay?" Ian shut the door, raced to her side.

"What are you doing here?"

"I'm your knight in shining armor, of course—" He stopped short, noticing the opened locks and chains on the floor. "Did you break these yourself?"

"Did you kidnap me?" She clenched her teeth, trying to sit up.

"I don't think you're technically a *kid* anymore." He leaned over her to whisper. "I mean, even dirty from your evening's events, and a night passed out on this old cot, you have me interested in more than a simple heartfelt thank-you."

Ashton gaped, but any response was trumped from pain.

"I'm kidding. Come on." He smirked, working to pull her up, but her sore body refused. Winking, he put his hands on her stomach. She half pushed them away but flinched from the stinging in her core. Warmth coursed through her body within seconds of contact, tingling as he healed her ribs and soothed her muscles.

After a few minutes, and with the ego of a hero, he lifted her down to the concrete floor.

"Where are we going?" Her head spun, the aftereffects of his magic.

"Shhhhh, we're getting out of here." He cracked the heavy door and peered out in both directions. Then he pulled her through a dark hallway. Filtered light spilled from high windows along the tall walls. From what she could tell, she was in an old building.

Ian stopped before each closed door and listened before moving on to a small opening at the end of the hall. The space, loaded with boxes, held a paper-strewn desk angled next to a door, and from the light glowing around the perimeter, it led outside. Just before cracking it open, Ian turned and handed her a pair of black sunglasses. She arched an eyebrow in confusion, but put them on. He slid on his own pair and then pushed the door open into the fresher, outside air.

The light blinded, even wearing sunglasses. Since Ian had started her body's healing process, she'd begun to think more clearly. The clicking sensation she'd experienced with Rory started like a small beat in the back of her mind, but fainter, and she pulled away from Ian to ground herself. Her tests with Rory were never under real duress.

Ian approached a black car waiting outside the door, then turned back to see she'd stopped. "What are you doing? We have to go."

"I can't go with you." She glanced around to get her bearings. "I don't know what kind of game you're playing. You're the one who took me, or arranged for it—" Shockingly, she recognized the waterfront, and the taller buildings set in the distance. She was in Seattle. She was *home*. "I know where I am."

Ashton's mind meshed into a series of miniscenes, as if the steps she should take had already happened, and she watched the replay on video. *Pulling Ian forward, she juts up her knee, surprising him with her new seam keeper strength. He bends over, and she shoves him left, leaping right with ease around the back of the car. She speeds across the lot without detection, into the city she's known since she was a child. From there, she contacts Mason, her family, and Max.* With a clear plan, her seam keeper inside revved up and grabbed onto Ian's shoulders, ready to star in the role already played out in her mind.

Ian countered, using her own energy against her, and swerving to miss her blunt knee-kick, he grabbed her before she could turn. He held her against the car. "Why are you fighting me? I'm trying to help you."

The images of failed scenes replaying in her head were astounding, but somehow, she slipped into seam keeper autopilot. It wasn't her human side, because that girl was cowering away, waiting for Mason. It was the warrior inside refusing to go down without a fight.

She twisted out of his grasp, on a second attempt to make a run for it, only to end up on the ground under his heavy knee. Even with Ian's healing touch, she didn't have the strength her mind was telling her she had.

All her energy drained in defeat.

Ian released his pressure, though still held tight. "Are you going to run? Because there are other demons out there who aren't as kind, or as good-looking, as I am."

Was he right? Were there other demons who wanted to hurt her? At least she knew Ian as an enemy. He would be a better captor over those slimy monsters she'd fought at the seam. And it would only be for a short time. She had escaped him before and would do it again, just not like this. She needed to heal and to think. Her confidence was wounded, but not broken.

Ian softened his grip, lifted her up, and opened the car door. It was a black sedan of some sort. Mason would have known the make and model in a glance, but it was just a black car with tinted windows to her. He motioned for her to move over, and reluctantly, she scooted to the other side of the bench seat. He sat down next to her in the back. In the front seat a driver waited, a young boy looking barely old enough to have a permit, and without a word, the car sped off.

"Thanks, Johnny." Ian patted the headrest behind the boy's head, then leaned back addressing Ashton. "Are you hurt anywhere else?" He grazed his eyes over her, stopping on his way back up at her neck. "Oh, that's pretty swollen. I bet you have whiplash." He laid his palm onto the curve of her neck. She didn't flinch, wanting the healing she knew his power would provide. Escape would only come in a healed body.

"What's really going on? You know who I am, and I know who you are."

"What does it look like? I'm saving you from the demons who stole you from your mission last night." He leaned in closer. "By the way, how does it feel being an official badass warrior?"

"I thought you were the one who took me?" Ashton was confused at his tactics, not about to respond to his last question. The buildings blurred together as the car whipped through the city.

Ian grinned, his signature charming smile. "I wanted to…take you away from all this. From all the lies." He swept a clump of fallen strands off her face and held them between his fingers. "But not as an evil demon. I like you, Ashton. I think you know it's more than that. I believe I've shared this with you before. I meant it." He leaned back, as if his response was enough.

Ashton's human side stirred. Had she misjudged him? Could he have been trying to help her? But her keeper side huffed a breath and moved farther away in the small confines of the backseat. "I want to go home."

His smile dropped, but he caught himself, lifting it with a curious expression. "Johnny?" His stare penetrated Ashton's tired eyes. "The young lady would like to go…*home*."

Johnny winked with black eyes in the rearview mirror, abruptly turning the car around.

They steered through heavy traffic. Ashton glared out the window as the city of Seattle buzzed past. Busy cars drove in a hurry from one place to another. She wished just one driver might take notice of her frightened face in the window, but the tinted blackness wasn't the only hindrance; overscheduled and stressed-out lifestyles had taken that prize long before the dark windows made any difference. She was on her own.

"Ashton, what can I do to make you believe I care for you?" He spoke sternly.

"We work for opposite sides."

"Opposites do attract."

She glared without saying a word. Hadn't Rory assessed her to be some kind of genius in getting out of situations? Wouldn't this be a proper time for those intuitions to surface?

He laughed, hopefully unaware of her thoughts. They were on the freeway now, heading east on 520. Was he really taking her to the clearing in the wooded area? Or maybe he knew of another portal back to Toria. Was this his plan, using her to get inside the Spiritual Realm? Speculation pounded behind her eyes. Her neck pain had subsided, but this was different, a twinge in her mind filling with tiny bursts, when the mental voice broke through.

Ashton, please! Say that you hear me.

Mason's desperation rambled through her mind, bringing tears to her eyes, and she knew for a fact her heart rate increased.

Ian glanced over. "Are you okay?"

Ashton shook her head and rubbed her temples. "I have a headache, probably the stress of being taken against my will." She hoped he couldn't sense Mason.

He chuckled in response. "I can fix it." His eyebrows rose in question, but he already had both hands resting on her neckline. Even in her vulnerable position, a demon's hands on her throat, Mason's voice in her mind, she couldn't stop herself from responding. *Mason!*

Just then, Ian's touch brought a familiar warmth coating her from the inside out. Whatever he was doing cured more than a headache. It stole her breath away, reminding her of other times her body filled with tingles from his touch. Like magic, her mind reflected the beautiful canvased background she'd first seen in her car. They were drinking lattes when he'd held her in his forest art, kissed her, protected her from the hawk attack. The painted scenes danced behind her eyes until finally her mind clicked into place, breaking the spell.

Heat rushed to her cheeks, and she pushed his hands away. "Don't touch me."

Ian smirked as she glared daggers. Had she fought off his magic again? But how? She hadn't thought of any memories about Mason. Or was it subconscious? She needed to avoid detection, fearful of losing her mental connection to Mason. Maybe her need to hold onto him was enough to cut through Ian's trance. Unable to analyze anything efficiently in her human state, her seam keeper side slapped Ian across the face.

Ian responded through gritted teeth. "We'll discuss this at—*home*." He turned his attention from her to a cell phone he pulled out of this pocket.

Ashton! Mason's voice rang again. *Ash!*

I'm here.

Oh my God. Are you okay?

I am, I just want out of here.

We're right outside the building. Be ready! I have to shift back.

No, wait! Ashton pleaded. *I'm not there anymore.*

Where are you? We tracked you here. Mason's tone altered.

I think I was there, but we left. Ian says he's taking me home. I don't know how—

Home? Mason questioned, but she felt the connection sever.

She strained to hear any sign of Mason's voice return. Hopefully, he could get to her. And she prayed the keepers were prepared for a battle at the seam. For now, speeding farther away from reality, she wished her dual personalities would mesh into one and longed to wield her gifts upon request. Until then, she would wait for a sign from Mason.

She would be ready.

****

Mason ran at track-speed, leaving the van in the dust. He bypassed Shunnar's original plan, heading back to the team. They had to be in the third building by now, but making his way around the forklift cemetery outside the second building was easier said than done. Cursing at having to climb over old machinery, he understood why Shunnar had gone through the building.

He zigzagged along the clutter of machinery, falling twice, until he reached the back corner of the second building. There was no sound, but his sense of danger heightened, like static in the air. He peered around the corner. Still nothing. He had to go for it. The door to the third building was maybe fifteen yards away. The sunlight seared against his forehead, sweat dripping, as he raced for the door at sprint speed.

Mistake!

Two men appeared from the opposite side of the second building. They wore jeans and T-shirts, but eerily, their faces and exposed arms were deathly gray. Mason's mind flew back to his dad's books on demons, the *fades*. Maybe Max knew more than Shunnar thought.

Evil brought him back to reality in a flash. As much as Mason dreaded running into trouble, they hadn't been expecting him either. The two growled like animals and charged. Mason's brain clicked into fighter-mode. Like a drill in training, he dropped down and swept his right leg low to the ground. The one on the right fell back. Mason jumped up to block the other beast's kick, then thrust his left elbow into its face. The demon stumbled back, tripping over a parked piece of machinery.

The first one jumped up again, coming down hard on Mason's back with both fists. Mason collapsed onto the blistering concrete. But the sunny day was a blessing after all, because the heat of the pavement sent his body reacting.

He sprang up, fumbled for a knife, and with adrenaline leading, slashed his offender in the chest, his knife and fist sinking into the cavity. The smell. It reeked of sewage, making his eyes water. Mason pulled back as if he'd touched a hot stove, and the gray man-shaped monster slid to the ground. He followed with a sharp stab to the right, catching the second gray-guy's shoulder, elbow. It didn't matter. The demon on the ground sizzled in the sun with a terrific screech before evaporating into a single black flame.

The smell was nauseating, but Mason had only wounded the other demon, who was now hurtling over his partner's remains with a small hand axe. He swung it over his head like an angry woodcutter. Mason retreated, hoping his long jump had improved since middle school track, away from the blade.

Just then, the door of the third building burst open, and his seam keeper team poured out. The startled gray demon turned as Connor released a knife swiftly into his chest, halting him in his tracks, while Mason took him down with a final blow to the back of the head. Stench of demon death filled the stale air, and it was over.

"Nice job." Connor stomped his feet, freeing them of sooty remains.

"I thought I told you to wait in the van?" Shunnar barked.

"What were those things? Half human, half demon-spawn?" The gray human-like monsters were far from the animalistic ones he'd hunted at the seam, and nowhere near the human-looking Ian.

"Fades." Connor snorted. "It's how lesser demons look in this realm. When negative human energy is strong enough, they can hold new forms."

"Can't humans tell the difference?" Mason thought back. His dad had written of something like this, but he had his facts mixed up.

Connor shook his head. "They look completely normal to humans. Depending on their power, sometimes people will get a bad vibe or feeling in their gut."

"Most humans are too busy to notice," Rory chimed in. "That's why it's crucial for us to keep them from the Dream Realm, where they syphon the energy to hold their forms."

"Ian didn't look faded."

"Ian's not a lesser demon," Des corrected.

Rory set a hand on Mason's shoulder. "This is what we're fighting for. Even though Ashton's connection has already been transferred, if she loses her free will to Ian, her connections and gifts go with her."

Mason had no words, no impulsive comeback. He didn't have the same memories pouring into him, like Ashton. But even with his unusual fit into this new world, Ashton was created for it. He knew that now. And rather than hiding from his dad at a human college without a plan, maybe being a seam keeper was exactly who he was supposed to be.

"You disobeyed orders. You were supposed to meet us at the van." Shunnar interrupted his thoughts, bringing him back to reality.

He ignored the rebuke. "I communicated with Ashton. She's not here anymore."

"We already figured that out. The building's empty," Connor said. Shunnar and Rory stared intently at Mason, knowing there had to be more.

"She said Ian was taking her *home*." He paused. It

had been bothering him since he'd heard it, but he was worried about being detected and getting back to warn the others. "I think he's taking her back to the realm. Is he starting some kind of war?"

Shunnar turned, clomping toward the van. The others followed. "He's not taking her back to our realm. He's taking her to her house in the Human Realm. This can't be good."

Mason's stomach churned.

They arrived at the van, and Shunnar tossed the keys to Rory. "Take this back and report to the council." He touched her shoulder, as if a private message passed between them, before facing the group. "Head to the alley. Be cautious. Shift. We can get there faster by flight."

Rory took off in the van as the four of them dashed across the street.

"Split up!" Shunnar called shifting in midair.

Mason had learned in training that their hawk forms were natural sized in the Human Realm, aiding their inconspicuousness. He figured Shunnar had them split up because hawks typically didn't fly together either, but right now, he could care less what anyone, in any realm, thought. He was getting to Ashton.

He had barely left the ground as his bones shattered into their new hollow forms and his wings lifted into the air. It was the first time he'd shifted in one continuous motion. But any celebration of progress was lost to the flight. He aimed straight over Lake Washington to his and Ashton's tiny suburb.

Chapter 26

Pain

Sleep held Ashton with an iron fist, and she stirred against whatever surface held her, sticky and hot. What dungeon was she in now?

She sucked in dry air and opened her eyes, quickly wishing she hadn't. A commotion roared in the distance, and from her twisted position in the backseat of Ian's car, her body shuddered, shaking off the mental lock in her brain. When she lifted her head, both Ian and Johnny were gone.

The noise outside penetrated the seclusion of the car. There was screaming and pounding and crackling, like an enormous thunderstorm. Scents of burning wood and smoke brought her to full awareness. She rose to see her house, the one she'd grown up in next door to Mason, ablaze.

"No!" She pulled on the door handle, hands shaking.

Monstrous flames swallowed the silhouette of her house. Black smoke billowed from every window, shading the bright day like night.

"No—no—no!" She pushed open the door, tears streaming down her face.

Firefighters worked in clusters around the yard.

Ashton climbed out of the car but clumsily fell between the door and the curb, her legs forgetting how to walk. "Help!" she screamed, the smoke already burning her eyes.

Visibility was difficult, silhouetted bodies coming and going. A police officer directed onlookers, keeping them away from the danger. Eying her, a uniformed man yelled to step back, but she ignored him, coughing, and ran toward the house.

"Mom, Dad!"

Out of nowhere, Ian appeared and swooped her up, backing them both away from the flames. He put a hand up to the police officer, and the man stopped, calmly turned, and walked away. At that point, an invisible wall went up, and her burning house took on more of a flattened façade, far out of reach.

Ashton screamed, "My parents!"

He carried her to the lawn across the street diagonally from Mason's house.

Her body was numb, but her emotions exploded into overdrive. "Put me down!"

Ian dropped to the ground, bear-hugging her into his lap. "Stop it, Ashton. Stop!" He pinned her arms to her sides. "The fire's out of control. We can't go in!"

"Let. Me. Go." She articulated through clenched teeth.

He refused. But then…she felt herself relax. Heat from the fire, or maybe from Ian's hands, seeped into each and every pore. She heaved out the breath she'd been holding and leaned back into his arms to watch the production on stage.

The fire was a masterpiece, filled with hues of ebony and amber. Scarlet flames scratched claw marks in the sky, blackened by dancing obsidian smoke. Inside the heart of the blaze, there were deeper colors of mulberry and wine, and a shade of purple she couldn't name, but she knew her mom could. Heat swirled around her like translucent waves. It teased with crackling pops and snaps drumming in her ears. The beat reminded her of the music her dad would play…Miles Davis. That was it, with the drums of Philly Joe Jones. Her dad beamed in her memory. He loved sharing his passion for jazz. Dad…

A new chill prickled her arms, cutting the heat. "I—I need to find my parents."

He released his grip to spin her around. "We can't do anything until they get the fire under control. It's too dangerous. I sent Johnny in. He will let us know."

She twisted back to see the huge flames engulfing the only true home she'd ever known. The fire was beautiful, though other adjectives hovered in the back of her mind—vicious, terrifying. Everything moved in slow motion as she watched through the bubble around them. The onlookers, the police, the fire crew. They couldn't see her. She looked around for familiar neighbors and found Mr. and Mrs. Williams, who had lived across the street for as long as she could remember. They were crying. But where was Mason's dad? He was on summer break. Would he already have forgotten them, traveling on a book tour?

She wriggled free of Ian's grip.

"I don't understand," she mumbled, a chilliness wafted through her like a draft. The cloudiness in her mind clearing—and then she knew. Her parents were dead.

Ashton's mind clicked in slow motion. How could she have fallen asleep in the middle of a kidnapping? *Click.* In the back of the car she had been very much awake. *Click.* How could her house of eighteen years randomly catch fire the day Ian brings her home? *Click.*

She turned to face Ian, chin up, shoulders back, fingernails drawing blood in her tightly clenched fists. "It was you. This was all you." She motioned to the fire as if introducing him to a friend. "You burned my house down to prove a point."

He would always find her. How many people would he hurt or kill in the process?

His expression faded. Glossy eyes, black as the smoke billowing in the place her house once stood. "What part of me caring about you makes you think I killed your parents?"

"I'm the Centennial. My elemental gifts create quite the powerful cocktail for you."

He flinched as if *she* had been the one to hurt him. "Perhaps that was how I felt in the beginning. And for that, I am truly sorry." He smoothed her hair before she backed away. "That was before I knew *you,* for who *you* are. I never expected to fall in love with you, Ashton Nichols."

****

Mason was the first to arrive at the horrific scene. Disbelief obscured his ability to communicate any logical thoughts to his team, to his own mind. He felt everything shut down as he landed and shifted in the same backyard he'd played in with Ashton as a child.

"Ashton!" He stormed toward the burning house.

A fire fighter dove at him, yanking him back roughly. He yelled something over the roar of fire, but his words were lost in the noise. Mason backed up, pushing away the hands clasping his shirt. The grounds smoldered in blankets of gray. He needed to get higher and ran to the opposite side of his yard, shifting without care of discomfort. People, firefighters, onlookers everywhere, but their focus wasn't on him while his

287

best friend's house melted to dust.

Unsure if he shed tears or sweat, his body morphed into his hawk form and took flight to the top of a neighboring tree. *Ashton!*

Visibility consisted of smoke and maddening flames. He made out figures in the street below, but no identifiable faces, save for a few neighbors. He flew to a cell tower to gain a better view. *Ash!* She wasn't responding. What could that mean?

Shunnar's voice seeped through the panic just when Mason saw it, a reflection flickering through the chaos. Quick bursts of light summoning him through his momentary alarm. Someone was signaling him. It had to be her.

Ashton's alive.

Mason soared at record speed. Any thoughts of responding to the hawks, lost. There was no time to wait for the team and follow whatever orders Shunnar might command, surely to sit back and let someone else lead. He was getting Ashton back.

Three houses upwind, a rooftop provided the perfect spot to perch and peer out with hawk vision. He wasn't gun shy, only skeptical it could be a trap. With the air less smoky, he made out a figure dressed in black, hiding between two houses. A small figure, face hidden in a hoodie, and alone; it had to be Ashton. She must have escaped Ian. Again.

He flew to a branch above her head, not wanting to startle her. With his heart, he longed for her to look up, for it to be her lake blue eyes, so cool and refreshing he could dive into them and relieve the heat of worry. But his hopes sank when the face in the shadows emerged. Losing balance, he plummeted to the ground, painfully shifting as he landed with a thud. The figure in black crept up slowly, cautiously, her eyes never leaving his, as he pulled himself up to stand.

Time stopped when the recollection of her face filled his mind, pushing him back to his knees. The woman knelt down, opening her arms to him.

"Mom?"

She nodded, touched his shoulders, pulled him up. "Mason." She embraced him.

He shrugged back, hands glued to his sides. "You're alive."

"It's a long story, and I will tell you everything, but not here. Come with me."

He shook his head, forgetting how to think at first, knowing he'd been on a mission. Somehow, he had to shove this painful blow to the back of his mind. "I–I have to find Ash."

"Ian's taken her. I know how to find her, but we can't do anything until morning. I can explain later, but for now, please come with me." Her golden eyes teared with desperation.

"My team—" He rubbed his eyes as if it might clear the fog filling his head. He should contact Shunnar. Why couldn't he hear their voices anymore?

"No. I can't let them find me. Come. I will explain."

He hesitated, but his feet followed on their own accord, away from the flames and commotion.

Mia Deed led him down the street to an old black SUV. He looked back once, thinking it might be a bad idea leaving Shunnar and his team, but when he saw his mom's face, his own eyes staring back at him, he climbed into the passenger seat.

She pulled out of the neighborhood they had both once called home, and he didn't care where they were going, his mind fighting too many questions. He leaned back against the seat, exhausted, and turned his head to look at her. He hadn't slept in over twenty-four human hours.

After she merged into traffic, he asked, "Why wait until tomorrow?"

"It will be dark by the time I can get us there, and I need supplies. I know you're scared, but if she's the Centennial and as strong as I'm betting, then she'll be okay."

"How do you know all this? How are you even here?" His voice a thin line. "How are you going to find Ashton? Tell me her parents and Dad are okay. Just start talking, please." His head swirled in pain, none of it from a physical blow. He wished someone would strike him, help snap him out of his daze.

"I told you, I know where Ian's headed. We just need to regroup before going in. The fire was already ablaze when I arrived. I didn't see Maggie and Drew Nichols or your dad, only Ian carrying Ashton to a car and driving off. Then I saw this crazy hawk flying over the fire, and I knew. I don't know how, but I knew it had to be you. So I waited." She glanced over at him before putting her eyes back on the road. It was well past five o'clock traffic. "You're a shifter now," she said, proudly.

Mason huffed. "Yeah." The news was anticlimactic, not that he'd ever imagined sharing it with her. Since she was dead.

"And your dad knows?"

"Not necessarily." He inhaled a breath. Could he trust this woman who had quit her mom job? The little boy inside wanted to cry out the anguish he'd grown up with, to scream at her for leaving him. But he couldn't unravel that thread, yet. "He knows I'm part of another world, nothing specific. I wasn't allowed to say anything."

She flinched but didn't speak after that. He guessed she knew all about lying to the ones you love. They drove in silence for a while. Mason stared at the dust on the dashboard. Even though his instincts nagged him to pay better attention, he didn't care where they were going.

"I didn't know about Ashton right away." She shook loose blonde curls, dancing at her shoulders. Her ringlets were natural, the cut more severe, like she had lopped them off in one fell swoop. "Of all places for us to hide."

Mason sat up straighter. "Why couldn't you stay and tell me about your world? I'm assuming it's *yours* because I'm a seam keeper now, and it's hereditary. I know Dad doesn't know about the other realms, apart from the bits and pieces he's put together."

"I had to leave to protect you both." Her voice saddened. "Demons started showing up, minor ones, and fighting them off was getting more difficult to hide. It wasn't until recently I realized who Ashton was. It was too late for me, but she was already under seam keeper protection, and you, who I thought I'd hidden so well, had been identified." She paused, looking remorseful, but Mason waited for her to continue. He needed to hear everything.

"I suppose it was futile to think I could hide you from them. Always forgiving, the Spiritual Realm. They protected you right alongside her..." She glanced over at him. "You're paired, aren't you?"

"Yes," he answered. The weight of the word was daunting. It only added to the realization he'd never had control over any part of his life. All beginning with her.

His mom drove. Mason stared. She looked the same, but not the same. Maybe his eighteen-year-old eyes had forgotten what she looked like. Her hair was shorter, but everything else was as his five-year-old mind remembered, or was it? There was *something* different, something hardened, cold.

She glanced over at him, choking back tears. "You're *good*. I mean, they trust you and you fight for *good*."

He could tell she was battling something inside. It seemed to matter to her that they trusted him, and he didn't know if he should share that they didn't. He hadn't been around her in thirteen years, and now she was crying. When Ashton was upset, he always tried to make her laugh, but this time, he bartered on silence.

His mom's voice broke the quiet. Her fingers clenched the steering wheel. "I was a seam keeper, like you, paired with a shifter named Chase. We grew up together." She stopped again, and Mason held his breath not to pound her with more questions.

They had already driven a long time, away from the city, somewhere backwoods. Mason kicked himself for not paying better attention. He hadn't even noticed what exit she'd taken. It wasn't like him.

"Chase was killed in battle," she began again. "I couldn't recover. He was my best friend, and the only love I knew. I felt so empty, so dead inside. I wandered off to the Human Realm. I guess I wanted to die, too."

"I'm so sorry," Mason slipped in, feeling compelled to say something.

She turned onto a dirt road that wound downhill several more miles before curving onto a small property. A tiny log cabin sat nestled in a valley, with a creek on one side and a slanted hill on the other, all hidden by a mix of evergreens. She pulled into a single car garage and turned off the engine.

"I know this is difficult for you to hear all at once."

"Is that when you met Dad? When you fled to the Human Realm?" he asked, ignoring her last statement, the sadness in her eyes.

"I wish I had. I mean, I had met Max, yes, but I had met someone else first. This other man was kind and patient and knew how to make me laugh again. I started to think I could create a new life. But before discovering a terrible truth about him, I became pregnant. I should have sensed the truth. I was a seam keeper. But my abilities were dulled in the Human Realm, and in my grief—I didn't care." She wept now, and Mason was lost between consoling her and feeling curious about the pregnancy. Was she talking about him?

"I had already met Max, and he had shown interest in me. He was a gentleman. So I started my life over with him. He doesn't know you're *not* his son. I had time because seam keeper pregnancies are slightly longer than human ones. We were married, and you bounded into our lives ten months later." She smiled, as if that was enough.

"So Max isn't my dad?"

"Let's go inside." She turned abruptly and stepped out of the SUV.

Mason growled as he climbed out after her. He followed her through a side door that opened into a kitchen. The sparsely decorated space was neat and tidy. The décor matched the rugged surroundings, with beige and green plaids, and even a deer head mounted over the fireplace.

She pulled out a chair from the kitchen table and motioned for him to sit. She didn't join him, instead rattled around cupboards. "I want to tell you who your father is. I do. It's just—"

"We don't have time for this. You do understand that Ian is a powerful demon and he has Ashton? Tell me the truth, I deserve that much."

"I understand how dangerous Ian is." She started to say more but busied herself chopping something green from a planter in the window. She heated up the contents of a glass container from the refrigerator and sliced bread onto a platter. Before he found the nerve to push her further, she placed a bowl of herb-sprinkled soup and a tall glass of milk on the table in front of him. All he could do was stare.

"You don't like potato soup?"

"No, I do. I've just only had it from a can. Did you make this?" He leaned in, inhaling the scents wafting from the bowl.

She sat across from him, sipped a spoonful of the steamy white liquid. It was only soup, but Mason felt a multitude of animosities toward her. She'd left him alone when he was five. She could have taken him with her. Anything would have been better than living in that giant house with his dad—make that stepdad—seldom making appearances.

"I'm sorry I wasn't there for you. Please forgive me. Leaving was the only way I knew to keep you and Max safe."

"Keep us safe?" Mason's voice rose. "You left me alone with a man who stocked the fridge full of packaged crap and stayed away working late every night. I've been alone for thirteen years."

"Not alone. You've had Ashton and the hawks.

And you had me. I've watched over you all these years. I *have* been there." She pressed a napkin under her eyes.

"How was I supposed to know you were there? Ashton was the one who took care of me. She was the one I went to when I needed someone. She was the one who told me everything would be okay. Not you. Not Dad, or Max—or whoever he is now." He glared across the table. Enough was enough. "*Who* is my real father?"

"I can't." She covered her face with her hands.

Anger pulsed through Mason's veins. He didn't care how upset she was. "Who is it?"

"Mason, please—"

He cut her off, his hawk cry inside, throaty and bold. "Who are you to deny me knowing who I really am? You didn't even share that I'm from another realm, entirely! You left me. You lied to me. You owe me. Who. Is. My. Father?"

"It's Ian!" she blurted, jumping from her seat.

Mason stood, his chair tumbling behind him. "What did you say?"

She bit her lip before responding in a whisper that grew in volume with each word. "Your father is Ian, Dark prince to Lucifer. He is much older than you can imagine but can look any age he wishes. He is charming and young-hearted and evil, Mason. Pure evil. He seduced me because he could, and I fell right into his trap. I knew better, and it didn't matter. I—" She dropped to the table, face buried under her arms, sobbing.

Mason thought about helping her. He would have, had it been Ashton. But this? This wasn't anything he was prepared for. *This* didn't fit anywhere in his already stretched-thin mind. He thought back to the day Ashton found out she was adopted. How the façade of her happy home made her question her reality. For eighteen years, he had been Max Deed's son, so he had no happy façade to grieve. But at least he was human. That had been his identity. And then, he was a seam keeper from the Spiritual Realm, paired with the Centennial to protect the world from unbelievable evil. Half human. Now—the son of a demon? The very evil he had just been trained to fight against? He didn't understand anything about his shifter genes, except that they were hereditary.

What did a demon bloodline mean for him?

Mason backed up all the way to the front room. Bumping into the living room window, he turned to see a colorful sunset merge with the tree line silhouette. Pressing both hands on the glass, as if all unwanted feelings could be released in two simple handprints, he called for Ashton in his mind. He needed her more than anyone right now. But then again, how would he tell her he was part monster? How would he ever face his seam keeper cast and tell them *he* was who they were fighting? They were right to be leery of him. He could never return. And Ashton...now she would be alone.

As his world crumbled, he pushed off the glass to the front door. He needed air. He needed out of the tiny confined space. Throwing open the door, he tore outside, leaping the front steps in one jump. Fight or flight mode ignited, and without anyone to physically hit, he ran. Heading away from the same road he and his *undead* mom had come down earlier, into the thicker woods, he ran.

Chapter 27

Surrender

Ashton's nose tickled. Her senses filled with a warm scent that was both Mason and Mom's sugar cookies. "What time is it?" She stretched lazily.

"Time for breakfast. How do you feel?"

Ian's voice.

She bolted upright in a bedroom with pink and shiny fabrics spilling from windows and pouring over bedposts. A mural of Japanese cherry blossoms crawled up the wall beside the bed she found herself. Ian hovered with a food tray, concern painting his brow.

Ashton frowned at her nightgown, pink to match the room. The truth resurfaced like fireworks. "My parents. I have to go." She crawled out of bed. "Where are my clothes?"

"You've been through a lot. You've slept. Now you need to eat." He set the tray on a tiny round side table. Sconces flickered dimly around the room suggesting the sun had long set, but Ashton felt as if it should be morning.

Her feet hit the cold floor, her body revived from its earlier soreness. "You did this, didn't you? I know what you are." Her voice rose in octaves. "You probably don't even look like you in your real form, do you? I've killed lesser demons, and they're black and oozing of stench." She traveled slowly up to face him, rattling in her tirade. "You just destroy and murder, like you did with my…parents." She dropped to the bed, confidence deflated, tears choking her scolding.

"And you judge and sentence me because of who my father is?" His voice cut sharp. "Did it ever occur to you that free will applies to us all? That I might reject my evil heritage?"

Ashton connected her gaze to his, glowing the perfect shade of an autumn storm. His rebuke had bulldozed the angst right out of her. He was a demon. She was a seam keeper trained to kill everything he stood for, or at least stop it. Wasn't it her divine destiny to protect the world from him? If not, then what was the point? Why choose her as Centennial to have everything go wrong?

"No, I don't believe you." She stood to move away from him, but her voice dropped in pitch. Rory had never mentioned demons switching sides.

Ian slipped forward, blocking her escape around the edge of the bed. "How do you think I found you at that party? I was protecting you from my father. If I'm so evil, why didn't I take you then? I've had a multitude of opportunities. I have known your whereabouts at every turn. I found you in your hiding place at the beach just as easily as I found you being carried away by those monstrous scum that worship my father."

He dropped to his knees before her. "I *saved* you."

****

Mason ran until his body spoke louder than all he was running from. With burning lungs, he threw himself against the rocky cliff bordering the edge of the property. Jagged rocks jutted out among smoother stones, cool under his palms. But could they hold up the fury raging in his mind? When he looked up, the cliffside he leaned against stood blunt, a giant stepping-stone cut like a pathway to higher ground.

Higher ground, he thought.

Catching his breath, swiping at dripping sweat, Mason looked ahead at the forest floor, piled with a labyrinth of fallen trees. Behind was a mom who'd been dead to him for two-thirds of his life, and the discovery of an unbearable truth, one that would isolate him from everyone. From Ashton. He cringed at what he was about to do, but he was desperate and spoke into the night.

"I know you're there, God. I mean, I guess I kind-of work for you. Or I did anyway. Oh, man." His voice shaking. "I don't know why I haven't done this before. I'm not comfortable praying. I guess I've never tried. But if I could just talk to you. If I could ask you one thing. I know I'm undeserving, or maybe you can't help me because I'm part...demon." His confidence slipped at the word.

He blew out trapped air from his lungs, forcing himself on. "God, I am sorry for what I am, but if you could help me find Ashton, get her to safety? Please, tell me what to do."

He spoke to the sky, tears welling in his eyes, but he wouldn't cry. Not yet. He had a million feelings wrenching inside, but the one fear he had to conquer first was getting Ashton away from Ian. Away from— *his father.* The words tasted foul on his tongue, and he pulled his hands down his face. He hadn't shaved in days now, his chin scruffy. Suddenly he laughed, drowning out the tears begging for release, because it only reminded him more of Ashton.

She hated when he didn't shave, refusing to hug him. But she was the same girl who also understood his

299

outlandish need to follow instructions from a dream. The one beginning this *otherworldly* fiasco. His entire world revolved around her. How could he not realize they were always more than friends. And now, even knowing he wasn't a pure shifter, he would always want the best for her.

Always. The word jumbled in his mind. That was it. He would always love her. Hadn't he always said that? Maybe he'd said it so many times he hadn't realized the truth of it. He would *always* love Ashton, and it wasn't because they were paired as seam keepers. He wasn't even a real seam keeper. He loved her because it was her, and him, and they fit.

With renewed conviction, Mason dropped to the ground on all fours. He hung his head, not desperate anymore, not pleading, but in complete surrender to everything impossible. "There is a verse I remember. I don't know why, when it didn't mean anything to me before." He paused. Whatever the world thought, he knew now what he believed. He had seen enough proof. "*With man, this is impossible, but with God all things are possible.*" The verse spilled from his subconscious, and he was suddenly thankful for the few Sundays he'd crashed church with Ash's family.

He knelt back, stared up at the first stars making their appearance. "I'm not even a man. But you are God. If I can't save Ash, because of the evil I am now, can I ask you to provide her with her gifts? Can you give her the strength to save herself? I would be forever in your debt. *Always.*"

He hoped his prayer was enough to be his last act of protecting Ashton. Then he let his tears flow, shielded by copious walls of evergreens, the rocky cliff, and blanketed cover of night.

After a long time, he wiped his last tear with the hem of his shirt. He stood and looked up into the growing dusk. He knew the way back to the cabin. At least his survival skills were intact enough this time, amid his breakdown. He would have to remember to thank Max Deed for that, if he ever saw him again.

****

"You came back." His mom's eyes brightened when Mason walked through the door.

"I needed some air." He strode across the room to stand by the empty fireplace. The bareness matched his insides. When he turned around, his mom was still standing. Colors from the lamps in the room bounced around the space. The golden glow caused his mom's face to look even younger than she appeared to be. "You look so young."

"It's an elemental thing. Once you turn eighteen, you age slower. But Mason, can we talk? I want you to understand why I left."

He nodded, sat next to her on the small plaid couch, as a memory triggered his thoughts. He was side by side with his mom, on their red sofa, in their living room. He was only three or four years old, the memory vague. But he recalled the red sofa and the stack of children's books. He remembered her reading each book to him, then helping him read them back to her. He had always wondered if he'd made it up, desperate for a memory of her. But the older he grew, the more his memories faded. Now, suddenly, they were sitting together again.

"I was nothing to Ian, just a distraction. But grieving over my loss, I guess he was my distraction, too. I regret that relationship, Mason, but I don't regret you. You were the only good thing to come out of all that pain. You are what helped me to heal." She never stopped looking at him, though Mason's focus bounced between the cold fireplace, the darkening window, and the mounted deer head judging his frustration.

"I only left to keep you and Max safe."

Safe? Now he studied her eyes, a reflection of his own, and they looked sad.

"I can't do this. I have to make sure Ashton's okay, and then…then I'll have all the time in the world. All I *need* to know right now is what it means for me that my father's a demon."

"Mason, you are *not* a demon."

"No, I'm only *half* a monster," he sneered.

"Stop it." She stood up, stormed to the window.

"It's the truth. I overheard Shunnar and Rory; they're the keepers in charge of training. They talked about keeping an eye on me. Why else would they be watching me? Was I even supposed to be a seam keeper?"

Her chin dropped. "Any child of mine, whether Chase had been your father or even Max, would become a seam keeper. A girl, a rider. A boy, a shifter. It's in your blood."

"I don't feel the same, and it doesn't change the fact I was being watched by the team you claim I'm part of." He rubbed his eyes, his body spent.

"I'm sure they were just being cautious. They were probably hoping to get to me." Her voice softened at the end, as if she were pondering the thought.

"Why do they want you?"

"Because they have always hoped I would return. But I needed to stay here to protect you. And now, it's been so long. I don't want them to find me." She left the room.

Mason worried he'd struck a nerve, but she returned with blankets in hand. "You may have my bed or the sofa. It's your choice."

He was more than tired. When he thought about it, he hadn't really slept in weeks, months. "I'll take the couch. Do you have the supplies you said you needed to find Ashton? I want to leave early."

"I have everything we need. We'll leave at first light."

Mason passed her to the bathroom. He couldn't look at her anymore.

Chapter 28

Invisible Gift

It was impossible to think. The vast emptiness in Ashton's surroundings made it hopeless to stay focused. There was daylight, but it was dim, as if the sun's rays were too far to find their way. Nighttime was even darker. Black skies without stars, no visible moon, nothing. She could have escaped the locked room; she knew how to do that. But to go where? Sneaking out the evening before had landed her in the middle of foggy nothingness. No buildings, no houses, no roads, no anything. From what she could see of the horizon, there was no end to the eerie, lifeless space. She didn't think she was anywhere human or in the Spiritual Realm.

"Word is out about you, Century-girl. I can't risk other demons preying on you until you receive all your gifts and can protect yourself," Ian had explained earlier, without touching her anymore. She supposed there was no need in this place. Everything felt heavier. Even breathing. According to Ian, no one knew about his tiny pocket between realms. Not even his own father.

Ashton listened by her locked door for sounds of Ian. Aside from his servant, Marta, who had delivered her food and fresh clothes, he was the only one who came to her room. He said he was giving her space to realize his sincere feelings.

Sincere feelings? There had to be more to his plan.

Ashton forced her mind to unlock the door, just as she had the night before. It took longer in the thick air, but it finally clicked open. She slipped down the stairwell one floor at a time, thankful this place absorbed any disturbance of weight. There were no creaks in the wooden planks beneath her feet. No shuffling footstep sounds to send alarm. Or if there were, they deadened before they registered. The house reminded her of an old colonial but topped with four extra floors and tall pointed peaks, like a castle. A wrapped front porch created a picture-perfect setting, if it weren't for the bare trees and dusty grounds as the only view.

When she had escaped before, she'd bolted out a side door straight for freedom. But when freedom wasn't found anywhere in the eerie atmosphere, she had no choice but to return to the confines of her room. But this time, she needed information. If Ian was a powerful demon, then why waste his time on her?

"But Master, bringing her here is dangerous for us all. Her power could be a beacon. Your father—"

"My father is none of your concern, Dominic! There is nowhere else to take her."

Ian's voice pricked under Ashton's skin, and she lowered herself to her knees, the conversation coming from the main hallway, one floor below. The vibrations of sounds clipped short at the end of each word, but she could still make out their meaning.

"You would risk the safety of us all for the hand of a seam keeper?" the one called Dominic chastised.

"A Centennial seam keeper. And you're crossing a line—"

"A rather worn one at that, Master. And I do

305

apologize. I've raised you from the moment you were born, need I remind you. But even for you, this is reckless. We escaped the wrath of your father to be free."

"Don't you see? I've created this place from dust with my own power alone."

"And the growing negative energy of human dreamers." Dominic's voice seemed to chide. "But we need to increase our collection. It's lifeless here. You're settling!"

"For us to have control of our own realm, free of the bonds of my father, we need more strength. Without it, this place will remain lifeless. Nothing will grow. We can't develop without her. When I have the powers of the new Centennial, joined with mine, I will build an untouchable realm. Then my father will look on me proudly, respect what I've accomplished over my brothers. That is why we protect her, Dominic."

Ashton fell back, knees shaking from her awkward position on the floor. The scuffle started to sound but faded. The voices from below quieted. Her heart thumped in her throat.

"And…" Ian's voice came again, somehow louder this time. "I love her."

"That I can see, Master."

Ashton scrambled to her feet, flew up the remaining stairs to her room, and locked the door. She took her place by the window, exhaled each beaten breath, and stared out at the un-bright day. She called out mentally to Mason, again and again.

Nothing…just like the grayness surrounding her. She pushed herself to feel the tingle of her gift again, to feel the clicks in her mind revealing more than unlocking doors. It would come as far as a staticky feeling on her arms, then promptly fade away. Her sadness overwhelmed, like thick fog claiming the day.

The loss of her parents stabbed in her chest, the blade twisting and turning with regret. Regret at never having said a proper goodbye. Regret she would never sketch something Mom might add her flair of color to, creating beauty together with her. And Dad. She could hear his voice now, sharing funny stories from work, laughing at his own jokes, reciting poetry that moved him, and so it moved Ashton.

Regret.

She cried for them, wept for the parents who would always be her parents regardless of where she came from, regardless of her adoption. The core of her heart longed for them to be her birth parents because they were perfect in her eyes. They always had been. They had worried she might not think they loved her enough, but now, how would they ever know how much she truly loved them? Mourning tears pooled the reality of her loss.

Her parents were gone.

When she wiped her wet cheeks, she found the backs of her hands streaked in violet, like watercolor smudges. She wiped more drippings from under her eyes—purple. The more she thought about it, the more it made sense. The purple markings on her hands told her exactly what she needed to know. There were no mirrors in the room, and any reflection from the window was dull from the unnatural filtered light.

Ashton closed her eyes, forced herself to think. This was a sign. It was a message, maybe from her own mind. Wherever Ian was keeping her, it couldn't block everything.

"Think!" she commanded herself. And when the

goosebumps on her arms rose, she knew what to do.

Guiltily, she tapped into her lament. She lifted her hands to her face, easily catching the tears flowing in her grief. At first, she feared she'd cried herself dry. But that was human thinking. She was a seam keeper, strong and fierce. The Centennial, who would soon have the gifts Ian coveted. And she wasn't about to join him in this dark excuse for a realm.

She threw back her shoulders and closed her eyes, allowing her tears to pool. She thought of the flames swallowing her parents, her home. She thought of Mason, worried, searching for her. Her eyes burned. What if she was too emotional for her plan to work? When, out of nowhere, a verse wove through her mind. *I can do all things through Him who gives me strength.* She wasn't sure where it had come from, maybe an Easter Sunday from her childhood. But the words repeated, over and over like a chant, spurring her on.

Ashton opened her eyes, tipped her chin, and caught the waterworks in her hands. She squinted into her violet-damp palms and pictured Althaia's tree—a portal between realms.

Before her next breath, she could see the strong oak standing tall and serene in the forest. The knotty bark rippled like a heartbeat. Her vision traveled along each crease; each smaller trunk twined with the others to create the massive portal that it was. The leaves, shamrock and seafoam, emerald and sage, waved for her to join them. They blew a cool breath on her face, welcoming. Her hair swirled up in the wind, pulling at her equilibrium. Every part of her body trembled until she found herself on the floor of Ian's room again.

"No!" She cried even more. If this didn't work, she would have no way of escaping. She had to try again.

Her hands were stained, as if she'd painted all afternoon with her mom. Just as they had one day last summer. The memory jarred behind her eyes. Her grandma's purple irises grew tall, as if standing guard outside Mom's childhood bedroom window. Grandma always teased it was to keep the boys away from her beautiful daughter. The three of them had giggled, reminiscing in the hospital room, just weeks before grandma died. After the funeral, Ashton and Mom painted abstract irises, as tall as trees. The canvas hung…Ashton choked back the sting of reality…*had hung* in the entryway of their home, now burned to the ground.

"I have to get out of here." She leaned over, pushed at her pounding temples. She'd seen the tree ripple in the strange double vision only moments ago. The verse filled her head once more. *I can do all things through Him who gives me strength. I can do all things through Him who gives me strength…*

Suddenly the oak streamed into view again, her vision tinted violet from her flow of heartbreak. The dizziness almost enveloped her body, so she fell to her hands and knees, steadying herself with tear-stained hands. In her mind's eye, she reached out and scratched at the bark, her fingers melting into the grain until she lost herself. Finally, as if stuck somewhere in between the visions and the pink room, she blinked, dropping solidly to the wooden floor inside the oak.

She scrambled to her feet, no time to spare. "Althaia!"

From room to room, she called for her birth mother. But the tiny space was empty. She couldn't let this stop her. The tree was a portal, she knew that. Running back to her birth mother's room, she found a full-length mirror. She grasped the sides as she pictured her room in Toria. She could see her bed on the north wall, her window that overlooked a garden of lavender and snapdragons. Her overstuffed chair—

"What was that?" Something nudged her senses from outside. "Althaia?" The external vision of the oak filled her mind, and the clamor she'd heard before sounded again. She still gripped the mirror, and when she looked back, it was too late. Her arms were already smoothing into a gooey haze, followed by her shoulders and torso and legs. In seconds, the energy carrying her essence poured her into the woods outside the tree.

The forest was heavy with the fresh scents of cedar and pine and sweet moss. Ashton breathed in deeply, distinguishing the heavy contrast between the Spiritual Realm and the one outside Ian's private lair. She also noticed the speed with which she'd just traveled. There was no comparison to the sludgy slow production from Ian's hidden realm.

She stalked around to the back of the giant trunk, extending her senses in every direction. The strength of them increased in intensity. They'd been lazy or asleep before, but now every nerve ending buzzed with life.

Suddenly, the forest was peaceful, too calm for what appeared to be late afternoon. There were no squirrels bickering in the tree branches, no prancing of deer feet, skittish of her presence. And there was no chirping of birds. But she had heard something, and it was more than the clicking beginning to tick in the back of her mind. Something tugged inside, telling her things weren't right. She squatted, scanning the area for signs of danger.

At first, she noticed a strong floral scent. When she looked down, she was surrounded by a patch of purple wildflowers. They looked like tiny stars with thick green leaves, reminding her of the trough of violets from her grandma's front porch. Her fingers, drawn to their vibrant hue, brushed over the soft petals, her mind distracted by their calling. Before she could stop herself, she pulled off several blossoms. Their silkiness hummed across her fingertips so strongly she thought she should drop them but couldn't bring herself to do it.

Ashton's teeth chattered at the buzzing, knocking her off balance, and she tumbled into the flower patch. She almost laughed aloud at the silliness of it but stopped short when she saw two dark figures approach. Could they have been what she sensed from inside? Or was it the flowers calling? From her position on the ground, she scrambled up without thinking, her warrior side making the decision.

It was too late to hide.

They looked like regular men, and for a minute, she wondered if they could be shifters, until their auras, thick with evil, infringed against her vibrating body. Now she was desperate for a place to hide, for a weapon.

Preparing for the worst, she widened her stance and thrust out her chin. Her hands still clenched the violet flowers, now folded into bits in her fists.

This was it.

And then…

They didn't stop. The two showed no acknowledgement of her presence, no signs of stopping. Before they could bulldoze her down, she leapt out of their path.

"Excuse me," she muttered, frustrated at landing on the ground again.

She climbed back up, dusting herself off, and in the

process dropped the flower petals. Just then, the two intruders turned, seemingly alarmed at her presence, and pulled out their weapons. The one on the right, pasty with a black beard, gripped a dagger in each fist. The one on the left, equally pale and bald, held a half-sword. They stormed toward her with snide grins.

"Now you notice me?" She assumed a fighting stance, even with her knees shaking. At least she was standing.

The two brutes chuckled at each other with a knowing glance, insider information passing between them. They must have figured out who she was, and if Ian was right, she was worth a lot. Her brain multi-tasked now, the clicking that had faded in Ian's hidden world was alive again. Bravery knocked her shoulders, but her opponents' enormous size still intimidated her human side. So she stepped forward, pushing back her human fear, and let the determination of her seam keeper mind rush over. They hadn't noticed her before—before the flowers! The vibrations had stopped once she dropped the purple blossoms.

Just as they closed in, she threw her body into the scented patch of violet blooms. Her arms spread wide, she grasped handfuls with both fists.

The two froze in their spots, looking from where she once stood, to each other, and back again. Confusion painted their faces.

"Where'd she go?" Blackbeard yelled.

"Vanished!" Baldy swore, scanning the woods.

Ashton held her breath, inching away in her strange form. Was she invisible? Branches snapped under her feet, but neither of them jumped. They couldn't see or hear her. Without another thought she ran, still clutching torn flowers in both hands.

The humming of the blossoms was unyielding, but she kept going until she found a trickling creek pulsing in the rhythm of the forest, a full orchestra of animal and bird song once again returned. It buzzed right along with the flowers she gripped, and she shoved the crushed petals into both front pockets. Then she closed her eyes and drew on whatever gifts she could summon.

The feeling was there, even with the distraction of flowers and forest. She opened her eyes and focused on the flow of water. Her reflection warbled as she pictured Mason's face, and only Mason. His big brown eyes, warm with glints of russet and copper, echoing in his golden curls falling in clumps around his suntanned face. It didn't matter where Toria was, or where Althaia was, she needed to be wherever he was.

"Mason," she whispered, and let herself fall into the liquid pull.

It took longer this time, though still not as long as it had in Ian's realm. Maybe it was the flowers keeping her body invisible. Maybe having a destination, rather than a person, was essential to the process. Too late now.

Finally, her body dropped to another forest floor, unlike the one outside Althaia's oak. The air smelled musty like Seattle in the rainy springtime. A low cliff edged along as far as she could see. The sun leaned west, though still high enough in the sky. She wasn't sure what realm she was in, but if she had to guess, the Human Realm. Even through the buzzing, she felt her senses dulling.

"Mason?" she queried the trees. Their silent response aided in her decision to follow the cliff, the biggest landmark she could find. She hadn't taken survival courses like Mason and getting any more lost was not in her plans. But if her gifts had brought her here, he must be close.

Her seam keeper side felt empowered, yet her human side felt strong too. With everything changed…burned down in the human world, there was only one thing left for her to do. It was time to forge a new path. And for the first time, she felt her two selves clasp hands.

Chapter 29

Pocket Of Discovery

Mason blinked as his mom shook him awake. Dressed in jeans and a zip-up hoodie, she was ready to go. Ashton was his only thought, so he didn't need time or caffeine to wake up and rolled off the sofa in one fell swoop.

Mia stopped him at the door. "It's a little tricky getting there. You'll have to trust me."

"I don't think I have a choice. But Ian's a high-level demon; will he sense us coming?"

"No." She pulled out a shiny stone, wired from a chain around her neck. "Black jade. It dispels the aura of any vulnerability, leaving you undetectable. It's from the Spiritual Realm, so it's been blessed." She pointed to his own vest pocket.

He slipped his fingers inside, retrieving a similar smooth black stone. Mason had wondered why Shunnar hadn't found him by now, hadn't tried to make contact, or at the least shock his spine into submission. He thought back to the day before, when he'd discovered his mom. She must have slipped it into his pocket when she hugged him. "This is why my cast hasn't made contact."

Mia nodded, threw him a granola bar, and led the way out the front door. He patted his other vest pocket, feeling the rounded shape of the malachite Connor had given him the day before. He must be double hidden now.

They traveled into the woods outside her house, perpendicular to the cliff, and walked for what seemed like an hour across uneven ground. It was littered with swollen branches, soft from the rise in temperature, still moist in the spots living amongst the shade. Finally, they came to a small swamp-like pond. The air reeked of damp mildew. The tree coverage was dense, with willow-like branches falling over the small bog. Even with the sun rising, its rays would never reach the water's surface.

"Ian's hiding place is lost between realms, and I'm sure only he knows about it. I was able to follow him years ago because of the protection stone. It will neutralize our energies." She tucked a curl behind her ear. "Are you ready to go?"

He gave her an uncomfortable *whatever* look and nodded. Then she pointed to the soupy black water and motioned for him to follow.

"Are you kidding me?" The water was flat-out gross.

She crossed both arms over her chest, closed her eyes, and stepped off the bank into the mucky liquid without a splash, gone before his mouth fell open.

He shook his head, mostly to erase the awful thought of jumping into the inky black pool, but then followed suit, letting his impulsiveness lead the way. He'd never turned down a dare and couldn't risk changing his mind. So he crossed his arms, closed his eyes, and pictured Ashton's face, before stepping off into the unimaginable.

He landed unexpectedly onto solid ground without a drop of moisture. He glanced up to find his mom waiting in what looked like a paper-thin forest. Sparse trees sprawled in every direction, backed by empty rolling hills that disappeared into gray nothing. There wasn't a speck of foliage on any branch. Where he imagined grasses and bushes to cover the low hills, he found chalk-like dirt. Nothing was dying, yet nothing seemed alive, the landscape colorless. Mason detected a dim source of light, like a bedroom lamp, trickling in through the emptiness from over a small hill. But the atmosphere was stale and lifeless.

"What is this place?"

"Like I said, it's not supposed to be here. I think it's a pocket inside a seam of the Dark Realm, or somewhere in between. At least that's my understanding." She moved on. "I think Ian created it. If he wanted to hide Ashton from every realm, this would be the place."

They followed no path and left no footprints. Mason had never seen soil quite like this. No matter how heavily he stepped, there was no sign of disturbance.

They soon came to a dwelling that looked like a modest mansion, or a small castle built into the cliff behind. Each level of height eased into pointy turrets as it rose. A large porch sat on the front as if a spectacular view awaited. Mason shook his head. There was no view. Then he followed his mom along the side of the house. They slid, backs against smooth ashlar, until they found a back door. Through the adjacent window, there was a kitchen with food preparations out on the counters and a pot steaming on a stove. His mom appeared unsurprised by the activity.

She continued along the stone bricks, to another window. With the faint light behind them, and a bright light inside, Mason peered into what looked like a dining area. A few men and women bustled around a grandiose table, while a couple sat at a large desk going over papers. One man sat alone in an overstuffed chair, reading a book. None of them noticed their intruders.

Who were they?

His mom motioned, and he moved along the way. Once clear of the window, they wound back up toward the front of the house. There were more windows, and the side of the giant porch protruded out. The whole scene took on the feel of a haunted house, created for charm right before a chainsaw monster dropped off the roof.

His mom studied each window along the sidewall, and he snapped back into focus. Finally, she stopped at a dark one and nodded to Mason. Pulling out another stone from her pocket, she traced it along the edges of the pane, and within seconds, the reflection rippled like water before disappearing completely.

Mason's expression must have been loud because Mia whispered, "It's only an illusion. Quickly, before it resurfaces." With that, she linked her hands together for Mason to climb up and over the sill. Once inside, he leaned over, grasping both her arms, hoisted her up. They snuck through the dark room to a door.

Mason whispered, "Where are the guards?"

She shook her head in response. "No need. He's the only one who comes here."

"Who are they?" He thumbed, referring to the people they'd seen through the window.

"Servants, I guess, to keep the grounds running. I can't tell if they're human or demon." She frowned. "We have to go."

They slipped through the door and down a long

hallway. No one was around, except short snips of faint voices coming from the dining room. It was a strange silence, matching the eerie feeling outside.

Mia led Mason up a grand staircase, slowly to the first landing. It held a lengthy hallway with four doors on each side. There were starts of soft voices coming from a room at the end of the hall, and after Mia snuck closer to listen, she inched the two of them back to the stairwell. "Servants."

After investigating the first four floors, each one narrower than the one below, they found every room empty. Eventually they approached a small corridor on the fifth and final floor. There were only two doors.

One led to a library with a sitting room. The bookshelves were impressive with hardcovers looking old and antique to new and modern. But what caught his eye, before his mom could whisk him away, was the pile of books scattered across a table in the center of the room. The cover of each one was familiar because he'd seen them in his childhood, hidden away with Ashton to read when his dad wasn't home. Max Deed's unpublished books on demons.

"Wait a minute." Mason strode to the table. "These are Dad's—I mean, Max's."

Mia had already picked one up. "Did he write these?" Bewilderment colored her face. "I don't understand. I kept this part of my life hidden."

"Not hidden enough." Mason slammed his fist down, causing a few books to jumble. "I didn't even check on him during the fire."

"He wasn't there." Mia put a hand on his shoulder. "He left weeks ago and hasn't been back. I've been checking. Mason, I need you *right* here, *right* now."

"Fine! Let's find Ashton, so we can figure this all

out." He stormed from the room.

Mia lingered briefly over the books but followed Mason to the other door. It was locked. The first locked door they'd come across. Mason eyed his mom, and she nodded in understanding. Her hands already working their magic with a similar stone to the one she'd used on the window. "Amazez, with…a little help," she whispered.

"Help?" Mason rose an eyebrow. But he hadn't heard of amazez either.

"Stones and minerals alone have special qualities, especially blessed from the Spiritual Realm, but sometimes they need a little extra help." The only thing his brain could conjure up was the power of his own blades or Ashton's weapons, they were all blessed. What kind of extra help was she talking about?

The door opened soundlessly, allowing them access and shutting down Mason's concern over the stones. It was another empty bedroom, only this one had an unmade bed with a pink silk nightgown on the floor. "She's gone."

"Are you sure it was her?" Mia held up the pink nighty.

"I don't know. But I feel like it has to be." It didn't look like anything Ashton would wear, but he wanted to be sure. Then it hit him—he knew what to do.

Dropping his fists to his sides, he focused on the bed. He called on his hawk vision, willing it to surface while keeping the change locked inside. His head filled with pressure, crawling up through each blood vessel to his temples, and finally behind his eyes. It seemed stuck there, pulsating, as if trying to make it through a heavy shield. But he pushed through the sluggishness as if his life depended on it. Finally, the new vision forced down his unreliable human sight, easily picking up the swirling shades of purple.

"Her mother pulled her out."

"Her mother?"

"Her birth mother. I can see the light residue. Purple is good, so she must be safe." He felt oddly surprised in his declaration of faith.

"Mason, there is no *good* way out of here. Do you understand me?" She was serious. "Even if someone tried to pull her through, it wouldn't work. Any gifts used here would require help from *other* sources. It can't be done."

"What *other* sources. Are you implying something Dark?"

"Mason, I can explain. But this isn't the time. We need to find Ashton, and I don't believe she would be able to get out on her own. I was stuck here for three human days until Ian left again, and I could follow. You don't return the same way you enter."

"She's stronger than you think. She can open locks and solve complex problems. And she doesn't need *other* sources." He peered with his hawk vision at the edge of the door, calling his ability to surface once again, willing it through the mental fog in Ian's hidden realm. Finally it worked, and his suspicions were right. He pointed to the gray-black stains tracing the edge of the door.

"What's this?" He knew she couldn't see what his hawk vision had revealed, evidence of the Dark on the door where she'd used her stone. But she was a seam keeper. Maybe she understood.

Mia stared at the door, her face solemn. "I've had to use extreme measures to survive. I'm hiding from three realms. Using dark magic with blessed stones

321

creates the invisibility I need. I'm ashamed, but I'm alive. Besides, it's allowed me to watch over you and Max. You had Ashton. I knew—"

"Knew what? That I was completely alone? Ashton and I were kids. I didn't just lose my mom back then...I lost a dad too. But he's not even my dad, so I guess it doesn't matter." He stormed out.

Without looking back, Mason sensed Mia's presence behind him and headed down the stairs. Without words or eye contact, he led her back into the stale, lifeless outside. New anger fueled his frustration. If she needed Dark help to survive, where would that leave him? He could only hope the purple light meant Ashton was safe, or at least that his prayer from the night before had meant something.

But buried deep inside, behind everything spinning out of control, he was so mad he wanted to kill something. And that single thought revealed who he truly was...the demon he was supposed to *claim*.

Somewhere along the way his mom stepped ahead, stopping them at a sparse grove of leafless trees. She held out her hand, and Mason reluctantly accepted. Then she touched a tree covered with dark ashy markings and pushed them through. The sensation was like walking through a waterfall, the pressure heavy on his head. The weight of impact caused him to almost lose consciousness. Almost. But once he touched ground on the other side, the effect dispelled. Daylight shone low in the Earthly sky.

They walked back through the woods toward his mom's cabin, unsuccessful in their mission. The path back reassured him they were out of the gray stale pocket between realms. Shades of green enveloped them, and the windblown branches crunching under his feet became music compared to Ian's desolate lair. When they passed the black water hole they'd dropped into earlier, Mason shivered at the thought of diving in again. He looked ahead, thankful for the hour walk back to the cabin. He needed time to think, his to-do list growing by the minute.

Find Ashton.

Kill Ian.

Figure out Life Plan B.

He didn't know what kind of future was possible when his own demon heritage bled out into his preplanned destiny. But he knew he'd end up alone. What other outcome could there be?

Chapter 30

Reunited

Circles. Ashton wandered in circles. She kept
letting familiar trees and rock-shaped landmarks pull
her off course. Finally, with Mason's voice mocking
her subconscious, she put the cliff on her left and
walked as straight as possible, ignoring the sun setting
and chill nipping her arms.

The vibrating flower power of invisibility felt more
comfortable, serving as a companion in the wooded
terrain. That is until mucky wet spots, forever in the
shade, swallowed her feet. This only reminded her more
of Seattle, her *home*, her family, her loss. Tears welled,
with memories of her parents weaving their way back
and forth along her thoughts. And Ian? She couldn't
think about him. He wanted her gifts to fortify his
secret realm. But was that all? Did he really have
feelings for her? Everything she knew to be true
muddled into fantasy.

I can do all things... began playing in the
background of her mind, and she switched gears. The
verse transformed into a chant, and her feet stomped out
their own path, the hum from her petal-filled pockets
offering the rhythm as she trudged along. And before
she could lead herself in another wrong direction, she
stumbled upon it.

The small cabin sat nestled behind a copse of old

cedars, at the base of the cliff she'd followed, rendered almost invisible by the umbrella of branches hovering atop. She had no idea if Mason was there, but something inside—faith she told herself—confirmed it was the right spot.

No one answered the door when she knocked. Walking around the cabin, she found every window locked and sat on the porch to think. She could use her gift to open locks. But would that be the right thing to do? Her heart told her the violet light was trustworthy. She'd used it to travel to Mason, and it brought her here. Knowing him, he was out looking for her, likely putting himself in danger. Again.

****

The front door clicked open effortlessly, after Ashton ordered her mind to do it. Her decision, as wavering as it was to break and enter, thrust her right across the threshold.

"Trespassing twice, check." She ticked off an imaginary list of badness, thinking of the many times Mason had called her a Goody Two-shoes. Maybe she *was* capable of more than she thought.

Inside, careful not to touch anything, she wandered around. In the only bedroom, she found a small brass picture frame on a dresser, next to a bed. The green plaid comforter and sparse room gave nothing away as to the gender of the homeowner. When she bent to open the dresser, the subject of a framed photo came into focus, Mason.

It was from his fifth birthday. She'd been a guest at the dinosaur-themed party. His mom had buried phony fossils for the kids to find in her garden. His toothless smile made her cry, and she ripped open the drawers with more vigor. She wasn't surprised to find women's clothing. This was Mia Deed's cabin. She *was* alive.

A thud sounded from the other side of the house, then voices carried. Ashton froze, sent out her senses. They were foggy in the Human Realm, but still worked. She could sense Mason's presence and bolted from the room, her joy bubbling over.

She rounded the corner and leapt into Mason's arms, bypassing his unemotional face. She needed his heartbeat next to hers, her body feeling whole once again.

"What the hell?" He pushed back, startled.

"What's wrong?" the woman with him asked.

It had to be Mia, Ashton thought, even if she hadn't seen her since she was five. They both wore stunned faces, and they were not *surprised-to-see-you* expressions.

"Mason, it's me." She stood in front of him, but his eyes still roamed the room.

"That was weird." He wriggled his shoulders as if shaking off a surprise spider and started forward again, right into her.

"There it is again. Something's here. I can feel it." His body fell into a fighting stance.

"I don't see anything." The woman held her ground but pulled a small dagger from her vest pocket.

"Oh my God. You can't see me." Realization flooded, and she emptied her pockets of wadded flower petals. Finally, materializing into view, Mason's expression shifted from ready-to-attack, to confusion, to surprise.

"Ashton?" He held out a hand, as if he needed to touch her, attest she was real.

"It's me." She leaned into him, not wishing to scare him, just needing him. His hands pulled her tight, his breathing staggered in her ear. They held each other, and Ashton inhaled his familiar scent, letting all her fears fall away. She cried for her parents and her confusion over everything real and unknowing. She cried, relieved to have her best friend back.

"Are you okay?" He pulled back to see her face. "Did he hurt you?"

"No. But he took me to an awful place, a barren land he created. He wants my gifts to help fortify his own realm. It took some time, but I figured out another gift to get back."

He raised an eyebrow, silently waiting for her to share. It was unlike him to be so quiet, but she inhaled a breath for momentum. "I pulled myself through to Althaia's tree with a reflection."

"You did it yourself?"

"Yes. It wasn't easy, but I'm relieved to see you." Her exhaustion wasn't only mental. He must have sensed it because he pulled her over to a small plaid sofa.

A soft voice came from behind. "Do you remember me?"

Ashton's lips parted when she saw her. Not because she was surprised, she'd already figured the woman to be Mason's mom. It was more the surreal sense that Mia stood there, next to her son who had grieved miserably over her death. Ashton struggled with words, unsure if she should hug her or attack. Mason hadn't been able to sleep well since he was five…because of her death. Yet there she stood.

"Ash, it's my mom. She's alive." Interpreting his tone was tricky, but maybe because he was just as confused.

"I do remember you. I'm sorry. It's just such a

shock." She worked to stay neutral.

Mia smiled. "It is for all of us. I can explain. It's just a lot to take in at once. I'll make something to eat and let you two catch up. How does that sound?" They both nodded.

"So new gifts?" He took her hand. "You can make yourself invisible now?"

She huffed out a breathy laugh, but there was no joy behind it. "It was the flowers." She glanced over at the scattered purple petals. Then, her gaze found his again, and she couldn't help blurting, "My parents—they're dead."

Mason didn't blink. He seemed to know already, or he was waiting for confirmation. "I'm sorry, Ash."

"Everything's out of control."

"I know. That's why I need to get you back to Toria."

"I guess that's our only home now?" She raised an eyebrow to Mason, but his gaze dropped to his lap. She leaned back and closed her eyes, picturing the beautiful city that provided every physical need imaginable, yet how un-home-like it felt. Mason hadn't mentioned getting back to his human life since they'd started their shifts at the seam. Fighting demons must surely be in their blood. But could it replace what she once had? Could it really become her home?

They sat together in silence. Ashton had lots to say, to ask, to figure out, but words wouldn't come. Mason would want the details of her escape. But somehow, grief won out. He leaned in next to her, and his presence alone comforted. After a while, thoughts began to form. It was time to check on Mason. Time to take care of him again. She could do that.

"Your mom." She sat up straighter. "Tell me about

her."

As if on cue, Mia returned carrying a tray of sandwiches, grapes, and glasses of what looked to be iced tea. "I know it's hard to understand, but I went into hiding to keep Mason and Max safe."

"We haven't really discussed the details," Mason said, flatly.

"The one important detail would be that I am a seam keeper who left to live in the Human Realm. But demons found me, and it became impossible to hide my battles. After a while, I knew I had to disappear. I couldn't take Mason with me *and* protect him. I thought he would be safer growing up unaware of this part of his life. Ashton, I didn't realize you were who you were until it was too late. I had already faked my death." Her sad eyes looked like Mason's.

"What about Max?" She nudged Mason with her elbow. Why was he being so quiet? "Does he know you're alive?"

Mia looked at Mason before answering, the awkward silence evident. "He doesn't know. And no, we don't know where he is, but—" She stopped as Mason turned his glare toward her, as if there was more, and he didn't want her to share. His mom sipped her drink to escape the silent attack.

Ashton glanced between the two of them. "But he knows demons exist, right? That's why he wrote the books?"

"Right," Mason said, still watching his mom.

"I didn't see him the night...the night of the f-fire." Ashton choked out the words.

Mason wrapped his arm around her.

Mia moved to sit on her other side. "Ashton, I'm sorry about your parents."

"Thank you." She swallowed tears. "I'm so confused. At first, I thought Ian set the fire, but I think maybe he was trying to save my parents—"

"Save them?" Mason jumped to his feet. "He killed them."

"He said he was protecting me from other demons." She stood to settle him but also to gather her thoughts. "Well, he does need my gifts to build his secret realm. But either way, we can't judge him because of his father."

Mason crumpled at her last comment but recovered quickly. "We aren't judging him because of who his father is. We're judging him because of who he is."

"And you know for sure he killed my parents?" Why was she standing against him? She wanted someone to blame for her parents' death, but she needed to know it was the right someone. Ian had ruined that possibility when he placed doubt in her mind.

Mia interceded. "I think *blame* isn't the real issue here."

"Mom." Mason's voice held warning. Ashton's eyes flickered between them.

Mia looked to Mason. "I thought the plan was to get Ashton back to the seam?"

"You mean get both of us back to the seam."

"No, Ash, we mean you. I'm not going back." He marched into the kitchen.

"What's he talking about?" Ashton's voice, barely a whisper, as she processed what she'd heard. She started after him when Mia reached for her.

"He's gone through a lot since you've been separated. Give him time, and he will tell you." She disappeared toward her bedroom.

Ashton huffed a breath and entered the kitchen. Mason leaned against the sink, arms crossed, eyes weighed with more secrets. She was surprised he spoke first.

"I'm not the person you—or I—thought I was." He paused, but Ashton thought better about interrupting. "Max isn't my father. Ian is."

"What?" So much for not interrupting. "What are you talking about?"

He pushed off the counter into his crazy pacing. "I'm talking about the dad I always *thought* was my dad *isn't* my dad. I'm talking about that demon spawn, Ian, being my father." He ranted, right brow twitching, fists tightening at his sides, and stopped to glare. "Yeah, the very one you thought you liked in a very un-fatherly-type way."

Ashton shook off his tone. It wasn't directed at her. This was Mason upset. Pain marked his face, yet a new realization slapped her just as hard…disgust. Suddenly, she felt dirty and ashamed. Her hands twisted into her hair, pulling and clawing as if she were clinging to a rope off the side of a boat.

Her mind pictured Ian from her memories. The boy from Hicks's party, the one standing outside the beach house with lattes, kissing her, claiming he loved her, nothing like a fatherly figure. "I'm so stupid. I'm so sorry."

"This isn't your fault." He closed the gap between them. "But it does change things."

Ashton dropped her chin. "I don't want it to change *us*."

She looked into his eyes, feeling a tinge of warmth, a touch of home. "We can figure this out, Mas. We always do."

"We've never had to figure out anything this serious before."

"But it's possible. We just need to get back ho—" She stopped, rephrased her words. "I mean, back to Toria. *I* can get us there, and we can talk to Rory and Shunnar."

"I can't go back. I don't belong."

"Of course you do. We're paired together."

"By mistake! They figured out who I am. That's why Shunnar was watching me." He slumped into a kitchen chair.

"If they knew, then why train you? Why let you join the cast? It must be possible."

"What's possible? That I could fight for their side as a…half demon? Do you really believe they can trust me? I already turned on Adam."

"Mason, *I* trust you." She stood in front of him, hands rubbing his shoulders, like she always did when he needed her. But was it enough this time? "I can't lose you."

His eyes met hers. "You aren't losing me. But I don't see how I can fly with the cast now. I'm going to stay here with my mom. I need to find Max."

She could tell it was difficult for him to call his dad by name. Her stomach flip-flopped. How could Ian be his real father? But then she remembered Althaia telling her he could look any age to anyone.

Mia turned the corner just then, pulling their attention. "She's right, Mason. You can't break from her now. You've been paired, and it would ruin you both."

"Mom, you know why it won't work," he argued, but Mia held up her hand.

"No. What *won't* work are you two severed. Didn't

you feel the frenzy in your soul to find her when she was lost, to fight until you found her again?"

"Yes, but that's because she's been my best friend since I was five. I didn't want anything bad to happen to her."

"I felt it too," Ashton said quietly, as if figuring it out for herself. She *had* felt an incredible need to get back to him. It's what drove her to try transporting to him instead of an actual place. She had thought it was their deeply connected friendship. Maybe it was more.

"You felt the same thing I felt. *Us*. It's always been us. Of course, we wanted to make sure each other was okay. Mom!" He turned his glare on her. "I already tried to kill one of my cast. I attacked him for no reason. I heard voices, *Ian's* voice, in my head, telling me I should claim who I am. Don't you see? Shunnar didn't trust me from the beginning. He's been watching me all along." Mason stormed to the front room window.

Ashton followed behind. The sky was dark, the bright moon casting an amber glow across the tips of evergreens. It had taken her most of the day to get to him, and she was tired, but the survival side of her, seam keeper and human both, would never give up this fight.

Mia interjected, "It's because they found my journal. They have suspected I was alive for a while now."

"You knew?" Ashton asked, somehow surprised.

"Of course, I knew. I've made it my job to keep the Dark *and* the Light off my back."

"But why?" Mason turned to face her.

Ashton was taken aback at how much they looked alike. The same coloring, the same caramel eyes, the same wrinkle in their foreheads when they worried.

"Don't you see? I abandoned my duty at the seam. I bore a child of the enemy. I can't go back to either side. Anyway, I couldn't live with myself if Ian got to you, Mason."

"Exactly why I can't go back. It only makes sense I stay here, hidden from both worlds."

"You don't get it, do you?" His mother cupped his face with her hands. "It wouldn't work. You can't be away from Ashton, without driving yourself crazy to get back to her. You'd be a danger to yourself and me. Ian would be able to find us both for sure."

"He already found me there," Mason countered.

"He found you, but he can't get to you. Not in the Spiritual Realm. You're safe there."

"That's where you're wrong." Mason's voice filled the tiny room. "He can get to me, if not through haunted voices tempting me to hurt my cast, then through her."

Mia's jaw dropped in surprise.

"He pulled her through a dream-like experience. She was with me at training one minute, and the next she woke up with him at the beach house. Well, her mind did, anyway. Her body passed out at training camp. If he can get to her, he can get to me."

Ashton butted in. "It was all very confusing. He had been charming and kind, and he wanted me to go with him. But I wouldn't. Somehow, deep inside I *knew* I couldn't go. My *memories* stopped him."

Mia smiled, knowingly. "And how did you escape?"

Ashton realized what she meant. "It was Mason." She smiled at him. "She's right. It was you. My mind generated memories of you, and my heart was filled

334

with love. For you. Mason, I love you."

"Can't you see it's because of our history? We do love each other." He paused, swallowing the words he was maybe going to say. "I've *always* loved you. That'll never change."

Why was he being so stubborn? "It's different for me now. But I get that you're not ready yet."

"Yet?" Mason coughed out a breath. "We have no choice in the matter. You're just accepting everything. So what? You're just waiting for me to cave?"

"Mason!" Mia seemed startled by his sudden cruelty.

Ashton's head spun. "That's not what I meant. I understand you need time to figure things out on your own."

"Mason, you love her already. What's the difficulty admitting the reality of it? It's an honor to serve the seam this way. I thought you realized that."

"An honor *I* should respect, but not you? I don't see you high-tailing it back there." Ashton could only remember Mason this angry with his dad, and it never ended well.

"Stop it, Mason," Mia warned. "Chase is dead. Ashton's still here."

All three of them froze, chins dropped. Finally, Mason shook his head, his mouth shaping words he didn't know how to say.

"I'm sorry, but I did my job for the seam. I did what I could to protect her. I'm still protecting her." He faced Ashton. "How do we get back?"

"I don't need your protection anymore. And I won't tell you anything unless you promise to go back with me." She crossed her arms.

"Then we'll go to Seattle. I know where there's a

portal." He stood up. "I'm taking a shower and going to bed. We leave in the morning." He left the room without another word.

Ashton watched him go. Mia tried comforting her with words she couldn't hear and touches she couldn't feel. She wasn't about to go anywhere without Mason. She could channel her own determination against him.

Just like old times.

Chapter 31

Return To Disappear

Mason woke as dawn broke, his body feeling unusually rested. He guessed getting more than a few consecutive hours of sleep was the secret. Only his heart dragged now, regardless of his alert state. No matter how he felt inside, he had to get Ashton to the Spiritual Realm...and walk away. He wasn't about to live where he wasn't trusted.

Maybe the time away would give him an opportunity to reconnect with his mom and to find Max. He may not have been father of the year in any realm, but when compared to the father from Hell, literally, Max surely won by a long shot. Time to mend old wounds.

He found his mom making breakfast in the kitchen, where a familiar scent drew him to the percolating coffee maker. It had been a while. He poured himself a cup, inhaling the caffeine-rich steam.

"Morning. Ashton is still asleep. She had a rough night." She motioned him to the table. "I got her to talk about her parents. To grieve."

"What's going to happen? There'll be a funeral. Won't people wonder where she is?" He slumped in his chair. "It isn't right. Her parents took care of me like their own. They didn't deserve this. And where's Dad?" He met her eyes with conviction. "Yeah, Max, my *dad*.

Where do you think he is?"

Her lips curved, and she blinked hard. Had he grown up with her, maybe he would've recognized her expression.

"I'm not sure where your dad is, yet. As for Ashton, Rory will oversee everything. I'm betting Bethesda is still present in the realm, and she heals in miraculous ways. Truths become distorted for human families and friends when the Centennial transitions back to the Spiritual Realm. They will remember her, but not focus on her. The healers manage the façade, and it's lasting. But I'm sure Rory will allow Ashton to say goodbye in her own way."

"That seems almost worse." Mason wondered how Ashton would grieve all alone.

"Ashton understands the people connected to her need this to move on."

"Did you know Rory when you were a keeper?" Mason sipped his coffee, hoping to sooth his nerves. His railroad of emotions could use a break. Maybe his mom had contacts in the pharmaceutical world who could prescribe anxiety medicine. Or maybe there was a stone for that. Ashton had always been the worrier, not him. These new feelings made the hairs on his arms stand up. If he had felt them before, he'd been too hyper to notice.

"Rory is younger, but as you know, we age slower once turning eighteen. She had just come to Toria with Shunnar when Chase…when I left. We worked together briefly before it all fell apart. Before—"

His mom stopped short, then shook it off. "Many seam keeper kids grow up in Valley, just south of Toria. A beautiful place. I would love for you to see it one day."

Mason stood to refill his coffee. He hadn't missed the hint of joy on his mom's face. If this place, Valley, made her smile like that, then it must be worth seeing, for Ashton anyway.

Soft rustlings drew their attention as Ashton appeared around the corner. She was unnaturally quiet during breakfast. The only words she muttered, as she picked at her food, was agreeing to take them back to the Spiritual Realm. The bonus for Mason, she hadn't asked him about staying. His mom was right. It must have been a hard night.

"You just need a reflection?" his mom asked Ashton after the breakfast dishes were washed and they all stood ready to go.

"Yes." Ashton walked to a hanging mirror. Mason followed.

"I've never taken anybody with me before. But I feel like it should work the same." She looked to his mom, who wasn't looking satisfied with her declaration. "What is it?"

"Well, I don't know how strong you are. I mean, you *should* be able to transport Mason with you, but without proper training, I'm not sure how well it will work. We don't have time to experiment. He could end up somewhere else, or you could. It's unpredictable." Mia hesitated. "I can help you."

She rummaged through drawers in the kitchen and rifled through the hallway closet. She walked back and forth from her room multiple times. Was she stalling? Mason imagined returning to the one place she'd successfully hidden from for eighteen years would be unsettling. Finally, she led them outside and away from the cabin.

It was still early, the forest gleaming with a foggy

layer of dew. They walked without speaking, Mason's heart heavy with his decision not to stay in Toria and the scene that would arise when Ashton realized the truth.

His mom stopped several times before deciding on a location. Then she pulled stones from her pockets, sorting through a variety. Mason remembered his house full of them when he was a boy. She had hidden them in his pockets, in his bed, and in the bottom of his toy box. What had she said before, that they warded detection from both sides? Some were shiny and colorful, while others were dull. But now, they were more than just rocks, some were blessed from the Spiritual Realm, while others were riddled with Dark Realm magic. Maybe both.

"All right, I think this will do," she announced, as if they understood her dilemma.

Mason looked over at Ashton, still withdrawn, which was typical back home around groups, but never with him. He needed to get her to Toria and help her find peace in her only home now. He had no idea how to talk her into staying there without him. How would he even live on his own without her? But they'd have endured it for college had none of this mess began.

He squeezed the bridge of his nose, the stress forming like a ball behind his forehead. Maybe they could visit if their parting became unbearable. He'd never needed Max like he felt he needed him now, desperate for the fatherly advice he'd never received.

The truth crashed down like heavy rain. Had he been destined to be alone all along? Ashton had been there for him growing up, but really, with a demon father and rogue mother, what did he expect? He groaned in frustration.

"Are you okay?" Ashton touched his arm.

"I'm fine." He turned to his mom. "What now?"

She stared at him questioningly.

"What's next?" He didn't want Ashton realizing he still planned to leave her.

His mom huffed. "Ashton, put a hand on Mason. I will stand on his other side and use your energy with this stone." It was bright red with tiny blue-gray veins. He remembered it from childhood, tracing tiny mazes in the faint designs and making up stories about where they led.

"Wait!" Suddenly fearing her use of Dark magic. "Outside of his realm, will Ian sense us using Dar—this energy?"

"It's okay." She nodded. "It's crimson culprite, only blessed, and brings transformation, spiritual in this realm but physical in the Spiritual Realm. It will enhance Ashton's natural gift."

Mason exhaled and took in Ashton's hopeful eyes, so blue he wanted to swim in them, to break the surface and find them both back at their neighborhood pool, silly and young and free. But that life was over. With heavy eyelids, he nodded back in agreement.

They clasped hands, as instructed. His mom closed her eyes, with the red stone in her palm. Ashton stared intently at a dewdrop on the low branch in front of them. Mason held his breath.

Swiftly, as if he hadn't anticipated it could happen, he felt his body liquefy, then solidify through cobwebs. Pressure closed in on all sides, and he gripped the hands he held tighter. His stomach turned over, then settled again. And it was over. Before he could swipe away imaginary silk strands, he opened his eyes to a green, park-like setting, Toria. He recognized the soft blue sky and inhaled the crisp, pure air. The tiny village they now called home sat just down the hill. Ashton's home, anyway. He stepped back, taking in another fresh breath. It was pure oxygen, filling him like he'd held his breath for too long.

"Everybody good?" he asked them both, but his eyes were on Ashton.

Ashton nodded, then smiled.

It was the gift he needed. Or curse. He was going to miss her. The past few days had been miserable when he couldn't find her. He only hoped the feelings would be less severe knowing she was safe in Toria.

"Let's go." Mason started down the short trail toward town.

"I'm going to slip back to the portal." His mom took steps in the opposite direction.

"No," Ashton said. "We just found you. I'm sure the council will understand why you left."

Mason said nothing. He knew she wouldn't stay; he wasn't staying himself. Their family didn't belong there.

"This isn't my home now. I'm better on my own." His mom looked to Mason, who tilted his head in question. What was she getting at? He hadn't actually asked to stay with her.

Ashton took her hands. "Mia, please stay. I know it would be easier for Mason."

"Yes, Mia, please stay." A female voice carried from behind. A woman Mason had never seen before stepped out of the trees. She was beautiful, wearing a wrapped garment of green and gold.

"Althaia," Ashton gasped.

Mason looked to his mom, but her wide eyes stared at the woman. Althaia stared back with familiar sorrow.

They knew each other.

"She's yours." His mom spoke softly. "I didn't know."

"Yes. But yours too. Don't you remember our plans?" Althaia walked straight to her.

Tears filled his mom's eyes. "Our plans were destroyed the night Chase died."

"Untrue." Althaia cupped her face, kissing each falling drop away. "My friend, how did you survive your mourning all alone? I searched for you."

"I don't belong here anymore. I've made choices that exclude me from this life. I did so because I grieved, but I committed them, nonetheless. I have no life here, Thaia." His mom didn't fight against Althaia's grip and instead fell into her shoulder and wept.

"You are forgiven. You know how this works. How could you lose faith?" Althaia cried.

Mason's head filled with selfish concerns. What if his mom returned to the Spiritual Realm? Where would that leave him? He would never seek out Ian, never accept his Dark side. And he wouldn't put Max in danger either. He already knew the answer to his own miserable question: he'd end up alone.

But wasn't that where evil deserved to dwell?

Ashton grabbed his hand, pulled him away, shattering the disheartening monologue in his head. "Your face?"

"What?" He shook off his torment.

"I've never seen your face so wrinkled with worry. Tell me what you're thinking? What's *really* going on?"

He thought fast. "It's a pretty emotional scene back there, don't you think?"

Ashton looked behind to the heartbreaking reunion.

"I don't know whether to be happy or sad for them."
Her eyes, now icy, blinked back in his direction. "But
that's not what I'm talking about."

Busted.

He knew this Ashton. The one who wouldn't stop
pressuring him until he gave in. He didn't have time to
wait out the silent treatment. "I haven't changed my
mind. I'm not staying in Toria."

Ashton's shock and hurt released in a burst all at
once. She dropped his hands. "You have a job here.
We're a team."

"I'm not really one of you."

Tears welled in her eyes, almost melting the ice
he'd just seen. "What do you mean you're not one of
us? You shift into a hawk. We trained to be seam
keepers. Together."

He checked over his shoulder, but the two women
didn't seem to notice Ashton's rising shrills. "Look, my
father—" His voice caught unexpectedly. "My real
father is Satan's own spawn. I *can't* be here."
Verbalizing the reality caused his arms to chill, his legs
to go numb.

"Then why did the council bless us for this
destiny? Don't you think *they* knew?"

It didn't make sense to him, either. The council had
to have known, if the hierarchy he learned in training
meant anything. They were there to serve the angels,
who served God. Seam keepers weren't angelic
themselves, but their blessed strengths protected
humans from the evil they unknowingly created. Then
again, why were Shunnar and Rory watching him
secretly, as if no one else knew? His confusion only
made him angrier and itching to escape. He needed to
find Max. He *wanted* to find him for reasons he

couldn't explain.

"I don't know. That's what I need to find out." He slid down into the soft grass, so different from his rain-filled yard back home. The home that was never really his. "I can't figure out who I am here. They don't trust me. I think it was a mistake they blessed me. But you." He pulled her down next to him. "You have always been destined to be here. You were planned as the Centennial, and I am so proud of you."

"Stop talking like this. I just lost my family. I can't lose you, too." Her tears held.

He'd prayed for her strength that night by the cliff. Maybe it had worked. She escaped captivity from a place hidden from every realm. He had to believe she'd be okay.

"You're stronger than you think." He rubbed her shoulders this time, switching roles from a time when they were human, from a time not so long ago.

Ashton opened her mouth to respond, her glare pierced with conviction and rage. But before a word flew, the ground beneath them rumbled.

They jumped to their feet, his unsteady on the moving ground. The light above clouded to dusky gray, a contrast to its usual serenity. Mason gripped Ashton with one strong hand and shielded his eyes with the other. Dust swirled the oak, set just behind the place they'd traveled through with Ashton's gift. Panic gripped with sharp claws, but he squinted through the winds to his mom and Althaia. He made out their silhouettes in the dust, just as their darkened forms vanished.

Ashton pulled him toward the oak without hesitation, and he leaned into the force of the wind. She ripped her hand from his grasp and threw both arms into the spinning air. The angry debris revolving around them didn't just stop blowing. It formed into what looked like tiny pixels before shattering onto the ground, disappearing.

"How did you do that? Never mind." It had to be another gift. But she wasn't stopping to chat about it, and he raced to catch her at the portal. "Wait!"

"He took them," she growled, paying no attention to him. As if the icy change he'd caught in her expression only moments ago had in fact occurred, and she wasn't the same Ashton from graduation day. She just might be the braver version he'd hoped to convince her she was.

"I know, you're right. But I think we need a plan." He'd barely spoken the last word when a familiar presence pulsed from behind. He turned, unsurprised, to find Shunnar and Rory.

Chapter 32

Realizations

Ashton sat in a conference room next to Mason. Their cast was to the left, the Blessing Council to the right. Mason had whispered the names Nurzhen and Isleen, representatives from the two realms, but didn't know the other members' names. Gavan sat next to Shunnar and Rory, directly across them. Shunnar was speaking.

"Ian's powers breached our borders, possibly due to his connection through Mason."

Ashton glanced at Mason. Aside from his jaw clenching behind tight skin, he showed no emotion.

Shunnar continued. "Ashton informed us of Ian's goal to join their powers and fortify his secret realm. But taking Althaia and Mia? He could have easily taken Ashton, and for that matter, why not Mason?" He gestured to Mason, sorrow in his eyes.

Ashton interjected before Mason could say a word. "We were farther away from the portal. Maybe he can't come in that far."

"He shouldn't be able to enter at all," Gavan said without looking at her.

Suddenly all their attentions focused above. Soothing circles of illumination forced down the burdens of frustration. Azure blue filled the space, drawing all eyes to its brilliant glow. The angel

Sandalphon hovered, so tall, so massive in power. The room stilled for his blessings.

Ashton felt it like a downpour, as if she needed to duck, but held steady. Musical notes vibrated against her eardrums. Her mind didn't have to work at interpreting the message. The melody filtered through any misunderstanding. Soon, the room filled with silent tones, and her lungs sailed with every breath. Rhythm flowed through her veins like rivers rushing to sea, then crashed to a halt. The melody ceased as quickly as it had begun, light retracted from the space, leaving a soft residual glow on the ceiling. It was the only physical evidence of the angelic blessing received.

Ashton didn't know if the angel's message was identical for everyone, but for her, she felt empowered, protected, and enlightened in her drive to fight for what was right and good.

Nurzhen, head of the Spiritual Realm, stood to address them. He wore authority with his white robes. "How this has occurred matters not. It is time for Mia to come home. The cast will retrieve both Althaia and Mia together. We are blessed and will carry out this feat. Gavan shall lead."

Gavan sat unmoved at the table—his facial expressions as intense as the last time Ashton had seen him. His eyes bored into hers, sending a chill down her arms. Was it the situation, or something more personal? Finally, he rubbed his jaw and stood.

"Thank you for your blessings, Council." He bowed his head to Nurzhen, then spoke directly to Shunnar. "Ready our cast. We leave in an hour."

"Do we have a location?" Shunnar stood.

Mason and Ashton rang out in unison. "I know where he is."

Ashton nodded for Mason to speak first. "I know where he is because my mom and I went there looking for Ashton before she found us."

The group remained silent. Mason nodded for Ashton to share her part.

"I don't know how I got to Ian's hiding place, but I left by way of my tears. I'd been crying over the loss of my parents." She dropped her gaze, a slight moment of weakness, yet pushed on. "They were tinged violet, which reminded me of the light Althaia pulled me through from the beach house. I don't know how I thought I could do it; I just knew." She shrugged at Mason. He reached under the table, clasped her hand. She felt the strength in it, but this time her confidence was already simmering. "I think I can get back the same way."

"We could follow with a back-up team. My mom showed me the entrance," Mason added.

Shunnar cut in. "The entrance to the warehouse?"

"No. He found a glitch. My mom called it a hidden pocket *between* realms. The entrance is due east, an hour's walk through the woods behind her house. I can find it again." He hesitated. "But…we will need some of her stones to help us."

Gavan shook his head at Mason. "This is precisely why we can't trust you. You have been tainted by evil, spawned by the Devil himself, and now you want to bring Dark practices into the Spiritual Realm?" He stepped back from the table, growing in bulk. "Goodness has overcome evil for thousands of years. We don't need your magic stones."

Mason shot up in challenge. The table of onlookers stood too, followed by an eerie silence. Everyone's unspoken thoughts froze in the thick of anticipation.

Ashton knew Mason's impulsiveness, and her heart pounded, fearing the outcome.

"Mason, look at me." She tried pulling his chin toward her, but his eyes remained glued to Gavan's.

"Ashton's safety is of the upmost importance. She isn't going. We've been doing this a long time. We will fight Ian without help from either of you." Gavan turned toward Shunnar, repeating his earlier command. "Now, ready my cast."

"No." Ashton shouldered herself in front of Mason, who she usually hid behind. Not this time. Her blood burned, perhaps the angelic blessing? Maybe the clicking that had begun in her head? It didn't matter. Her gift of *knowing what to do* seeped from her mind, even before she understood it herself.

She met Gavan's icy stare. "None of this is Mason's fault. The Blessing Council must know that, if they are all powerful."

She looked to the robed leaders. "Tell him, *please*. Tell him he was chosen, that he was destined to be here *with* me. Why else would you train him early, trust him to protect me all those days before my birthday? Hasn't he done everything you've asked?" She turned her attention to him. "Mason, you are my paired partner. We are *both* seam keepers, and we'll fight together." She returned her glare to Gavan, unafraid of his piercing stare. "Those are our mothers. Mason and I are going."

Mason found his voice, anger seething. "I'll fight with Ashton. I don't need your approval. After that, you won't need to worry about me. I'll leave the seam for good."

"No!" Ashton didn't care how hysterical she sounded.

Finally, Isleen of the Dream Realm, raised a hand, demanding silence. She moved slowly around the table to Mason, her glowing aura trailing behind her indigo gown. Her black hair flowed like ripples in water at night. When the table settled for her to speak, Gavan and Mason were the last to sit.

"You question our faith in you, Mason Gabriel. Did Lucifer himself not begin on the side of good with our Almighty? Do you not believe his sons would be formed of the same light? He, of good Light, paired with Mia, of the Spiritual Realm, would only create a son of good faith."

Ashton could see the wheels turning in Mason's head, his right eyebrow twitching, but his chest, unmoving. He wasn't remembering to breathe. She moved her fingers behind his neck, gently squeezed, pushing into the hidden worry. "Mas, it makes sense."

She needed him to understand. Finding Mia and Althaia was their primary concern. She also needed to finish things with Ian, put an end to his torment. But more than that, she needed Mason to stay. Her heart, no matter how torn with grief and anger, would never fully heal without him. They were destined. Maybe that's why she'd lingered in his shadow for so long. Maybe that's why she couldn't see her future without him, even when she was only human.

"Do you see now, Mason? You have a choice, just as we all do," Rory added, and Ashton sent her a look she hoped carried appreciation.

Mason was speechless.

"I mean no disrespect to the council," Gavan interjected, popping the moment with a pin.

"I am aware of your mistrust, my Gavan." Isleen spoke gently, placing her hand on Mason's shoulder.

351

"Though Mason paired with Ashton not so long ago, do not mistake God's timing. You need not fear for Ashton's safety. She may be your daughter, but she is the realm's Centennial."

"What?" Ashton felt the shock like a blow to her stomach and bolted out of the chair. "*You're* my *birth* father?"

Gavan winced. "I understand her fate, but she is young and only *just* trained. As I do have faith in above, I am only suggesting we take a seasoned cast to fight the demon prince."

"Wait a minute! If you are my father, then you're the man who left Althaia. Because of me." She gripped the edge of the table with both hands. Mason stood up, his hand on her back.

"My decisions are not your concern. I can explain my part after the mission. But all is futile if you're taken to the Dark Realm. And putting your trust in Mason is unpredictable for us all."

"He's right about me being unpredictable." Mason's voice was barely audible. "When Ian called to my thoughts, I attacked Adam."

Ashton knew, even though Adam had forgiven him, he hadn't forgiven himself.

"Mason, we're good—" Adam broke in, but was interrupted by a higher power.

Nurzhen's melodious voice rang. "Cillian is clever, Mason. Just as Ashton has learned he has no power over her, you must learn you have equal power against him. He can tempt you, but he can't decide *for* you. You were raised in the Light, as his father was. It is by choice one retreats to the Dark. *Choice*, Mason. We all abide by free will, including you." The healing of his insight spilled through the room as he moved behind

Mason.

Skipping over Gavan, Ashton regarded the entirety of the room, meeting hopeful expressions along the way to Mason's tear-filled eyes. He said nothing, and she knew he didn't want to lose it in front of his cast. She ran her grip along his neck, roughly digging in to ground him. He needed that, and she would give it to him regardless of the shock coursing through her veins. He didn't have to be the strong one all the time.

Nurzhen touched Mason's head with both hands, whispering a blessing inaudible to the surrounding audience.

Gavan exhaled a heavy breath toward Ashton. "How would you presume to stop Ian?"

"I've found my gifts, or at least enough of them for this mission. I don't know how to articulate it, but my mind clicks into place when I need it." She left out the part where it didn't always work on command. "You'll have to trust me on that part. I have invisibility with a kind of purple flower. I know where to find them. And I *think* I can pull others through reflections with me. My mind can open locks, and—" She stopped, refusing to sound desperate to prove herself. "I stopped Ian's whirlwind with my hands, my mind. My own strength. I have completed my training as a seam keeper. I am trusted to fight demons in the Dream Realm. If I am the Centennial, then why shouldn't I be included?"

"It's not only about you or your gifts. Ian found his way *in*—here to our realm. That's never happened before, and it must be due to his connection with Mason. We can't overlook that detail, regardless of free will." Gavan glanced exhaustedly at Mason.

"All the more reason to stop him." Mason turned, took both Ashton's hands, ignoring the crowd of

353

onlookers. "I'm choosing the side of good—here in the Spiritual Realm. I choose you, Ashton. You're strong and I believe in you. You've fought Ian all along. We know where he is, so let's end this. Together."

Ashton glanced across the table to Bronwyn and Hannah. They were smiling. She saw Nigel and Adam nodding. The rest of their cast...their friends, standing tall in support.

She blinked back to Mason.

The fire in his eyes burned into hers, and she felt his energy run through his fingertips. She wasn't sure if it was Nurzhen's private blessing, the truth finally revealed, or the challenge of proving Gavan wrong. But Mason's determination was medicinal, and she drank it down.

****

The buzz of the impending mission weighed on everyone, emotions sizzling like static. For Mason, releasing the fear of his evil heritage was a coup. He had no idea how much he wanted to live in the Spiritual Realm, or the deep pride he'd felt in becoming a seam keeper, until he'd almost lost it.

His mom had been right. He wasn't a demon because of who his father was. He only had to keep a strong will and not claim it. Could it be that simple?

For now, he buried any thoughts of the place he'd call home because battling Ian had him panicked for another reason altogether. He believed in Ashton and knew she almost believed in herself. As he finalized his weapons in the armory, it hit him. He had to share *exactly* how he felt. So when he heard Ashton come into the gear room, he took it as divine intervention. Time to be the man he was destined to be.

"Hey," he whispered, closing the door.

"What is it?"

Mason flipped the light off. He needed complete privacy, and with fingers to his lips, he walked her backward into the darkness. The only light glowed from an artillery locker in the back of the room.

"Ash." Mason's voice reached through the quiet dark. He wrapped his arms around her waist, afraid she might fall away. She stared up at him, biting her lip. She wasn't afraid, Mason knew that. It was fear of the unknown, the invisible monster they had been fighting for some time. Their connection undefined.

He didn't want to ruin their friendship. He only needed it to be honest. She was worth that. He stared into her eyes, drowning in the blue of them. It didn't matter that he was *supposed* to be paired with her, forever there to serve. If that be true, let this be his first genuine act of service: to love her for all she was because he *wanted* to. Because he *chose* to. Because he had *always* loved her, for her, before their lives were turned upside down.

He loved her as his best friend, clumsily falling out of trees, a scaredy-cat afraid to be social, but always there for him. He loved her nurturing ways, because he needed lots of it, especially in the absence of his mom. Ashton Magnolia Nichols...lovely and soft like she always felt, even if he noticed it differently growing up. She was beautiful. Didn't she wonder why he always needed her to play the *best friend card* when other girls got too close? Maybe he didn't understand it then, but no one ever compared to her, to the comfortable her that she was, the Ash who knew everything about him and still believed in him. She'd fought for him even when others feared his connection to evil. Even when he didn't trust himself.

Finally, his voice soft. "I *more* than always love you, Ash. You're my everyone and my only." Moving his hands up her arms, he gripped her shoulders, pulled her close, their faces mere inches apart. He wanted to kiss her with every nerve in his body. He could risk being vulnerable with *his* heart, but *she* had to choose him back. He took in a breath, unsure it might be his last, and waited.

"Mason." She exhaled, reaching the distance between their lips. She moved her hands behind his neck, gripped the collar of his vest to pull him even closer, and kissed him.

Her heart thrummed against his chest. The rhythmic beat like a song he always hummed but couldn't place until now. He knew she felt it too, when her wall of uncertainty tumbled away. When she squeezed him tighter, kissed him stronger. Somehow, pressed together as one, he wondered how he'd ever breathed without her.

"Ash, say it." He pulled back and held her face with both hands, soft and secure. She dropped her eyelids, but the smile on her lips was full of knowing. He couldn't help joining in her realization that together they were more than the best friends they'd grown up to be. They were more than Mason's typical flings he'd dabbled with at school. And they were more than seam keepers destined together.

They were each a half of one heart, one soul, one life...

"I choose us too, Mason. I've always loved you. And—"

Mason consumed her words in his kiss, discarding every ounce of frustration and fear filling him these last weeks. He found inexpressible joy lingering at every resting place on her lips. He searched her soul in that kiss, his thumbs swirling gentle circles at her jawline, until finally he drew back…curious.

"And?" He gleamed down at her bright eyes, her flushed cheeks.

Ashton exhaled a breathy laugh. "And, well, technically you *are* mine. My seam keeper *and* human side have *always* known that."

He narrowed his eyes, carefully slipping his right ankle out and around her left one, in a sweeping motion only too quick, she was on the ground beneath him.

She read his intentions and braced herself. "No tickles, Mas—"

"I know." He brushed long wisps of hair away from her face. "We have a demon to stop. We have our mothers to bring home." He wasn't fooling around anymore, but for the first time in a while, he felt a hint of his old self settling back where it belonged. "Are you up for this, Ash?"

She tilted her head, as if considering his question. He knew it wouldn't be easy for her. He wanted to give her the space to answer honestly but hoped she already knew she held the power.

She was the Centennial.

Her responsive nod was all he needed, and before pulling her up to join their cast, to claim the man he knew he was, he kissed the keeper he was honored to be paired with.

Chapter 33

Angry Oak

Ashton perched with Mason at the edge of nothingness, in Ian's pocket between realms. Their cast had headed to the portal outside Mia's cabin when she realized she could only bring one person through a reflection at a time. Rory promised to work with her once they had Althaia and Mia safely back and things returned to normal.

Normal. There wasn't anything normal about her life, let alone the colorless terrain surrounding her. The trees with their bland branches, drained of any pigment, perfectly matched her heart. She felt joy because of Mason, sadness from the loss of her parents, courage in her seam keeper confidence, yet fear her human soul was slowly slipping away…and there was no color for that.

"We can do this, Ash." Mason's encouragement was typical. Only this time, he was holding her hand, pulling her close. It felt like they'd been together their entire lives, without ever knowing the power they truly held.

She stood taller.

Mason's voice whispered on. "We *will* end Ian's connection to the both of us and avenge our parents at the same time." His lips touched the soft spot under her ear as he spoke.

Just then, movement from behind startled their intimate moment. Hushed wisps of air trying to disturb the listless place raised alarm, until she realized it was their cast. She glanced at Mason's proud smile. Their mates walked toward them wearing pride like honor badges, Nigel and Bronwyn, Adam and Hannah, with the rest just behind. Of course, Shunnar and Rory led the way. Gavan accompanied them, but Ashton ignored him.

"Unbelievable," Gavan muttered to no one in particular. Ashton assumed he was referring to Ian's hidden estate, or possibly that Mason's directions actually worked to lead them through the swampy portal outside his mom's cabin.

"Look at this place." Rory shook her head, taking in the grim scenery.

Ashton had stared for hours at the dull-edged view while imprisoned inside the castle-like house. The trees were undead, yet still not thriving. The ground traceless, the air soundless, the sense of stillness thick, holding every ounce of eerie a place could hold.

"It's unnerving," Bronwyn said, daring to touch a branch. "Whatever light it's seeking won't be found here."

Gavan noticeably avoided Mason, but Ashton caught him glimpsing at her. As the others took in the surroundings, preparing to advance, he moved next to her. "I need you to take it easy in there. Stand down if you can."

Ashton rolled her eyes. Gavan was supposed to be her birth father, head of casts, a leader in the Spiritual Realm. But he didn't believe in her, even when his entire realm chose her to be their Centennial. She stalked away, regretting any time spent wondering about her birth father. She was the Centennial whether he approved or not.

"There's his estate." Nigel pointed off in the distance. The group closed in, looking in the direction he indicated.

"Surely there must be some shields," Adam said, always thinking logistically.

"We only saw servants before. My mom had stones that hid our energy, and others that cut through glass and wooden doors," Mason said. He walked over to Ashton, noticing her edginess as Gavan retreated. She shook her head not to worry, and he squeezed her hand.

"Jasper, maybe azeztulite to cut through glass?" Rory speculated about the stones and then looked at Shunnar, who looked to Gavan, who only nodded, his face stern.

Shunnar spoke, yet Ashton knew they were Gavan's words. "The entire pocket *is* his shield. But Adam's right. It's much too quiet." He motioned for the groups to split up. But before anyone moved, thunder rumbled above them in a disturbingly unnatural way. The sound, like breaking glass, shattered across the sky, but sank as if the soundwaves had nothing to vibrate against.

Ashton's eyes flew up to find the colorless excuse for a sky tainted with ominous black splotches.

Demons.

Time stopped pressing and froze altogether. In slow motion, Mason's arm ripped Ashton down, his knee buckling her leg and rolling them both over, just escaping a monster dropping. No one screamed, though a few choice words flew as everyone dispersed.

Mason leapt to his feet, hovering protectively over Ashton as a knife flew from his right hand into the head of an oncoming demon. He glanced over wide-eyed, and she remembered him saying at training he hoped his seam keeper sense of aim held up because his human side would only have a few lucky shots.

There were hundreds of them, black with a sticky tar-like substance oozing over their hairless skin. Each was about the size of a small black bear, with no visible ears, but long snouts with vicious teeth protruding awkwardly. They looked like giant, angry moles burrowing through the clammy air.

Ashton saw Hannah across the knoll, Adam back to back with her. They had their weapons drawn and sliced through demons dropping like rain. Rory was fighting off a mass of beasts two-handedly, so Gavan and Shunnar could shift. Once in hawk form, their screeches just pierced the stale night before the thick atmosphere extinguished them. But it was enough to draw the attention of the bulk of demons. They must have had ears somewhere, because instantly they swarmed the two hawks.

Shunnar dipped for Rory to mount, but her size hadn't adjusted, slower in this pocket of Hell. Ashton swiped a throwing knife from Mason's vest and hurled it at two demon-moles approaching them. She missed, but the interference gave Rory the time she needed. Nigel and Adam took the gift of distraction to transition themselves.

Ashton backed against a tree, a violet light from her weapons belt illuminated. She unsheathed her amethyst-handled knife, the slender blade like an extension of her arm. Her seam keeper inside pushed out, and she was ready to fight. Crossing her right hand to her chest and down, she sliced lengthwise into the ribs of a monster snarling from behind the tree. Mason peered in her direction. They had only slain a few demons together, but she didn't think it would have surprised him. His look of pride was a gift, as she knew he intended. She had come far from that scared little human girl. They both had.

Grasping Mason's vest, she glared at her ichor-smeared blade, picturing the pink bedroom Ian had kept her. She envisioned Mason and herself together in the quiet space, behind the safety of the locked door. And even though Mason's body heaved with tension as he reached and lunged, fighting the monstrous beasts, she pulled them both through the mucky reflection before he could shift.

They crumbled to the floor in a heap, Mason swearing from the shock of it.

"Are you okay?" He gave her a quick head-to-toe check.

She nodded. "We're inside the house." But when she looked around at the messed bed, her nightgown still balled on the floor, it brought back a storm of emotions.

"I can't really kill him, right?" She gulped, though she already knew the answer.

Mason raised his eyebrow in question.

"I know we only banish them for a hundred years, but this feels different." She held a finger to her lips when he started to interrupt. "Don't worry, I want him gone as much as you do. I just have this strange feeling it's going to take a lot more of me. He isn't a demon creature like those monsters outside. He looks like a man, like Nigel or you. He gets in my head."

"Are you worried because of the feelings you used to have for him?"

She cringed, wishing he hadn't picked up on that.

"I'm worried about hurting someone who looks so human and who, in his own misguided way, claims he loves me, and…he's your father."

"He'll never be my father. And I'll be right behind you. You distract him, and I'll be happy to stab him in the heart," he said with a hefty dose of vengeance.

Just then, screams from outside seeped through the stone walls. Ashton pulled Mason along as she twisted the doorknob and headed for the staircase. More shouting rose from downstairs, so Mason pulled her back toward the only other door, the library. Rows of bookshelves lined the floor around every wall with several in between.

Mason traced his fingers along an empty table.

"What is it?"

"When we were searching for you, my dad—Max—his books were here on this table. The ones about demons, remember?"

Then, as if on cue, a small explosion jarred them from the floor below.

Mason pulled her to the back of the room. No sooner had they slipped out of sight, the library door burst open to angry voices. Mason motioned for her to stay silent, and she held her breath, her back pressed against a bookshelf.

Ashton didn't have a vantage point from their position but thought the first voice sounded familiar. And the second? She would have known that voice anywhere, Max Deed. She looked at Mason. His mouth dropped open. He was just as surprised. They were talking about Max's work. The first voice, a man, demanded he retreat to his room until things settled. Max argued about needing titles in the library to cross-reference his research.

"I don't care what's happening outside. This is the Dark prince's estate, am I right?" Max's voice gruffer than usual. "Control the situation and let me finish my work. A deal's a deal."

"A deal *is* a deal, Mr. Deed," the man's voice cut in.

Could it be Dominic, the one she had spied with Ian? She wasn't sure.

"I guarantee the contract will not be broken, but alas, we are under attack. The Master wants you protected in your quarters. This room is off limits without him."

"This room holds the information I need to revise my work. If you want me to publish anything remotely believable to the human world, then you're going to have to allow me to cross reference everything I've alluded to in my research. There is no room for error. And then, you will return my wife, son, and Ashton, alive and safe, as promised."

Ashton glanced at Mason. His face drained of color. What kind of deal had Max made with the Devil? The same dad Mason believed never cared.

Look what he'd risked!

She squeezed his hand, and he gripped hers back like a vise before letting out a slow breath. Their eyes met again, flecks of garnet glinting in his amber gaze. She loved him so much. More than she ever thought possible. Suddenly, she realized she was right where she was supposed to be. She would handle whatever was coming now, and even if it was too late for her family, she could bring Mason's back together.

He nodded, and she nodded back. Then he inched her along the shelf, away from the two voices, until they hit a spot that collapsed behind them. Anticipating a portal-hole in a shelving unit wasn't on her radar of possibilities—even in an unimaginable space between realms. Before she could react, the spot pulled them both away like a raging river.

The sensation of warm water rushed down Ashton's forehead, blurring her vision. She lost Mason's hand as she tumbled through the portal's sticky pull. A membrane-like web engulfed her feet, while her torso pushed to the side and back. Her body stretched and retracted while knocking sounds hissed in her ears until she dropped in a thud to the ground.

Opening her eyes, she knew instantly they weren't in Ian's realm anymore. Too much fresh air. Too many trees growing green.

Mason scrambled toward her. "Are you okay?"

"Creepy portal." Ashton shakily scanned the forest for demons. For Ian.

Mason pulled her up and moved them forward. He led her to a small cluster of birch trees, wound together with low brush. He pointed into the makeshift shelter. She plunged inside the bushes.

"Stay here. I'm going to shift to get a better view."

"Wait a minute. I can fight. I'm not hiding." Why was he protecting her? Hadn't he said himself she was strong enough?

"I know." He clasped her shoulder. "I'm just being cautious. We don't have our cast, and this could be a trap. Let me get better view from the air, so we can make a plan."

Make a plan? Where was the impulsive boy she'd grown up with? But she nodded as he turned, changing into a hawk midair. Not even a talon touched the ground before he was airborne. It was breathtaking. She'd never seen anything like it, and her pride in him soared.

A single feather drifted down, swirling in a moment of stopped time. As she bent to pluck the delicate plume of amber softness, a melody caught her ear.

With the feather pressed securely in her palm, Ashton scanned the area. A sense of déjà vu flooded her mind. She knew these woods.

Just then, the music strummed louder. Bells, flutes, and chimes enchanted her awareness to its intended message. It reminded her of the angel Sandalphon, but she sensed it differently. Listening with purpose now, the melody came from under her skin, coaxing her out of her hiding place, and away from the direction Mason had flown.

The melody rang louder, pulling her from the cover of trees. She sensed Althaia close—and in danger.

The song.

It was a message from Althaia. She felt her birth mother calling but couldn't decode the message, unsure why its entirety was scrambled. With hands on her weapon's belt, she felt the jade dagger warm against her leg. Unsheathing its trapped glint of green, she traipsed along the natural path toward the oak, her feet in tempo with the music.

"Oh my God!" Ashton rushed to the alarming scene before her.

No wonder her song had been jostled. Althaia's body was strung up, suspended, and imprisoned by the same oak she'd called home. Something meant to be beautiful, a portal between worlds, gripped her birth mother by the scalp. Her eyes were crescent moons shadowed along the delicate place above her cheeks, sunken and pale. But she was alive. The song was proof of that.

Her body swayed like a hammock between two weeping willows. Each strand of hair, unnaturally thick and long like rope, twisted around branches high off the ground. It weaved back and forth securing her body in a kind of net. Sky, the color of a brewing storm, illuminated the oak's limbs clawing at her lifeless form. The whole scene looked like a lion's mane, enormous and frightening, her body suspended by cords of hair, like ivy growing wild in a jungle.

Ashton crept forward, careful to approach in silence, when she saw Mason's strong wings stroke above. She inhaled slow and shallow, relieved he was there.

Always. His voice soothing, the reinforcement she needed. *But you should have waited.*

No sign of Ian? she sent, ignoring his warning, itching to move. Her fingers clenched the dagger.

No, but it feels too easy. I still think it's a trap.

The battle's back in his realm. We have to help her. And before waiting for a response, she leaped.

Her arms clung steadily to the trunk of the tree, and even when the scar under her right eye burned with the memory of the tree she'd fallen from as a little girl, she didn't stop. She gripped her dagger and swept up and over, climbing as close as she could to her birth mother. Her feet clutched the bark as if she'd grown up climbing trees, her boots stuck with each step, and in no time, she found herself so far up, she leaned down over Althaia's dangling body. Her seam keeper inside beamed proudly as her human side climbed next to her.

"Althaia," she whispered.

Mason screeched in warning above. The sky darkened but let in streaks of light through cracks in its angst. A new energy surged her soul, as if light filled her from the inside out. She had no idea what time of day it was. Jumping between realms was confusing enough. But there was no time to question. The melody strummed in her mind again. Althaia, though her eyes shut tight, called to her.

Something's coming. Mason's voice broke through. *I feel it.*

Just then she sensed Ian's presence. She heard the cries of faraway commotion, the other hawks fighting the demon prince's mole-creatures. They were nearer somehow, maybe even through the portal, closer to the oak. She had to act fast.

Her final thought was for Mason. She sent him her heart and then sliced her jade dagger through the first locks of chestnut hair.

The oak shook like a grizzly waking in surprise. Her arms and legs clung tightly to the angry tree as Mason flew down, willing her to mount. She'd learned how to do that, to adjust the size of her body, but outside the Spiritual Realm it took time. Time, she didn't have. She refused.

Inching herself across the limb, she cut another strand of hair clumped in the oak's grasp. Again, her arm flew down with force, slicing back and forth, jade light trailing behind, freeing more mounds of tangles from captivity.

Ash, we're being set up. We need to move. His urging filled her mind.

She couldn't stop, impulsivity surging, her body on a mission of its own. She climbed and sliced, clambering up and around Althaia's swinging body. She chopped hair, then squeezed through the flurry of swinging branches, chopped some more. The thought of losing another mother pushed her onward.

Mason landed on a higher branch and began helping, clawing at the strands, ripping at the clutching bark with hooked beak. Ashton worked her way down, opposite from Mason. Althaia's eyes never opened, but she couldn't focus on that. Instead, she strained to hear the fading song from her birth mother's weakening heart.

They labored over each branch freeing locks of hair. Ashton could almost taste the success, of having Althaia liberated from her prison, when the magic in the oak awoke completely. Rumbling, it fought against whatever dark magic was swollen inside, and with retribution, deepened its violent attack.

Time to retreat. The oak's waging its own war. Ash!

Finally, she looked to him, but he wasn't looking back, he was gripping the tree branch with sharp talons, his head tucked awkwardly under his wing. The branch shook brutally, and in that moment, she realized she'd pushed their luck beyond repair.

Mason's bough swung fiercely. He was a blur of amber and ivory melded together, a brushstroke painting the distance between sky and ground. She opened her mouth to scream, but her own branch veered wrathfully, flinging her body wildly against the trunk, the wind knocked out of her.

Panic shot through her chest. Coughing and hacking, she tried to catch her breath, tried forcing air back into her lungs, when Mason squawked desperately. She knew he worried about her, even amid his own plight.

I'm okay. She hoped her message delivered through the chaos quivering around them.

But she wasn't okay because the roots of the oak broke surface, bulging from under the earth. Ashton held on with both arms and legs, still trying to breathe, yet frightened by the silence of the song she'd clung to. Squinting through dusty air, she saw a sea of worm-like roots breaking free of their earthly blanket. Steam from the depths of Hell rose. The smell was horrific, unlike anything she could name. Coarse bark tore against her face. The oak moaned and belched its temper, as she clung for life.

The spinning.

It was too much.

Too fast.

Her head pounded under the pressure, and she felt herself pass in and out of consciousness.

Mason! Her mind called, but there was nothing but the tornado tearing her world apart.

Somewhere behind her eyes, she saw her turquoise bedcovers tucked neatly in place. Her e-reader on the pillow, right where she'd left it. She pictured her mom painting in her studio, music blasting, with paint jars cluttering every surface. She saw her dad at the end of a long shift, sitting in his car for a full two minutes longer, to de-stress before entering into dad-mode. Her favorite coconut ice cream sat in the freezer, top shelf, left side, like always. Her favorite mug, steaming with jasmine tea, sat waiting on her window's ledge. She pictured every part of her old life as if she could reach out and touch it. What she couldn't imagine…what she refused to see in her mind, was Althaia's body being torn from its imprisonment. Or Mason, clinging for his life to a vicious tree limb. No, these thoughts were stricken from view.

Abruptly, the winds dispelled, and her branch

creaked when she finally opened her eyes. The storm had slowed, leaving tree roots arched below. A faraway glimpse of Mia making her way toward them brought hope, like a rainbow in dust-filled skies. Had Mia calmed the strange attack? She wondered if she could have stopped the storm herself, as she had at the portal in Toria? But her ripped flesh, caught on the branch she'd clung to, revealed her answer. There hadn't been time for her to stop something that fierce. Maybe she wasn't as experienced as she thought. Angry visions of Gavan asking her to stand down filled her mind. His icy blue glare figuratively gloating. "I told you so…"

Ashton loosened her grip from the limb she'd sworn allegiance to. She perched low, suspicious of lingering danger, looking through the debris for Althaia and Mason. Althaia was in the same position she'd been snared, though her head and shoulder dangled lower from where strands of hair had been cut. Her left arm swung free, at an unnatural angle, broken. She glanced to where she'd last seen Mason, but the entire branch was gone.

Mason, where are you? She coughed, gasped in dirty air from the raised earth below, straining to see across the far widths of the tree. She could just make out her cast and Mia. They were far in the distance, but in the same realm, still fighting a constant stream of black demons peppering the sky. Slowly her gaze lowered to the forest floor, uprooted and tangled.

"Please don't be down there. Please," she petitioned aloud. The earth so mangled, she knew her plea was too late, even before the truth came into view.

Her heart split, sinking to the depths of her stomach, when she saw Mason right where she pleaded not to find him. Ivory and amber feathers littered the broken ground, floating like snow in the air atop the surface. It would have been beautiful if it hadn't been the most agonizing sight since seeing her house ablaze.

Ashton's stomach churned so quickly, she could only twist her head to vomit. Her balance quivered, and she barely caught herself when a dark shadow loomed above, like night closing the shutters on daylight.

Chapter 34

Battle Lost?

Ian shook his head, disgrace pelting Ashton's shoulders. The winds whipped his black hair, longer now. He looked much older, evil eyes reflecting how small and frail she stood in comparison.

A feather, suspended in unsettled dust, broke her connection, enough to bring her back from his forceful glare. How had she ever wavered on Ian's ability to change? Shame on her. And Mason. How could he be gone after everything they'd gone through? How could he have ever imagined himself evil like this monster?

He didn't deserve to die. It wasn't supposed to happen this way. Hadn't they been destined together?

"You did this, Ashton." Ian's voice amplified deep inside her chest.

She glared, wiping away strands of hair. Her tears, only hinting to fall. Now balanced on the tree limb that once sought to hurl her away, she forced a breath and prepared for what she knew was coming. The battle she was destined for. *This* was her mission. It was supposed to be with Mason, but she could do it. He had said so himself.

She would kill Ian *for* Mason.

"If only you had joined me, none of this would have happened. All of it preventable, Ashton. You. Did. This." His tone cut like a knife.

Ashton buried all the unthinkable words she wanted to hurl. She worked to keep her head as the clicking of a solution tapped its song. Somehow too late, she knew what to do. And she needed every emotion. She needed her feelings to grow inside, to hold together, to burn and rot and fester. She would make him own up to the fire that burned her parents, to the trauma he'd caused their families, and for Mason's horrific death. With new strength, she bounded to the base of the tree, slipping and scraping her way down, but landing upright. She locked her feet into the torn, uneven ground.

Ian walked past her to Althaia, whispering something inaudible to the wind, before the branches released their hold. Althaia fell forward, still unconscious, into his arms. He carried her through the filthy air to a soft mossy spot, her chest rising and falling. She was alive! Ashton's heart sparked, practically knocking her off balance.

The melody that had drawn her to the tree sounded quietly in the back of her mind, and she was grateful as it attached its magical strength, one ligament at a time. The light of her birth mother's weak spirit found its way through every part of her body, starting in the charm on her wrist. Absorbing through broken skin, it carried to her veins, to her bones. She had Heaven on her side. She *could* do all things. Standing in the misery of the reality surrounding her, it was all very much worth fighting for.

Ashton stood taller than she knew herself to be. And it was enough. The seam keeper inside pushed to fight. But inside she stayed; it was her human side she needed now. The angel had blessed her with energy, enhancing her courage, and even as her seam keeper gift was clicking the solution into place, it was her human side who would carry out the final blow. She was the one who had always held the power to conquer Ian. Only she'd worried it away like the world at sleep, empowering Ian's darkness through anxiety and fear.

Enough!

"You're right." She glued her gaze to his glare. "I did this. We all did, sleeping off our dark fears, our dreams giving you power. I never thought I could do anything on my own. I hid behind Mason for years. You're the first one to cause me to rethink my lack of confidence. *You*, Ian. You are the doubt that I gave life to, but it's given me new strength."

"You didn't give me life, little girl. You chose selfishness instead of power, weakness over the strength we could have gained."

He strode closer, but she stood her ground. She needed him close.

"And what a father you are. Thank God, Mason inherited nothing of you." She baited him, luring him, bit by bit.

"You have no idea. Maybe he was everything I needed him to be. Look at you now. You're a mess, Ashton. A beautiful, delicate mess, talking of such power. I've taken everything from you. But I can give it all back. I can give you everything you want." He gestured to her birth mother lying vulnerably on the mossy ground and to the lifeless hawk body stained crimson at her side. "The Spiritual Realm is only using you for patrol duty. It's embarrassing, really. You're worth much more."

"Yes. I am. But I will be the one to decide, though it's not my seam keeper side you should worry about. It's me." She took a step closer, fear forgotten. Grief

375

ignored. Suddenly she was fighting for something bigger than herself. She saw the faces of her family, her cast, the Blessing Council, and the radiant blue light from the angel Sandalphon.

Her fingers inched toward her weapons belt. "I gave you power by doubting my strength because God knows I never knew why I was chosen for such a cause. But it's my human side that gives life to evil like you. I gave you power with my doubt, so I can take it away. I don't need to fight you on a spiritual level. I can save that for my destiny at the seam, where I am proud to serve its borders. I can stop you right here, right now, with only my human side."

"Oh, really." He leaned in, a mere inch from her face, no concern for her power across his brow. He smugly brushed her cheek. Ashton felt the tingle pierce her mind. The warmth attempting to turn her thoughts, as it had before.

He was always too confident, sweeping her off her feet. But her free will wasn't for sale. She had a choice, and she'd made it. Peering squarely into his dark eyes, she spoke through gritted teeth. "I have already won against you because I have faith. Good will prevail over evil. You are nothing. At first, I called it luck that I was chosen Centennial, or that the realms made a mistake trusting me with this responsibility. But they didn't. I did. So you were right when you said, I did this. I let you knock down my faith, but I'm not letting it happen again."

"I'm all that's left, Ashton." His breath hot against her cheek.

She clasped both hands up to her chest, as if bracing herself against his declaration.

"I'm the one standing here. You have no parents.

Soon, you'll have no birth mother. Your God is not here. Your angels are MIA. And where are your beloved hawks? Where's Mason? Even he couldn't stand against his true bloodline, falling so easily. He's no son of mine. No one holds the power to get close enough to me, to cause any amount of damage. My demons are keeping every one of your cast at bay, so I can be here with you. Alone. You must already know you can't kill me. Join me in creating a whole new realm, and I'll bring everyone you love back to life."

"No." Her answer, quick and blunt.

His expression shifted to surprise when the single word escaped her lips, followed by the three whispered names he was known by. "Ian. Cillian. Demon prince." She spoke into the palms of her hands, into the single rose soul-spherule nestled between her fingers. Then she opened her palm revealing the small sphere and pushed it against his chest.

The heat of his body pulsed under each fingertip, but the soul-spherule blossomed like a flower, wrapping long winding tentacles around his body. So close in proximity, she caught the shock in his eyes, blue, then green, then black, before he vaporized. Black like the eyes she'd accidentally sketched in her tree drawing the morning after they'd met. She winced at the eerie connection as the dark gray mist of his body swirled together with the soft pink-bleeding spherule.

He had underestimated her. Rory had too, assuming that, like most keepers, her emotions shut down in battle, hindering the effectiveness of the spheres. But Ashton wasn't any seam keeper; she was the Centennial.

She'd been human first.

There was no color now, only smoke and soot and

377

ashes and death and hate and betrayal and pure ugly evil, swirling away into a glop of nothing. Ian's body rose in the air, fading as he soared up and away in a windstorm that wasn't there before dropping against the hard ground.

The forest floor opened along the edges welcoming him home to Hell. The ooze that was Ian spread itself thin, finding hidden crevices in which to sink. Steam emitted, while final pieces of earth replaced itself, dissipating. The cry of demons behind flew off in the dust. It was over in a matter of seconds as Ashton stood in the forest at Althaia's oak, the surroundings demolished. Strands of her birth mother's hair snagged on branches like Christmas tree tinsel.

She glanced to Althaia, relieved to find her stirring, and hobbled over exposed roots, kneeling at her side. "Are you okay?"

"You decided to be the warrior you're meant to be." She lifted her workable arm to rest on Ashton's shoulder. Her touch should have felt cold, she was so near death, but instead it was warm.

"A little too late." Ashton twisted to see Mason's crumpled body, now an empty human shell, under a broken limb. She hadn't seen his hawk shift back. Grief notched at her heart.

"*Not* too late," a voice cried. "Just in time."

Mia fought her way over the uprooted land, blackened and bloody from fighting demons. Ashton only wished Mason could have known of his mom's freedom before his own life was taken.

The cast behind watched as Mia made her way to her son. Dumping her pockets of stones, she placed them all over his torn body.

"No, Mia, don't call on Dark magic. It won't bring

you peace," Althaia cried out, unable to stop her, her own body broken.

Mia put one hand up to stop Althaia's concerns, the other outstretched to the sky, palm opened, head bowed. "Father, please forgive me for my absence and my choices in not trusting You. Ian's blood does run through my son's body, and with these stones, I pray to do what is right, to fix the bloodline I wronged. Please take these stones from me, allow them to purify the strength of his free will, to fortify his seam keeper blood. The power is all yours. Please forgive his doubts and mine. If not for me, for Chase's soul. I know he is with You. I love You, my Father, and I wish to come home. Please send us your miracle."

Ashton felt the warmth of a summer day fall over them. She bent down to steady her swaying legs, and the rough ground she'd recently wrestled against nestled into place. As the Heavens opened above, the oak tree leveled itself back into the ground, bursting with leaves in every hue of green, surely impossible to mix with cadmium yellow or phthalo blue.

The rainbow she'd seen in Mia spread to every branch. Althaia stood on her own, healed. When she looked back, her cast knelt to the ground, heads bowed, no longer filthy or exhausted from battle. She looked down at her own body. Her hands weren't scarred from the branches, her keeper uniform unmarred as if she'd just stepped out of the armory…with Mason.

Mia's gasp pulled her attention back to the scene. Tears of joy shed from his mom's slumped form, as she hovered over her son.

Mason was alive.

Epilogue

Sunshine danced across the church's stained-glass windows. Ashton peered inside, recognizing family and friends. Colorful reflections cast bright hues across sad faces. Pictures displayed on a buffet table next to a few of her mom's paintings brought her much needed relief, because she was there. Her smiling face visible in the photos, just as she should be.

Grief filled the chapel, though no one seemed to be searching for her presence, or questioning her absence. Rory had told her as much, explaining how the healer, Bethesda, had coated every mind connected to hers. They would remember her but not pursue any further thoughts about where she was. In the end, she knew where her parents were, that they were safe, and one day she would see them again.

It would be enough.

Mason squeezed her shoulder, pulling her to step away. They ambled across the parking lot unnoticed by anyone, save a few hawks on the roof. Without a word, Ashton turned into his strong hug, and using a single tear, carried them back across the realms to the seam.

"Are you okay?" He led her to sit against the very tree they'd sat under when first arriving to Toria. It was a beautiful day, as usual in the Spiritual Realm. A Georges-Seurat-painted afternoon with a soft breeze blowing long flyaway wisps of hair across her cheeks.

Mason tucked them behind her ears.

"I will be."

Mason had awoken from death with a whole new appreciation for the struggles his mom endured. He was determined to find the only dad he wanted to know, Max. Their next mission was retrieving him from Ian's hidden realm. But they'd agreed to wait until after her parents' funeral. Hawks were on watch, though the council felt even that was unneeded. With the realm's hidden existence, how would anyone get there to take over? Shunnar had explained the lesser demons were just mindless bats without orders.

But the thought of Max still captive struck a nerve.

"It's time to get your dad out." She sat up ready for battle.

"Slow down, warrior-girl. Shunnar's researching the deal he made. It may be binding."

She leaned back against the tree's trunk. Neither of them knew what a contract like that would mean. But then, there was Mason, showing more patience than ever. She wished for her sketchbook. Maybe there was a way to draw out all these feelings, the way she used to...*gain a new perspective*. She smiled at her mom's familiar words, and this time, with her mom's memory as inspiration, she vowed to use color.

"Will your mom work at the seam again? Maybe reteam with another mate?" Ashton couldn't help thinking how she'd almost lost Mason.

"Maybe they'll use her another way, like making Althaia the portal keeper, and Gavan the chief of casts."

Thoughts of working solo in the most beautiful location imaginable made Ashton sad. Thank God, she had Mason back. She squeezed his hand. That loss, no matter how short, tore away every worry she'd ever felt. Her adoption made sense. College didn't matter. They were already employed at the highest level of importance. She knew her parents would be proud. For that, she was grateful. And though it would take time, she was finding more comforts in her new home. It didn't matter where they were, just that she and Mason were together.

She would fight for *that* ending for the rest of her life.

"Speaking of Gavan, have you two talked?"

Her blood cooled with the thought of this icy man being her birth father. The one who'd asked her to stand down in battle. The one who'd glared at Mason as if he were the Devil.

"No, not ready for that," she said, mood shifting. "Did you know he hasn't even—"

"Apologized yet? I know." His pinky finger traced the scar under her eye.

"Well, he should. He was wrong. He should be—"

"Thanking you? I know." His lips curled at the corners.

"Mason!"

"Listen, I get the angst against evil birth fathers. Mine showed his true colors, malicious and vile, and he's dead to us. But yours? We don't even know Gavan, or anything he's gone through. Just don't wait too long."

"You don't know everything, Mason Deed."

"I know you're my everything. My everyone. My only." He pulled her gently to his shoulder. "And I know we're home now."

"I didn't think it was possible, but I feel it too."

She let out a breath, and they leaned back, embraced as one, watching the trees sway in the breeze. Tiny wrens hopped from branch to branch. "Once Max is safe, maybe things can fall into more of a routine."

"I'm trying out that patience thing my dad seems to excel in. How do you like my poker face?" He looked at her with pursed lips and wide eyes, goofy like she hadn't seen since…they were human. But there he was again, his humor trumping her need for order.

Quietly she closed her imaginary file drawer.

She poked him tenderly in the chest. "I wondered how you were holding it together. I thought you'd already be scheming to sneak out and find Max on your own."

"Well, I am anxious to get my family back, if that's even possible. That's part of why I want you to talk things out with Gavan. But it's more." Mason's eyes grew hopeful. "I want to honor my duty at the seam. The Big Guy's taking a chance on me, right?"

"I think *He* already believed in both of us from the beginning." She smoothed his right eyebrow, still and unmoving.

He caught her hand, held it to his heart. "I'm sorry it took me so long to figure things out, but I—"

"Always love you," Ashton finished, free from the need to ever hide again.

A word about the author...

Celaine Charles lives in the Pacific Northwest where she teaches elementary students, writes poetry and fiction, and blogs about her writing journey on her site, Steps In Between. Her young adult fantasy, *Seam Keepers*, is her debut novel. She is also a published poet.

When Celaine isn't busy writing or teaching, she can be found walking or hiking around her beautiful surroundings with family and friends. Follow her on social media to see the gems she finds on her walks, as she is always snapping and posting pictures. She claims the walks clear her mind and the pictures inspire her craft.

www.celainecharlesauthor.com

https://stepsinbetween.com/